The Cabi

Alan Jones

First Print edition

Copyright © Alan Jones 2013

Published by Ailsa Publishing.

A dictionary of Glasgow slang and a glossary of woodworking terms are available at the end of the book and at www.thecabinetmaker.info

For Mary

PROLOGUE

[Sunday 27thApril 2008]

I stood in the warm April sunshine watching the flames curl and twist, destroying most of what remained of Francis Hare's life.

Thirty years after the death of his son, Patrick, I spent the whole day in the yard behind the workshop loading up the wood-burner with all the papers, photographs and newspaper clippings that Francis had collected since Patrick's murder.

As I loaded it up I glanced at the odd item, but I only kept one; the front page from the *Sunday Mail* of 30th April 1978. The headline read:

GIFTED GLASGOW STUDENT MURDERED BY GANG OF THUGS

I read the story again slowly, even though, like most of the stuff I was burning, I knew its contents only too well:

Student Patrick Hare, 20, was beaten to death in an apparently unprovoked attack close to Byres Road in Glasgow's West End. The attack occurred between 11 o'clock and midnight on Saturday, and police are appealing for anyone who was in the area at the time to come forward ...

I laid it aside and got on with the task in hand. It barely all fitted in the furnace, but I managed, and I doused it with diesel to make sure that the fire took hold. By the time the sun was going down, all that was left was a thick layer of ash settled halfway up the glass door of the cooling stove.

1

I had kept it all, even after I retired, having been a detective in Glasgow for over twenty-five years. I'd wrestled with thoughts of telling someone about the events of the last thirty years, but in the end I couldn't bring myself to tell a soul, not even Andy.

Until now.

CHAPTER 1   CRIME

[Sunday 30th April 1978 4 p.m.]

I took to Francis Hare from the first time I met him. He had a dignity and inner strength about him and, despite the circumstances of our first meeting, there was a warmth that showed through at unexpected moments, when you got to know him.

We met in Partick police station not long after his only son had been brutally beaten and left bleeding to death in the street. I came into the investigation on its second day, having just been transferred from uniform for my probationary period of six months in CID. At first, as the most junior member of the team, and "brand new, out of the box" as Gallagher liked to say, I was expected to watch and learn, and do menial tasks for ninety-five per cent of the day.

That day, as was usual in the office, there was a buzz of conversation: the odd laugh, a bit of banter between two of the shift's comedians, and Detective Inspector Gallagher trying to make himself heard above the clamour.

I probably noticed Francis first, which gave me a chance to watch him as he stood in the corridor with a WPC, waiting to meet with Gallagher. He was a tall, angular man with dark, slightly receding hair. I would have guessed mid-forties. His "old-fashioned" look reminded me somewhat of a black and white photograph of my grandfather at a similar age.

Everyone in the room gradually noticed Francis standing outside, but it must have taken a couple of minutes for the room to quieten, until finally the two comedians were the only ones who hadn't seen him. Unfortunately, they were verbally abusing each other about their respective Old Firm teams, who had both won the day before. To avoid further embarrassment, DI Gallagher made a beeline out the door towards Francis, took him by the arm, and led him into the room, coughing loudly.

"'Scuse me guys, let's have your 'tention. For anyone here who hasnae met him, this is Francis Hare, Patrick's father." He turned to Francis. "I'm sorry, Francis, I have to go. I've got a meeting with Chief Inspector Donaldson in two minutes, so I'll leave you with Dave; he'll fill you in on how the investigation is proceeding." He looked around. "Dave, come over here a mo', and tell Francis what progress we've been making." He turned to me. "McDaid, offer Francis something to drink, instead of standing there like a spare prick."

Francis looked around the room, and for a moment caught my eye. Gallagher turned away, saying, "Must go, Francis, I'll give you a bell tomorrow to keep you in the picture."

Francis didn't glance round as Gallagher left the room.

"Cup of tea?" I offered Francis nervously, as he still hadn't uttered a word.

"Aye, that'll do, lad," he answered. "And who might you be?"

"John McDaid," I said, shaking his hand. "I've just started my training in CID. I was transferred over from uniform yesterday and they put me in here to help out with the paperwork. I'll get your tea, if you want to talk to Dave."

When I came back Dave was giving Francis the latest stuff we had.

"We're close to getting them; we have four or five witnesses who saw a group of youths running down Byres Road about ten minutes before your son was found. One of them had blood on his T-shirt and trousers, according to the best of our wits …" he turned and picked up a folder, "… a university lab technician on his way home from a late night film at the GFT. He assumed that they had been fighting, and only contacted us today after seeing the *Sunday Mail*. We've had some good info from a few local pubs about this crowd, one or two names being bandied about and some excellent descriptions. We're hoping for a result by the end of the week. I'll remind the DI to phone, like he promised, if there's any progress." He turned to me as I returned with the teas. "After he's finished his tea, show Francis down to his car."

I must have looked taken aback; I was surprised that Dave had been so dismissive. To be fair, Francis never said a word; he just took the tea from me and proceeded to walk out the door, into the corridor. I followed him, spilling some tea on my shoes as I banged through the door.

"Listen, sorry about that, I think everyone is under a bit of pressure," I spluttered. I made some lame excuses about how busy the investigation was, but Francis' attention seemed to be wandering, as if he had something more important think about.

"Listen, John," he said suddenly, handing me his almost-full cup, "you get back in there and I'll find my own way out. You might miss something."

"Nah, it's OK, I'll see you out. It's nearly five o'clock and my shift's just finishing; I'm heading anyway." I deposited our cups in the waste-bin, and we walked along the corridor towards the stairs. I asked him where he was parked.

"Round in the station car park," he answered, and I showed him the quick way down and out through the back entrance.

I felt a deep sadness surrounding him as I watched him slowly walk away towards his car, then I headed to Duke Street for the train, and a night out with some of my mates that had been arranged the previous week.

~~o~~

The following morning I awoke, if that is the best term for what seemed at the time to be part of an ongoing horrible dream. Clothes still on, a mouth that tasted like shite and a basin overflowing with last night's regurgitated kebab. Despite the use of a pen to clear the blocked sink, a double dose of aspirin, a pint of Irn-Bru and a long shower, the little workmen inside my head were still pounding away at the back of my eyes with pneumatic drills when I entered the CID general office. The saving grace was that everyone else seemed to be in a similar condition.

"You lot out on the batter last night?" I asked no one in particular.

Danny Simpson lifted his head from between his hands, elbows still on the table. "We all ended up at the Balmoral – they had a stripper on last night, bit of a dog but ..." he looked round, leaned over and whispered in my ear, "... Peter Dalry shagged her in the toilet after the show."

"Piss off," I said, "not Peter. He's not that long married again."

"Naw, Gen, straight up – we bloody saw him taking her into the cubicle, and if he wasn't in baw deep, they both deserved a fucking BAFTA, wi' the sounds that were coming out. Anyhow, seems she lost her panties and Tommo saw her on the way out and he said the stuff was runnin' down her leg."

I grimaced. "I didn't need to know that, but thanks for sharing it with me anyway."

I began to feel a bit guilty, not only about the state I was in, but also about the whole squad. I had an awful feeling that if Francis Hare walked in now, he would be absolutely disgusted with us. I knew that DI Gallagher was of the "work hard, play harder" school, and most shifts would end with a few pints at the Crammond, or the sharing of a bottle of whisky. If you didn't take a regular part in these sessions you could be made to feel pretty much an outsider. I considered myself a drinker, but I could see I was in exalted company with this lot, who could drink for Scotland.

6

Shortly after, we were all at our desks when Gallagher sauntered in.

"Cup of tea, John," he shouted over, "and see if you can rustle up a couple of paracetamol." He looked around the room and asked about Peter, Chris and Dave.

As I wandered over to put the kettle on, I heard him say something about "dirty bastard" followed by a laugh. I returned with his tea and he was still laughing with Danny and Andy. "What's happening this morning?" I asked.

"Hold on, give us all a chance to waken up. Anyhow, we'll give the other piss artists ten minutes to show up."

"Only place Peter'll be showing up today is at the clinic," quipped Danny.

There was more laughter which I joined in with, feeling a little uneasy at the thought of Peter's discomfort, which could prove to be more than just physical: his new wife was a feisty girl of Scouser extraction, quite capable of making him suffer for his lapse.

By ten thirty, there were still only the eight of us.

It was such a contrast to yesterday, my first day, which had been pandemonium. Everything had been new to me, and chaotic. I'd wondered if I had done the right thing by joining CID, and had hoped I would be able to adapt to the pace at which everything seemed to be happening.

There had been plain-clothes officers everywhere you looked, and everyone had been busy doing something. There was a large whiteboard at the front of the room with a blank flipchart next to it. Gallagher had given out instructions from the centre of the room.

"Right," he'd said, "I want a photo for each of the names we've got, and two or three of the other scum that we know they hang around with. I want a short bio for each of them, and any other relevant info you can get me. Most of it is already in the room. There's a Xerox at the side, so get moving. Here's the list."

He had handed the list to Danny and I'd looked over his shoulder as he read it. Gallagher had left the room, presumably heading back to his own office.

Kevin (Nolman) Nolan

Lee (Scouly) Scoular

Derek (Spaz) Davidson

Malcolm (Malky) McGovern

James Sornie

Stewart (Pinky) McNiven

John (Whitey) White

Billy Green

"Kevin, they call him Nolman, short for 'Nolan Man', is the leader of this gang of bampots. Thin, ugly fucker, bad breath." Danny had grinned, then continued. "They've all got previous. Nolan and John White have done time, young offenders mainly. Most of the stuff they've done is petty – vandalism, breach, shoplifting – but White got the jail for bottling some Paki's heid after he had been caught stealing the charity box outside the poor cunt's shop."

"It's a big step from that to kicking some poor bastard to death, though," I'd said. "Were they all involved, d'you think?"

"There's various reports of the gang, all at different times and places. Sometimes there were five or six of them, at one point there could have been all eight, but we think the six on the left of that sheet were all definitely present when Patrick was killed. Having said that, the other two were more than likely present."

He'd gone on to show me the photos and give a brief description of each of them.

"Nolan I've told you about. Scoular's a bit less ugly, short hair, and his ears stick out. They're both about five feet

8

ten. Spaz Davidson's slightly smaller, dark hair, and his eyes look as if they are too close together. Inbreeding, we think; his ma's his sister."

I'd laughed. "What about the rest?"

"Aye, they're all inbred too." He'd smiled. "Pinky McNiven is a short wee fucker, round head, small piggy eyes, hair cropped into the wood. Billy Green is small as well, probably about five seven. He's got a scar on his forehead from a knife fight. James Sornie, they call him 'Pervo', looks like one. David Johnstone, probably the least hard out of them all, gets the piss ripped a lot. Ginger heid. That leaves John White and Malky McGovern. White's just a thug, but Malky's a slimy bastard, you've got to watch him. Better looking than the rest. Always has a decent-looking bird. Mind you, they're jakey birds, so that's not saying much."

I had looked at the photos, thinking that they all looked like evil bastards.

That had been my first day. Naively, I had thought that every day would be the same, but here we were a day later, seemingly in the doldrums, doing nothing constructive.

By lunchtime it was obvious that we were going to be a depleted unit, and in fact by now two of them had phoned in "sick". Gallagher suggested a pub lunch, but in the end we made do with a few sandwiches ordered in from The Crusty Loaf across the street.

~~o~~

"Right," Gallagher said through a mouthful of chicken mayo as we gathered in the incident room to eat our lunch, "I'd meant to send eight teams out to do some preliminary interviews on as many of this crowd as we could, but due to staff illness ..." he paused, allowing time for dutiful laughs all round, "... due to staff illness we'll have to tackle them in four pairs. John, you come with me, Andy and Danny can go together, Pete and Dave, Joe and Chris, you pair up today. Make sure we get together between times to pool our information."

He had a list of eight names from the previous day's briefing and he handed them out, keeping three for us to do, for some reason. He threw me the keys and we set off for Clydebank, where all the "turns" were to take place. The place had suffered massive unemployment over the years as a result of the closures of the shipyards and the Singer Factory.

It was nearly two thirty by now, and our first call was in a block of flats in Glazer Street.

"It would be the fucking top floor," he wheezed, as we climbed the stairs. Gallagher wasn't the fittest and the stairs were bloody steep. As flats go, these weren't too bad; very little graffiti on the walls, plant tubs outside the doors on the landings, even a few window boxes on the outside. There was a mixture of small and large flats, and the top flats were of the double storey type. It was in one of these that our first suspect allegedly lived. We knocked on the inner door of the small porch leading off the landing, which was essentially a long balcony running the entire length of the building.

The woman who answered the door was obviously not the boy's mother, I reckoned, but I was wrong. She didn't look to be over thirty, and OK, despite being dressed a little, well, skanky; to be honest, she rather suited it. This one was definitely a goer and as I glanced at DS Gallagher, I could see he was thinking along similar lines.

"Aw right, hen, I'm Detective Inspector Gallagher, and this is Detective Constable John McDaid. Is Kevin home, em, Mrs Nolan – it is Mrs Nolan, isn't it?"

As soon as she opened her mouth, I instantly had her shifted from a "Yes" to a "No chance". She had one of those voices that would have killed the hardest boner.

"Yes, I am. I suppose you're gonnae say that you thought I was his fucking sister. Anyway, what's the wee bastard done now?"

I could see that, like me, Gallagher couldn't equate the shrill jarring voice with the good-looking woman standing in front of us, but he kept his composure and replied, "Just routine enquiries, Mrs Nolan. Can we have a chat with Kevin?"

"He's no' in, so you cannae, but I'll tell him you were sniffin' around." She closed the door partially, leaving just her head out. "You might get him down at the puggys this time of day." She withdrew her head to close the door, but Gallagher put his hand on it to hold it open.

"Have you any idea where he was on the evening of April twenty-sixth? That was last Saturday."

"Fuck, I can't remember where they all are every day of the week; I've got three sons and they're all out most of the time anyway, Christ knows where."

"He's not frightened of talking to us, is he, Mrs Nolan?"

"The only thing thon cunt is frightened frae is dentists, don't flatter yersels." She closed the door even further. "Now I've got to get on, I've work to go to, if you don't bloody mind."

Gallagher, however, had his sizable foot against the door, stopping it from shutting. "Now look here, you little tart, I don't give a shit if you've to get to work, I'm sure your punters will wait," he sneered.

I don't think he expected her to react so quickly. I was amazed that she managed to slap him so cleanly round the partly opened door and without him trying to fend off the blow. I was still stunned by this when he reached through the gap between the door and the wall to try and grab her arm. At this point she managed to push the door sufficiently hard to dislodge his foot, and she would have got it fully closed if Gallagher's arm hadn't still been through the gap.

With a bellow he pushed viciously on the door, throwing her back against the wall.

"You little cunt, I'm going to have you for that, you've broken my fucking arm." By this time he had her by the hair, and she was trying to bite and scratch him, but he just kept repeatedly banging her off the wall. I finally woke up to what was happening and tried to put myself between them.

"Inspector," I said, "we're in the fucking house, let's go." He seemed to snap out of it then and although she managed a swipe at him as he let her go, he moved backwards towards the door.

As I ushered him out, I happened to glance up the stairs. One of the doors was slightly ajar and I could have sworn that I saw someone peering over the banister and down the stairs. He was only there for a few seconds; I caught sight of a heavily tattooed chest, then the door closed gently, as if he'd seen me. I knew at once it was Kevin Nolan, but we'd already done enough damage so I didn't even mention it to Gallagher.

As we returned to our car, our footsteps echoing in the concrete stairwell, he seemed to have brushed the incident aside.

I waited for him to say something about what had just happened, but he just turned to me, grinning, and said, "What did you think of that? What a fucking whine of a voice, and on a bloody fit bird, too!" I was still feeling shocked at the way things had developed, but I kept my thoughts to myself.

I had anticipated an afternoon of knocking on doors and searching snooker halls and amusement arcades, so I was surprised when we drew up at the Stone Lion, one of those "drinker's pubs" where nothing gets in the way of a good pint.

Gallagher ordered a pint of heavy and a whisky chaser. "Yerself?" he said, and I ordered a pint of lager shandy, much to his amusement. "You'll have tae let your hair down a bit if you're goin' tae fit in with us – all work and no play makes you a right dull bastard." I stuttered a reply about having a hangover, but I could see he wasn't convinced.

"Where do we take it from here?" I asked, curious to know if he had some sort of strategy.

"We were all supposed to meet up here, but there's no sign of the others. We'll give them half an hour, then we'll take a look at a couple of the other cunts' hooses before we head back, and tomorrow we'll get warrants to get them all in. Let them stew for a day first; we know the bastards are guilty, it's just gettin' one or two of them to make a slip."

"Won't the extra time let them dump any evidence and get their stories straight?"

"Listen, these guys are as thick as shite. They'll make so many mistakes when we get them in, we'll have them shafted by five tomorrow. Have another pint." He lifted our glasses, and placed them on the bar. "Same again, Jim, then we'll be off."

"I'm OK, honest, I'd rather just have one when I'm driving."

"Fuck off, d'ye want me to drink on my own? I'll drive the fuckin' car."

I left it at that, but I could see he wasn't impressed. I could just imagine the conversation later: "Fucking new boy isnae up to much – bit of a mummy's boy, wouldnae even take a pint wi' me."

Gallagher changed tack, trying to needle me. "So whit the fuck makes you think you can be a detective?"

I half muttered, "I just fancied it. I'd watched a couple of CID guys on a case and after speaking to them, I thought I'd apply for the training."

"Mmm. You just fancied it," he said, aping my slightly nervous manner. "Don't you think it will take a bit more than that?"

I said nothing. He continued. "There's too many o' you clever young fuckers comin' in to CID, not realising what

13

it's aw aboot. I bet you've got a college-fucking-degree and no common-fucking-sense."

"As a matter of fact, I don't. I've got five O' grades; I left school when I was sixteen. Can't vouch for the common sense, right enough."

"Aye, well, you know what I mean," he said, slightly mollified. "How long were you in uniform?"

"I started when I was twenty. About five years. Before that I was an apprentice at Yarrow's, but most of us were going to be laid off before we finished and I decided to jump ship, so to speak, and join the police."

"So, aw right, yer thick like the rest o' us, but we'll see if ye can hack it at the sharp end."

We went on to our next port of call, one of the older terraced houses up the back towards the old Singer factory. It was obvious when we arrived at the house that they'd been forewarned, which made it even more likely it had been Kevin Nolan that I'd seen. The thug that answered the door was probably the father, but I had a feeling we were only seeing an older version of the son, Lee Scoular.

"Yeh?" he grunted

"Mr Scoular?"

"So?"

"We'd like to talk to Lee, if that's possible," Gallagher replied, his voice dripping with sarcasm.

"Well, it's no' fuckin' possible, cos he's no' in, so piss off back to where you came from."

"Do you know when he'll be back?"

"Not while you're here, anyway, so gie's peace and fuck off."

Gallagher turned to me. "Nice to see where the boy got his intelligence from, anyway." He turned back to the door. "Tell him we want to talk to him; he'll know why."

With that we turned and started down the steps onto the cracked, rubbish-lined path. It wasn't until I was almost at the gate that I realised that Gallagher had turned back and leapt up the steps again. He said a few quiet words to Lee's old man, there was a small scuffle, and then Gallagher was coming back down the path, grinning and making tossing-off gestures to me, directed, I hoped, at the now closed doorway.

I didn't even ask what had gone on and Gallagher was disinclined to let me in on the joke. On the way back I asked him about our other call.

"I thought we had to go and see John White as well?"

Gallagher laughed. "The wee cunts all knew to get out of the way. Nothin' to be gained from chappin' his gran's door. We'll keep that one for later."

"I'm surprised you'd take an old woman's health into consideration in a case like this."

He nearly choked laughing at that. "Mags Smith is no frail old lady, she's a hard cunt o' a woman who'd run riot over you, new boy." I thought he was going to lose control of the car; he was nearly doubled over the wheel. "Aye, big Mags is quite a girl."

"How do you know her?" I asked, and I couldn't keep a small grin from my face.

"Oi, you little bastard," Gallagher swore, "I wouldn't touch her with a fucking bargepole, if that's the way your foul little brain works," but I could see he was pleased that I could join in the piss-taking. "No, she's got all sorts of previous convictions, anything from hooring to serious assault, and she's done a wee bit of time here and there. She's one of these fat, hard cunts that keeps the whole scheme terrified, and the rest of the family arenae much better – there's always one of her sons inside for one thing

15

or another, and her granweans are just going to be the same."

I asked him how we'd got all the names and he said that as soon as they'd talked to the wits and some of the landlords in Partick, they knew right away which crew the bastards belonged to. "It's just a matter of getting one of them to shop on his pals, although we'll probably end up getting some forensics too … mind, you, there's enough witnesses to get them anyway." He continued, more to fill me in on the case than anything. "From what we can gather, Patrick was out with his girlfriend and a friend at a party. They'd just left there when they were verbally abused by a gang of about seven or eight youths. They hurried round to her flat in Frankland Street. Patrick stayed for a while, but then left to go home. As he walked back down to Byres Road, he must have been jumped by the same lads. Maybe they didn't like the fact that he had a nice looking girlfriend, or perhaps they just didn't like students in general, but ten minutes or so later he was beaten and left unconscious in her doorway, dying, as it turned out. A man out walking his dog found him, thought he was just drunk until he noticed the blood trickling off the step. They tried to resuscitate him at the Western, but they failed. We don't think there was much time between him being attacked and his death. The post-mortem showed severe head injuries consistent with his head being jumped on, but there were also five broken ribs, a punctured lung, ruptured spleen, a broken left arm and extensive bruising. Cause of death was a massive subdural haematoma."

"Could these guys have any previous with Patrick? Maybe he'd had a run in with them before."

"I suppose it might be worthwhile checking out, but I think it's bloody unlikely. Those cunts wouldn't go intae places students would use."

"Couldn't we check that out with some of Patrick's student friends and see what they say?"

"That's not bad thinking, son," he said, then added, "nice to see you've got a brain," as we turned into the station car park.

The others hadn't had a great deal of joy either.

"Fuckers should have probably all been picked up today," muttered Andy, not loud enough that Gallagher would hear, but I did, and I gave him a nod of agreement. Nice to know that someone else thought things were a bit sloppy.

Gallagher had a word with all the DCs then he and Danny went to organise search warrants for the next day, while Andy and I wrote up the day's actions, as our submitted notes were called; I wondered if he had to leave out as much as I did.

Andy turned to me. "Gallagher wasn't impressed with you."

"Why, did he say something to you?" I asked, anxiously.

"Don't worry, it's not a bad thing. He just said you were a bit of a pussy, but a thick cunt like the rest of us."

"I refused a drink when I was driving. He took the pet at that. Then he accused me of being too fucking clever." Andy could see that I was more than a bit angry.

He laughed. "I heard that you told him you worked in the shipyards. I bet that shut him up."

It was my turn to smile. "Aye, he didn't say too much after that."

"As I said, don't you worry about him. Anyway, from what I've seen I think you're a bit brighter than you let on."

"I don't know about that. My mum was always convinced that I would do well at school, but to be honest I just got bored and dicked around a lot with my mates until I suddenly realised that I'd left school without much to show for it. Also, I was brought up in Shettleston, and if you did well at school, you usually ended up getting a bit of a pasting most times. Anyway, I was lucky my old man got me a job at Yarrows. Funny thing is, I finished top of my course when I joined the police and was first again in the CID module I just finished. It was just a bit more interesting so it was easy to get stuck in."

Andy nodded his head. "I was a bit the same. I didn't really grow up until I was in my twenties. All I was interested in at school was girls and bevvy. I had to go back to college even to get O' grades."

I was surprised. We talked a bit more while we were working and discovered we both liked reading and were fans of science documentaries on TV, something that neither of us would particularly want Gallagher and his cronies to know.

We were just finishing off when the phone rang. Andy answered it. It turned out to be Francis, looking for an update. Andy, who was obviously trying to get away sharp, was pulling faces at me, which I read as, "Be a mate, take this for me, will you?" I walked over to the nearest phone, pressed the line button and motioned him to get the fuck off home. Andy quickly spoke to Francis, saying that the inspector was out but that I had all the news to hand and that DI Gallagher would speak to him later.

"Francis," I said, "nice to speak to you again." I cringed at my choice of words, but Francis didn't seem to notice.

"How's progress?" he asked bluntly.

"Well ..." I hesitated. "We tried to interview a couple of the suspects today, without much success. But we got quite a bit of background info from their families," I added lamely.

Francis must have known I was struggling, but he didn't push it. He surprised me, however, by asking that I come round and meet him at his shop for a chat. Normally in an investigation like that we didn't get too close to the deceased's relatives, partly because we couldn't always be sure that they weren't involved in the crime, but in this instance we were one hundred per cent sure that Francis wasn't.

"OK, I said, "I'll be around in twenty minutes. Where exactly are you?"

"Just along from Jordanhill station, near the lights, you'll see the sign outside." With that he hung up.

CHAPTER 2   FRANCIS

I picked my kit bag out of my locker in the corridor and got a lift from one of the "woodies", or uniforms, as they were more correctly known. My car was still at home – I hadn't risked driving that morning after a night on the batter.

Francis' shop was in a substantial red sandstone building. It had an old fashioned half-glass door and one large window elegantly displaying a couple of smaller pieces of furniture. The doors, and all the wood surrounding the window, were painted dark green, and there was a small sign above the door indicating that this was the business premises of "P. Hare & Son, Cabinetmakers and Finishers". Connected to the shop was a stone arch incorporating two large wooden gates, also painted green, and with a small door inset into the left hand gate. Carved on the stone above the arch was the year it was built, over a century ago, and I wondered if it had been built by Francis' family.

As the shop door was locked I tried the small door within the gate and found it to be open. I stepped into an enclosed yard, large enough to comfortably hold an "M" registration Jaguar and a large green van, with another couple of vehicles parked behind it. The yard was surrounded on two sides by what I took to be the house. There was a narrow gap between the part of the house facing me and the other side of the yard, which was lined by a large wooden workshop and a low woodshed, the latter extending from the back of the workshop. I shouted a "Hello," and was relieved when Francis poked his head out of the workshop door.

"In here," he said, beckoning me over.

"I don't think I've ever been in a joiner's workshop before." I looked around at the neatly laid out benches and machines, racks of tools and stacked wood extending almost to the roof in places.

"Don't confuse this with a joiner's workshop." He smiled. "Most cabinetmakers would be offended by that."

"Sorry," I said, "I didn't know there was a difference." I noticed a wooden staircase going up to a kind of balcony, with what looked like a tree house at one end of it.

He saw me looking. "That's my office." He started up the stairs. "Come on, we can chat in there."

I climbed up the stairs, intoxicated by the unfamiliar smell of sawdust, oil, glue and varnish. As I entered the poorly lit office, he nodded for me to sit down on one of two old carvers, both a bit worse for wear but well suited to the rest of the room. Tea boxes containing rolled up plans cluttered up the back of the room and a wide shelf ran along one side; Francis was fiddling with a coffee maker that sat on this.

"I asked you here for a reason," he said, then he paused. "Now, you know and I know that this investigation is being run by a bunch of useless morons." He glanced at me, and said, "No, don't deny it," as I tried to interrupt. "My son has been killed and as far as I can see, those investigating his murder are in danger of screwing the whole thing up."

"Listen, Francis," I said, having managed to butt in, "I don't know where you got that idea from, but I'm sure this will be done in the right way eventually." Even to myself, it sounded trite, and I could see Francis shaking his head and sighing.

"Look, son, I'd expect you to show a bit of loyalty, but can you try and tell me that, as a complete newcomer to that place, you are not disturbed by anything you've seen or heard?"

My face must have turned a shade of red, but I tried to bluster. "I can't comment about the investigation to the public, Francis – I know it's your son, and you have a right to know what's going on, but you've got to go through the right channels."

He looked at me rather strangely, his head slightly to one side and a quizzical look on his face. "I don't think I got you wrong – I'm usually a good judge of character and I had you down as someone with a bit of integrity. All I'm looking for is for someone to keep me informed of developments, and to enable me to have some input into this investigation. I can't afford to rely on 'official channels' or being shut out."

I had a cold feeling in my lower abdomen – I knew what he was suggesting was wrong, but ... the only reason I was still even considering his request was that, even though neither of us had any experience of a murder inquiry, he had come to the same conclusion I had.

"I'll need to think about it," I said, but a big part of me was saying to myself, "Get out of here, walk away from this."

"Think of it this way, John," Francis said, "in some countries, the police assign somebody to be close to the deceased's family as a sort of family liaison officer – think of yourself like that. Anyway, take your time, and be assured that anything you say will stay between us, I can promise you that. If you feel uncomfortable with it, I can ask the inspector if he can assign someone to keep me in touch. I could probably suggest you in a roundabout way."

Despite hardly knowing Francis, I believed him. But it didn't make it any easier. In hindsight I can honestly say that I never regretted agreeing to help, but I can also say that the decision gave me more than a few sleepless nights.

I thought about it for a while, but he seemed quite relaxed about that, as if he knew that I would come through for him. After going downstairs to the workshop and wandering round for a few minutes, I retraced my steps back up to the office and told Francis that I would help, but only where I felt that it did not leave me with a moral or ethical problem. These words had sounded laudable during my three month CID training, but now they just sounded crass and pompous.

I felt more relaxed after I had made the decision to help, and we passed half an hour or so talking about what we knew of the case so far, and what way it was likely to go.

Finally, I said, "By tomorrow night, we should know a lot more. There's talk of us making some arrests in the morning."

Francis merely raised an eyebrow, then frowned. "I'm hoping they've got some strong evidence to back that up."

I shrugged, not knowing quite what to say.

As we walked back out through the workshop I looked around with interest, never having seen anything like it. There was almost a religious feel to the place. Wooden handled tools hung in racks between the large cast machinery. Everything looked so old and solid, and in its place.

"My grandfather started this workshop, you know."

"It must give you a great feeling to keep it going after all these years. Has it changed much?"

"My father put in most of the machinery, but the rip saw was my grandfather's, and most of the benches are his originals. I've replaced a few machines and added a couple. Virtually all of the hand tools and clamps are either my grandfather's or my father's, although I've managed to pick up a fair few second-hand tools as all the old craftsmen have retired."

He dragged an old wooden toolbox from under the bench, placed it on top and opened the lid.

"This was my father's first toolbox – he made it as an apprentice when he first left school. Look at the way everything fits in little trays or drawers and niches in the lid."

I looked closely at the box – the corners were beautifully dovetailed, and tools fitted everywhere inside it, like a three dimensional jigsaw puzzle. I closed the lid and noticed that, inlaid into the top, in a darker wood, was the inscription "M. Hare ~ 28th January 1922". It was then that I realised that the "son" in the title was not Francis, but his father. Suddenly, it crossed my mind that Francis was the last of them. Even if his son had survived, having chosen to go to university he probably wouldn't have followed in his father's footsteps.

"Was Patrick never interested in any of this?" I asked.

"No, he always hated the workshop. I suppose it was my fault really – I expected him to be like me. I used to spend hours in here from an early age, watching my father, doing little chores for him, but Patrick was bored to tears with anything to do with wood or making things."

As a way of changing the subject I asked Francis what he was working on at the moment. Despite his obviously melancholic mood he became by his standards almost animated, and he took me through to what he called his clean room, where he told me the "finishing" took place. In the centre of the room stood the most beautiful piece of furniture I have ever seen. I can honestly say that in some respects that moment changed my life – it was the start of a lifelong love of traditional workmanship and materials, and a lifestyle more reminiscent of my grandfather's time than my own.

Francis' piece of furniture was a solid oak bookcase, with latticed glass doors and drawers and cupboards underneath. The finish on the wood was incredible – the flecked black grain stood out from the rich golden brown surface, and the finish had an astonishing depth to it. Everything seemed to be in perfect proportion; in fact, it almost seemed a shame to spoil it by ever putting any books in it. I opened one of the doors. It felt at the same time heavy and light, as if the solidity of the materials was balanced by the precision of the construction. The door clicked closed again with a sound so soft that I had to open and close it once more, just to hear it. Even the back of the bookcase was finished immaculately, all the wood planed and varnished to the same high standard as the rest of it. There was a small metal plaque screwed to the frame. Stamped onto it was the following inscription:

P. Hare & Son, Glasgow.

FH 1978

Francis smiled gently as he saw the effect his work was having on me. "Open a drawer," he told me, watching as I did so, my jaw almost dropping with the smoothness with which it slid open. It reminded me of the time my dad took me, as a small, awestruck boy, to the motor show at the Kelvin Hall, and we got to sit in a Bentley; the soft click the doors made when they were closed and the way the ashtray popped up slowly when you pressed its lid screamed money and quality, but also demanded an admiration for the unseen craftsmen who had achieved it.

"That is stunning, , I can't believe that you made this."

"People have different reactions when they first see furniture of this quality. I pride myself that my work is as good as any being made in the country today." He said this without any conceit, just an honest belief that he was as good as the best in his trade. "Some people are amazed by the technical quality of the construction, others see it adding to the beauty of their home, but there are some who have an almost spiritual reaction to it, as if they see the humanity, the blood, sweat and tears, the emotion, that goes into something like this. They realise that what they see in front of them is the end result of generations of craftsmen who have honed their craft to reach as near to perfection as is possible." He let that hang in the air for a little while, then turned to me and said, "What did you feel when you first saw it?"

I hesitated for a few seconds. "I can't easily put it into words, but I'll never think of wood in the same way again." I felt stupid, and not a little embarrassed.

He looked thoughtful as he replied. "To me, it's not dissimilar to the effect a great piece of art or music has on you, but it's more subtle and personal."

The customer had ordered a matched pair, so he took me back through and showed me the parts he had already made for the second bookcase. It became obvious why the finished bookcase looked so good – all of the joints fitted precisely and many of them were of the "hidden" variety. Years later, when I started to dabble with a little cabinetry of my own, I tried to make similar hidden mitred dovetails for a small cabinet that I wished to give to my sister as a wedding present. It took weeks to cut the joints and in the end it required the judicious use of strong gap-filling glue and some hastily-cut matching wooden wedges to get the joints to look acceptable from the outside. (I lined the inside with cherry, which hid the internal cock-ups.) For years after, I recognised my limitations and stuck to biscuit joints, mortice and tenons, or standard dovetails.

Francis started to fiddle with the carcase and I'm sure he very quickly forgot that I was there. I watched him work as he planed an edge, and even my untrained eye could see that the plane was an extension of his arm, the shavings coming from its mouth so thin as to be almost translucent. I could have watched him for hours, but a shout from the yard interrupted my reverie, and Francis asked me if I wanted a lift anywhere.

I was a bit surprised. "Don't suppose you could drop me up at Anniesland Cross? I'm playing football up there this evening."

"No bother, it's not that far away."

He locked up the workshop, spoke briefly to someone in the house, and led me over to the car. "Here we are," he said.

Fuck, it's the Antiques Roadshow, I thought to myself, as I surveyed an old Morris Traveller in a corner of the yard. This one was immaculate; the curved wooden struts and the gleaming bodywork panels glinting in the sun. Sitting in the soft cracked leather of the strangely upright seats,

26

Francis explained that he'd restored the car after inheriting it from an old guy down the street whom he used to help out a bit from time to time.

After we had passed through Anniesland Cross and stopped at the sports ground, I crossed around in front of the car to head for the changing rooms. He wound down his window, stuck his head out and motioned me back over.

"Who's playing?" he asked.

I told him that we were taking on a bunch of academic dickheads in a match that had been arranged by some "fast-track-ex-university-prick" from Pitt Street who had organised his old "Uni" team to play against our largely successful, but now mostly ageing, B division team. "Some of us have gone to seed a bit, but there's enough of us still playing regular football to hopefully give them a humping."

"Mind if I watch a while?" he said, as he got out of the car.

Although I was a wee bit self-conscious, I nodded. "Yup," I said, "but you may regret it. It won't be pretty." He followed me in as far as the changing rooms, which were, to be honest, more reminiscent of a rugby or cricket club than the usual parks we normally played at. The boys were fairly upbeat about the game until Brian Fleming mentioned that our opposition was virtually the same university team that had reached the second round of the Scottish Cup and had given some third division professional side, Montrose or Brechin, he thought, a real bloody fright before going out to a dodgy penalty in the replay.

A voice from the shitehouse shouted, "Aw fuck, we've been set up by that fanny, Johnston: this is his revenge for all the shite he's had from us since the stupid cunt arrived." That was Stu Mack, one of the Pitt Street wide boys who was probably responsible for most of the proverbial shit that seemed to fall on the heads of all the accelerated-promotion officers who just happened to be heading up the ranks a little bit quicker than the rest of us plodders.

We trudged (not a good sign) out on to the park, which was at the far corner of the playing fields. Needless to say, the "rugger" pitches were clustered around the clubhouse, which had a kind of balcony where non-participating students could stand with their jolly pints and cheer on their varsity fucking fellows. Having said that, once we got to it, the pitch itself was bloody fantastic, best I've ever played on: big (almost the same size as Hampden, I've been told); flat (unlike some of the hillsides we've visited) and green, so fucking green all over, even in the bloody goalmouths. I lay down on my back in the centre circle.

"This is more comfy than my bed," I said to Tommo, who was reverentially rubbing the grass, muttering that it was a bit too much to expect us to play on a decent pitch.

"Aw, shut up … would you rather play on red blaze?" I asked him, referring to the ex-power-station ash and cinder parks that could shred skin from your legs faster than a cheese grater.

"As a matter of fact, I fucking well would. At least it would even it up a bit if we were playing at the Red Road pitches."

As I warmed up I was surprised to see the ref walk over to the corner of the park and speak to Francis, who had been watching us go through the motions of jogging and stretching and eyeing up the opposition's warm-up drill. (They were like some demented wasp army, swarming about with these horrible multi-coloured horizontal stripes that you normally see on rugby's fanny boys.) Francis and the ref talked for what seemed to be an age, then he handed Francis a flag to run the line, the other one going to some bespectacled student in a bloody duffel coat.

I would like to say that we played them off the park; I would even like to say that it was a fairly even game and we just lost it at the last gasp. What I can say is that we were red rotten. Not all of us. Some, including myself, if it doesn't sound too arrogant, really played our guts out and in short spells actually played some nice football. But for most of the game it was backs to the wall and, to coin a phrase, they looked like scoring every time they came up the park. To be fair, we had several large slices of luck and it is perhaps a reflection of how well our goalie played that we were only two down at half-time.

If the first half had been one-sided the second half was, for the most part, even worse. The game was played almost exclusively in our half, as our goalkeeper's weakest point was his kicking. It was a good job that we'd changed round at half-time, otherwise one half of the pitch would have been mud, while the other wouldn't have looked out of place on a golf course, except for the muddy path that their goalkeeper had trodden back and forth across his six yard box in boredom, like some demented polar bear.

Despite their dominance and bombardment of our goal the gods of football shone on us for a while, even to the extent of providing us with a breakaway goal set up by a lovely long pass from deep inside our own half, which Stu Mack had threaded through their defence. They probably had gone to sleep waiting for some action – a couple of them even seemed to have joined their midfield's siege on our goal. Anyway, Tommo uncharacteristically latched on to this pinpoint pass, ran twenty yards to the byline and stroked a vicious curving cross straight on to the frantically flying head of yours truly, and from there it looped into the top left corner of the net. At this point our heads could have lifted, and we could have perhaps scrambled an undeserved draw. What actually happened was that even the fairly fit players among us ran out of steam all around the same point, thus joining the six or seven fat bastards who had been completely cunted since half-time. After the score reached five-one, and five of our team looked like serious candidates for the Western Infirmary's cardiac resuscitation suite, the ref put us out of our misery by blowing the final whistle a full five minutes early. Johnston, at that moment, actually lost all the superiority that he had gained in winning the game by trying to argue with the ref that full time was at least eight minutes off, taking into consideration the time that the game had stopped to allow Colin "Donkey" Harvey to vomit in three different places along the touchline.

We trooped off miserably to the changing rooms (big hot communal bath and showers – fucking amazing), and as I shook the ref's hand in the corridor, he asked me if I'd known Francis long. When I replied that I'd known him only for a short while, he looked at me strangely and said, "You must be honoured, then. Francis doesn't usually go out of his way for anybody."

Feeling slightly uncomfortable with this, I asked him how he knew Francis. "I've been refereeing for twenty-four years, and Francis Hare is one of the best amateur footballers I've had the privilege to referee."

"Don't you mean used to be?" I asked, laughing.

"No, he still plays amateur football, and after seeing your performance none of you could hold a candle to him, even at his age. I'll tell you, he could have outlasted ALL the players on the pitch today. He probably could have gone professional, but I suppose he thought he would get caught out for speed at that level. He did play junior football for quite a few years."

I thanked him for the game and the information, and we both went to get changed. We all met in the bar after the game, and I waved Francis in. Although quiet, he seemed very much at ease, talking quietly with a few of the opposition, whom he obviously knew. I caught up with him as he stood at the bar on his own, nursing an orange juice.

"You never told me you played," I said, sounding slightly miffed as I said it.

"You never asked."

I had to grin at that; I deserved it, really.

"Who are you playing for at the moment?" he asked me.

"Oh, just a Sunday league mob, and sometimes with the division team. Why d'you ask?"

He didn't reply, but I was getting almost used to the sudden gaps in the conversation that were his trademark. We stood sipping our drinks and just as it was beginning to get a bit awkward Francis put on his coat and wished me all the best, and said that he'd see me again sometime.

CHAPTER 3   SARAH

[Tuesday 2nd May 1978 a.m.]

I found a note on my desk when I came in the next morning. I made my way to the DI's office, as requested, knocked on the half-open door, and took the vacant seat in front of Gallagher's desk.

"I want you to do some more background on the kid," he said, "seeing as you came up with the bright idea of looking at his haunts and habits. Start at his house, look at his stuff, and see if you get anything on where he hangs out. Just fucking remember to phone the parents first to warn them you're coming."

"OK, sir, but aren't we detaining the suspects today?"

"Yeh, but I've got enough guys for that. We've got an extra eight DCs and a whole pile of uniforms, and you're the one with the least experience, so see what you can dredge up. Talk to his pals and his girlfriend, and see if you can speak to some of the other students in his year. Don't complain. A lot of new cunts wouldn't even get out of the office for the first month!"

In fact I thought this sounded like a good idea, but I was a bit disappointed to miss out on the arrests. At the back of my mind I wondered if I was being deliberately left out of it. Had Gallagher sensed my disapproval?

"Very good, sir. Do I go on my own?"

"If you're frightened, take a WPC in case it all gets a bit too hairy for you." He laughed, obviously delighted with his ready wit.

"No, sir, I think I'll manage," I retorted, shrugging acceptance that the joke was on me.

"Don't be fucking slow, you daft fuckwit. You can go with Joe; he's got a doctor's appointment later, so I don't want him sloping off halfway through something more important."

"Right, sir, I'll hook up with Joe and get moving."

"Off you go then." He pointed to the door, and just as I was going out, he asked me if I knew where the house was.

"Aye, sir, Mr Hare gave me a lift to my football game the other day, and he stopped off to get something at his shop first – my game was just up the road from his house." These small fucking lies have a habit of catching up with me, but it was all that I could think of at the time. "I'll get the rest of the addresses from the incident room. Am I OK to visit the university to try and see his classmates?"

"Yes, but don't make a spectacle of yourself. Be a bit fucking subtle."

I made myself scarce, finding a spare phone and speaking, as it turned out, to Mrs Hare.

I told her what I'd been asked to do and explained that it could help in finding Patrick's killers. She said that Francis would be away all day, but that I was free to come over anytime as she would not be leaving the house. I wrote all the other relevant details from the central file into my notebook and found Joe, who told me he'd meet me downstairs in ten minutes.

I waited in the car and Joe eventually stuck his head in the passenger door. "Hey, John, I'm really sorry to do this to you, but any chance you could cover for me?"

"Go on; what's up?" I liked Joe, but I wasn't sure what he wanted from me.

"I kind of lied to Gallagher about the doctor thing, gave him the impression I had something wrong with me. Well, I am going to see a doc, but not for my health. The wife and I, we've been trying to have kids for a few years now, and it's not happening for us. She's getting a bit antsy about it. Anyway, we've got an appointment at the fertility clinic today. If we don't take this one, it'll be months before we can get another date."

He looked so miserable, I felt sorry for the poor bastard, having to tell a near stranger he was having trouble getting his missus bairned.

"Listen, Joe, you're all right with me, I'll not say a word."

"Thanks. My car's parked up at the university so no cunt would see me leave. Drop me off at it, would you?" He jumped in and put his belt on.

"Nae probs, consider it done," I said, as I pulled out into the traffic. "Will I just go ahead on my own, or would I be better waiting for you to come back?"

"No, just carry on. I'll catch up with you later and we can go over anything you get. Meet me at the Koh-i-Noor about lunchtime. If I've got time we'll have a curry. Hey, that's my car there, pull over."

I pulled in to let him out and watched in my rear-view mirror as he got into the car and headed for his spunk test, or whatever it was they were going to do to him.

I set off for Jordanhill. It only took a few minutes, as traffic was fairly light after the rush hour. I let myself into the yard and knocked on the front door of the house.

Mrs Hare was one of those women you would call "handsome" – tall, perhaps severe looking, and to my mind a little bit "superior". You could see that she would have been attractive as a young woman, but daunting at the same time. When she answered the door she had obviously been cooking, as she had an apron on and the smell of home baking pervaded the hallway. She motioned me in with a nod of her head, and I closed the door behind me then followed her along the passage and up the stairs. She showed me into a large bedroom at the rear of the house, saying, "I'll be downstairs if you need me. Please don't make a mess, and please ask if you wish to take anything away."

I stood and looked round the room. It was tidy as far as students' rooms go, and I wondered if she'd tidied up after his death. I placed my notebook on the desk in the corner and started to look around.

A guitar sat on a stand by the head of the bed, but I couldn't see any music lying about – probably a "dabbler", I thought.

The room was a peculiar mixture of solid old and tacky new. The bed was a beautiful old wooden three-quarter size bed, with inlaid headboard and footboard. With the matching wardrobe and tall chest, it would not have looked out of place in Francis' showroom, but in front of the old wooden fireplace, sitting like a fat filthy squatter at a royal garden party, was a cheap chipboard and laminate monstrosity in "light pine effect", long and low with smoked glass doors and shelves holding records and books. On top of it there was some rather expensive hi-fi kit, rather than the ubiquitous cheap music centre.

Although most of Patrick Hare's record collection was housed in this unit, there were also a couple of burgundy PVC LP cases, each holding about forty or fifty records, and more than a few singles cases of the same design, but in black. Blaming thoroughness, I took a good look through his records. I liked what I saw; our record collections were kind of similar. Most of the "biggies" were there, especially in the singles department, but there were enough differences for me to think to myself that this lot would fill a few gaps on my album list. There were some nice twelve inch EPs, and a few early picture discs.

Pistols, Ramones, Skids, The Clash; they were all there, but he had a wider taste than I had expected; there was also some older stuff, including The Kinks, Stones, Beatles, early Bowie, a bit of Dylan and The Who. Most of the modern stuff was punk and new wave, but he had a bit of reggae and more than a few modern folk albums.

I checked the desk out next. It was largely unexciting, apart from an economy pack of condoms (I made a note to ask the girlfriend about birth control). I had assumed that his relationship with her had been a longstanding one and that she would have been on the pill.

The other items in the desk, apart from the usual stationery, were mostly university related objects, from notebooks filled with writing in a neat but light hand, to textbooks and printed lecture notes in loose-leaf ring binders.

There were a few bank statements – he had an overdraft, not massive, but big enough to make it likely that he took part in the student lifestyle to the full.

I crossed to a built-in cupboard to the left of the fireplace and opened the door to reveal a fairly deep and well-filled glory hole, the obvious depository for anything not needed for everyday use. Ski boots, boxes of books, an old skateboard, and a box labelled "Natural History" vied for space with various assorted jackets, scarves and hats. There was also a stack of *New Musical Express* papers: he hadn't kept every one, but he'd certainly held on to the most interesting issues. It was like a musical history of the mid-seventies.

At the back of the cupboard I found a box containing an interesting collection of items. Hidden beneath a pile of ten or twelve records, which included Gordon Lightfoot, ELP, Genesis, Mike Oldfield and Supertramp albums, there was a small but well-thumbed collection of porn, mostly your mainstream stuff, but also a couple of slightly more hard-core mags of Dutch origin. Obviously the porn was only slightly more embarrassing to him than the dodgy vinyl. I myself had furtively dumped my early record collection when I was trying to become "cool" at seventeen. As for my porn, well I got rid of that when I moved in with my girlfriend, stuck between the rock (my mum finding it if I stashed it at home) and the hard place (Moira finding it at the flat). I deposited it in a skip outside my dad's nosy neighbour's house – you know, the type of prick who used to chase us as kids when we played football in the street and complained to everyone's parents about each and every sub-criminal act that was perpetrated in the area. I tipped off the local gang of fourteen-year-olds that old Pettigrew was dumping his porn collection in the skip and for the next twenty-four hours, they were like wasps round a picnic – wee boys in and out the skip, pages of choice porn fluttering about the street and into Pettigrew's front garden, the old bastard running about with plastic bags trying to gather it all up to burn in his little garden brazier.

More interestingly, below the porn mags I found a tobacco tin containing a partly used half ounce of Golden Virginia, some Rizlas and a small block of cannabis wrapped in some thick cling film. I looked round to see if his mother was lurking, picked it up with a T-shirt from one of the drawers, and stashed the tin under a loose floorboard at the back of the cupboard. How long it had been there I didn't know, but this was purely for personal use and I sure as fuck wasn't going to be the one that would provide any crumbs of comfort for the defence to use. If it ever turned up I could just say I missed it during my search of the room.

I felt that I had seen everything I needed to, so I went downstairs and shouted through the back to Mrs Hare. On the way out I told her that Patrick and I had had similar tastes, and that he had quite an interesting record collection.

"Oh, I don't like all the stuff he likes, but I suppose our parents said the same about our music tastes when we were young."

I noticed her avoidance of the past tense, but I didn't comment. She gave me the names of a couple of his university friends when I asked, then I shook her hand and left to make my way across to the home of the other female in Patrick's life, his girlfriend Sarah. I found the close where she lived and started climbing up the polished stone stairs, admiring the wrought iron and polished wood banisters, the half-tiled walls, the well-kept painted doors and the potted plants on each landing, the sign of a slightly superior Glasgow tenement building.

I eventually found myself on the top floor and as I knocked on the door of the left hand flat, the door of the flat opposite opened behind me a crack and I could feel someone looking at my back. By the time I had turned round, the door had closed – some nosy bastard neighbour, or perhaps some friend just keeping an eye open for Sarah? Eventually the door was answered by a skinny scarecrow of a girl who assured me that although she wasn't Sarah, if I came in and took a seat Sarah would be through shortly.

Sarah Anstruther was more or less what I'd expected. She was really good looking, but dressed down for two reasons that I worked out later, apart from the obvious one of avoiding being constantly leered at by members of the male sex, myself included. Firstly, and this was confirmed swiftly during our chat; she seemed to want to be taken seriously in some intellectual context, and if looking drop dead gorgeous was going to get in the way, she was more than happy to tone it down. Secondly, I think she saw herself as a left wing moderate-radical, and dull drone was the order of the day among that section of the university intelligentsia.

As far as I was concerned she didn't succeed in being asexual, but it certainly helped to let me have something approaching a normal conversation with her, without my tongue hanging out or my eyes darting too often to her more interesting physical attributes.

Surprisingly, and perhaps because of this, her most noticeable feature was her hair –brown, but in certain lights it could have been almost red, and short in style. She had quite a pretty face, no makeup or jewellery, and she wore jeans and a baggy jumper, which was meant to hide, but gloriously hinted at, a beautifully proportioned figure below it.

I installed my so-sorry-about-your-bereavement face and told her that I was sorry for her loss, I was a detective on the investigation, and I wanted to ask a few questions. She asked me for ID, which surprised me, as very few people do. After looking at my warrant card, the issue date – which screamed "rookie" carefully hidden by my thumb – she motioned for me to take a seat in the kitchen-cum-dining-cum-living area of the flat. Her pal, the stick insect, made it clear that she was not going to leave the room, and I assured her that I was fine with that, although I could have done without the hostile glare that she was giving me.

Anyhow, I kicked off with, "When did you last see Patrick?"

For a moment she couldn't really say anything, and when the words did come out they were sort of half muffled with a sob. "He left here about eleven o'clock on Saturday night, he just left and I never saw him after that." A few tears were running down her cheeks, but she seemed to ignore them. "I told the other policeman about this the night it happened," she added.

"I know," I said softly, handing her a fresh tissue from the box sitting on the table. "I saw in the notes that you'd made a brief statement. This interview is to expand on that and maybe give us some background on Patrick, what he liked, what he did with himself, etcetera, etcetera. If it's any consolation, it will help us a hell of a lot if you can give us as much detail about him as you can."

She gave a barely perceptible nod, and I waited for her to go on. "He thought it was safe to go back to his flat. He could have stayed the bloody night, and it would never have happened."

"You said in your statement that you had been hassled by a crowd of youths earlier. Was that why you were worried about it being safe?"

"We were on our way back from a party in a flat just off Dumbarton Road." She turned to her friend. "What was the name of that street?"

"Gardener Street," came the sullen reply from the twiglet.

"That's it," she said, turning back to me. "We'd left early because Paddy was working in the morning. I suppose he wanted to go home so that he would get a good sleep, but he always walked me home first."

She blushed as she realised what she'd said. "Not that he wouldn't have slept here, but we would have stayed up later."

She looked at her friend, who gave her a little smile of encouragement. "Shit, I'm digging myself in deeper here." She was beginning to get angry with herself now, but I put my arm out and touched the back of her hand. "Hey, it's OK, take your time, this isn't easy for you."

The stick insect glared at me as if I had applied electrodes to her friend's nipples and gradually turned up the power. I gave her what I thought was a dismissive glance and concentrated on the next few questions.

"What actually happened on the way back from the party?"

She gathered herself together. "We were just walking along, talking as usual, and we were just about to turn into Byres Road when six or seven youths who had been standing in a pub doorway moved over to us. Patrick gripped my arm and tried to cross over the road, but two of them moved in front of us."

I nodded, taking brief notes as I went along.

"Patrick asked them if there was a problem and said that he didn't want any trouble, but the smaller of the two said something about not liking him or his type, and did he ..." She paused, biting her bottom lip and shuddered. "He said something really nasty that I really don't want to repeat."

I told her that it was important for us to know everything and that she shouldn't feel bad about repeating what had been said.

"I can't remember the exact words, but it was to do with Patrick having sex with me."

At this point the stick insect butted in.

"The wee bastard's exact words were to ask if he was going to give her a proper shagging, from behind. Sarah, you may as well tell him what these thugs were really like."

I was astonished at the sudden change of heart by Twiggy until I realised that she probably hated all men, but at the current moment I was lower down the hate score than the ones that had killed Patrick.

"I'd rather Sarah answered the questions," I said to her, then I turned to Sarah. "Sarah, is that what he said?"

"Yes, and even when we got past them and seemed to be getting away, they were still running after us, shouting. I can't give you all of it exactly, but it was horrible."

I suggested that she should write down what she could remember, and then I would read it out and she could confirm that it was correct. I didn't want to tell her that she would probably have to get up on the witness stand and tell a packed court all of this; I decided we could cross that bridge when we came to it.

I asked the friend for a piece of paper and slid it across the thick varnished surface of the cheap pine table, then sat quietly watching her as she started to fill the page with neat girly handwriting. Later, as I read it back, I could see that parts of it were shaky, and there were quite a few smudged words where she'd wiped a tear off the page, leaving a bubble of crinkly paper with a washed out letter or two. She had paused at some words as if writing them gave them too much substance. I copied it all into my notebook, as any statement taken had to be written down in my handwriting. As she listened to me reading it out, the twiglet sat beside her and put a hand on her shoulder and it suddenly struck me that Sarah was more than a flatmate to this girl, although it was probably one-way traffic.

I finished reading her words back to her, and to be honest, most of it was the usual stuff you would hear on the streets of any housing scheme, especially at closing time.

She looked pretty numb as I finished and confirmed that, as far as she could remember, that was a fairly accurate record of what had been said. I asked her for descriptions but I wasn't expecting too much as most of the schemies looked, spoke and dressed the same anyway. However, she surprised me with a couple of details which I hadn't heard before, including Billy Green's scar and Nolman's bad teeth.

I asked her if she had ever seen any of them before that day and although she briefly hesitated, she was almost certain that she hadn't. When I asked her if she would be willing to identify the suspects for us her face paled and she looked away, but she agreed to give it a try.

"What sort of mood was Patrick in when he left?" I asked, trying to deflect her from the prospect of an identity parade.

"He was OK – more tired than anything else, but he was really just his usual self."

The twig interrupted indignantly. "He asked you if you would be OK on your own, like as if I wasn't in the flat."

"He didn't mean it like that, he was just thinking that I might have wanted him to stay because I was upset. I wish now I'd made him stay." She started sobbing again and her flatmate didn't waste the opportunity to console her by putting her arm around her shoulder.

"Have you not upset her enough already?" she spat at me.

I stared her out, directing another question to the quietly sobbing girl.

"How long had you and Patrick been together?" I asked quietly.

42

"About a year and a half," she said. This seemed to steady her, and I asked her some bland questions about where they'd met, and what they liked doing, etcetera. She yapped away about how they just liked each other's company and that there wasn't anything particular, but, "Oh, we do both like long walks and we both feel strongly about the environment." We all noticed her use of the present tense, and this led to her face crumpling into tears again.

"And did you always get on really well? You hadn't fallen out over anything, had an argument?"

I thought her pal was going to burst an aneurysm – the eyes blazed anger – but she managed to keep her mouth shut. Sarah looked slightly guarded, as if she'd relaxed too much and suddenly realised that I wasn't as friendly as I seemed.

I went on, "I'm sorry, but I've got to ask these questions. We need to understand Patrick's state of mind when he left." I made a point of scribbling a few extra notes in my book to give her a bit of time.

Eventually she replied that they had had the odd disagreement, but that in general they really got on as well as two people could. She added, "I loved him, you know, and I'm not embarrassed to say it, even to you," meaning, of course that this cynical bastard probably wasn't capable of understanding the concept, far less being able to have feelings for another human being. I didn't seem to be making a very good impression, but I suppose that's part of the job; you really need to have a bit of a shell.

That was me about done. I couldn't think of any more questions to ask her, but as soon as I'd left the flat I remembered that I'd meant to ask her if she knew if Patrick was a heavy drinker, or if he was into drugs. I made a note to call back at some point and see her, but thought perhaps that a phone call might do it. Shit, I'd also forgotten to ask about the birth control method they used. I smiled to myself at the thought of the reaction of her feminist friend if I'd asked Sarah if she was on the pill!

While I was in the area I thought I'd call and see a couple of his friends, but neither of them were in their flats. There was a note on the door of one that said "BB". It didn't take a detective to guess that it referred to the Beer Bar at the Student's Union. Although never a student, I'd been in the Union a few times, trying to pull the nicely uninhibited female undergraduates at the disco in the extension.

Leaving the car parked, I walked briskly up over the hill to the Union in Gibson Street. I entered the old building, took the stairs down and turned left into the Beer Bar. Sartorial drinking it is not. Laminated tables and hideous vinyl cushioned booths, coupled with a floor that almost always seemed to be swimming in beer made it suitable for only one purpose – getting students absolutely pished. To be fair it was cheap and you certainly got a quality pint. Not only that, but women of any description were completely banned from the whole Union, except for the previously mentioned disco. This made the place a haven for the more politically incorrect male student; they even had a soft porn show every Thursday lunchtime called "The Freds".

Anyhow, when I walked in the bar was almost empty, apart from a group of four students sitting in the corner. After collecting a pint at the bar I moved over towards them.

"Is one of you guys Keith Davies?"

They looked at me, sort of surprised – I suppose I didn't look like a student, but I didn't look much like a rozzer either. The one with the cropped hair pointed to one of his mates, the tallest of the four and said, "He is."

"Thanks a fucking lot," said the newly identified Keith. "Why are you looking for me anyway, and who the fuck are you?" he said, turning to me.

I flipped my warrant card across the table. They looked a little less cocky after that, but Mr Hairless was the first to speak. "This about Paddy, then?"

"Yes," I answered, "this is about Patrick – did he get called Paddy normally?"

44

"His mother goes scripto if she hears him called Paddy or Pat, but we generally call him one or the other."

"Listen, if you want to have this discussion elsewhere, I'm happy to oblige." I had thought that somewhere more private would be better, but when they replied that "here will do" I realised that I would probably get more out of them in these surroundings.

I got a bit of background on their friendship with Patrick which, to be honest, wasn't much help beyond confirming what I knew already – that he was one of the lads, had a nice girlfriend ("very nice girlfriend"), got on well with his parents, but rebelled a little in token ways, such as having the odd spliff, not going home some nights (although he usually phoned), and arguing politics and values with his dad.

They got up to the usual student things, pretty harmless fun, but it seemed a fucking waste of the taxpayers' money if you're working class and helping to pay for it. To be fair, this crowd seemed to have come from similar backgrounds to myself.

As I said, the chat really wasn't doing much for me, but when one of the four, I think it was the one called Alex or Alec, said, "He did like to feel he could go anywhere and still be one of the crowd," I felt a little tingle of interest.

"What d'you mean by that?" I asked, probably a bit sharply, because he gave me a funny look and hesitated before answering.

"Well, we all know where we can go and where it's, how can I put it, not advisable to go."

"What, like areas in Glasgow, or pubs and stuff?"

"Anything really – he would drag one of us down to some new pub he'd found, and we would stand and have a pint, me shitting myself and him talking to some old bloke about welding or dog racing. He sometimes even took Sarah with him."

"You're joking," I said.

"Nope, I think she might have got a buzz out of him being able to mix with the 'common man', because she never complained about it."

At this point, Keith butted in, "I don't think he did it to show off or anything. I'm sure he really believed that people should be able to mix with any social class or group, no matter who they were. The silly bastard even went to the odd Rangers pub, and him called 'Patrick'."

"Did he ever get into any trouble when he went native?" I asked.

They all shook their heads and Alec, or whatever he was called, said, "No, the funny thing was he always got on really well with them all. Even in diehard Hun pubs, I've seen him getting pissed quite happily with a crowd of loyal bluenoses."

"Surely they didn't know his name?" I asked, agreeing that Patrick wasn't the best name to have in a place like that. I had another thought: "Was he a football fan?"

"He was a Celtic fan, but he never went to a game as far as I know. He was one of those guys who was equally at home at a rugby international – anyway, I think the fact that his old man was so keen on football was a bit of a turn off for Pat. He liked to make it obvious that he was not a chip off the old block."

"Listen, back to Patrick's love for a bit of rough, did that ever go further? What about rough tarts? Did he ever go to any of the schemes or anything stupid like that?"

"No, not as far as we know," one of them replied.

Another thought crossed my mind, and after I'd asked the question, I thought *what a silly bastard*, because when I asked them where Patrick got his stash, it was like a shutter coming down.

"Listen, man," Keith said, "we all have a little smoke now and again, but there's no heavy stuff and it's all small amounts – Pat was the same, so where he got it is his business. He didn't supply anyone with anything, if that's what you're asking."

"No, no, nothing like that," I quickly retreated, saying, "I just wondered if Patrick got his stuff on his 'travels'."

"Look, you're the police, so we're not going to say anything that will cause the guys problems here – surely all you need to know is that that side of it had nothing to do with anything."

"OK, subject dropped," I said, but I thought it would be worth following up with his girlfriend at a later date.

I bought us all a pint each and chatted for a while about life in general, trying to be vague when they asked when the funeral would be, then I left, heading down to Gibson Street for a businessman's lunch at the Koh-i-Noor – one pound fifty, three courses, and one of the best curries in Glasgow.

I sat at the table eating my bhuna and reviewed my afternoon's notes – you had to do that as soon as possible, while it was still fresh. I left most of the cannabis references out, referring only to "the odd spliff". I was just finishing up when Joe came in.

"How did it go?" we both asked simultaneously, and then burst out laughing. "You first," I said.

"Oh, you don't want to know. Good thing is, my side seems to be OK, although officially I've got to wait a bit while they do some more tests. The doc also seems to think that the wife's OK as well. He says that barring any other results, chances are that if we stop worrying about it, it'll happen sooner or later."

"That's brilliant, but I can't call you Jaffa now." I grinned.

"Jaffa?"

"You know, seedless." I laughed, and to be fair, he did too.

"How did things go with you?"

"Very good," I replied, "here ..." I handed him my notes, which he read, nodding from time to time.

"I'll make a few notes and that's us done for the day. Can't say thanks enough, man."

I phoned Francis to update him on progress. After I'd finished, he said that there was something else he wanted to speak to me about and I cringed inwardly, wondering what he was going to ask.

"I've had a word with Mike and he'd like to take a look at you, if you can come to our next training session."

"Mike being ...?" I interjected, rather stupidly.

"Mike Moffat, manager of Glenhill, the team I play for – we're always looking out for younger players, if they're willing to learn, and I told him I thought you were worth a look."

"Yeah, well, OK," I stammered, surprised, as I had always considered myself to be just a Sunday league player and Glenhill were one of the old, established amateur sides in the Glasgow area, maybe slightly fading from their post-war "glory years", but still in the amateur elite.

"Thursday night, then, I'll pick you up if you like, from the station."

"No, I'll meet you at the house," I answered, not quite knowing why I said that, but aware at the back of my mind that I did not want the boys to know I was on first name terms with Francis.

CHAPTER 4   ARRESTS

When we got back to the office, around four-ish, there was no one in the incident room, so I asked the duty officer where everyone was.

"Most of them are along at the interview rooms," I was told. I returned to a spare desk and wrote up the actions for my interviews, then headed along to the other end of the corridor, meeting Danny on the way.

"What's going on?" I asked him

"We've got them in, about an hour ago it was, and we're nearly finished with the first sessions," he replied as he disappeared into the bog. I followed him in, suddenly realising that I needed a piss.

"How's it going?" I asked.

He grunted non-committedly and checked his hair in the mirror above the sink.

I asked him again if there was any progress, but he mumbled something about it being early days yet and left the toilet. I got the impression that things weren't going that well and that I wasn't the most popular member of the squad. I made my way along to the interview rooms and as I turned the corner I could see Danny standing talking to Tommy Thompson and Pete Jones, "the two fat sergeants". I went to walk past them but Tommy, or "Tommo" as he was known, stopped me, saying that no one was allowed to disturb the interviews.

I stood with them for a while, but no one was saying very much. Tommy offered a fag to Danny and Pete. Just as he was about to put the pack back in his pocket, he glanced at the other two and offered one to me.

"Thanks, but I don't smoke."

"You must be the only one in here that doesn't."

I told him that smoking would fuck up my football, but I could see that they weren't impressed.

"The boss says you don't drink either," he sneered.

"No, that's not true, I just don't drink if I'm going to be driving or if I've a game the next day."

"Oh, I thought you might be 'God Squad' or something. You know, a fucking Quaker."

"Or even worse, a Tim," Pete interjected, enjoying the smirks of the other two.

I kept a smile on my face.

"I was brought up a Tim, but I haven't been to mass in years, haven't been to church at all except for our Stevie's wedding." I wondered why I'd said that – I'm not usually defensive about being a Catholic. All I needed was two more answers like that and I'd feel like Peter the fucking Apostle.

"At least you're not on your own – there's another Fenian in the building. Joe'll be pleased that he's got someone to talk to 'bout his altar boy experiences."

I forced a laugh. It becomes second nature over the years to deal with bigots this way. Laugh with them and drop them in the shite somewhere along the line without them knowing who it was, or why. I wondered if Gallagher had told them that he'd teamed me up with Joe today.

"Maybe Joe and I can start up a wee Celtic supporters club in the station – we could even use the same room that they use for the station lodge meetings."

An angry look passed across Pete's face, but he joined in when he saw the other two laughing, and he slapped me on the back, turning to Tommy.

"Cheeky cunt, isn't he?"

I knew the bastard didn't like me, but I wasn't going to let him see that I was rattled. I also knew that if I stood up to ignorant twats like him I would survive my first spell of CID. There would also be chances to move on to a better section if I kept my head down and got on with the job as best as I could.

Danny turned to me, still grinning. "How did you get on with the girlfriend, then?"

"I got on fine with her until we got engaged, but it's been downhill all the way since then."

"No, you stupid arsehole, not your girlfriend ..." He realised at that point I was winding him up. "OK, smart arse, you know fine well what I meant."

"Sorry, ," I said, laughing. "She's a looker, alright. The guy had good taste. We got a bit of background stuff and some details on the timeline and some more info on the possible suspects from her. I've put it all in the incident room."

"Worth a ride, then?" What a surprise, a sensitive question from Pete the caveman.

"Out of your class, mate," I replied, "out of your class."

"You little cunt, you think you're so fucking clever." With that he stormed off up the corridor in the direction of the bogs.

I turned to the two others, who were obviously taking great pleasure in seeing Pete getting riled, and said, "And probably mine, for that matter."

After a short while Gallagher came out of room one. "Give me a fucking break," he complained. "That wee bastard is being a right stubborn little cunt." He looked at me. "Where's Pete? I want him to do a spell in there. Where the fuck is he?"

"Away for a slash, sir," Danny informed him.

"Go and fucking tell him to get his arse in here, pronto." He was looking at me as he said this, so I made myself scarce in the direction of the toilets. On entering I couldn't see anyone, but one of the cubicles was closed, so I shouted, "Are you in there, Peter?"

"Christ, can a man no' have a crap in peace around here? Fuck off and leave me alone."

I walked back and told Gallagher that Peter would be busy for the foreseeable future and that judging by the smell he was processing the curry that he'd had last night. Gallagher wasn't exactly impressed, but he turned to Tommy Thompson.

"Go and put a bit of pressure on the scummy little ned, we've only got six hours with them."

I stood about waiting in the corridor, the walls grubby and the roof yellow with smoke, waiting for Gallagher to explain what was going on, but he launched into a story about playing two brothers off against each other, eventually getting them to compete in giving details about a gruesome double murder from the late sixties.

I felt pretty marginal: I'd half anticipated that anyway, being new to the job, but I hadn't expected to have the feeling that I was being deliberately excluded from parts of the case. I tried talking to Gallagher, reporting on the interviews of that afternoon. He asked me to clarify a few things and then told me to make sure it was all documented. I said that I wanted to go back and have another chat with Sarah, and Gallagher and Danny gave each other knowing looks.

"Taken a shine to her, have we?" Gallagher asked.

I denied it, but I could see that they were going to have their bit of fun no matter what I said, so I just looked slightly sheepish as I leaned against the wall and waited for something to happen. I yawned, trying to stay awake in the cloying, smoky atmosphere. As a result of being half asleep, I nearly shit myself when all of a sudden there were loud bangs and a clatter from the room that Tommy Thompson had gone in to. I made to open the door, but Gallagher put himself in between the door and me, opening it a crack to see what was going on inside. He closed it again, and turned to us, grinning. "Just young Malky trying it on with the lads." He opened the door and glanced in again. "I think he's just regretting it now."

"Wouldn't it be an idea for us to get in there and help them?" I asked, naively.

"Nah, they're managing just fine on their own." He smiled. "Leave them to it. We'll go and get a cuppa."

With that he started walking back up the corridor to the incident room. As he passed the toilet, he pushed the door halfway open and shouted, "C'mon, you smelly bastard, we've got work to do. Can't have you sitting about getting your piles aired." He turned back to us, and said, "Come on and give us a hand, you lazy twats. Let's get this place in order, before the statements start coming through," then headed off to the incident room.

Danny and I looked at each other, and followed him into the now deserted room.

"How many have we got in custody?" I asked.

"Just the six – we're going to leave the other two to stew a bit yet, now that they know their friends have been lifted. We'll get them in later."

"Do we have much forensics, yet?"

"We searched their hooses earlier, but we got hee-haw."

"No wonder – they'll have got rid of anything that we could have used long ago. They had plenty of time."

"They're too fucking stupid for that. They were just lucky." He started pulling out papers and files. "Right you two, get this lot copied and filed, pronto."

Boring as it was, it needed done, so we just got on with it. Danny pissed off back to the interview rooms after a while, leaving me on my own. Every so often one of the others would come in briefly and, despite their general lack of enthusiasm for giving me information, I gleaned enough to get the feeling that they were really getting somewhere with the interviews. The only bit of excitement came when I heard a commotion in the corridor. By the time I reached the door, Pete and Tommy had already passed. Pete seemed to be holding a wedge of toilet paper to his face and there were a couple of drops of blood splattered here and there in the corridor. Later, someone told me that Pete had "walked into a door" on his way out of the interview room. I briefly saw a couple of the suspects on their way to the cells and they looked as if they'd been roughed up a bit; nothing broken, you understand, just bruising and cuts that would be later explained away as resisting arrest. Into the bargain, one of them would later be additionally charged with assaulting a police officer, hence the disappearance of DC Jones in the direction of the Gartnavel Casualty Department.

I had wondered why there was a distinct absence of legal representation until quite late on in the day, but I had been informed that the little bastards had been so cocky, they'd thought that it was unnecessary until things started to go pear-shaped. Then there was a scramble for lawyers such as hadn't been seen since the Tolpuddle Martyrs decided to say "screw you" to the establishment. By early evening the place was crawling with defence lawyers. I know someone has to do it, to protect punters against the likes of Gallagher and his cronies, but how the fuck these guys go home at night to their wives and kids after protecting the scum they have as clients, I don't know. Christ, some of them even admit that they often know that their clients are as guilty as fuck, so how the hell can they stand up in court and terrorise some poor bastard witness who's already probably shiting himself because the accused's family or pals are already threatening him with physical violence?

Anyway, these lawyers were all milling about, as Gallagher refused to allow them access to their clients. This he was allowed to do on the grounds that there were still two arrests to be made. Obviously, once they were charged, the suspects would be entitled to talk to their briefs before the remand hearing.

When Danny came back we worked away, selecting key pages from the copied files, sticking them on the board with pins. Andy came in and muttered something about "that arsehole Gallagher". I glanced around to check that Gallagher wasn't within earshot.

"Watch yourself, Andy," whispered Danny loudly. "If he hears you talking like that, you'll get clobbered."

"You just look after yourself, Danny boy, and I'll look after Andy. I'm thinking of asking for a transfer anyway. If I can't get another CID unit, I'll go back on bloody traffic."

"You can't be serious," I said, shocked.

"No, you're probably right, but there's times I feel like it." He looked at Danny and me. "And don't you two go bleating to Gallagher about it, OK?"

"Don't be daft," I said, "I'll not say anything."

"Me neither," said Danny. I vowed to have a pint with Andy sometime, just to have a bit of a natter, but I didn't say anything in front of Danny who, despite his assurances, could well go back and report our conversation to the rest of the squad.

We chatted for a while, mostly about the names on the board – it was useful to me, as these guys knew the area and the people and for once seemed willing to get me up to speed on the whole culture of the place. As usual, as I knew from the areas I'd worked in uniform, it was only a small number of evil bastards that made the place smell of decay and violence – ninety five per cent of the folk were decent, but they often lived in fear or intimidation of those few fuckheads.

About an hour passed, then the boys began to filter into the room. There wasn't much chat; to be honest the atmosphere was subdued, despite the underlying tension. One of the guys said that the police surgeon was in seeing Malky, but he would more than likely live. There were a few nervous laughs at that.

Gallagher eventually came in, and apart from Pete Jones and Dave Woodman, the whole lot of us were there, mostly sitting about in small groups, quietly talking. Cups of tea had been handed round and the air quality was not being helped by the inevitable series of fags that were being lit up by most of the squad.

"Right, let's get down to business." Gallagher pointed to the whiteboard. "I see that Danny and McDaid have got the incident board up to date – over the next twenty-four hours I want a summary of everything new we get on there, and Joe, I mean a fucking summary." There were one or two laughs at that and when I turned to Danny he whispered that Joe was famous for his lengthy reports about everything. Gallagher continued: "Malky has given us quite a bit of stuff. Mind you, we've given him quite a bit as well." This time there were more laughs, but I could see that one or two of the lads weren't entirely comfortable with it – Andy for one.

"The other wideos think they're being clever, but they've been making one or two mistakes – seems that two of them were shagging the same bird in different pub toilets at the same time – she must be a right slag to let that happen." This time the laughter was more relaxed, and Gallagher waited until it had died down before continuing. "We're going to put a bit more pressure on Malky, and I think David Johnstone will be our next best bet. He seems to harbour a bit of resentment against John White. Let's try and use that.

"For all of you doing interviews, keep at them, and keep talking to each other. I keep telling you to communicate – these bastards hate to see notes coming into the room 'cause they don't like it if they think we know something. Later on, change them round; let them see Malky's face in passing, but no talking – only take one back to the cells at a time. Wind the bastards up, talk about their women, especially their schemie boiler girlfriends and their poxy slag mothers."

He looked round us all, making sure we were all hanging on his every word.

"Now, those of you that aren't doing interviews, make yourselves busy. Get as much stuff up on the board as you can, get some phone calls made – there's a list of outstanding calls as long as my dick, and before any smart arse comes back at me on that, it's a fucking long list."

Again, the laughter was a bit louder and more relaxed.

At that moment Pete Jones walked in and Gallagher turned to him. "Nice of you to join us, you fat prick," he said, but they were both smiling as he said it.

"Sorry, boss. spot of diarrhoea."

"Well, it's better than gonorrhoea I suppose." Gallagher looked at Peter Dalry as he said this, and the place erupted, Peter spread his hands wide and put on a sheepish look, and the laughter continued for another thirty seconds.

Gallagher tapped on the desk for order. "After we've finished the interviews, I want everyone back here to find out what we've got from the house searches. You all know what we're looking for, so get your actions all done and dusted. Again, those of you not assigned to this, there's plenty to do otherwise. I'll put a list up of who's doing what. That's all for the moment."

He turned to me. "John, I want a word with you before you fuck off anywhere."

Some of the others were already making their way out of the door when Gallagher seemed to suddenly remember something that he'd meant to say.

"Hold it a mo, boys, I forgot to say that *Chief Inspector* Donaldson will be down first thing to give us all a pep talk." The emphasis on the rank, and the sarcastic manner in which he gave this information made me think that he didn't have a great deal of time for Jim Donaldson. I'd only met the inspector once, when I started at CID, and he seemed a decent sort of gaffer, although he looked the slightly nervous, reserved type. He finished with, "I'm sure it's something we'll all look forward to at the start of a long day." With that he waved us towards the door. "Well, on your bikes then."

He turned to me after everyone had noisily left the room. "Listen John, I'm not putting you on any of the interviews. It's not fair to drop you into these situations too early. I've also got a couple of things I want you to help Andy Craig with tomorrow; I'll get him to fill you in on that." With that he walked out, leaving me slightly annoyed but not particularly surprised.

Andy came up behind me. "Listen, pal, you're better off out of it, if you want the honest truth. Just do your job and get out when you can."

"Is the whole of CID like this?" I asked. "Because if it is, I can do without it."

"It's not all like this, but believe it or not I've seen worse." He looked a bit like I felt.

"What have we got, anyway?"

"Shite, kid, but some cunts's got to do it. Gallagher wants us to finish off the house to house at the scene – they got some done the other day but we've to do the rest."

"Oh," I said, disappointed, but in a way relieved to be doing something at all. "Hey, can we call in with Sarah Anstruther? There are a couple of things I need to get back to her for."

He looked at me slightly strangely. "Go on ..."

I felt a bit stupid, but I told him a couple of ideas I'd had. "Patrick definitely had the odd the odd reefer, so I just wondered if she knew where he got it, whether that had anything to do with his death."

"Not bad thinking, mate, but you're on the wrong track – these bastards that we've got just now, they did it, we know they did it, and they know that we know, but we need to know the details to make sure they don't walk. Gallagher wants to do it the easy way because basically he's a lazy fucker. What we need to do is find some stuff to back up the confessions that he's going to rely on. So keep thinking, ask the questions, but at the end of the day the poor bugger got snuffed for being in the wrong bloody street at the wrong time of night."

"Does that mean that we shouldn't bother looking elsewhere?"

"No, you aren't listening – we'll look everywhere we have to, just don't get your hopes up that it will make any difference."

~~o~~

When I arrived at work the next morning I could feel that something significant had happened – there was a buzz around the station, starting at the front desk where the duty officer was talking to two journalists from the *Daily Record*. Although he was telling them that there was no further progress, I could see that his body language was getting the journos interested. The last thing I heard as I went up the stairs was him telling them that they'd be better to hang around as things could change at any time.

Only Danny was in the squad room when I got there, and he was just leaving.

"What's happening?"

"Six of them have been charged, and the other two are getting picked up today. We got a couple of them talking last night, and Sarah and her pal identified three of the suspects as the ones who'd hassled them on the way home that night. The boss managed to get some stuff out of David Johnstone and when they confronted Malky with it, he initially tried to get himself off the hook by saying he was there, but he hadn't taken part in the assault. He said that he didn't want to shop his mates but he 'wasnae gettin the jail for thae cunts', but when we told him that his story didnae tie in with rest of them, he admitted that he was involved with some of the violence."

"Did we get any forensics yesterday?" I asked, despite knowing the answer already.

"I haven't heard yet if we've got much, not that it matters if they're all squealing. Quite a few of the statements indicated that Billy Green was more involved than we'd thought, so he's being pulled in now, along with John White."

"Did Gallagher say anything about what Andy and I were supposed to be doing today?"

He looked anxious to leave, but before he did he told me that he hadn't seen Gallagher since about half past seven that morning.

"How early was everybody in?" I asked.

"Some of them only went home for a wee while last night. Interviewing went on pretty late. Most of us were in about seven."

"No one told me it would be an early start," I complained.

"Oh, I think the boss would be thinking you weren't needed until later. I wouldn't worry about it."

After the morning pep talk from Donaldson, the DCI, which was received with barely concealed disdain by most of the squad, Andy grabbed me and we walked out to his car. As we got in he asked if there was anything else I needed to ask Patrick's girlfriend, as we would be in that area.

I thought that he was one of these quiet people who actually knows when someone else has something to say and would listen when they did, so I took the opportunity to update him. "There are a couple of other things I'd like to ask her. His friends said that Patrick liked to go native, drink in pubs at the rougher edge and stuff – he liked to think he was a friend of the working classes. Also, I wonder how he got on with his father. I've got slightly different slants on that from different people already."

"Hey, whoa, Trigger, you're going off at a tangent now. The old man's not involved. Firstly, he's stone clad somewhere else at the time of the murder, and secondly ... well, there isn't a secondly, but he just didn't ..."

I butted in. "I know that, it was more for background, to try and see how Patrick fitted together. I mean, maybe he felt he had to prove something, and doing that put him in risky situations."

"Doesn't matter what motivated him, it's what motivated his killers that's the important bit."

He suddenly seemed to remember something. "Aw, fuck, talking about Patrick's old man, there was a phone call for you earlier, he said to contact him when you could manage, something about football." He looked a bit embarrassed. "Sorry, I should have told you earlier. Look, there's a phone box over there, give him a call."

I nipped out from the car and phoned Francis. He wasn't in, but his wife said that he had left a message about remembering training tomorrow night at seven, and that I should meet at the house after work.

When I got back to the car, Andy gave me a look.

"I've started training with the same team as Francis," I said. I tried to sound as matter of fact as possible. "He saw me play the other day and put in a word for me with his manager, so he's going to give me a go."

"Just watch Gallagher doesn't find out – he might use that to get at you or Francis." Andy still looked thoughtful. "How did he get to be watching you silly bastards trying to play football anyway?"

"He gave me a lift the other day as the ground where we were playing was just up from where he lives, and he stayed to watch a bit of the match. He knew the ref, and a few of the opposition players, as well."

"Yeh, you lot got stuffed, didn't you, by Johnston and his posh brigade? He was slagging you lot off all over the division."

"Aye, it wasn't pretty, but a few of us actually played all right. Francis asked me after if I'd be interested in trying out for Glenhill."

He whistled, impressed at that, and said, "That's a not bad outfit, from what I hear."

"Do you play then?" I turned and asked him.

"Naw, at least not since I was a kid, but I hear the boys talking, you know. Anyway, enough of that; just watch yourself and don't tell any of the lads any more than you have to."

For him that seemed to be the end of the conversation, and besides, we had reached Byres Road.

I can't say the next few hours were the most exciting I'd spent in the job, but there was a quiet satisfaction to be gained from doing the donkey work that filled in some of the gaps in the case. I can't say we learned much new, but we made sure there that no one had seen or heard anything that would conflict with what we already did know.

Just as we were knocking on the last door of the morning, Andy turned to me and said, "Do you still want to see the deceased's bird?"

"Is it not getting on a bit?" I replied, thinking of my stomach.

"Don't worry, we can grab a bite later."

We proceeded up to Sarah's flat and this time the flatmate looked more like an emaciated Rottweiler when she saw who was at the door.

"Can't you people just leave her alone? She's having a really rough time of it at the moment. That parade thing last night really freaked her out."

Andy put his hand up to cut off anything I was going to say and instead, in a voice designed to charm the fiercest of harpies, told her that we were very sorry to do this to her friend, but that we needed a couple of pieces of information that might help us to nail the suspects who had been charged late last night.

She obviously was impressed with that, because she grudgingly let us in and we were ushered into the now familiar room. Sarah was again sitting down at the table and Andy asked the flatmate to get a cup of tea for her. He added that a cup of tea for all of us would help and I was pleasantly surprised, and not a little impressed, when she disappeared into the kitchen to comply with Andy's request.

I looked at him admiringly, but he had a bigger agenda. In the absence of Sarah's minder, he asked if it was OK to ask another couple of questions. When she nodded weakly, he explained that a few of Patrick's friends had been interviewed, and that a couple of things had come up from those conversations. He then gave me the nod to carry on.

"Sarah, before I ask you anything, can we just tell you that six of them have been charged, and two others have been detained today. We know it was very difficult for you to identify the suspects, but it was so critical in this case, so really well done. Now, are you OK for a few more questions?"

"Yes, carry on," she said, making an effort to give me a hint of a smile. The identity parade was still obviously worrying her, because she suddenly said, "I could only say for sure with three of them, the others I couldn't be definite about. Lesley identified the same ones I did, we think."

"Don't worry," Andy chipped in, "some of the other witnesses identified them as well." He turned to me. "John …"

I took a deep breath. "Did Patrick ever take you to any pubs or places that you thought were a bit rough or you felt uncomfortable in?"

She looked a bit taken aback at this, but obviously caught on that I already knew about it, and answered in a way that I thought must be pretty close to the truth. "Pat did go to some pretty rough pubs and clubs, and he would occasionally take me, but we never saw any trouble and the majority of the people were really friendly to us."

"Did you ever see any of the guys who were abusive to you on the night of Patrick's death at any of these places?"

She started to bluster that she'd already told me that she didn't recognise any of the men, but she sounded less convincing with that answer than the previous one.

I pressed on, despite noticing that she was beginning to look a little agitated.

"Are you absolutely sure that you hadn't seen any of them before – think really hard before you answer."

She started to sob a little and Andy handed her a paper hankie, which he conjured from his jacket pocket.

"I wasn't really sure, to be honest, but I may have seen a couple of them before – I just don't know for certain." She seemed to pull herself together a little. "I didn't want to say in case I was mistaken. I was worried it would look as if I was making it up."

I softened a little. "Look, we just need all the help we can get to get these bastards, pardon my French, so if you just let us decide what is important and what isn't, we'll get on a lot better." I looked at my notebook, more to create a pause than anything else. "Where did Patrick get his dope from?" I asked, expecting another tearful reaction.

Surprisingly, she answered very matter-of-factly. "I know he had a place down in Dumbarton Road he used to go to, but he only ever had enough for him and me. We often shared with both my friends and his – we all had access to it, really, but no one in our lot really goes over the score."

I told her that I wasn't interested in what they smoked or when, I just needed to know where his source was.

Andy interrupted. "Were him and his friends big drinkers, then?"

Again she replied calmly. "They drank too much, probably, but no more than the rest of the students around here. Sometimes we'd go weeks without a drink, or for that matter, a smoke. The only thing I can say to help you about where he got our grass is that it is up the stairs from an off-licence, I heard him mention that once."

She was trying to help, but that only narrowed it down to half the buildings in Dumbarton Road.

Andy asked her one last question, just as the tea arrived. "How did Patrick and his parents get on?"

"He got on well with his mum, although I don't think she approved of me over much, but him and his dad had a funny sort of relationship."

"What do you mean?" I asked.

"On the surface they seemed a bit distant with each other, and they had quite a few arguments about politics and the environment and stuff like that, but I still think that beneath it all, they loved each other."

"What made you think that?" Andy asked.

"You know when you know someone really well, you often get a feeling about what they're thinking? I just know, that's all, that Pat loved his dad. Anyway, when I first saw Pat's dad after he was killed, I don't think I've ever seen someone so hurt – he didn't really show it much, but I saw it in his eyes. He likes to be the strong man and carry on as normal, and perhaps that is his way of coping, but he is as sore inside as Pat's mum and I are."

"Have you had much contact with them since Patrick's death?" I asked on the spur of the moment.

"Francis has been to see me every day, but I haven't seen his mum. I think she blames me in some way for letting Pat leave that night." She gave a small choked laugh. "It's ironic – she used to give Pat a hard time for staying over, and now she's angry because he didn't stay that night."

"I'm sorry we had to drag you through more of this, but it will help us, rest assured about that. Now, you look after yourself, OK?"

She sniffed. "OK, thanks, I know you have your jobs to do."

We could both see that she really had had enough, so we gave our thanks and left. At the doorway, Andy thanked the flatmate for her patience with us, for the great support she was giving her friend, and for the tea, and asked her to contact us if there was anything they needed.

"You smooth bastard!" I said to Andy as we walked down the stairs.

"Sssshh," he whispered, putting his finger to his lips.

Once we were outside, he turned to me and said, "Sometimes you have to kiss a little ass to make things happen. Anyway, you were pretty touchy-feely with Sarah, so don't start about me."

I grinned as we walked back to the car, thinking that I could learn quite a bit from Andy, and contrasted his style with that of Gallagher and some of the other bully-boys in Partick CID.

As we got back into the car, I suddenly remembered what I'd forgotten to ask. "Fuck it, I meant to ask her if she was on the pill." I explained about the box of condoms I'd found in Patrick's room.

"Chances are they could have been there a while. She's probably on the pill if they've been together for a more than a few weeks."

I looked through my notebook. "Eighteen months or so, they've been going out."

"Maybe his parents made sure he had a supply – you know, didn't want an unwanted kid to fuck up their son's education."

I didn't think so. "Mum's a bit prim and proper, and I couldn't see Francis discussing Patrick's sex life with him. Perhaps he was Jack the lad before Sarah."

"Or maybe he shags about behind her back and wants to avoid giving her a dose."

I was strangely surprised; I'd not even thought of that. "If she was my bird, I don't think I would be playing away from home."

"Ah, but no matter how gorgeous she is, and I'll admit she's all that, some women just don't provide everything a bloke wants, so don't rule it out completely."

I grinned. "OK, the old blow job complaint. But, being honest, from what I've heard of these two it seems as if they were completely into each other."

"You can ask her if we interview her again, that will make you popular with the angry lesbian."

"Yeah, she does seem a bit protective – fancies herself as the bull dyke in that relationship."

We got back to the station, and Andy was called away to the interview rooms by Tommo, one of the two sergeants, leaving me to get back to the drudge of sorting and sifting through pages of notes and collating the information into some semblance of order. I didn't see him until much later, when he poked his head round the door and asked if I'd eaten.

We nicked over to Doloni's for a pie supper each and sat on a bench in the small park down from the station eating them. In between blowing on chips to cool them down, Andy told me about one of this afternoon's interviews. "I was in on Billy Green's. Now, he's just like the rest of the little bastards, he's an evil little cunt, but I still didn't like what they did to him today."

"What happened?" I asked, as I stuck a piece of steak pie in my mouth. Next thing I was sucking air in to try and avoid scalding my tongue on the pie – my reward for not checking how piping hot the fucking thing was. I spat the offending item on to the grass and took a quick slug of Irn-Bru to cool my mouth down.

Andy laughed. "Serves you right, you could see that was roasting hot."

I repeated my question. "What happened?"

"Well, the wee cunt was just stringing us along, and Gallagher came in with this inhaler in his hand, you know, for asthma. Anyway, he says to Billy, 'Lost something, Billy?' as he was waving it from side to side. So Billy, who had been cool as fuck up to that point, suddenly felt in his pocket and realised that Gallagher had pulled a fast one on him. To be fair, the little fuck shrugged and tried to look like he didn't give a toss. We just watched him for a while and you could see that it was getting to him, he just started breathing a bit faster, then the little bastard started sweating, you could see the drops forming on his forehead. I thought I could hear a kind of whistling sound every time he breathed in.

"I asked Gallagher to give him a puff to calm him down a bit. Gallagher just smiled, and said, 'No fucking chance, not unless he gives us a bit of information about his poxy mates, then I might think of giving it back to him.' I could have punched the sick bastard; he was as bad as they were. I realised that Gallagher had put me in there for a reason – it made him look like a right hard bastard if someone else tried to stop him and he just laughed in their face. It wouldn't have been so bad if he'd warned me, or maybe it would have, but anyway, I was fucking annoyed. I stayed anyway, and by the time they gave him his inhaler the poor cunt hardly had the breath left to use it – it took him about ten minutes for his breath to stop rasping."

I listened, wondering why Andy was even telling me all this, but I suppose he had to get it off his chest to someone and he seemed to trust me. He carried on with the story.

"After he'd settled down, they took the inhaler away again. He asked to see a doctor, but Gallagher dismissed that request as well. Well, that went on for a while, and at one point I thought we were all going to be up on a murder charge. I actually asked permission to terminate the fucking interview. In the end I think wee Billy was more scared of breathing his last than of his so-called-mates because he started to talk. They're still working on him."

"Fuck me gently," I said, shaking my head, "they're a bunch of nutters. Does Donaldson never do anything about it?" I added, thinking that surely someone could keep Gallagher and his team under control.

He laughed at that, looking at me as if I was stupid. "Donaldson couldn't see shite at the end of his nose. Anyhow, he's scared shitless of Gallagher and a few of the others. As long as Gallagher gets results, which to be fair, he does, Donaldson'll just let him run his own show. He makes the odd appearance, to make it look as if he's in charge, but everyone just laughs at him behind his back."

He continued, bitterly. "You want to know about Gallagher and his mates? Just ask around. When Gallagher started with plain clothes, in the late sixties, he was a member of this task force that was set up to try and rid the streets of the knife gangs that were rife at the time. Laugh if you want, but they called themselves the 'untouchables', and they consisted of a core of hard-as-fuck cops who would patrol in the well-known unmarked 'Black Maria' vans, going right into the gangs' strongholds, bursting out the back doors of the vans and rounding up as many of the knife thugs as possible. Sometimes you could see the vans swaying from side to side as the thugs were ferried back to the local station, justice being meted out to the occupants en route with fists, boots and truncheons. Once there they were charged with breaches of the peace, resisting arrest, possession of offensive weapons and the like, basically jailed for fuck-all half of the time, but it did clean up the streets, right enough.

"Anyway, as usual, there were always individuals who pushed the boundaries far and above what was generally accepted as 'within reason'. Gallagher was one of those … it was well known that when he picked up a ned who was in possession of a razor or knife, he would slash him across the face with his own blade, permanently scarring the individual for life, and to ensure the poor cunt really got the message, he would then deposit him deep into a rival gangs' heartland, to make his own way back to safety with half his face off."

"How did they get away with it? Did no one say anything?"

"Eventually it was disbanded, but by that time it had done its job anyway."

"Were the other two in it as well?"

"Tommo and Pete Jones? No, but they weren't much better. I heard a story about them when they were younger, working uniform over Baillieston way. They tanned a door in this pub, I can't remember its name, then they helped themselves to a couple of crates of spirits, planked it somewhere, and called in a suspected break-in to control. The keyholder was contacted and turned up at the pub, which Tommo and Pete were 'minding' to make sure nothing else was stolen. The keyholder, who was one of the barmaids, was grateful to the two nice officers for checking the property and noticing the break-in, and for keeping an eye on the place – so they got a lock-in with unlimited booze and no doubt one of them would have given the barmaid a ride into the bargain, while they waited for a joiner to turn up and make the place secure!"

I couldn't believe that sort of thing had gone on, and although he said that it wasn't the same now, he assured me that it had been like that back in the sixties and early seventies.

When we got back to the station everyone else had disappeared. Some were in doing interviews, and I supposed that the rest of them were still doing the last of the house searches. I talked to the duty officer, but he didn't know much about anything. Andy told me to bugger off and said that he might do the same, seeing as we didn't seem to be part of the team anyway. I could see that he was totally pissed off, and was about to suggest a quick pint, when I saw that there was a message pinned to the noticeboard for me.

"I've to give Francis a phone, probably something to do with the football. I'll see you in the morning."

Andy gave a wave as he went out and I dialled Francis' number.

This time he was in. I told him that I'd got his message about the training, and that I would meet him at his house the following night at half six.

"You do that," he replied. He paused, and added, "But that wasn't what I was phoning about, John."

Immediately, I looked around to see if anyone was watching or listening. I must have looked as guilty as fuck.

"Listen, Francis, I can't say much here. Can I meet you somewhere?"

He hesitated for a few seconds. "Do you know the Clan Head?"

I knew where it was and had been in it once or twice. I told Francis that I could be there in ten.

When I arrived he had just ordered a pint for himself, and one for me. He didn't say much until we had sat down and had a few satisfying gulps of our drinks. I noticed that he was a "heavy" man, but he'd bought me a lager.

I looked at him expectantly, but he just took another long swallow of his beer. I didn't have the patience to wait him out. "Well ...?"

"They got nothing on the house searches."

I nearly choked on a mouthful of Tennent's.

"Jesus, Francis, what are you trying to do to me? Where did you get that from?" I blurted out, looking round to see if anyone else in the dimly lit pub was looking at us.

"Let's just say that I've no reason to doubt its trustworthiness, and there's no secret about where it came from. I phoned Gallagher not long ago and he told me that, although he'd got no forensics to speak of, he was very confident about the suspect confessions and the witnesses."

I gathered my thoughts together before speaking.

"That seems to be the way he works – if it's any consolation, he seems to have a fairly good success rate."

"But you have misgivings about it?"

I fidgeted a bit as I answered – I didn't feel comfortable with this at all, but deep down I felt that Francis had a right to know what the score was.

"As far as I can tell, Donaldson, the DCI, more or less gives Gallagher a free hand to run the investigations. The two DSs are cronies of Gallagher's and are happy with anything he says or does. The result is that Gallagher runs the show. From what I hear, some of the other sections are the same, but Gallagher's seems to be worst. He gets away with it because he has a good conviction rate, and Donaldson can just gloss over the detail."

"And you don't think that's a good thing, I take it?"

"Probably not. He seems to take too many short cuts. As far as I can see the whole squad is sloppy, and there's other things going on as well."

Francis gave me that knowing look again. "Something you don't want to talk to me about? Don't worry, I can read between the lines. Don't say anything that you don't feel comfortable with."

"It's just that ..." Francis reached over and put his hand on my shoulder.

"Listen, I'm not stupid, I can see that the whole thing is run by some second-rate bully. To be honest, you and I both know that these guys they've got are the right ones. I don't mind if Gallagher uses methods to get them which we might be squeamish about," he said, glancing at me as he did, noting my slightly surprised look, and giving me a sardonic smile, "but I am really concerned that they are going to make an arse of this and let the little bastards get away with it."

I must've had a sick look on my face, because Francis just inclined his head towards me and finished, "You too, obviously?"

"Look, I think there is a danger that something like that could happen, and I can't say too much about how the interviews were conducted, but I hope to fuck that the result will go the right way. Apart from anything else, there are a couple of DCs on the case who are trying to do all the other stuff that should be getting done while Gallagher and his cronies get on with their bit."

I hesitated slightly, and then plunged on.

"There are a few things which could come out that you won't particularly like ..." I tailed off, waiting to see what his reaction was going to be, but he didn't flinch, so I carried on. "Patrick smoked cannabis from time to time and it's nearly bound to come out at the trial."

"I had an idea that he did, and although I can't say I approved, I never broached the subject with him. Of course his mum never knew and she might get upset if it comes out."

I told him it might be an idea to tell her before it came out in public. "The defence are going to bring up anything which might make Patrick look less than perfect, so be prepared for some crap in that department."

"Anything else?"

"How can I put this? Patrick was guilty of putting himself in situations which were a bit risky at best, dangerous at worst; mostly places that weren't what you'd call suitable for a student from a middle-class background. Did he ever tell you anything about the pubs he went to?"

"Not really. We sometimes would have a pint or two together somewhere local. I've been a few rough places after games in my time, but I've never had any trouble."

"Yes, but there are pubs and there is Beirut," I said. I named a few of the bars, and for the first time, he looked a bit surprised.

"I've heard of most of them – quite a mixture there. Some of them are just houfs in no-go areas, some are hard-core sectarian places, some I don't recognise." I could see that he was trying to work out why Patrick would have wanted to drink in those types of places.

"That's the nice ones you've described, the rest of them are either gangland pubs or drug dens." I told him that we had a couple of theories. "It could be that he and Sarah got off on danger." I was reluctant to go into details of how some couples heightened the excitement of their sexual encounters by being involved in real or perceived danger. That could mean anything from shagging in a place where they might be discovered to fucking after a car chase, or shoplifting for the adrenalin surge rather than financial gain.

Francis shook his head and I thought that he hadn't understood the connotations of my statement, but he dispelled that idea with his answer. "As far as I know, they didn't need any extras in that department."

"Yes," I said, "I don't think I would need much encouragement if she was my girlfriend either, but ..." I kind of realised what I'd said as soon as I'd said it, and my

face turned an appropriate shade of red. "Oh, I didn't mean
..."

Francis smiled "Don't worry, I know what you are trying
to say – she is a stunning young lady. That's not why I
don't think their choice of drinking den was some sort of
sex game. Beauty and sexiness don't always go hand in
hand, but if you had ever seen the two of them together
you would have realised that they had no need to add a bit
of zest to their love life."

Francis said this without the slightest sign of discomfort or
embarrassment.

"Don't you feel a bit awkward talking about it?" I asked
him.

"When Patrick was alive I don't think we ever discussed
the subject, and I now regret that it was one of the many
things that we should have been able to talk about. The
things we did speak about latterly usually ended up in an
argument, more often than not about politics or religion."

Glancing at him, I could see some tightening of his face as
he talked. I turned away to give him a chance to gather
himself together.

"Why do you think they went to those dives?" he
eventually asked.

"Well, I agree with you that it probably wasn't for cheap
thrills. He didn't always go with Sarah, for a start. As often
as not he would be on his own or with his pals. I think it
was more a kind of liberal-leftish kind of thing – I think he
probably saw himself as a man of the people who could
mix with any social group, that there were no barriers."

Francis thought for a spell. "He certainly always
championed the working man and the supposedly
disenfranchised when we discussed politics. I thought that
it was in the main a reaction to my conservative outlook,
that he needed to be different from me. The way I see it is
that you don't deserve anything without hard work, and
although there should be a basic protection for the poorest

in our society, there are far too many wasters and scroungers about. Needless to say, Patrick thought that my politics were somewhat to the right of Genghis Khan, and he frequently told me so."

"So Patrick was as left wing as ... what, labour party, socialist worker, communist?"

He mulled that one over before he replied. "I don't think he was really as organised as that, it was just a general outlook he had, that everyone deserved a chance, or needed looking after. I don't think he joined any parties or anything, but I know for a fact that he had been on a few marches, you know, CND, Save the Whale, etcetera."

"I'll check up on that, so that we're covered when the trial comes round. The defence will try and muddy the waters as much as possible, and the more we know the better."

Nothing was said for a few minutes, but I can't honestly say that it was an uncomfortable silence.

Francis dragged me back to the conversation. "Sarah was probably his biggest influence in that respect – she was more ideological than Patrick was. Up until he met her, he was more of a liberal, middle of the road type of boy."

"I can imagine that her flatmate was also an influence – have you met her?"

"You mean Lesley?"

I nodded "Uh-huh, that'll be her, I suppose."

"A bit of a dyke that one, I think."

Again I nearly choked on my drink. "Christ, Francis, not the sort of thing I'd expect you to come out with."

"I may live a quiet life, but I have seen a bit of the world, you know."

"Right," I said, "but getting back to Sarah, how well do you know her?"

"Oh, I know her fairly well – she always insisted on making the effort to come and see us with Patrick, and although Deborah sometimes gave her a bit of a hard time about their 'intentions', we used to really enjoy her visits. She would sometimes come out and sit and chat in the workroom with me while Patrick wound his mother up in the house one way or another."

"So you've seen her quite a bit since Patrick died?"

"Yes, I've gone to see her every day. I know she must be feeling this as much as we are – she and Patrick were very close."

"I went back to see Sarah, today, just to clear up a few things up. She might mention it to you."

With that, we said our farewells, and I drove home thoughtfully. I made a mental note to myself to ask Andy if it was worth chasing up a few of those pubs to see if any of the suspects were regulars in them.

~~o~~

The next day, Thursday, the inquiry room was quiet when I got in, just before eight. Only Danny, and a WPC filling up the kettle on Gallagher's orders, were present. I asked Danny where everyone was, but he just shrugged and told me he didn't have a clue.

"After the other two were charged, the remand hearings were organised and all the paperwork was tidied up. It was quite late last night before we finished. A few of them went for a drink, so nobody will be in too early today. Didn't you know they'd all been charged now?"

"No, I seem to be the last to hear anything in this place. Has Francis Hare been told yet?"

"Gallagher phoned him late last night. He has seemingly asked to talk to the Fiscal after Donaldson and Gallagher are finished, but I doubt he'll be given the meeting."

I changed the subject. "Where's Andy, then? I've got something he was looking for."

"Andy? I haven't seen him today – have a look on the duty roster to see if he's down for court or something."

Danny left and I looked around the room. There was nothing on the noticeboard for me, so I went over to Andy's desk and had a look to see if he'd left a note of where he was. The duty roster showed that he had been in, at about seven-thirty. I strolled down the corridor towards the toilets and as I turned the corner, I bumped into Joe Harrison coming the other way. I hadn't really seen much of Joe since I'd covered for his visit to the clinic, and he didn't seem to hang around with the rest, but Gallagher seemed to tolerate him more than Andy. I guessed that he was more inclined to keep his head down and say nothing rather than try to fight against them.

"Hey, John, how's it going?" he said.

"Fine," I replied. "I was looking for Andy, you seen him about?"

"No, but Gallagher was looking for you, oh, here he is." Just as he said that, Gallagher came round the corner.

"Who's looking for Andy?" he asked.

I replied that I had been looking for him, but hadn't been able to find out where he was.

Gallagher gave me a funny look, but I didn't let on that I'd noticed. "What were you wanting him for, John? Because you'll not see him till this afternoon – he's doing a wee job for me with DC Woodman."

I told him that I had something to ask Andy about yesterday's interviews, and he asked me how they'd gone.

"OK, I suppose; we didn't find anything that would lead to any other lines of inquiry. The only question would have been whether Patrick and his girlfriend had come across the gang before."

I didn't know if he was entirely pleased with my contribution, or my interest in finding Andy. I was intrigued to find out about the job Andy and Dave were doing, but I wasn't going to say that to Gallagher.

Gallagher more or less dismissed the likelihood of prior contact between the deceased and his murderers, but said that I could pursue it with Andy later on. "I don't want you going off half-cock on your own, though," were the words he used. That being said, I also got the impression that he would be quite happy to keep Andy and I out of his hair until he could wrap up the investigation.

"In the meantime, get on with some filing – the pile on the desk at the front needs copied and the highlighted bits put on the board. File the rest as per usual before the pile reaches the fucking roof."

"OK, sir," I said, thinking that it was better to keep on his right side if I wanted to stay in CID after all this was over.

By lunchtime there was still no sign of Andy, so I nipped out for a bacon, egg and fried tattie scone roll at Jimmy's Joint, a nutritional error if ever there was one. When I returned, I found Andy talking to Gallagher in the corridor. Although their voices were not raised, I could see by the way they were standing that there was some sort of argument taking place. I slipped into the incident room and made to continue with my filing chores. By the time Andy stormed into the room, I had almost finished the task.

"Right, let's go," he said brusquely.

I followed him out, curious as to what had gone on between him and Gallagher, but I managed to resist the impulse to ask him, hoping instead that he'd tell me in his own time. I hurried to catch up with him as he made for his car. Andy, with his black leather jacket and quality sideburns, just had to drive a Capri – not just any Capri, but a GT with the black vinyl top. "Jump in," he said, as he unlocked the car, got in, and reached over to unlock the passenger door. I complied as quickly as I could, and even before my door was shut, he was reversing the car out of the parking space, nearly knocking down a startled traffic warden in the process, then with a squeal of tyres, we surged forward out of the car park. Despite the impressiveness of this manoeuvre it didn't get us very far, as the traffic in Dumbarton Road was nose to tail. As Andy fumed silently and the snarl-up continued to hold us up, I decided to tackle him about his differences with Gallagher.

"What was that all about?' I asked. "You and Gallagher, back in the office."

"If you really must know, we're being fucked over by Gallagher and his cronies, and the whole investigation is based on shite. It's all very well having confessions, but you've got to back that up with good solid evidence and witness statements."

I kept pretty quiet at this, and he continued.

"I shouldn't really be even discussing this with you, and I don't know why, but I think you're all right. The thing is, there's a fair chance that Gallagher and his mob are gonna fuck this up. As a matter of fact, they've been getting away with all this crap for years. Sooner or later things are going to go tits-up and I've got a bad feeling that it might be on this one."

"If they get the convictions, does it really matter in the end?"

He looked at me witheringly. "I thought you seemed to be different." As I started to protest, he silenced me with a glare, and carried on. "Yes, they get convictions, but in the time I've been with them, I can think of two cases where I'm not sure we got the right guys. Even when I raised the possibility with Gallagher, he just laughed and told me to get tae fuck."

"Why don't you go higher up than Gallagher, then?"

"I've already told you; Donaldson is shit-feart of Gallagher, and the bastards above him aren't going to take my word over Donaldson or Gallagher. I'm hoping for a move elsewhere in the division, but it's not easy to get out without it looking bad on your record. Anyway, I get the feeling that I'm getting on their tits now, and they may ship me out anyway."

He paused; he obviously felt quite bitter about the whole situation.

"What are we supposed to be doing now?" I asked.

"That's the annoying thing. We're going to follow up some of the stuff that you've been doing; you know, about Patrick's liking for the rougher side of Glasgow. It's fucking diabolical that someone like you, no offence, but you're just new on the job, is doing the proper investigative work that should have been done by these other lazy cunts."

He smiled after he had said that, as he could see that I was pleased at this backhanded compliment.

"The other reason Gallagher wants us to do this is that if we can show that the deceased was known to the suspects previous to that night, it makes it easier to show a degree of premeditation. So, we're out of his hair and we might turn up something of use to him."

I nodded in agreement, and asked where we were going to start.

"Close to home. We start down at Clydebank, and then work our way back to here."

As we drove along Dumbarton Road, up to Anniesland Cross and down towards Clydebank, I was amazed, as usual, at the juxtaposition of "well-to-do" areas with the less affluent ones. You could see passing through Jordanhill that the large sandstone houses and wide tree-lined streets were the homes of your professionals, businessmen and the odd senior teacher. In contrast, sometimes within a few hundred yards, the houses became smaller, closer together and the only stone involved in their construction was in the crumbling roughcast of the gable end. As we got further into the estate, the roughcast gave way to the monotonous grey of the numerous monolithic flats that surrounded the dirty concrete shopping centre, half of the shops' metal roller shutters closed for security even when the shops were open. There always seemed to be a cold wind blowing through the urine stained passageways under the flats which gave access to the shopping centre's square; a solitary tree with a partly burnt trunk raised its near-lifeless branches to the sky in some attempt to grasp on to life. The boarded up windows on the lower flats made the whole structure look more like a medieval fortress constructed from graffiti-covered reinforced concrete than a place where families could live and shop.

On one corner of the square, next to the Asian mini-market that boasted that it opened "eight-till-late", sat a public house optimistically named the Blue Lagoon, colloquially known as the Bar-L: some comedian had named it before the bright new dawn that was the modern high rise housing estate had foundered on concrete, antisocial families, a lack of community and sheer poverty. The sad fact was that many of the clientele had probably sampled the accommodation of the other "Bar-L", as the infamous Barlinnie prison was known in Glasgow.

As we entered the bar and showed our ID to the barman, the few regulars that were present, nursing their half and halfs, stared at us. Despite looking at photos of Patrick and Sarah, the barman couldn't recall anyone remotely resembling them ever being in the bar. He did, however, easily identify our suspects from the pictures we showed him, but he informed us that they hadn't been in for over a year, having been barred for a string of violent incidents. It had culminated in the near rape of an older divorced woman who had made the mistake of assuming that the young man that had been chatting her up and buying her drinks was not the evil bastard he later proved to be, when he followed her to the toilet and attempted to gang rape her with the help of his friends. Only the intervention of a suspicious barmaid had prevented the obvious outcome.

"The thing is," said the barman, "Sadie, the barmaid who interrupted them, said that the most horrifying thing about the whole incident was the way they had just laughed at her as she threatened to call the police, knowing that the woman wouldn't even report the assault through a combination of shame and fear."

He asked what had they been up to now, and Andy told him that it was a murder investigation.

"Right, I saw that in the papers – some young student was done in, wasn't he?"

"Aye," replied Andy, "but we think we've got them; we just need to tie up a few loose ends."

"I'm not surprised, they were a bunch of bad wee bastards, ask anyone in here."

I thought that the rest of the inhabitants were less than happy with the idea of talking to the rozzers, but showed the pictures around anyway. They reluctantly answered questions confirming the barman's story that the gang hadn't been in for a year, and that somebody would have recognised Patrick and Sarah if they had been in, "especially the girl", a few of the blokes had said.

We checked all the dives in Clydebank and up around Anniesland, and came up with nothing that added to our knowledge of the gang or their victim, but we struck luckier in Dumbarton Road, where in three of the pubs Patrick and his girlfriend had been noticed, and in one of them, Strachan's Bar, the gang had also been seen. Neither the landlord or his barmaid could say if there had been an occasion when both were in together, but then told us to contact a bloke called Dougie Jamieson, who worked in the bar most evenings. We decided to come back at five when he started his shift, so we checked out the remainder of the pubs in the area in the meantime. Despite coming up with only another couple of vague possible IDs on both Patrick and the gang we both felt that we had covered the lead sufficiently, with only the guy Dougie left to speak to.

We returned to Strachan's at about four-thirty, and each of us had a lukewarm pie that had probably been cooked three days ago and kept warm since then in the heated glass food display on the top of the bar. We washed it down with a pint as we waited.

Dougie arrived sharp at five, and the landlord stayed on for a while to allow us a bit of time with him without interruption. Although he seemed reluctant to commit himself at first, Andy's deft manipulation of the situation soon yielded results. Yes, on a couple of occasions they had all been in at the same time. On the first occasion Patrick had been alone, talking to some of the regulars, when the gang came in. They had had a few pints, and after verbally abusing a few of the older soaks, had been asked to move on to avoid any trouble. On the second occasion, which as far as Dougie could recollect was no more than a couple of months ago, the gang had already been in for a couple of hours, getting to the loud-drunk stage when Patrick had walked in with Sarah. Apart from a few catcalls and whistles at first there seemed to be no problem, but as the gang left about an hour later, something appeared to have been said to Patrick as they passed on their way out. A couple of the larger locals had stepped in to prevent any aggro and the gang had left, shouting abuse at Patrick, Sarah, the locals and the staff.

As we returned to the station I asked Andy if this would be as useful, as I thought it would be, and he more or less confirmed what I thought myself, namely that it might help Gallagher build a case of pre-planned murder.

Andy told me as we got back to the station that he would handle Gallagher, but that I should write up everything that we had done that afternoon. "Don't you want to check it all over together before going to Gallagher?" I asked him.

"No, I'll just give Gallagher a brief verbal, and we can cross check the actions in the morning. You can bugger off now if you want."

"Hey, thanks man, I was hoping to get away sharp to get to football training."

"You'll see Francis at this training of yours?"

"Aye, he'll be there, I hope – he's the only bugger in the team that I know."

"You can tell him what we've found out today, I'll square that with Gallagher."

I wondered if he knew that I talked to Francis, and I had a few uncomfortable moments thinking that I'd been caught doing something I shouldn't, but then it suddenly gelled with me – Andy was Francis' other source of information.

CHAPTER 5   GLENHILL

After going home and having an early tea, I left Moira a note saying that I might be late home after football training. Although our relationship was a bit rocky by then, given the right "time of the month" and with half a bottle of wine inside her, Moira could still be her old affectionate self, but it was becoming more and more infrequent.

With thoughts of a scantily clad Moira receding from my mind, I began to concentrate on my first training session with Francis' team. To be honest, I was a bit nervous – apart from my lack of fitness, I wondered if I could cut the mustard at this level. I'd always thought that, with a bit of effort, I could make a half decent player. Well, this was my chance to prove it. Being a bit anxious, I arrived early at Francis' place. I sat in the car for five minutes, and then went in through the yard gate and rang the doorbell. Deborah, his wife, answered the door.

"Oh, hello, John. Francis is upstairs, he'll be ready in five minutes. Come in and take a seat." She showed me into the sitting room and sat down on one of the armchairs. I must admit that she was holding herself together well despite having just lost her only son, but as I had realised earlier, she was a very tough woman. Like Francis, I think she saw any show of emotion in front of strangers as a weakness. I stood awkwardly until she motioned for me to take the other chair.

"I hope you don't mind me asking, but how is the investigation going?"

"The suspects are all blaming each other, so we shouldn't be long in getting the full story. We are still trying to piece all the evidence together, but they've all been charged." I wondered how much Francis had told her about our discussions and I looked at her face to see if there was any clue to what she was thinking, but the woman should have been a poker player – she betrayed no emotion at all, although I knew from a couple of comments Francis had made that she was taking it all very hard. Francis' arrival saved me from further awkwardness.

"Bye for now, Mrs Hare," I mumbled.

"You're welcome any time. Francis seems to think highly of you."

I beat a hasty exit after Francis, who had already left the room, and we walked to the training ground, which took us about fifteen minutes. Francis talked a little, mainly about the players in the team, but he also gave me some advice on how to handle the manager.

"Mike's pretty firm, but fair. If you don't piss him about you'll get on just fine. The lads are on the whole a good bunch and they all take training pretty seriously."

We arrived at the park and, after being quickly introduced to the other lads, what followed was the hardest training session I had ever experienced. Mike Moffat took us through a well-structured series of fitness routines, ball skills and tactical drills, and you could see that everyone was up for it. There was intense competition in the sprint exercises and much derisory shouting when someone screwed up in passing practice. At the end of training we played a couple of small sided games and although I had expected these to be of the non-contact variety to avoid injuries I was surprised to see some pretty hefty tackles going in. Mike would occasionally shout to us to tone it down a bit, but in general he seemed unconcerned about the rough stuff.

I had struggled in the fitness training and not surprisingly I found that the training games really stretched me, but I thought that I had done reasonably well for my first night. At the end, after announcing that everyone apart from Derek, a player who was still recovering from a longstanding injury, and I would be required for Saturday, Mike took me aside and asked if he could have a quiet word. I nodded, still breathing hard from the evening's exertions, and we walked round the touchline away from the changing rooms.

"Firstly, I think you should keep coming to training. I think we can make a player out of you."

I must have looked pleased at that, because the next thing he said wasn't as flattering.

"Your fitness is very poor and it's going to take you at least five or six weeks to get anywhere near being able to play, and that's only if you take it really seriously. Even then, you will have to fight to get into the team. If you are willing to do this, I think you'll like it here."

"No problem, Boss", I said, "I'll try and make a go of it."

"Francis seemed to think you would, so don't let yourself or him down." He paused, then added, "And by the way, 'Mike' will do, but don't be getting any ideas that I'm your friend. If you don't hate me most of the time over the next three months there'll be something wrong."

"Thanks, B … I mean Mike," I replied, grinning. "Anything else I should know?"

"Yes, as a matter of fact, there are a couple of things. Firstly, I would strongly advise you to cut back on boozing if you're a heavy drinker, and definitely NO drinking the day before a game or training. Now, diet. Just be a bit more careful. Eat less crap, and drink plenty water. Thirdly, we don't tolerate hotheads here, so make sure you stay disciplined. If you want to come to watch the games in the meantime, just let me know. We have an old minibus we use for away games, and there's often a spare seat. Any questions?"

I shook my head. "No, I think I'm OK with everything." With that I ran and got showered and changed. Francis and I left the training ground along with two or three of the boys, and made our way to the Esquire for a pint.

Most of the team were in, but practically all of them were drinking pints of orange and lemonade, and we ordered the same. I got chatting with a few of the younger players, mainly about how much football I'd played, who I'd played for and so forth. None of them asked me how I'd met Francis, so I presumed that they already knew that I was working on the investigation of Patrick's murder. I got the impression that Francis had quietly requested that things should go on as normal, at least as far as football was concerned. Some might say that Francis was being a bit insensitive in carrying on with these aspects of life as if nothing had happened, but I can only say, in his defence, that people can sometimes cope better with bereavement by continuing with as much of their everyday routine as possible.

There was a good mix of lads in the team and, although there were a few characters, the atmosphere was more subdued than the post-training binges I was accustomed to with my Saturday morning league team. As this thought crossed my mind, I realised that I hadn't told any of my mates that I was leaving my old team to join Glenhill, and I wondered if Mike would have any objections to me playing with them on Saturday mornings until such time as he considered me fit enough to play for him. I drifted over to ask Francis about it, but he was talking to another player, Barry Miller I think it was. I stood for a few moments as they finished their conversation, then Francis turned to me and said, "John, has Mike said anything to you?"

"Aye, he says that if I train hard for a couple of seasons, I might get to carry the water bottles on at half-time," I replied.

Barry laughed. "Was Mike a bit blunt with you? Let me guess, he told you that you were unfit, you should drink less and that you weren't good enough to clean the boots of some of the players he's played with."

"Well, two out of three anyway. He didn't mention the boots," I said with a grin.

Francis chuckled, and told me that every new signing got the same lecture. "Don't worry about it; he just likes to put the frighteners on new players. There's nothing wrong with you that a few good weeks' training won't sort out. We can even get you doing an extra bit of training if you like, just to sharpen you up."

"Thanks, I might take you up on that," I said, inwardly cursing myself as I found fitness training in small groups even worse than normal training. "Do you think Mike would mind if I played with my old team for a couple of weeks, just to keep me playing? It'll also give them time to find another player. I'm not a hundred per cent happy about leaving them in the lurch."

"Mike can be a bit funny about that," said Barry, "but one of us could have a word with him to see if you can give them a few weeks."

"I'll do it," Francis said, "but you really want to do it for no more than a couple of games, or Mike will think you're not committed enough. Have you signed forms yet?"

I shook my head. "No, I think he wants to see how I train for the next few weeks."

"Aye, that sounds like Mike, right enough. If he hasn't signed you, I can't see how he can object." With that, Barry looked at his watch and added, "Got to fly, I've got an early start in the morning."

When I arrived home a bit sooner than I'd expected, Moira commented that I was sober, and early. I may have taken advantage of this and implied that I had left the rest of the team drinking to rush home into her arms.

I could see that this approach was going to pay dividends, and sure enough, as I entered the bedroom after brushing my teeth, I saw that a bottle of red wine and a couple of glasses had appeared on the bedside table, and Moira had lit a few candles and placed them strategically around the room. As I was having a quick shave, I heard the phone ringing. "Fuck it," I muttered, and thought to myself that if that's my work or her mum, there'd be the end of the erotic delights I was so looking forward to.

"John," I heard her shout from the bedroom, "it's for you." My mood didn't improve when I saw the look on Moira's face. For fuck's sake, it wasn't my fault if my work occasionally interfered with our love life.

"It's Francis Hare," she said.

Puzzled, but relieved that the evening's sexual extravaganza might yet be back on track, I smiled at Moira and gave her the thumbs up as I took the phone from her.

I was still watching Moira's face as I spoke into the phone.

"Francis, what's up?"

I was only half-listening as I watched Moira extinguish the candles and lift the wine bottle and glasses and leave the room. I half hoped that she'd decided that the fireside rug was more romantic, but I didn't like the look of her body language.

"Sorry, , could you say that again." I'd completely missed what he had said.

"I was saying that I'd spoken to Mike on the phone, and he says that you are all right to continue playing with your mates for a couple of weeks. I thought you'd want to know."

"Thanks a lot,. I'll see you on Saturday, I'll probably come and watch the game."

Francis hung up after saying goodnight, and I hurried through to find Moira.

As soon as I saw her face, I knew I'd blown it.

"What's up?" I stupidly asked

"Nothing."

"Come on, , something's up. Was it something Francis said on the phone?"

"I hate being lied to," Moira replied, and once she had started, I was going to get the full works. "According to Francis, everyone left the pub early, and no one really drinks much after the training sessions anyway, so why did you tell me that you had left early to get home to me?"

Technically correct, but unwise in retrospect, I replied, "I never said at any point that I had left early or that the rest of the lads were drinking, although I did say that I wanted to get home to see you, which was true."

Angry and increasingly tearful, she tore into me. "You bastard, you maybe didn't say it exactly, but you gave the impression that you were so bloody romantic that you left your precious mates to come home early to be with me, so don't bloody lie about it."

Moira didn't often swear, so I knew that I was in deep shit. Fuck, you'd think I'd been caught having an affair, for god's sake.

"I came home, didn't I, instead of going on somewhere else for a couple of pints?"

"That's not the point," she said. "If you'd come home and said training had finished early and you didn't go for a bevvy afterwards I would have been fine with that. It's the fact that you tried to make yourself out to be so-o-o considerate, when all along it was just that nothing better had come up and you thought you'd be bloody clever and take advantage of the situation to get in my bloody knickers."

Then I began to lose it myself: "Keep your bloody knickers on, then. The way you're talking you'd think I was a fucking criminal. Anyway, it's getting more and more difficult to get sex around here nowadays, so you can't blame me for trying to increase my chances."

"Do what you bloody well like," she said as she stormed out of the room, "just don't come near me." With that, she slammed the door of the bedroom, leaving me to ponder how easy it was to screw things up when it came to women. I took a duvet from the linen cupboard, switched the TV and the lights off, and settled down for an uncomfortable night.

The next morning I made sure that I had left for work before Moira was up, having cleared away my temporary bed. When I arrived at the station I met Joe Harrison, who asked me if I'd heard about Andy. For a brief moment it crossed my mind that something had happened to him, but Joe immediately smiled and told me that Andy had just found out that he'd been made up to Detective Sergeant, having completed his divisional and force panels six or eight months before.

"Is he staying here?" I asked hopefully.

"No, of course not – he's moving down to Ayr. Starts at the beginning of next week."

"That's great," I said, not convinced. "Will someone else be taking his place, d'you think?"

"Gallagher says it will be a while before he gets a replacement, but he's not that bothered, as this inquiry is nearly finished."

"Where is Andy at the moment?" I asked

"He's up with Donaldson, but he'll be back down soon. I think we're all going out for a few pints tonight, to celebrate Andy's promotion."

"Right, let me know where you're heading. It'll be better than going home, anyway." I said, still pissed off at last night's fiasco.

Joe laughed. "Wrong time of the month, or did you step too far out of line?"

I smiled ruefully. "A bit of both, I think. Anyway, she's out tonight with the girls, so it would have been a boring night in watching the TV. And I like Andy; he seems one of the good guys."

Joe looked sideways at me. "You and Andy friends, then?"

Cagily, I told him that I'd been with Andy for the last couple of days and I liked the way he went about the job.

"Listen," he said quietly, taking my arm and leading me along the corridor, "Andy's ruffled a few feathers here over the last few months, and a lot of the guys will be quite glad to see the back of him. If I were you, I wouldn't discuss Andy with any of the others. Having said that, I agree with you – he is one of the best. I've been here eighteen months and I reckon I'm due for a move, so I try not to get their backs up like he does – I just keep my head down and get on with the job as best I can. I'd advise you to do the same. I've heard Gallagher and his cronies moaning about your attitude, so unless you want to get sent back to uniform, don't get under their skin."

I was a bit taken aback. "Surely it can't be that bad?" I asked.

"Why do you think Andy's been trying to get out for months, and I've been keeping my ears open for any moves worth trying for?"

"Bloody hell, you're not joking about this, are you?"

Joe shrugged and walked off, his warnings ringing in my ear. I thought about what he'd said and seriously wondered if I could come to work every day and keep my mouth shut and get on with the job. I knew that if I went back to uniform I might never get the chance to work in CID again, so I tried to resign myself to seeing it through with Gallagher's squad until something better came up.

Just as I was thinking of going to get a cup of coffee, Andy walked in.

"Andy, congratulations," I said, shaking his hand.

"Thanks a lot,. I can't say I'm sorry to be leaving this lot. I'm going to clean out my desk, make sure all my case-related stuff has been handed over, and then I'm out of here."

I must have looked disappointed, because he added, "Don't worry, you'll not have to put up with it too long. Gallagher will have you shifted pronto if you don't fit in."

Changing the subject, I asked him if he was going out that evening with the rest of the squad.

"Yes, I'll go for a while, but a few of us might disappear early – Gallagher and his pals won't miss me. It'll give them time to slag me off behind my back."

I told Andy that I'd see him that night and I headed back in the incident room. It was beginning to look a little busier, with Tommo, Pete, Dave, Chris and Danny all there. There was an end-of-case atmosphere. Everyone was tidying up loose ends; writing up and cross-referencing all the paperwork that would now go to the Procurator Fiscal. It would obviously be a couple of months before the trial, and as I had only a peripheral part in the investigation, it would be unlikely to involve me directly. I hoped fervently that the convictions would be straightforward, but at the back of my mind there was a vague uneasiness about the whole thing.

The rest of the day was one of those wasted days when nothing much happened. At about three o'clock I buggered off home after clearing it with Tommo and checking out where we were meeting up that night.

After a sleep and a shower, I caught the train back into town and got off at Charing Cross. I headed up Sauchiehall Street, finding Bar 101 easily, and spotted Gallagher. I could tell from his ruddy features and the way he was slurring his speech that he was a few drinks ahead of me. I could now make out at least three or four bodies slouching in the corner, to one degree or another. There was no sign of Andy yet, and Joe Harrison seemingly had a family engagement on. "At the fucking pineapple, more likely than not, to christen another of these Fenian nephews or nieces," jeered Pete Jones. He turned to me, grinning. "No offence, Johnny boy."

"None taken, big man," I replied, chalking up one for later.

As the evening got into full swing, I tried my best to limit the damage by missing out a few of the rounds, remembering that I was playing football in the morning. About half past eight, in walked Andy. By the time the bouncers came on duty at about ten o'clock, our lot had got pretty loud and obnoxious and I watched as the bouncers and the bar staff glanced over in our direction as they talked. Nobody had done anything really stupid, but you could sense that everybody in the bar wanted us to leave.

At about quarter to eleven I bumped into Andy in the bogs and he mentioned quietly that he was going to make his exit. "Listen, wait five minutes then tell everyone that I spewed my ring in the bogs and pissed off home."

I was just about to ask why, but he went on, "Leave it another ten minutes, then meet me at the Shish for a curry – Joe's meeting us there if he can get away."

I tapped my finger on my nose. "Shtum," I said, and wandered back to the table. Gallagher and Tommo had engaged a couple of tarts from the next table in conversation. The blokes that were in their group looked a bit pissed off at this, but the girls had obviously thought that ours was a more interesting crowd. When Gallagher told them that we were all CID, doing murder inquiries, the girls squeezed in between Gallagher, Tommo and Dave. You could see by their faces that all the gutter talk and the sense of danger was giving them the equivalent of a right good hard on. To be fair, the tarts were having a similar effect on all the lads sitting round them, each of them vying to shock the girls with gruesome descriptions and filthy stories. The blokes from the tarts' table had legged it after discovering that we were the filth, thinking better of making a scene once they knew who we were. The remaining two girls joined us at that point and I could see that there was a fair chance that all four of them were going to get shagged by our lot tonight. I told the lads I was off, as I had football in the morning. After a hail of derisory jeers, Pete shouted, leering at the lassie to his left, "All the more poontang for us, you boring little arse."

I waved my hand and smiled, departing to raucous laughter from the whole sorry group.

Andy and Joe had already ordered, so I added a chicken dansak, two chapatis and a veg pakora to the order. I asked Andy when he started down in Ayr, and whether he would find it a bit boring after working in the city.

"Listen, , I would have taken anything to get away from that bunch of morons, so the fact that it's a promotion and I'm still in serious crimes is a bonus. Anyway, if I do a couple of years down there, I can always come back up if I want."

Joe interrupted. "You'll fit in all right, as long as you don't end up with another Gallagher."

Andy smiled. "Don't worry, I checked it all out – I spoke to the DI, a couple of DSs and a few of the plods, and they all say it's a good place to work."

Our food arrived and I mostly listened as Andy and Joe reminisced about their time on Gallagher's team. About midnight, we decided to call it a night, Joe and I promising to keep in touch with Andy. Joe hurried away and Andy took my arm and said quietly, "John, just hang in there and something will come up. Gallagher doesn't want you in the squad anyway, so you'll be moved on." I thought he had finished, but he added one last thing. "Keep in touch with Francis for me, I feel for that poor bastard."

I said that I would, and with a, "Bye for now," he walked out to the edge of the road and hailed a passing taxi.

~~o~~

Before Saturday's game, I knew I had to let my old team know that I was leaving. I mentioned it to the manager first and he was kind of philosophical about it, but seemed disappointed.

"I've been telling folk for ages that it was a matter of time before you would move on, so it's no surprise. It'll leave me looking for some other wanker for your position, but good luck anyway. If it doesn't work out, you can always come back." He shook my hand which, to be honest, took me by surprise.

I blustered, covering over any possible show of emotion. "Piss off, don't go all soft on me, I'll start crying in a minute."

He just laughed. "Come on, we'll go and tell the rest of this sorry bunch."

So after he had hushed the changing room, I told the boys that I was training with Glenhill with a view to signing and their response was predictable. There was a chorus of jeers and whistles, "Smart bastard,"; "Toooo good for us, then," a few strutted about with their noses in the air, and Jerry used a pair of rolled up socks as a microphone and, in his best Archie McPherson voice, announced: "Young John McDaid has today signed for Glenhill for a fee reported to be in the region of ... em, sorry, the fee seems to be undisclosed at the moment, but we understand it will be in the region of ... fuck all." The rest of the lads were pissing themselves at this, and he went on. "Glenhill issued a statement saying that they were delighted with their new acquisition and that they expected a big improvement in the quality of their kit now that they had obtained the services of a new bag man."

I laughed along with the rest of them, and the comments and barbs continued as we got ready for the game. I told them that I would be playing for the next couple of games while they found someone else and that produced another stream of abuse: "Naw, fuck off tae yer fancy friends,"; "Are you sure you don't mind getting your boots muddy with us?" and big hairy Tam started taunting me in a very feminine voice; "We are sooo grateful. Do you wish me to suck you off in gratitude now, or do you wish to wait until the end of the game?"

As we ran out, we were still all laughing. The opposition must have thought we were all on drugs. We might as well have been, right enough. We lost four-two after having led two-one for most of the second half. Two silly errors in defence and a raft of wasted chances meant we were chasing the game for the last five minutes. The usual story; while we were pushing, a long ball over the top by them, a slip by our usually cast iron right back, a wee fast-as-fuck left winger, who for once kept his composure and slotted one over our flailing keeper to kill us stone dead. For about the tenth time this season, we had thrown away a game we could have easily won.

After the game, I drove up to watch the Glenhill match. I arrived well before kick-off and spoke to a few of the team as they went in to get changed. I found a bench and sat outside in the warm sun, leaning against the whitewashed wall and almost dozing off, when I felt a tap on my arm.

"Francis," I said, "you gave me a fright."

"You were somewhere else, just then," he said. "Tired?'

'Just a bit," I replied. "Hard game this morning, and I had a few drinks last night."

"Shame on you." Francis smiled. "Did you not listen to Mike's lecture?"

"Aye, I did, but it would have been hard to get out of it last night and I did keep it down to a reasonable level."

"Oh, was it an end-of-case night out?"

"Aye, partly, but also Andy's leaving – he's been made up to DS, and he's moving out to a new post."

"That's a shame," said Francis, "I quite liked Andy; he seemed to be one of the more decent guys on Patrick's case."

I paused and looked at him. Because he was so good at coping, you could easily miss the small cracks that occasionally appeared on the face that he put on for the outside world. I could tell this morning that he was feeling the full weight of his loss; it was obvious in his eyes.

Natural, I suppose, as there were the beginnings of justice for his son's killers, but still a degree of uncertainty about the outcome of the trial, along with the traumatic experience for Francis and Deborah of the trial itself. The fact that Patrick had been their only child made it doubly unbearable. If there had been other sons or daughters, there would have been more to look forward to once the trial was over. Even more than most couples who had lost a son or daughter, their lives would never be the same again.

I spoke gently to Francis. "How are you both coping? I tried to get hold of you yesterday, but you were out most of the time, and I was late back last night."

"Deborah said you'd phoned; I appreciate that. We're both doing all right, but after the last few day's hectic activities, today is a bit of a downer."

This was the worst I had seen Francis. "I thought that you would feel better at this point, now that things were moving."

"I probably would feel better if I didn't have the feeling that the wheels could come off at any moment."

"Did you get to speak with the PF?"

"Who?"

"You know, the Procurator Fiscal. Andy said you were trying to fix up a meeting."

"Yes, I did, but Gallagher insisted on being present and there seemed to be a bit of friction between the Crown Lawyers and him."

"That's not surprising; the PF would rather have some cast iron physical evidence in this sort of case, bloodied clothes, hair, fibres, for instance."

"Why do YOU think they didn't get any?"

"They just didn't move quickly enough. I think they all thought that this was going to be easy, that they were dealing with wee thick schemie bastards who wouldn't have the brains to cover up the crime."

"I don't like the lack of physical evidence and the Crown Lawyer doesn't, either, but Gallagher just laughed it off," said Francis, and I could hear a concern in his voice that mirrored his worried frown.

"I think that there will be enough to get them with the confessions, and don't forget there are a few witnesses as well." I tried to play down my own concern in saying this, but Francis wasn't convinced.

"There are only a couple of witnesses, and no one saw the actual murder, only the gang before and afterwards."

At that point, the rest of the team started trickling out of the changing rooms.

"I'm sloping off sharpish after the match, but I'll phone you tomorrow."

"Right, I'd better go and warm up. At my age I need to do a bit extra to avoid injuries. I'll speak to you later. Why don't you pop round tomorrow?"

I left immediately after the match, which finished in a three-one victory for Glenhill. I had watched Francis during the game and quickly realised that he was a bit special, in a quiet sort of way. Over the next few years I came to rate him as one of the best players that I ever played with or against, even though I only saw him when he was considered to be well past his peak. Don't get me wrong; there was nothing he was spectacularly good at. He could trap the ball, pass accurately, and his attempts at goal were generally on-target. They even occasionally had the venom or guile that is needed to produce a memorable goal. He was good in the air, defensively and in attack, and he seemed to have no fear of putting his head into situations where it was as likely to make contact with a fist, a head or a stud as it was with the ball. He most definitely could tackle, although eight times out of ten he didn't need to, as he was a great reader of the game. He wasn't the fastest, and it was this that probably kept him from playing professionally. Like everything else in life, he played football with a quiet passion, not suffering fools gladly, but occasionally he could have patience with a younger player that could be surprising. More than anything else, he kept it simple, very rarely giving the ball away or putting a teammate in trouble with a "hospital pass".

You had the feeling that if he were on the same side as you, you could always rely on him to back you up. That mattered to me as much as anything and, although I have played with more skilful players and players with more genuine pace or finishing ability, at the end of the day he would have been one of the first picks on my team sheet.

I wondered again if I was good enough to get a game with Glenhill, but I supposed I had nothing to lose by trying, apart from a little pride. At worst, I would have the humiliation of going back to playing in the Saturday morning league, and the derision I knew I could expect from my former teammates.

~~o~~

I called round to see Francis early the next day and found him in the workshop. We chatted for a while about football, then, looking round, I asked Francis about some of the tools and machinery. He showed me around in more detail, explaining what each machine was for, showing samples of turnings and mouldings produced on the lathe and the spindle-moulder. He seemed to take my interest quite seriously and in the light of my enthusiasm offered to teach me the rudiments and perhaps let me build a few small pieces for the flat.

"I'll look forward to that," I said, not realising that I had just opened the door to a lifelong fascination with furniture-making that I still have to this day.

"Seeing you are in your Sunday best, we'll maybe not start today. I have some books you can look through to get an idea for something simple to start you off. Have you done anything with wood at all?"

I replied that I had put up the odd shelf, but that was about as far as it went. Strangely enough, Moira and I had been looking around for a small bookcase for a while and I thought that perhaps I could give it a go, something simple and plain. "Surely I could manage that?" I added.

Francis smiled. "I was thinking of something smaller, what we call an apprentice piece. It is designed to give you practice with basic techniques and also to be a showcase of the skills you'd have learned as an apprentice. It is usually something modest, quite often it's a toolbox to hold all your newly acquired tools, so I think that would be a better idea."

"I do have an electric drill, a saw and a wee screwdriver set, but I don't suppose that is what you were meaning by tools."

"It's a start, but I can also give you some tools to start you off." He opened a cupboard at the far end of the workshop, and after rummaging for a while, came towards me with a square canvas tool bag, which he placed on the bench. He opened the bag and pulled out a small jack plane, a block plane and a few other tools.

"Patrick never got round to making a toolbox for these and to be honest, I don't suppose he ever would have."

"I can't take these if they were Patrick's – you should keep them for ..."

I couldn't find the right word, "keepsake" or "mementos" both sounded trite. I finished, "... you to remember him by."

Francis sighed. "John, I bought these for Patrick when he was eleven or twelve years old, and I don't think he'd have used them more than once or twice in the last five years; he never was interested, so I don't feel as if these are part of Patrick. I would rather see somebody make good use of them than have them sit in the cupboard."

I handled one of the planes. It had an oily, gunmetal smell. Francis pointed at the plane. "I oil them all regularly to stop them rusting, that's what the smell is. Watch you don't get it on your clothes."

I didn't know what to say, so I took a leaf out of Francis' book and said nothing. We sat in silence for a while, then he returned the tools to the bag and put it under the bench. "We'll get you started on a toolbox next week."

By his manner I knew that there was something else Francis wanted to talk about but, being Francis, he took his own time.

"The funeral is to be on Tuesday."

"I hadn't heard. Do they know at the station?"

"Yes, the body was released last night. Inspector Gallagher was informed by the Fiscal at the same time as I was."

"Where is it to be held?"

"The Mass will be held at the Chapel near the house. It's on Mitre Street, just off the Crow Road, followed by the burial in Duntocher Cemetery."

"It's been a long wait for the body, with the post-mortems and everything; it must have been very difficult for you both."

"Aye, Deborah especially, she's more deeply religious than I am and she desperately needs to bury her boy."

Heavy duty stuff for me, I barely knew what to say, but Francis didn't expect me to say anything.

"Feel free to come if you can manage."

With that he got up from his stool and motioned for us to go over to the house. "Come on, we'll be in trouble if you don't say hello to Deborah."

~~o~~

A couple of us had been left "on the book" to cover the day-to-day running of the general office, but most of the guys had taken re-rostered rest days as there was really very little to do. I went in on the Monday morning and footered about for a bit, until Gallagher briefly popped his head round the door and gave me instructions to start photocopying everything and boxing it up. He gave me a list of documents he wanted extra copies of and told me that there would be a WPC along to give me a hand, but that I was in charge.

"D'you think you can manage that, McDaid?"

"No bother, sir. Who's the WPC?"

"How the fuck do I know? Play your cards right and you might even get a ride. Some of these uniform birds like the idea of a bit of CID meat." He grinned. "Oh, by the way, the funeral is tomorrow. The deceased's, that is, so we'll not likely be in, got to put on a show at these affairs. If you just get on with this, I'll see you Wednesday."

With that he turned and left, leaving me in charge of the clear up. The WPC turned out to be "Titclops" as some of the boys had cruelly christened her. She'd been in the force for about twenty years, and like the mythical Cyclops of ancient Greece, who had one eye in the centre of its forehead, Titclops' large breasts seemed to merge into one in the centre of her chest. She had legs as thick as the columns on the Parthenon and you could have projected movies on to her arse. Her hair was heavily lacquered, like some medieval helmet, and the only way you could tell she was female by looking at her face was the bright red lipstick she wore, that made it look like a Greggs' Halloween cake. I had overheard Gallagher once say that "you widnae ride her intae battle".

It wouldn't have been so bad if she'd had a nice way with her, at least then you might have had a bit of sympathy for the woman, but her personality matched her looks and virtually no one in the station liked her. Anyway, Titclops and I spent the rest of the day together, and I realised that it was probably Gallagher's idea of a joke to pair me up with her.

~~o~~

I went into work on the morning of the funeral and we got a fair bit more of the paperwork tidied up before I left to go to the service, which was at one o'clock. I think Gallagher was surprised that I'd turned up, but I was pretty discreet, staying at the back of the congregation in the church and on the periphery of the large crowd at the graveside. It was a large funeral, as tends to happen with a combination of popularity, youth and a violent death. As well as a few of our guys, including Gallagher, Andy and I, all Patrick's university friends were there, along with his friends from school, Sarah, and the Stick, of course, plus lots of older mourners that I presumed to be friends and family. I thought I saw Mike, the Glenhill manager, and a few of the players, but they were at the other side of the grave so I didn't get to speak to them. I briefly shook hands with Francis at the graveside and he gave me a small nod of thanks, but I didn't go to the "do" afterwards. I can't even remember which hotel on Great Western Road it was in.

The next day Pete Jones made a comment about my attendance at the funeral and added something along the lines of "you papes like to stick together". I just turned away, ignoring him, and he left shortly after that. The incident room was amazingly quiet after the chaos of the previous week.

When I next saw Francis he barely mentioned the funeral, just said a quick thanks for the fact that I'd turned up. Just about the whole football team had been there and I think Francis was quite touched by that.

For the next few weeks I got into the routine of knocking off early doors Thursdays to spend some time working in Francis' workshop on my toolbox before heading up to training. Francis showed me how to mark out and hand-cut dovetail joints on a few wood scraps, and then told me to draw out a design for my toolbox. "Keep it simple," he told me, "but leave room to add trays inside later."

I looked at a few of the toolboxes in the workshop and thumbed through a few old carpentry books that Francis left out for me. I had done "techy" drawing and metalwork in school, but had missed out on woodwork due to some nutter burning down the woodwork department when I was in my first few years of secondary education. In between work, two lots of football training, playing on Saturday morning and watching Glenhill on a Saturday afternoon, I managed to knock together a plan for what I thought was a nice toolbox. When I showed it to Francis, he clicked his tongue a few times and said, "Hmmm."

"Doesn't sound good," I said, fearing the worst.

"No, no, it's not bad, but ..."

"Go on, what have I left out?"

"Well, did you measure your rip saw first?"

"Ehmm, no. I didn't actually measure any of the tools," I replied, feeling more than a bit foolish.

"Your box is perfectly well designed and drawn, but if I told you that the longest saw you will have in your box is twenty-two to twenty-eight inches, perhaps you would like to change a few of your measurements."

I smiled sheepishly. "I should maybe measure the other tools as well, just to make sure they all fit."

"Aye, and leave a bit of room for a few extras. You haven't got the full complement yet, and you might if you keep at it."

After I had altered my plans to Francis' satisfaction, I gradually marked and cut out the pieces, taking my time and doing it as thoroughly and neatly as possible. Francis explained that the dovetail joint, which pre-dated written history, was not used for its beauty, but for its strength – it can only be fitted or pulled apart in one direction, and once glued, the intermeshing pins and tails gave enormous strength in all directions. I can't say my joints were anywhere as neat as the ones Francis produced, but I was quite proud of my initial efforts. Francis had donated a fair bit of "scrap" timber, some of which looked more like normal stock timber to me. I did offer to pay for the wood, but he simply ignored that suggestion.

Slowly it came together. Francis showed me how to rebate the hinges for strength and appearance; I made shaped wooden toggles to hold the three handsaws in the recess inside the lid. Inside the box, on each of the ends, I attached some small supports for internal trays which would sit in the space above the loose tools and hold small tools: drill and auger bits, chisels and gouges, along with all the marking out tools that I would eventually acquire.

At this point, although it would have been easier and probably more accurate, Francis would not let me near any of the power saws, planers, or routers that were around the workshop. "No point in using these if you haven't mastered hand tools," he countered, when I wondered aloud if it would be quicker than cutting all the pieces by hand.

I nearly screwed up by being impatient – after all my pieces were cut, I had the glue out ready to stick everything together when Francis looked over and coughed. I think he was keeping an eye out to see if I had the sense to stop and think the thing out first.

"A few tips to avoid cock-ups," he said. "Firstly, always dry assemble and clamp your piece first, this lets you see if it all fits together correctly; you can easily take it apart and make adjustments, and you also then have all your clamps set at the right sizes for when you are ready to start to glue it. Also make sure you get rid of any of your pencil marks at the same time."

It was like being back at school. "I should have thought about that. I'll try it together now and I'll call you over to keep an eye on things when I glue it."

"One other thing," Francis added. "After you have got it all dry-fitting, use some fine sandpaper to finish all the inside components – they are much more difficult to sand after they have been assembled."

He showed me a small writing bureau that he was working on, with lots of little compartments and drawers and a fold down front.

"You see, it would be difficult to sand all these nooks and crannies after it's glued together. You'll also notice that the insides are all varnished before being glued together, as it makes it much easier to wipe any excess glue off when it has been assembled."

I admired the bureau, even though it wasn't finished. Francis leaned over and told me to pull one of the small drawers out. I did as he said but it didn't quite come out all the way, so he showed me how to release it by pressing a small metal clip at the back of the drawer.

"Now put the drawer in the other way round."

I turned the drawer over, and started to slide it back in.

"No, you idiot," Francis said, smiling, "the other 'other way round'."

I turned the drawer back over, then pushed the front in first.

"Go on, all the way," Francis instructed me.

I pushed the drawer firmly and as it went in I felt a little resistance and heard a soft click. I looked at Francis, puzzled, but he just smiled and pointed to the small inlaid decorative panel in the centre of the bureau. I looked closely, and I could see that the previously flush panel had now sprung open. I gripped the edge with my fingers and flipped it open. Underneath there was a shallow space, just big enough to store a packet of cigarettes if you were a secret smoker.

"I put these in quite a few of the pieces, sometimes as a surprise for the customer, sometimes on request." He then explained that one guy even liked to be kept in the dark about the secret compartment, spending endless hours trying to find it when he got the furniture home!

He closed the lid and pulled the drawer back out, using the tiny little finger grip in the back, designed to make it easier.

"How does it work?" I asked

"There's a small series of rods and cams. I'll show you sometime, when I'm doing another one."

I grew to love these workshop sessions of ours; we didn't talk a great deal – I would ask the odd question and he would give an occasional instruction – but when I was waiting for glue or varnish to dry, or just had half an hour to spare, there was nothing better I liked to do than to stand and watch Francis at work. Whatever task he was doing, he always applied his full concentration to it and I'm sure he often forgot I was there. Now and then he would explain something, or even give me a go at it, to let me try out a technique for myself.

We didn't discuss the case much; I don't think he saw any point in raking over ground that had already been covered, and nothing new was going to happen before the trial. I did have in my possession, however, a pile of documents which I'd copied during the clear-up after the inquiry had closed. Once the PF's office had their copies, everyone apart from me had been assigned to other cases. Gallagher had asked me for copies of the core documents for himself, and it was technically straightforward to take additional copies, but in reality, I was bricking it on every occasion I took a sheaf home in the evening. My parents had bought me a black leather lockable briefcase when I was initially transferred to CID and although I didn't foresee me using it at the time, it became the repository for these purloined papers. Something held me back from giving them to Francis; I suppose that keeping them at home under lock and key for my own information felt less of a misdemeanour than "leaking" them to someone outside of the force.

~~o~~

Doing two lots of training a week and still playing on a Saturday with my old team soon had a beneficial effect on my fitness, and by the third week even my teammates noticed an improvement in my game, when we hammered our nearest rivals six-one. Even though I say so myself, I more or less ran the show, completing what was probably my best performance in the shirt with a brace of goals; a looping back post header and a drilled shot low from the edge of the box.

Although I'd cut back on the booze, I allowed myself a bit of a bevy that afternoon instead of going to see Glenhill, as I had to tell the boys that my best game for them was also my last. Mike Moffat had taken me aside the previous Thursday and told me that I could play as a trialist for Glenhill and that I would have a place on the sub's bench for the next few games at least, but I would have to be released from my current team to allow that to happen.

The boys gave me a rough time that afternoon, sitting in the pub watching Scotland being beaten by England, great preparation for the impending World Cup in Argentina. To be honest I had expected to be slagged off and would probably have been disappointed if it had been otherwise, but in between all the banter, they were keen to find out what the Glenhill players were like, what the training consisted of, and did we really have a team bus? Deep down, I knew that some of the fun had just gone out of my football with the move – I doubted very much if there would be any more all day sessions or as much piss-taking in the changing room or on the park, but I felt that I would have regretted it if I hadn't given it a go at the higher level.

But it was another black mark in Moira's book. To be fair I was absolutely moggered that night, and Moira's planned trip to umpteen furniture warehouses on the Sunday had to be postponed while I suffered in my pit most of the day. We were barely speaking now, and any sniff of sexual activity had completely disappeared. I was glad of a couple of scenarios that I'd put in the "Wank Bank" earlier that month for just such a drought. Worryingly, I just couldn't get it going with a picture of a semi-naked Sarah Anstruther in my mind – perhaps the proximity of Patrick's demise and my friendship with Francis was the problem, but it was soon solved by a visit to the bit of rough in my imagination that was Mrs Scoular, although in my version of the tableau she didn't open her mouth once – at least not to speak, anyway.

I had fully recovered by the Thursday and at training I was told that I might even get a start the following Saturday, as there were three players with niggling long-term injuries. The training was the best yet and I felt that I was ready to give it a go. I think Mike was less reluctant to start me as we were playing what was, on paper, probably the weakest team in the league.

Saturday came and I was untypically nervous. The game itself was perhaps a routine match for everyone else, but I played for three quarters of it and didn't disgrace myself, and we won comfortably, three-one. The following two weeks I started on the bench, but in both games I got a decent run out in the second half and scored a couple of useful goals from right midfield. Francis, as usual, was ever present and as he played just behind me I began to appreciate just how good he was, covering my back, giving me instructions or encouragement and occasionally a verbal kick up the arse if I was being lazy or too smart for my own good. Overall I liked to think I was building a good rapport with the team, and with Francis in particular.

CHAPTER 6   TRIAL

[Saturday 14th October 1978]

"I'm not looking forward to this."

Francis and I were in the workshop. The trial was due to start on the following Monday and he was voicing his unease. I had ostensibly gone over to do some work on my oak bookcase, as I had been doing regularly over the last few months since finishing my toolbox. We had remained in frequent contact, even during the close season when there was no football training, and often I would spend a few hours at the workshop, two or three times a week. Occasionally I would even work there on my own if Francis wasn't there, when Deborah would let me in and lock up afterwards.

"I'll try and get over on the first day if I can but, as you know, I'm not Gallagher's flavour of the month, so I'd like to keep out of the way."

Shortly after we had cleared up the inquiry room, Gallagher had called me in to see him in his office on the top floor. I hadn't told Francis the full details of the conversation but I think he'd read between the lines and got a pretty fair picture of what had taken place.

Initially Gallagher had been friendly and jovial, asking how I was enjoying CID and saying he hoped that I'd get into the swing with the rest of the department, maybe get a bit more involved. I had no intention of getting "involved" with those guys – I didn't fancy ending up fat, sloppy and with zero integrity – so I made a non-committal grunt and waited as Gallagher summed up how successful the outcome of the investigation had been and stressed that you "don't always have to stick to the book".

I was saying nothing and I could see him beginning to get a bit annoyed at my lack of co-operation, but to be honest I didn't give a toss.

"Right, I just need to get us square on a couple of things. Kevin Nolan's old dear is making accusations about us being a bit heavy-handed with her. I just need you to back me up that we responded appropriately to her violent behaviour." He paused and glared at me. "Have I got your word on that?"

I could feel parts of my colon turn to jelly but I somehow I managed to look him straight in the eye.

"To be honest, sir, I don't think it's 'us' we're talking about here, and there's no way I'm going to lie about what happened. The best I can do is to say as little as possible, but if they ask, what am I supposed to do – drop myself in it?"

"You sanctimonious little cunt, you've only been here a few months." He was almost spitting at me. "You do know that I can get you transferred from CID so quickly you'll not have time to shite first."

"Listen, I don't think you'll do that, because if you do, I'll blow the whistle on everything I've seen here and there's a lot of stuff that you don't want to be made public." I couldn't believe I was standing up to the bastard like that but I could feel a grim determination that I wouldn't be cowed by him.

"You're as bad as that cunt Andy – the pair of you are so stuck up your own arses following the fucking Scout code, you couldn't catch a fucking cold without worrying about the fucking rule book first. Neither of you will touch me for getting cunts the jail, so just get to fuck out of here. I'll get you transferred to another division if you want, as long as you keep your fucking gob shut."

"That suits me, sir, but if the shite ever hits the fan, don't expect me to cover for any of you."

"Firstly, nothing will hit the fucking fan; I've been doing this since you were in short trousers and we've never had any problems before. Secondly, if I ever catch you mouthing off, you'd better watch your back – I've got a lot of friends all over the force."

I couldn't believe what I was hearing. "Is that a threat, sir? Do what you like, I'll be glad to get out of this place."

With that I had stormed out the room, and Gallagher had been as good as his word – by the end of the end of the week I'd been moved to CID Kirkintilloch, in D division north, just up the road from Glasgow. I phoned Andy to tell him what had happened.

"I told you they'd shift you out if your face didn't fit. You'll be fine out there; from what I hear it's a good place to work. Don't worry about Gallagher. He hasn't got as many friends as he thinks."

There was more travelling involved and the sub-division was much quieter than Partick, but if Gallagher meant it as a punishment, he failed miserably – there was a good young team in place. The DCI, the DIs and the sergeants got on really well, but there was no doubt who was in charge. They didn't cut too many corners, but at the same time they were quite creative when it was asked for. The guys at Kirkintilloch made it pretty easy for me – a couple of them had worked with Gallagher previously and I think they realised that I was probably a bit disillusioned. For me, working out there was like a breath of fresh air.

One day in Francis' workshop, as the trial approached, I asked him if he knew what to expect.

"I've got a fair idea. I've read up a bit about it, and the prosecution lawyers have been very helpful. I've had quite a few meetings with them and they've run through the whole thing for me."

"Are you both going to attend the trial?"

"I fully intend to. I've cleared most of my backlog of orders and there's only a few on-going things that I can work on evenings and at the weekends. I feel that I should be there, for Patrick's sake. I don't think Deborah can face it, though."

"I can understand that. If you need any help with work … I know I'm not up to much on the skills front, but if there's anything at all you need done, I'm here."

He smiled. "Thanks for the offer, but I think I'll manage. If there's anything, I'll let you know. You can still come round and work away on your own stuff if you want. In fact, I would like it if you did. I may be in need of someone to bounce things off over the next few weeks."

I was happy to be of any use to Francis. Both on and off the football field we had developed a good relationship in a relatively short time, and I think it surprised many of those who knew him as someone who was difficult to get close to. As I left that evening, I wished Francis all the best and shook his hand. As it turned out I didn't see him for a week, as I worked as much overtime during that spell than I had in the previous two months – two of our guys went on the sick and although we had additional cover supplied by another section, three serious assaults happened within twenty-four hours. I found myself running about like a blue-arsed fly from seven in the morning until ten or eleven at night. The only good thing was that Moira could see a nice holiday coming out of it, if the overtime continued for another few weeks.

I even missed training that week and, because I knew that I was also going to be doubtful for Saturday, I phoned Mike and told him that I wouldn't be available. He told me to turn up if I could and said he would stick me on the bench. By now, through hard work, some good coaching and a lot of support from Francis and the other players, I had made my position in the team secure on the right side of midfield, helped by the sad fact that Derek Bell's recovery from his long term-knee injury had taken a serious setback. The poor bastard was only twenty-three, had already been out for seven months and was now talking about having an operation to remove part of a torn

116

cartilage. Despite feeling sorry for him, I was still going to make the most of the opportunity.

As it turned out I made the kick-off but, as promised, I was on the bench. We won comfortably but I only played the last fifteen minutes, presumably as a reward for making the effort to turn up. I had a brief word with Francis, who seemed to be reasonably satisfied with the way the trial had been going. I had, of course, kept myself up to date with progress (I still had friends in B Division, even if not in the CID section). Andy, whom I had also stayed in touch with, kept me informed as well and, although I didn't know the source of his information, it must have been someone inside the court, as he didn't miss much. There was less than I had expected in the press; I don't suppose the case was so unusual that it merited many column inches in the *Glasgow Herald* or the *Evening Times*. From what I could gather, the prosecution were making steady progress towards an almost inevitable guilty verdict for six of the eight accused, with the other two likely to be convicted at least for obstruction, if not for something more serious. Most of the statements made by the gang seemed to tie up together, even if a few of them had descended into blaming each other. I promised Francis that I would pop over the next day, round about eleven-ish, and made my way home.

When I arrived at the workshop the next day Francis was hard at work, catching up on the few projects that he had taken on for regular clients despite his lack of available time.

"Remember that offer?" he asked, pointing at a stack of oak planks on the bench in the middle of the workshop. "If I show you what to do, can you cut those for me and I'll do the moulding and the jointing?"

I must have gaped at him.

"It's fairly straightforward. I'll show you how to do it, you can have a couple of practises first, and I'll keep an eye out that you're doing it right."

"OK, if you think I'm up to it I'll give it a go."

He handed me a dust mask and took one himself. "Here, wear this. It could get quite dusty."

He showed me how to clamp a piece of scrap wood to the back fence on the saw, to allow me to make repeated cuts of exactly the same length without measuring every one individually, and demonstrated the technique of cutting across the wood without it catching or breaking out into splinters or, worse still, jumping forward dangerously and removing part of a finger or thumb. "Always keep your hands away from anywhere the saw will cut, and also watch out for the wood springing up and catching you in the eye."

I was getting more concerned, but after trying a few cuts in some waste wood I felt that I could do it if I just took my time and was extra careful. There were over fifty cuts to be made and I completed them within a couple of hours. Francis came over periodically to check that the cuts were clean, the measurements were correct, and that I was doing the job with safety in mind. He discarded a couple of bits that had small defects in them and told me that it was fairly typical to get the odd split, but I thought that there may well have been no waste at all if he had been doing it himself. Overall, though, I was quietly pleased with my efforts and I think Francis was also satisfied. He had been taking the sawn lengths and, using a clever self-made jig, cutting dovetails with the band saw. He would finish them off with a sharp quarter inch chisel, and then use the spindle moulder or planer to apply an edge profile or rebate, a kind of slot, to hold the drawer bottom in place.

After I had finished I stood and watched as Francis completed all the sections, and then helped him to assemble the drawers, intended for a large chest, part of a set including two matching wardrobes and a dressing table. I was surprised that he'd taken on a job of this size while the trial was on, but I think he found it difficult to turn work away. We left the glue to dry and retired to his office for a cup of coffee.

"There's a bit of shortbread in that tin," he said, pointing to the top shelf on the old secretaire that sat at one end of his loft. "Thanks for that, you have no idea how much of a help that was."

I felt inordinately pleased. "I enjoyed doing it. Any time I can help and I'm available, just give me a shout. I would feel a bit nervous around the heavier machines, though."

"Fair dos, you gave it a very good crack, but it will be a while before I let you loose on the spindle moulder." He then proceeded to tell me tales of horrific accidents in which spindle moulder blocks had flown off, spinning at over two thousand revs per minute, and torn chunks out of people, sometimes killing them in the process.

After that we sat for a while just drinking our brew. I could see that Francis probably wanted a chat but I let him take his own time. The smell of the resin from the wood blended with the aroma of the freshly made coffee, and a shaft of sunlight shone through a skylight window in a haze of settling dust. I looked around and thought to myself that there were worse places to be.

It was some time before Francis broke the silence. Finally he said, "Have you had a chance to catch up on the trial?"

I told him that I had more or less managed to follow the progress of it so far, but I had gleaned most of my information from talking to others, including Andy.

"Aye, I saw Andy one day outside the court. I think he just wanted to see how we were getting on. A nice guy, Andy. It was good that he got his promotion."

I had spoken to Andy a couple of days before, when he phoned me and told me he'd been made up to Acting Detective Inspector incredibly quickly after his last promotion which, to be fair, had been long overdue. He still seemed to be enjoying his move to Ayrshire. I was quite surprised he'd been up in Glasgow as he hadn't mentioned it, and I said so to Francis.

"Oh, he was up anyway, something to do with a departmental exchange meeting he was attending over at Pitt Street." This was the Strathclyde Police Headquarters,

119

and I wondered if Andy was angling to get back into the Glasgow area, even though he seemed to be happy living just outside Ayr at the moment. He was still single and perhaps Ayr was a bit too quiet for him. I knew he liked going out at the weekend with a few of his mates, mostly frequenting the classier clubs and the casino. Compared to us he had a bit of a playboy image, and even his clothes and haircut gave him what we all thought then was a more sophisticated look.

"You quite happy with the way it's going?" I asked him.

"happy is maybe the wrong word, but all in all there's been nothing to worry us so far – all the witnesses have been good and the defence hasn't been able to shake any of their statements. We are just getting to the confessions that they made, and what has been good is the level of consistency across all the evidence."

"What are the lawyers like?"

"It's like a scrum in court. I hadn't realised that each of the bastards would have a senior counsel, a junior counsel and a solicitor. There wasn't enough room for them in court, some of them had to sit in the public gallery."

"Aye, the senior counsel is the QC; who have they all got?"

"our guys seem to be pretty good on the whole, very professional I would say, but their lawyers are quite a show. Malky has managed to get hold of Martin Hempleman as lead counsel; he's been involved in quite a few high profile cases and seems to be flavour of the month in defence circles. They've got a young lawyer on the team, some high flyer, thinks he's got the biggest dick in the place. Can't remember his name offhand, but he's a cocky bastard. I heard some of the others call him 'the White Rhino'. Most of the other defendants have got well-known lawyers as well, according to our boys."

I had been told that the defence team that had been assembled was the best in Scotland, and it made me feel slightly uneasy – these guys only usually take high profile cases that are either winnable, or where they think there may be an angle for them to shine. What worried me in this case was that it wasn't particularly high profile, so it begged the question – what did these guys see in it for them?

Francis must have sensed my misgivings. "You too?"

"I've got nothing solid, I just feel nervous. I think the way the confessions were obtained is a possible problem, but it's pretty obvious that they are all guilty to one degree or another, and I think that the jury will more than likely see through any crap the defence throws at them."

We spent the next hour going over the build-up testimonies from the witnesses who put the gang in the area before and after the murder. The witnesses' statements that blood had been seen on their clothes came out as well, with no convincing rebuttal by the defence counsel.

"Sarah was very good; it obviously cost her a good deal to stand up there and go through it all again. It pained me to watch her, but she is one strong girl." Francis was quite obviously a fan of the beautiful Sarah.

"I'm glad she did OK. I was very impressed with her when I interviewed her. I thought that it would be difficult for her, but I knew she would be good in court." When she'd given evidence, I'd been told that she'd dressed down even more than normal, looking almost drab and unattractive, if that was possible. I wondered if that had been part of the strategy of the prosecution team.

"Her pal did well too, but she came across as a bit too angry. I think the jury might question her impartiality."

I smiled at that. "No surprise there, I've never actually seen her when she wasn't angry."

Francis held up his hand. "You're being a bit unfair. You've only seen her in stressful situations. She can be all right at times – she's been an absolute godsend to Sarah in the last few months."

121

"Aye, but probably with an ulterior motive," I countered, rather cheaply.

"John, give the girl a break. She's on the right side, and she surely must know any hopes she has in that direction are a bit of a long shot."

"OK, but I can't bring myself to like her. Even so, I'll give her the benefit of the doubt."

"Your guys started well, though, going through the various statements they'd taken from the defendants. Although they gave the impression of being hard men, that didn't seem inappropriate in the circumstances – I think that the jury will see the need for a robust approach by the police in this type of crime, as long as they don't think it went too far."

"That's my main worry, along with the fact that we were too slow to get physical evidence to back it all up."

Francis looked weary. "Let's hope it doesn't come to that. Anyway, I'd offer you some food, but I need to spend some time with Deborah before it all starts again tomorrow, to kind of reassure her that everything's OK. She hasn't been to court at all, so everything she gets is second-hand from me, and she can read me too well. She knows that I'm concerned at the moment and if you come in, I think it will only make things worse."

In the end, Deborah did not attend a single day of the trial. It wasn't, as she told me a few years later, that she couldn't face hearing all the details of Patrick's last few weeks of life and his horrible death, but that it would be heard in the presence of complete strangers, including the ones who had taken her son's life.

Francis and I went down the stairs and towards the door, switching off the power as we left. He locked the workshop behind him, and as I turned to go he asked how Moira and I were getting on.

It was typical of Francis to think of someone else when the weight of the world must have been on his shoulders.

"OK," I replied, not even convincing myself, but Francis just shrugged and said, "It's not easy, son, but if it's worth it, give it everything you've got."

I muttered something bland in reply about seeing him at the training, and left by the yard door.

[Monday 23rd October 1978]

The next week wasn't quite as hectic, but it was busy enough. I spoke to Francis briefly at a break in the trial. I had to run an errand into the centre of Glasgow in the late afternoon and took the opportunity of calling round by the High Court to see him. He told me that it had been much of the same. They had been presenting evidence about Billy Green's confession, and the defence had so far not challenged the methods used in obtaining it. In fact, all the defence QCs were all beginning to look a bit deflated.

We went for a coffee at one of those uber-modern places that look good but don't feel as comfortable as a wee shabby cafe with rickety wooden tables, but the place was busy, and the service and the coffee were good.

"Are you going to manage training this week?" Francis asked me.

"I hope to," I replied. "We're a bit short-handed, but not as busy as last week. If I work late for the next few nights, I can knock off early Thursday. I'm off the weekend, so I'll make the game on Saturday."

"It's a Scottish cup game, second round, remember?"

"Aye, we've had a pretty easy run so far, haven't we?"

Francis laughed. "This will be a tougher round. This lot are top of the Central League, some good players in their squad."

"It's a cup game – always a chance, I suppose."

We spent a pleasant half hour further discussing our prospects and past cup games we had played in, then Francis headed home to supper and a late night in the workshop, while I headed back to work.

There wasn't much happening, but it gave me a chance to catch up on some paperwork without the usual interruptions. Part of me knew I was also avoiding going back to the flat – the Moira situation had gone from bad to worse, we were barely talking, and part of me almost couldn't give a fuck. I was beginning to think that we'd be better off without each other.

I got home just after eleven and Moira was in bed, so I watched some late night documentary. I went to my kip just before one, and was up and out well before Moira got out of bed at eight o'clock for her work.

~~o~~

We were still quite busy, and when I got back to the office at lunchtime there was a note on my desk to phone Andy urgently. Puzzled, I phoned him, but I just missed him. He was expected back within the hour, so I promised to phone back later. "Tell him John McDaid returned his call," I said to the WPC on the end of the line. She sounded nice on the phone and I started wondering if the looks matched the voice or would meeting her in real life be a real disappointment, as was often the case.

When I phoned back the next time, it was Andy himself that answered. I asked him what the panic was.

"John, man – haven't you heard?"

"Not heard what?" He had me worried now; I thought that someone we knew had been injured or killed or something.

"I'll meet you after work and we'll head over to see Francis – there's been a fucking disaster; the trial's all gone to fuck. He's going to need a couple of friends."

I couldn't believe what I was hearing. "What the fuck's happened?' I blurted, looking round the office at a few concerned or curious faces now looking towards me. I waved them away, pointed at the phone and mouthed "an old mate". I turned away from them, cupped the phone and lowered my voice a bit. "Andy, what's happened?"

"You know how Malky McGovern made a confession? Well, this morning, his clever fuck of a defence lawyer drops the bombshell that Malky wasn't even there. Get this – the day of the murder he was visiting his brother in Broxburn, near Edinburgh; they'd got hammered and his brother put his hand through a pane of glass inside some pub. Malky took him to casualty at Edinburgh Royal and he got it cleaned up and a couple of stitches put in his arm."

I groaned inwardly – I could tell what was coming.

"By the time they got to the hospital it was about nine to nine thirty p.m., they waited nearly an hour and a half to get seen by a nurse, and the fucking casualty records show that the houseman who stitched up his brother's wound didn't go on duty until eleven that night. The doctor is to be called to corroborate this, and he'll say that it was after midnight, at the earliest, when they left the hospital, with no chance of catching the last train to Glasgow fucking Queen Street."

"And the doctor can positively ID Malky?'

'Yes, it seems so, and if necessary there are a few nurses and other staff who can also place him in casualty at that time as well."

"Fuck. Fuck. Fuck. Fuck. Fuck." I couldn't get my head round it, but a little voice in the back of my brain was telling me, "I knew it," over and over again. "You're right, we've got to get hold of Francis." I tried to think rationally. "When will the court recess today?"

"It has already – the shit hit the proverbial fan, there were accusations and counter accusations from the QCs on the defence side and the AD for the prosecution, the judge was having a blue fit and the public and press galleries seemingly erupted. I was told that Francis just sat in the middle of the clamour with his head in his hands."

"How did you get all this?" I asked, wondering even at this moment how Andy had learnt all this so soon when he wasn't even there.

"One of the clerks was at school with me. I once got him out of a scrape when he was having a rough time and he has always kept me up to date with anything that I'm involved with that comes through his court, but it's all common knowledge, anyway."

Just not as quick, or in as much detail, I thought.

"So if this is all true," I said, "why did it not come out before now, like when he was fucking well interviewed?"

"Oh, this is the clever bit. He's acting the dumb fuck, saying he got the dates mixed up and that the police beat him up to get him to make the confession, and that it had been self-defence that had caused him to resist and hit out at the DC who was attacking him. The right honourable Martin Hempleman, QC, is innocently claiming that these facts have just been brought to his attention.

"There's worse," he continued. "There have been further allegations made regarding the method of 'extraction' of confessions obtained in this case."

"Billy Green's asthma?"

"Got it in one, probably, but hey, take your pick."

"And once it goes that far, you can bet your last tenner that Tommo's spat with Malky and Gallagher's tête-à-tête with the Scoular woman will be dragged out as well." I felt a deep lurch in the pit of my stomach as I realised that I might have to give evidence against Gallagher, which could lead to the guys who killed Patrick walking free. I said as much to Andy.

"I don't think it will come to that. The AD will concede a lot of material to get this trial over quickly when they see that it can't be won."

"You think they'll just throw the case out?"

"Naw, but I think it will finish quickly, with the bastards walking, and all because Gallagher and his pals were too fucking lazy to back up the case with some good physical evidence and a bit of thorough research."

I arranged to phone him back shortly and went into speak to the DI, as my DS was on a half day. I explained the circumstances, and he kindly told me to "fuck off out of here". I phoned Andy and arranged to meet him in Glasgow.

"Give me an hour to get there; I'll meet you round at Francis' house. Park down the road a bit."

I agreed to that and made my way round by Torrance, Milngavie and Bearsden to avoid the traffic, then down the switchback to Anniesland. I found a space a few hundred yards from Francis' front entrance and sat in the car and watched. After a while I saw Francis in the mirror, walking from the direction of the train station. He passed by on the opposite side of the road, within thirty yards of me, but if he noticed my car, he didn't react in any way. He just walked on and stepped through the small door into the yard.

I waited for Andy and I saw his Capri pass by me in the opposite direction, then turn down the side road behind me. I got out of the car and made my way to meet him as he locked up.

"Francis arrived about ten minutes ago," I told him

"How did he seem?"

"He looked OK. Kind of more determined looking than normal, if that's possible."

"Right, let's go."

We went over to the yard gates and stepped through the door that Francis had gone through. We walked over to the house and knocked. Deborah answered the door and motioned for us to come in.

"Can we speak with Francis?" I asked, taking the lead, as Deborah probably knew me better than Andy.

"Francis hasn't been in the house yet. He went straight to the workshop."

I hadn't noticed on the way in if the workshop door had been open. I didn't know if Deborah had been told about today's events, so there was an awkward silence until she said, "I know." A tear slid down her cheek and she gripped the back of a chair to steady herself. I took her arm and guided her to a chair by the window. Andy nodded in the direction of the kitchen and left us, coming back five minutes later with a strong, sweet cup of tea. We had not said a word in his absence, but she had not let go my arm during that time. She sipped at the proffered cup, even though I knew that she did not normally take sugar.

We must have stayed like that, two sitting and one standing, for the best part of ten minutes. No more tears were shed and, as she sat there, her back seemed to stiffen and she gradually released the pressure on my arm.

"Go and see Francis," she told us. "I'll be OK now."

"If you are sure you're OK?" Andy asked her.

"Yes, I'll be fine. Go and talk to him. I think he needs the pair of you more than me."

I couldn't work out what she meant by that – you could take it either of two ways and either way I could feel a crushing weight of sadness in her that I would never forget.

As we got up to leave, she turned to us and just said, "Boys, thanks."

I glanced at Andy as we made our way over to the workshop. I noticed the door was very slightly open, but I could not see any lights on. A sudden horrible thought crossed my mind and I wondered if we would find Francis on the end of a rope, but I banished it quickly; he just wasn't the type to take the easy way out, no matter what the world threw at him.

Another glance at Andy told me that the same thought had occurred to him. With a deep breath I pushed the quarter door open and entered the gloomy workshop. It was only then that I noticed that the office lights were on, illuminating the wooden stairs leading up to the half-open door. I could just see the back of Francis' head through the window that overlooked the workshop.

I nodded towards the stairs and we climbed up, Andy just behind me, and knocked gently on the door.

There was no answer, but I went in anyway. Francis was standing, leaning against the desk with his head almost bowed. I slowly walked over to him and took his hand as if to shake it, but he surprised me by grabbing me in a heavy hug and drawing me to him. After a few seconds he released me and did the same to Andy.

"Thanks for coming," he said quietly, with a catch in his voice. "I knew you would."

"Francis, we are so, so sorry." Andy, who like me was a bit choked up, spoke for both of us.

Francis turned, reached up and unlocked a tall slim cupboard, and pulled out a bottle of Scotch and two glasses. He then rummaged around in the desk and came out with another glass, which contained an assortment of elastic bands, drawing pins, paper clips and a couple of random cubes of wood. He emptied them on to the bench, wiped out the glass with a piece of rag, and poured three over-generous measures.

"I keep this for the odd time customers expect a little hospitality when they come to pay for a finished item. This is the first time I can ever say I've actually needed it."

I didn't know what to say, and Andy obviously was feeling the same way. We stayed silent and let him carry on.

"You know, when I got the news about Patrick I thought that it was the worst feeling that I ever could have." He paused, took a stiff swallow of his whisky, and grimaced – I don't think he drank whisky too often by the look on his face. "But today, I just realised that I couldn't have been more wrong, because this is easily ten times worse. We aren't even going to be allowed the comfort of seeing Patrick's killers punished."

"Francis," Andy put his hand on Francis' shoulder, "is there anything we can do to help?"

"There is one thing you can both do, because this is not finished by a long way. If I have to go down the line of private prosecution or civil proceedings, I will. Can you two take a few days and write down everything that you know that's connected with the case? Don't put your names to it. I'll give you my word that I'll not divulge where any of the information came from, but if you don't feel comfortable with something, don't put it in."

Andy was the first to respond. "I can do that. I don't think there is much that I could say that would get me into bother, but I would prefer my name kept out of it."

I agreed. "I'm the same. It would be better from our point of view that any information implicating others was anonymous. It's different if we dish the dirt later under questioning."

Francis looked at me.

I explained. "Obviously the whole thing is going to come out into the open. If Andy and I are seen as whistle-blowers, then it is going to make our jobs a bit more difficult. If we are seen, however, as giving honest answers to questions from other officers about criminal or negligent acts, then it will have less impact on our reputations."

I could see that Francis was a step ahead of me. "I have already considered that. Neither of you would want to be known for 'grassing up' your fellow officers, even if they are unfit for duty. I can live with that. Again, I'll not use any information that you give me in any way that would put you in an awkward position." He waited a few seconds. "From saying what you have just said, you obviously have realised that I will try my utmost to make sure Gallagher never heads up a team again."

"Yes," I replied, "I thought that you would. It is down to him at the end of day that these guys are going to walk."

Francis, his voice almost inaudible, whispered, "Yes, they are going to walk, aren't they?"

We sat in silence for a while, all three of us deep in our own thoughts.

Andy was the first to get up. "I'm heading back down the road. I'll keep in touch, Francis, and I'll post that stuff up to you once I've done it, hopefully by the end of the week."

"I'm going to head off as well," I said. "I'll see you Thursday. Will you be OK?"

"I'll cope. I'd better away in and see Deborah, let her know the details. I phoned her earlier with the bare bones of it, but she'll want to know the rest."

Andy and I walked back to our cars. "Never seen Francis look so down," I said, as we reached my car.

"No, but he'll bounce back, he is one of the strongest people I've ever met."

"You know him quite well, then?"

"Funnily enough, I don't really know him that well, but I just think the guy is one hundred per cent and doesn't deserve all this."

"I can only hope that the pair of them get through all this somehow ... but whatever happens, their lives will never be the same again."

"No, I don't suppose they will." He changed the subject." How are you enjoying Kirkintilloch?"

I told him that it was living up to how I'd imagined the job to be, that I was beginning to feel much more involved. "The team's great, and they're all very helpful. I'm learning a hell of a lot more here than I ever did at Partick."

He laughed. "No, you actually learned more than you think, but just about how not to run an investigation!"

He added that he was looking at a possible move back to Glasgow and that if it came off and I was interested, then we could try and organise a move for me.

"Leave it as it is at the moment. I feel as if I'm just settling in where I am, but I would like to work with you again at some point, so perhaps down the line a bit ..."

"Aye, OK, that's fair. Anyway, keep well."

I waved and drove home, finding it difficult to get Francis out of my mind.

By the time I met Francis at training on the Thursday night, there had been further developments. The alibi that Malky McGovern had so belatedly provided had stood up to cross examination, the casualty records bore it out further and the evidence given by the doctor who had treated Malky's brother, a Doctor Deepak Rajendra, had nailed it down tight. Medical evidence showing that Billy Green had a history of severe asthma attacks added weight to his allegation of treatment being withheld to try and force a confession. Further allegations of brutality were being made on behalf of two more gang members, and two other unnamed witnesses had come forward supporting the additional allegations of unlawful entry on at least two occasions. I knew deep down that one of those would be the visit that Gallagher and I had made to the Scoular home and I waited for the phone call informing me that I was to appear as a witness.

Francis put everything into his training that night – he was like a man possessed. Nobody said anything, we all knew what he was going through and everybody upped the tempo to try and match him, but the harder we pushed, the harder he tried. It was probably the hardest training session I had ever done, and I hoped we wouldn't all be knackered for Saturday! I had only the briefest of words with Francis at the end of training, but I handed him my envelope containing twenty typewritten sheets of everything I could remember about the case. It also contained all the photocopied material that I'd obtained when I was clearing away all the case files. To be honest, I was quite glad to see the back of them. It would be difficult for anyone to prove Francis had got them from me. Even if it came down to fingerprints, I had handled all the originals and copies as part of my general duties anyway. I felt a weight lifted off my shoulders.

Just before the cup game on Saturday, in the changing room, Francis looked over at me and nodded. That was enough for me. I knew he'd never say anything further about the documents I had given him – as far as I was concerned, my part in the "leaking" of the case details was over.

We managed to do just enough to earn a trip to Renfrew for a replay. The game ended in a scoreless draw, which was unusual for us – I can't remember ever playing in more than a handful of nil-nil games wherever I'd played. We could have won it at the death, but two good chances went a-begging.

~~o~~

I called round with Francis the following day and managed to get a bit more of my bookcase done – Francis was at a point in his furniture order where I couldn't really help. His skills in finishing his furniture almost seemed better than those he used in making it. He would spend hours applying the various shades of shellac, rubbing the surfaces with a

133

constant, controlled series of sweeps. I lost count of the number of layers he laid down, producing that depth of surface where the grain of the wood seemed to float in a clear, utterly smooth layer of varnish. Depending on the customer's preference, the finish could be anything from the dark, rich red of a mahogany table to the deep golden brown and black grain of an oak desk.

Again, we didn't say much about the remaining days of the trial or when the verdict would be expected. I was fairly sure that Francis had written off the rest of the trial and was gathering himself for the battle he intended to fight to try and get some sort of justice for Patrick.

By the time training had come around again, it was all over. The previous day the jury had surprisingly returned "not proven" verdicts, a Scottish legal anachronism that leaves both sides in limbo, on almost all the accused. The only exceptions were the "not guilty" verdicts given to Malky McGovern, who had a blue chip alibi, and David Johnstone, who was at worst peripheral to the murder, and may possibly have made attempts to pull some of the gang members away, even if only with self-preservation in mind. To my mind, this was a small victory – deep down the jury obviously thought that they were guilty, but felt there were enough inconsistencies in the prosecution's case to make it unsafe to convict. It also occurred to me that not only had the gang killed Patrick, but they must have boasted about it, at least to Malky. His "confession" had too much accuracy. As he hadn't been there, he must have heard the full details of the attack from someone who had been closely involved. It also meant that his so-called confession was pre-planned to purposefully mislead and discredit the prosecution case. Gallagher had seriously underestimated their abilities – it was hard to imagine, having seen all of the gang close at hand, but at least some of them were more intelligent than they looked.

After training I looked around for Francis, hoping to have a word, but he had gone. I thought about calling round to the house, but I knew that if Francis had wanted to speak to me he would have made some indication. In fact, I didn't see him for nearly a fortnight. He did leave a message at the station saying that he was going to deliver his finished order and that he and Deborah were then going away for a short while.

I wasn't initially worried, but towards the end of the fortnight I began to have doubts – Francis virtually never missed a game and, while he'd cleared it with Mike, I was still surprised. Mike told me that the two games he was missing were against two of the poorer teams in the league and that it was a good chance anyway to give Lennie Foster a wee run out. Lennie was a seventeen-year-old that Glenhill's scout, old Dick Adams, had spotted playing youth football at a tournament recently. Dick had acquired quite a few players for Glenhill, but Lennie was one of the most promising. Within three years he would be playing professional football for Clydebank in the lower Scottish leagues, and from there he struck it lucky with a big money move to English club Middlesbrough, who were in the old third division at that point.

We won that game and the next one without having to play at our best. At that point we were one of three unbeaten teams at the top of the league. There was a buzz around the training ground and in the dressing room a quiet confidence was growing with every match. However, the upcoming away match against Kilbarchan, a difficult trip down towards the coast, would be a sterner test. On the same points as us, they had a long football pedigree and a crowd who took their football very seriously. Although the atmosphere was not as intimidating as some of the Ayrshire junior clubs like Auchinleck Talbot or Kilbirnie Ladeside, you could still feel the intense hostility that these small towns held towards visiting teams.

On the day I travelled down in the minibus next to Francis, who had turned up at training the previous Thursday. We steered clear of any conversation about the trial, or his time away with Deborah.

I knew that Francis was returning to the starting line-up, but I told him that Lennie had put in two very impressive performances and that he might not be best pleased at being relegated to the bench.

135

"The lad's young with plenty time, but I hope he is annoyed – he should be, if he is desperate to play – but he needs to learn a little patience and self-control. I suspect it won't be long before he is a regular, from what Mike and Dick have told me about him."

As it turned out, Hammy, one of our centre backs, took a head knock just before half-time and had to be taken off. When I say head knock, I really fail to give a true picture of the incident – the opposing centre forward nearly took Hammy's head off with a vicious elbow to the left temple. The ref obviously hadn't seen the challenge for what it was, and there was brief moment when we lost our discipline and it could have developed into a full-scale riot, but Francis and the ref moved in to separate the protagonists, including, I must shamefully add, yours truly. As Hammy was half-carried to the side-line, Lennie came on in the right back position and Francis moved in to take Hammy's place at the centre of defence.

The sense of outrage seemed to spur us on and, coupled with a cleverly subdued team talk at half-time by Mike, saw us a goal up midway through the second half. A quick breakaway move down our left wing produced a bizarre own goal after a colossal mix-up between two Kilbarchan defenders and the goalie, leaving us to defend the lead for the rest of the game with some backs-to-the-wall stuff by our makeshift back-line. There was one notable moment right at the death when, from a Kilbarchan corner, it looked like the centre forward should have headed the ball into the top corner of our net for an equalizing goal, but a towering headed clearance by Francis saw the ball in the relatively safe area of the centre circle and the unlucky centre forward writhing on the ground holding his head and moaning loudly. As the challenge had been perfectly fair, the ref signalled for the game to go on and eventually the player, urged to his feet by his teammates, desperate to salvage at least a draw from the game, staggered round the park for the last few minutes not quite knowing what park he was on and which end was which. As the ref blew for full time, I wondered fleetingly if we were going to get to the changing rooms in one piece and if our mini-bus would still be there to take us home after we had changed. I needn't have worried. All the players shook hands as normal at the end, including both mildly concussed players from each side. God knows if they knew who they were or who they were shaking hands with – Hammy was still holding his head to one side at the following week's training. The crowd must have thought that this degree of violence and retribution was fairly normal so, apart from a few bits of rather endearing abuse, they dispersed quietly to the rows of council houses surrounding the football park.

On the way back I again sat with Francis, who had a decent sized bruise on his forehead by then but seemed none the worse for it. I knew that he had bided his time, waiting for the first legitimate chance to teach their thug of a centre forward a lesson, but I didn't say a word about it; we just had a bit of a laugh at the comedy of errors that led to our winning goal.

Francis asked me if I had any plans that evening and I had to tell him that I had arranged to take Moira out to a film followed by a late curry in town. I was annoyed with myself. I'd have liked to spend some time with Francis, as I felt he would probably have spoken about his plans for the next few months. He said that he was heading down south to an exhibition of woodworking machinery and tools in Leeds, and that he would be away for three or four days. If I'd been available, I think he may have suggested that I went with him. I said to myself that it was probably more important for me to take Moira out and spend some time with her in an effort to revive our relationship which, if it had been in hospital, would be described as critical.

CHAPTER 7   INQUIRY

[Saturday 14th April 1979]

Almost six months had passed since the trial had finished. By then I probably spent more time at the workshop, with or without Francis being present, than I did at home. I had my own key, but I still preferred to work while Francis was there; I enjoyed the company, as he did, and he was a great teacher. I learnt as much, if not more, by watching him and I think my most pleasant memories of that time were of quiet winter evenings surrounded by the smell of newly sawn wood, watching him chamfer a drawer front, turn a table leg or apply an inlay to a door panel.

Francis would patiently explain every tool and machine, and demonstrate how they were used. He would then make me practise on off-cuts until I was competent enough to use each tool for real. He showed me strange contraptions like steaming chambers, used to bend wood, and vacuum presses, for applying veneers. There were objects that I wouldn't have expected to find in a workshop, like the old brass microscope kept in a wooden box in the office and which Francis used when examining insects or fungal spores from infected wood.

My repertoire of furniture was gradually increasing. I had made a few small pieces for family and friends, which were well received. I had given my first bookcase to my mum and dad, as I was homeless by the time I finished it.

Moira and I had split up just before Christmas and I moved back temporarily with my parents, before finding a one bedroom flat of my own in Denistoun. It wasn't up to much and I furnished it with a small amount of second-hand furniture from the Barras, the famous Glasgow market just off the Gallowgate, not too far from my flat.

Things had gone from bad to worse for Moira and me, constant rowing and lack of intimacy leading to a complete breakdown of communication, which culminated in a farcical episode involving a Christmas tree, of all things. At the heart of the problem was my apparent intransigence in procuring a "real" tree for us to make the flat "nice" for Christmas. I was busy at work and spending a lot of time at the workshop on a nice jewellery box with a beautiful brass lock and inlaid mother of pearl lid, which I was making as a Christmas gift for her. On a couple of occasions I forgot to collect the tree on my way home from work, and when I eventually did pick it up, I neglected to purchase a suitable container to "plant" it in. After a long and acrimonious argument one evening, I ended up telling her exactly where she could put the tree.

Shortly after that she suggested that it would be better if I left. I was more relieved than sad. It took a few weeks, the festive period making it awkward, for me to collect all my stuff from the flat in Francis' van.

I still gave Moira the jewellery box for Christmas. I left it in the flat when I'd picked up most of my stuff. I'd made it for her and wouldn't feel right giving it to anyone else. (In addition, it had her name engraved on the underside.) For all I know, she may have used it for firewood.

Francis had spoken once or twice about the trial and its aftermath. He initially wanted to push for a public inquiry, but that request had been refused on a number of occasions and was unlikely ever to happen. The press had made quite a thing of the latter part of the trial, in contrast to the paucity of its early coverage. Francis seemed to catch on very quickly to the fact that he could use the media to put pressure on the Chief Constable to act and to a certain extent he was successful. An initial local inquiry by the Discipline Department of Strathclyde Police was held, but for some reason no action was taken. Francis doggedly made enough noise and stirred up enough people to finally force a full independent internal inquiry fronted by the Chief Superintendent of Midlothian and Borders, David

Bryson. Although the results were to be published, the inquiry itself was to be conducted in private, so none of us ever got to see the full evidence given by those who participated. All of us who had been involved in the case in any way were called in to answer questions about our part in the investigation and, if my experience was typical, they were very, very thorough. Andy and I did not hold anything back, apart from not telling them that we had provided Francis with information connected with the case, and I like to think that we gave a fair account of our part in the investigation. Neither Andy nor I had technically blown the whistle; we had merely responded honestly to some intensive questioning from the inquiry team.

It wasn't pleasant, as we received a bit of criticism for not making certain facts known to our superior officers, but this was tempered with an admission on the part of the Chief Superintendent that there was an ineffectual chain of command that would have been difficult for us to access and a culture of intimidation and bullying which discouraged such communication.

During the key part of my interview I did not try and hide the fact that I had felt more empathy with the deceased's family than my own team, and that I had developed a friendship with Francis. A couple of the inquiry members had questioned the wisdom of this and one asked if I had not seen that there could have been a conflict of interest.

I had replied, "In the circumstances I may have been a little naïve, but Francis Hare was never in any way considered a suspect, and the way in which we got to be friends was only partly connected to the investigation and primarily through our interest in football."

"Even so," I was told, by the third member of the group, "it didn't show a great deal of prudence on your part." He went on: "However, I understand you both play for Glenhill and as that situation could hardly have been manufactured by either of you, we can assume that there were no ulterior motives on either part."

They went on to ask a few questions about the case generally, and then grilled me specifically about the incidents that had caused me most concern.

"You were present when Inspector Gallagher called at Kevin Nolan's home?"

"Yes, I was."

"And what was your recollection of that visit?"

I proceeded to give my account of that day, culminating in Gallagher's entry into the house.

I was then asked: "And did you think that the Detective Inspector's response to Mrs Nolan's provocation was in any way justified?"

I replied honestly, "No, I feel that Detective Inspector Gallagher overreacted. If I hadn't intervened, he would have made a serious assault on Mrs Nolan. I was also aware that we had no justification for being inside the house."

Later on in the interview, they asked about the confessions. "And moving on now to the interviews of the accused. Were you present at any of them?"

I replied that I was never in the interview rooms when the suspects were being questioned.

"But you were in the building?"

"Yes, for some of the time I was in the corridor outside the interview rooms."

"And did you see or hear anything that you would have considered to be excessive force during the questioning of the suspects?"

"I was not in a position to see or hear anything like that."

"Mr McDaid, this is not a court of law, and you may indicate if you heard something being spoken about, even if you did not witness it yourself."

I wondered how much they had been told, and by whom. "I did hear that Billy Green had his asthma medication withheld, and that there was a physical altercation between Malky McGovern and DC Thompson." I added that I had seen the injuries to the DC, but hadn't seen the state of the suspect at that time.

The Chief Superintendent then changed direction completely.

"You helped to clear up the inquiry room after the case had been handed over to the Procurator Fiscal, didn't you?"

I think I answered calmly, but I suddenly felt uneasy. "Yes, along with WPC, em ... sorry, I can't remember her name. No wait, Helen somebody, McCulloch or McClymont, I think."

"We have her name, no matter; it was McClymont. What duties did you actually perform at that time?"

"We took all the documents and photocopied them for our records, then boxed both sets and had the originals delivered to the Crown Office."

"And were any other copies made?"

"I was asked to make additional copies of some documents for Detective Inspector Gallagher."

"And there were no other copies made?"

"Not that I know of."

"We have a record of the copier counter before the case started and after it finished. Can you account for the large discrepancy between the number of documents produced and the number of copies made?"

I was now really worried. "No, I can't, but you will always get some of the guys using the copier for some home stuff and occasionally, if copies don't turn out, we have to do them again." I didn't mention that there might have been a

142

few extra copies flying round the station, with people being asked to guess whose genitals or backsides had been copied.

"Would it surprise you if we told you that there were a significant number of documents missing, both from the Crown's copies and the files kept at central records?"

It did. "I can't see how that happened as we packed everything away; we loaded all the PF's stuff into the van, and the rest we left stacked neatly in the inquiry room."

"Did you deliver the documents to the Fiscal's office?"

"No, we didn't."

"Did you see who made the delivery?"

I realised that it would have been easy for any number of people to remove papers, but they would have had to remove them from two separate piles of documents. "No, I couldn't tell you when they were taken over, or who did it."

"Thank you, that will be all for now."

I stood up and turned to leave, but I had to ask.

"How do you know there are items missing?"

"Mr McDaid," said the Chief Super, "since you ask, copies of some documents that would seem to be connected with that case have turned up, and it has been found that they are missing from both sets of original files."

I wondered if they suspected me of leaking the copies and were trying to gauge my reaction, or if they even cared where the documents had come from in the first place. I had to stop myself asking them which documents had been missing, as this would have gone beyond the realms of idle curiosity and might just have made it obvious that I had had a part in their removal or subsequent return.

I spoke to Andy afterwards and his experience sounded very similar to mine. Both of us felt that we'd done enough to make sure that the truth came out, without it appearing that either of us had put the boot in for personal reasons. Andy also reassured me that neither of us had done our future prospects any harm as nearly all the major players in the original investigation would all be severely discredited and that, by distancing ourselves from them, we would be unaffected by the fallout from the whole thing.

The inquiry lasted four and a half weeks, longer than the original trial, and in the end the report stretched to two hundred and thirty pages. As well as looking at the murder investigation, the inquiry had also looked at the management structure and procedures in the whole of the CID, and was in part the catalyst for the wider ranging review of the whole force carried out two years later by the new incoming Chief Constable.

Anyway, the 1979 report was hedged in terms designed to deflect any serious criticism of the force as a whole, and it was not in its remit to provide evidence that would lead to convictions or even disciplinary action against individuals, but in reality there were repercussions for nearly all those involved.

Francis spoke to me shortly after the inquiry had finished. "There will be a clear out of Partick CID when this report is published," he told me, as we sat in our usual spot in his upstairs office.

"Really?" I said. "You think so?" I was not convinced and had the suspicion that the whole thing would be brushed under the carpet.

"I don't think anything will happen which will lay the force open to accusations of negligence, but I'll hazard a guess that there will be significant changes made fairly quickly to keep the press happy, and there will be a lot of behind-the-scenes stuff going on to tighten things up and avoid the same thing happening again."

"Do you think Gallagher will get sacked from the force?" I asked hopefully.

"No, that won't happen, but he'll never take charge of anything again and I wouldn't be surprised if he and a few of his friends ended their careers behind desks, shuffling paper, having been told to shut up and keep out of trouble if they want to keep their pensions."

He proved to be almost right – Gallagher was demoted, and neither he, Tommo nor Peter Jones ever saw the inside of a CID room again. Quite a few of the others were gradually sidelined, as no one particularly wanted to be associated with them.

DCI Donaldson took immediate early retirement and opened a second-hand shop in a fashionable part of town, selling overpriced tat to people with too much money who had watched too many house-makeover programmes on TV. I gather that he had moderate success, and eventually ended up with a small chain of shops in Glasgow and some of the provincial towns close by. Francis told me he had been contacted by him about a year after the inquiry and he'd offered his sincere apologies at the way things had turned out. He had admitted that he had felt out of his depth, and had been wrong to let Gallagher more or less run CID in Partick without any intervention from him. He conceded that his excuse that Gallagher and his cronies had severely intimidated him didn't really wash, but that confrontation was something he had always tried to avoid at all cost.

"What are your plans from here?" I asked.

You could almost see his back stiffening. "Our lawyer is looking at the possibility of civil proceedings, but he has warned us that it would be very difficult, very expensive and with no certainty of success."

I personally thought that it was a waste of time and money, but I knew that Francis needed to believe that there was still a chance of justice for Patrick.

"Here, have a look at this for me." He handed me a box full of foolscap lever arch files. "This is a summary of the case up to date, as I have recorded it. Can you read it over and add anything that you think is missing?"

I turned to the front few pages, and in Francis' neat, almost technical, handwriting was a journal of the trial and a large amount of additional information taken from a number of sources. There were court transcripts, Francis' own notes of the trial, the document copies I'd acquired, a copy of the inquiry report, and some transcripts from that inquiry. There were also a series of photographs of the accused and one or two of the crime scene that I remember giving to him, having taken them from the discard pile during the original investigation. Francis had also made a dossier for each of the gang, with a bit of background information on each of them.

"I hope this is never seen by anyone, Francis. It would be pretty obvious who gave you these photos if it came to light."

"This is strictly for me. It was something I needed to do, to have a complete record of everything; I owe him that."

"I'll look over it here, I'd rather it didn't leave your office, and even then, it would be better kept in a safe place."

"I've got a very safe place for it, don't you worry yourself."

Over the next few visits to the workshop I read through the whole pile of documents, amazed at how full and accurate everything was. Francis had collected his information from a wide selection of places and people, although a large part of it was his own recollection of the trial. He had either been able to take shorthand or he had a very good memory, as the notes he had taken at the trial were very close to the trial transcripts. They added something, though, as he described gestures and facial expressions, made a note of the comings and goings in the court, and gave accurate descriptions of the legal teams and the judge. I knew that this was bordering on the obsessive, but I was also aware that this was one of his coping techniques.

146

It must have been hard for him to write. Parts of the testimonies, especially those concerning the confessions given by Malky and Billy Green, were horrific in detail and graphic in their description of the violence. As I read I could just imagine them being read out in court.

I got an idea of how harrowing it must have been for Francis when I read Billy Green's statement. "It was Nolman or Sornie who hit the cunt first. Up until then he had been tryin' to talk his way out of a kickin', saying stuff like 'look guys, take my wallet, I'll even go and get some more money at the Cashline for you', and 'this is stupid, I've never done anything to you', but Nolman hated guys like him, and I think his fucking whining was making it worse. Anyway, he didn't go down when Nol pushed him, he just put his hands up to try and fend him off. Then Nolman headbutted him right on the hooter, the guy's hands went up to his face, they were covered wi' blood, which was pouring through his fingers, then Nolman swung his boot right into his 'nads. He went down, and was kind of wailing at his point. Nolman turned to us and said, 'let's show this fucker who we are'. A couple of the others started kicking him in the guts and the back, I think it was Spaz and Scouly, but then we all had a go. I saw Nolman stamping on his head, and blood was starting to run out of his fucking ears. I sort of moved back a bit – I didnae like the look of it, being honest, man. I hardly touched him, maybe one or two kicks to his legs, you've gottae believe me, man."

I saw that he had been asked who had done what, and when. "It was a frenzy, man, everybody was just jumpin' in and kickin' the cunt. I would say that Spaz was wan of the worst apart from Nolman, he was still kickin' the fucker after he had stopped moving."

There were a few inconsistencies in the gang's testimonies, but it was easy to see that most of them had taken a significant part in the attack, apart from David Johnstone, who seemed to have been the least involved.

The pathologist's report, also included in the files, bore out the ferocity of the attack, as it described over eighty individual injuries on Patrick's body, with at least four of those being potentially fatal. The one that killed him was one of the head injuries, which had caused a massive subdural haematoma.

When I handed the box back to Francis I told him that there was nothing to add, that everything was there.

"I just needed someone else to read it, someone besides me who will never forget."

~~o~~

My visits to Francis over the next few years continued at the same level. Two or three times a week I would go over and work in the workshop, either on my own stuff or as an unpaid apprentice for Francis, helping out with simple repetitive tasks which let him get on with the highly skilled stuff or, more usually, assisting when the two of us working together made the job easier. This particularly applied to assembly and gluing up, and I loved that part; it was the point in the process of making a piece of furniture when everything came together and you saw the final form appearing on the low assembly bench in the middle of the workroom.

We always used to have problems with glues and varnishes becoming too thick to work with on really cold days, despite Francis having installed a couple of trickle heaters at each end of the workshop; then one cold day when I turned up, he very proudly showed me his latest acquisition.

"There," he said, pointing.

"What is it?" I could see a sort of white painted metal and glass box in the corner of the workshop.

"It's an incubator." He looked at me as if I was a bit simple.

"What, like the ones they use for babies? What do you want one of those for?"

148

He shook his head. "It's similar, but it's not for babies. I got it at an auction they held when they opened the new laboratory building at the University – all the equipment from the old building that they didn't use was being sold off. I heard about it and wondered if I could replace that old microscope with a more modern one, but as it happened, they weren't selling anything like that. When I saw this incubator, I thought, *Francis, that's the answer to the problem*, so I bought two for fifty-two quid. What do you think?"

"Well …" Not wanting to appear any thicker than I was already, I hesitated.

"Look inside it." He motioned for me to go and look.

I opened the catches and hinged back the lid. Francis had filled it up with various pots of glue and varnish, and some other chemicals that I'd not yet seen him use. A green indicator light showed that it was switched on.

"Ah, I see." The penny had dropped. "No more hassle with the glue on cold days." I could see that the temperature readout on the front indicated thirty-two degrees centigrade.

"Yes, and we've got a spare one if this one ever breaks down."

I don't know if he noticed his use of "we" rather than "I", but it made me feel, for a short time at least, part of the this old established company of craftsmen.

Francis had also purchased a camera, one of these fancy professional looking things with detachable lenses and more knobs, buttons and sliders on it than Apollo 11, because he wanted to take high quality photographs of his furniture suitable for an up-market brochure that prospective customers could be given. He must have got some advice from someone with expertise in photography because he seemed to know what he was doing.

When Francis wasn't working on commissions, he would make various items for his small shop showroom or window display. Some of these were purchased by people who came into the shop for a browse, although given the price, there were a limited number of customers who could afford them. Every so often Francis would feel the need for a clear out of his stock and he would select five or six pieces and take them to one of the fine furnishing exhibitions around the country. Occasionally held in Edinburgh, they were mostly down south, although the up and coming oil town of Aberdeen was fast becoming the place where people were spending big money. I got into the habit of going with him, which gave us a chance to talk as we travelled around the country.

On one occasion we travelled to Harrogate, a journey of about six hours. We listened to music and chatted, mostly about his decision that the football season we had just finished had been his last. We had won the league over a month before, although it had got a bit squeaky at the end after two draws had left us needing a win to claim the title. I don't know about the rest of them, but for that last game I was the most nervous I had ever felt, having never previously been in a position to win anything of note. I hadn't slept much the night before and struggled through nausea to keep my breakfast down. I didn't even attempt lunch and had a couple of extra visits to the toilet as my guts got the better of me. I thought we would all settle once the game started, but we made more misplaced passes in the first ten minutes than we had for the whole season. The only two players who were keeping us in the game were our goalkeeper, George Hunter, with four or five top class saves, and Francis, who shouted at us, organised us, and made so many crucial headers and crunching tackles that I doubted he would make half-time, far less play for the whole game. Lenny settled quicker than the rest of us and after that we felt much more solid at the back. It wasn't really until shortly before half-time that I felt we got into the game, and unfortunately we conceded a goal just as we started to play some decent football.

Driving down the M6, Francis chuckled as I parodied Mike Moffat's half-time talk. "Well, boys, there is one thing for fucking sure, there's no way you can play any worse in the second half, excusing Francis, Lennie and George from these comments. You are giving them the bloody league title. Is that what you want? I've seen my wee sister play better." To be honest, his younger sister had played for Scotland and Fulham Ladies, so that wasn't as big an insult as it sounded, but his team talk then went on to crucify each of us individually in great detail.

"We were a different team in the second half," Francis observed, whilst taking the turnoff for Harrogate.

We had equalised within ten minutes of the restart, but a draw would have meant that the opposition would still have won the title, if only on goal difference. As it got closer to full time they began to play deeper and deeper, hoping that they could keep us from scoring by packing their own half with all their players. With just over five minutes to go, we forced a corner on the left hand side. Francis and Lennie went up for it, I held back to cover in case we lost the ball and we got caught on the break. When the ball floated over, I had a great view from behind Francis as he rose and powered a glorious header into the top right hand corner of the opposing net. As the net bulged, I turned and ran back to celebrate with George on his eighteen yard line, but Francis jogged back to his position at centre half and told us all to concentrate right up to the final whistle, as we wouldn't have time to recover if they scored again.

"We looked more like scoring again after that than they did," I said.

"Yes, everyone got their act together for the whole of the second half. In the end, over ninety minutes, we probably just deserved it."

Francis had waited until the celebrations had subsided before stunning us all by announcing that he was retiring from playing. Mike Moffat had known before the game, but to the rest of us it came as a shock as he had been the best player on the park that day, and arguably the best all season.

I asked Francis if he had reconsidered the decision he had made six weeks ago.

"No, it was the right time to stop. I was taking painkillers for the last few weeks of the season and I can see that I'll start to struggle if I play on, and I don't want to do that. I've played long enough; it's time for someone else now."

"Will you not miss it?"

"Come the opening day of the season I will be probably be wishing that I hadn't made the decision, but that will pass very quickly. I've watched too many players stay one season too long, and they have regretted it." He turned to me and grinned. "Anyway, you're not getting rid of me that easily. I'm giving Mike a hand with the coaching, so you'd better be prepared for some hard work. And don't look so pleased. I'm going to make sure you lot are even better this season, and that means an extra night's training every week."

I must have looked dismayed because Francis grinned widely and asked me if I was looking forward to pre-season training.

"I was, until now." I grinned back, but to be honest, I had started to enjoy training, and it wouldn't do our fitness any harm either.

Over the next twenty-odd years I accompanied Francis on quite a few of these trips and I never tired of them. Apart from enjoying Francis' company and the break from the grind of police work, it fed my passion for wood and beautifully made furniture. It inspired me to learn and improve my skills and, although I knew that I could never reach the standards that craftsmen like Francis attained, it gave me something to aim at and an incredible sense of satisfaction when I produced something that came anywhere near their levels.

On the last night in Harrogate we went out for a meal as usual and then had a few drinks in the hotel bar when we returned. Francis seemed to be in a mood to talk about the outcome of the trial.

"Do you know what was the worst bit of it all?" he said.

I didn't answer, as it wasn't really a question.

He went on. "When the verdicts were read out there was a cheer from the public gallery behind me, and those bastards in the dock were hugging each other and doing that 'high five' thing. I wanted to shout that the jury hadn't returned 'not guilty' verdicts, but I wasn't going to give them the satisfaction."

"Don't beat yourself up. Scum like that don't care what folk think."

"Aye, you're probably right. But to see and hear them celebrating made me almost physically sick. If I could have, I'd have happily wiped them all out and gone to prison for it."

I'd heard that Francis had been very dignified afterwards, thanking the prosecution team and shaking their hands, before leaving on his own.

"When I got outside, the whole crowd of them were still on the steps. They were jumping up and down, dancing with each other, making obscene gestures to the reporters, photographers, and the one cameraman there from STV."

I'd seen the footage – I had felt gutted for Francis at the time, but I'd hoped he hadn't seen it. Lee Scoular had gone right up to the camera, two fingers up, shouting abuse, which of course had been bleeped out, although it didn't take an expert to lip read what he was saying. Some of their women were tarted up to the nines; others had the standard issue shell suits and designer trainers. The TV reporter had tried to have a word with some of the group, but had been shouted down and pushed away.

I'd heard through guys in the force, who had received reports throughout the rest of that day, that the newly released gang and their followers had left a trail of carnage in their wake as they moved from bar to bar, gradually meandering out from the city centre towards Clydebank. The uniformed branch had been told to play it softly to avoid accusations of over-reaction, so they were left to get on with it as long as it didn't become a riot.

"I saw it on TV. Didn't realise you were there, Francis. I thought you had already left."

"No, I made myself watch. A couple of them looked over at me and Kevin Nolan actually had the gall to wink at me. I'll not forget that, or any of the rest of it either."

After a while I asked him if there was any progress with a civil prosecution.

"We have been advised that the costs would be prohibitively expensive and there would be no chance of legal aid or government intervention. I am going to keep pressing for a public inquiry, but that seems to be a non-starter, too. All in all, I think we have just about exhausted all the avenues we had available."

"How has Deborah taken it?"

"She doesn't know all of it, but she is finding it very difficult to come to terms with. She has spent a bit of time away, visiting a friend who moved down near London a couple of years back. She has been very supportive to Deborah. She is down there at the moment and probably won't be back until the middle of next week."

"So what do you intend doing?"

"I intend to get on with my life. We know nothing will ever be the same again, but we still have to work and eat and I'm going to carry on looking for ways to get justice for Patrick, no matter what happens."

I offered him any help he needed and we left it at that. For the rest of the evening and on the journey back home, when we did speak, it was about sport, books, the weather, or the success of the trip.

CHAPTER 8   SEPARATION

In November of the following year I left Kirkintilloch CID and joined Andy Craig at Springburn. Andy had been there since August as a DI and when one of his DCs left he contacted me and asked me if I wanted to be recommended for the vacancy. It wasn't cut and dried for me – I really enjoyed the section I was with and had learned a hell of a lot from both DSs and the DCI.

By piecing together information I'd gleaned over the years since the internal inquiry, I knew that Gallagher's squad were not faring well. Peter Jones retired in June of 1980 at the age of fifty-five, and was dead within two years. A heart attack, I heard, and not a surprise – he was overweight, ate a full fry-up every morning, drank like a fish and smoked like a chimney. You could often hear him coming before you saw him, coughing and wheezing as he climbed the station stairs.

Tommy Thompson retired shortly after Peter Jones, on grounds of "ill health". It was convenient for everybody – the brass were relieved to be rid of him, no one particularly wanted to work with him, and he was happy to get away from the menial desk jobs that he had been reduced to since the inquiry. Three weeks after he retired he took up a new post as security consultant at Spangles Nightclub on Clydeside. It was owned by a couple of businessmen with what you could call questionable business ethics who'd been been investigated on a number of occasions, but never prosecuted. Illegal booze, cigarettes and prostitution had been mentioned in connection with the nightclub, and extortion and intimidation rumours surrounded their security firm.

Tommo seemed to do a selection of jobs for them and he came to the attention of Strathclyde Police on more than one occasion but, like his bosses, nothing could ever be proven. From all reports, he seemed to spend a lot of his time in the club, even when he was not working, but he had always been a heavy drinker. As well as that, as "management", he probably had access to some of the girls, purportedly exotic dancers and topless barmaids, but well known to provide other services if the price was right.

Just before Christmas, 1983, outside the nightclub, a punter stabbed Tommo in the thigh during a brawl. He was taken to Glasgow Royal and the wound was treated, although it did involve a trip to the operating theatre. About a month later it seemed to have healed up well and he had started back at work, albeit with a limp, when he was again rushed to hospital, something to do with a blood clot from the original injury moving down and blocking one of the main blood vessels in his leg. Despite extensive surgical and medical treatment, the leg was amputated one week later.

Drew Rutherford, one of the guys who investigated the brawl, which had involved three people being stabbed and four people being charged for attempted murder, told me that they couldn't say why Tommo had been stabbed and, when he had done a follow-up interview with him a couple of months later, he said that Tommo was in a hell of a state, living in filth and drunk most of the time. He said that he had seen a couple of crates of mostly empty whisky bottles sitting in the kitchen, and discarded fast food containers were lying everywhere.

As for Gallagher himself, he continued in the force for quite a few years until he was caught drink driving, convicted and banned for two years; more importantly, he was thrown out of the force without his pension. At that point I had heard that he was living on his own, in a vandalised council flat in Keppochill Road, close to my new patch. I hoped that I wouldn't run into him.

When I'd found all this out I told Francis, but while he didn't seem to derive any great satisfaction from it, neither did he have much sympathy for them. I think he had just written them off in his mind once he'd made sure they wouldn't screw up another investigation.

As for Francis, things hadn't worked out the best for Deborah and himself. Out of the blue one day he phoned me and told me that they had separated.

"I didn't want you to hear it from anyone else, so I'm telling you first. Can you let Andy know?"

"Of course," I assured him, stunned by his news, "I'll do that." I hesitated, and then asked, "Christ, Francis, why?"

He sighed. "You can't realise the pressure on a relationship when something as terrible as Patrick's murder happens, especially with the trial falling apart as well. No matter how close you think you are, you both handle it differently and neither of you can understand why the other is not reacting in the same way. I think I may have become a bit obsessive about the whole thing, but it was just my way of handling it. Deborah wanted me to let it go in the end and I just couldn't do that."

I had known that Deborah was away more often, but I had assumed that she was spending some more time with her friend down south who had been, according to Deborah, having a "bad time of it". In addition, she had started an Open University course, on human psychology of all things, and I had supposed that some time away at college would be part of that.

He went on. "Did you know that Deborah wanted us to retire, pack up here, move down south and try and build a new life?"

"Deborah never would have said anything like that to me."

"Oh, I just wondered. I had seen you two talking occasionally, and, well ... you know."

"We had a few conversations, mostly about the trial and what went after, occasionally about how you were coping. What's going to happen to the house and the yard?"

"We are fortunate that there are no financial repercussions. We have always been fairly thrifty and we have a decent nest egg to fall back on. It will allow me to keep the house and yard, and Deborah can afford to buy a place of her own somewhere. She will get a good allowance from this place, even if I have to work a bit harder." I didn't know if he was being serious, but I doubted it. On reflection, the house and the workshop had probably been handed down to Francis virtually debt-free by his father and it was a thriving business, even if it would never make Francis a rich man.

"So you'll carry on the same?" I asked, deep down hoping that he would.

"Yes. I really know nothing else. But I will take a little bit more time to myself. I'm not getting any younger and there's a lot of things I've always thought of doing, but have never got round to."

"Like what?"

"I'd like to do a bit of travel, see some of France, for instance."

"On your own?" I said, surprised.

"Yes. I can be quite happy with my own company, there's freedom when you can do as you please and not have to answer to anybody else."

Strangely enough, I could just see Francis going from village to village in provincial France in his little Morris Traveller. He did most things well and I guessed that would include quickly picking up a smattering of French. I also knew that if he did, he would end up gravitating to places where there were craftsmen to talk with or handmade furniture to see.

My thoughts turned to Deborah. I didn't know her very well but she was always very kind to me and I had a lot of respect for her. She was very strong and dignified in the face of all that had happened. She had surprised me one day when the three of us were having lunch in their kitchen, Francis and I halfway through our regular Sunday session in the workshop.

"John, I'd like you to have Patrick's LPs. Francis tells me that you have a similar taste in music to Patrick, so you just help yourself to anything."

Francis had just smiled at me and I took it that he was happy with all of this. I had quite a few of the same records and there were some I wasn't interested in, but on the whole they filled certain gaps in my collection. I also took a few of the classic issues of the *NME* music papers that I'd noticed previously and thought of maybe getting a few of the covers framed for my flat.

That was probably the last time I saw Deborah before they separated.

I still saw Francis three or four times a week, at training, at matches and, usually on Sundays, at the workshop. We got into the habit of working all day if I was off, then heading somewhere for a quick meal and a couple of pints. I would often kip at his house afterwards and we would have a quiet drink in his front room, him with a small malt, me with a larger one, on the rocks. He would sometimes take me into his "study", where he would show me his latest design on a large drawing board he kept for the purpose. On one occasion he very excitedly dragged me through to the office to show me his latest acquisition – an Apple Mac computer. I asked him why he'd shelled out so much for something I didn't think he would find much use for, but he showed me an early mock-up of a new brochure he was putting together and, I have to admit, I was impressed by his expertise with it, his photographs, and the brochure itself.

I began to get a real handle on what was involved in designing a piece of furniture and the range of tasks I

159

could do for Francis expanded every month. I was becoming more useful to him by the day.

As a favour to a pharmacist friend who had lost his delivery driver temporarily through illness, Francis had volunteered to deliver prescriptions to those people, mostly disabled or elderly, who couldn't manage to get out to collect them. It was typical of Francis and it meant that for six weeks he was struggling to keep up with his own work. I took a couple of weeks' annual leave and did my best to help him out. He often left me with a list of tasks to complete while he was away and I would have them finished by the time he returned, so that he could get on with the next stage of whatever he was working on.

One of the jobs Francis gave me to do was to make the small gunmetal maker's plaques that he screwed to the back of all his furniture before it left the workshop. I would take one of the small dull blanks and drill a hole in each corner for the screws. In pencil, I would draw a couple of lines to help me line up my lettering then, using a set of cold punches, I would carefully tap out "P. Hare & Son, Glasgow" along with Francis' initials and the year of manufacture. I would then polish the plaque, initially with steel wool, then with a fine buffing cloth, until it came up with a dull shine, like a gun barrel. A final coat of clear lacquer would keep it like that for years to come.

Working with Andy Craig was also a joy. I knew he was a good officer, but he had become even more confident, with a real knack for getting the best out of his people. I noticed as soon as I arrived how efficient and smooth the whole place ran and, although some of this was down to a good solid DCI who let the guys get on with it, a lot of it could be put down to the abilities of Andy and his DSs.

Compared with Kirkintilloch it was a busy station, with a much higher proportion of serious crimes. The area had a large percentage of low-income families and some of the most deprived housing in Glasgow. There were as many murders in the first month of my new job as there had been in the previous year up the road, yet there was less than five miles between them. Every Saturday and Sunday night there were a spate of serious assaults and pub brawls to sort out. Monday was always busy, because of having to deal with the backlog from the weekend.

[Sunday 3rd June 1984]

I'd had the odd girlfriend since I'd split up with Moira, but I was enjoying being on my own again. Perhaps I just never met the right girl, or maybe I was too selfish to give up what was, for me, an easy lifestyle, with no one to nag me for playing too much football, working too late, spending hours and hours at the workshop, or chilling out with a beer and a pizza in front of the box.

Andy would occasionally stay over; we'd get a curry and a bottle of wine and sit and watch a video. Although he was now my boss we managed to stay friends outside of work, but I was careful not to step over the line at any time when we were working. We were sitting in my flat watching football on the TV when Andy suddenly sat bolt upright and turned to me.

"I knew there was something I meant to tell you!" he said, "Remember a guy called Davie Erskine?"

I knew I should have, but I couldn't just place him.

"You know him. He used to annoy Gallagher when we were in Partick, he never let him bully him like he did with the rest of the uniforms."

"Vaguely," I said, "but remember, I wasn't there very long."

"Aye, but you'd know him if you saw him. Anyway, it doesn't matter. I bumped into him the other day and we got talking. He knew that I'd been on the Patrick Hare investigation and asked me if I'd heard about Lee Scoular. Turns out that Scoular's dead. He died of some disease you catch from rats."

"You're not serious," I said. "How'd this Erskine guy know?"

161

"A few of them were asked to do traffic control at the funeral. He recognised Scoular's name when he got there and asked some of the mourners what had happened. He noticed that most of the gang were present at the cemetery and when he met me he thought I would be interested. Big funeral, too. Most of the lowlifes from miles around were there. Scoular must have got to be a bit of a player, with all those bastards going to see him off."

"Was Kevin Nolan there?"

"No, he's doing a six month sentence for assault, doesn't get out for a couple of weeks yet."

"Was it some sort of yellow fever or something?"

"Nah, you moron, you only get that in tropical countries. Doesn't matter, anyway; the bastard's dead, and I, for one, am not sorry."

My first thought was to tell Francis. I phoned him that evening, but I was slightly disappointed with his muted response; I supposed that he thought that nothing was going to bring Patrick back again and that he was beginning to move on.

He'd been as good as his word and was now taking the odd weekend away from work. Once or twice a year he would disappear for a week or so in the old Traveller. He tried to make this coincide with my taking annual leave and I would mind the shop and get on with the few jobs that he would leave me to do. He insisted on paying me the going rate for a trainee craftsman and I took the money in good grace, knowing that it would keep him happy. It suited me, anyway, because I had plenty time to get on with my own carpentry, which was getting harder to fit in as I worked towards getting made up to Detective Sergeant. I'd just about sat most of the panels and was hoping to get an acting sergeant's post shortly, which would give me the experience needed when a full time DS's position came up. Francis didn't say too much about these trips away other than where he was headed, but I do know he did get to France, and he confirmed my predictions by telling me about a fantastic little

162

"craftsman's commune" he'd found in the Dordogne, where young carpenters, blacksmiths, and glassworkers, among others, lived and worked with their families in a small village in the hills, sharing resources and collaborating to produce work of exceptional quality and individuality. He would come back from these breaks refreshed and full of ideas, with a sheaf of photographs of craftwork of all descriptions, which he would refer to when needing inspiration.

~~o~~

I couldn't stop myself being curious about Lee Scoular's death, so I knocked off early one afternoon a few weeks later, meaning to call in at a few of the hospitals to find out a bit more about it. I started at Stobhill, as it was just up the road from the station and, after flourishing my ID and explaining that it was part of an ongoing investigation, one of the medical records staff had a look through the microfiche records for me. I was not surprised to learn that they had no record of a Lee Scoular, as his home turf was on the other side of Glasgow.

An almost identical process took place at the Royal Infirmary and again I came away empty handed, but I was now heading back to his neck of the woods. My next call was at the Western Infirmary and, ironically, as this was where Patrick had been taken and was pronounced DOA after the attack, I struck lucky. I was told by a medical secretary that a Lee Scoular had been a patient there but that she couldn't release any information without talking to a doctor first. I hadn't really wanted to leave any official record of my enquiries, but I agreed that she could contact the doctor involved with the case. She told me to come back in half an hour so I had a cup of coffee in the canteen, watching all these poor bastards shuffling about in their dressing gowns and wrist tapes, their skin varying in shades of grey, with sunken faces marking the pain and suffering they were enduring.

I couldn't hang about any longer watching the day of the living dead, so I was back at the clinical records office a bit sharper than necessary. I took a seat for ten minutes, waiting for the doc, and whiled away the time looking at the health posters on the wall, informing me that if prostate or bowel cancer didn't get me, a stroke or "furred-up" arteries would, leaving me to come to the conclusion that hospitals were the most depressing places on earth.

When the doctor arrived I was surprised that she was female, young and Irish; she looked about mid-twenties, tops. I introduced myself, showed her my identity card, and explained that I was just tying up some loose ends in a high-profile murder investigation that I was involved in, where Lee Scoular had been one of the main suspects.

She explained that she was doing a medical residency with the consultant, Mr Cooper, and that he was unavailable but that she had authority to provide limited information about the case. I told her that I would keep any information off the record anyway, as this was merely a follow up to a closed investigation.

"Firstly, what is your name?"

She smiled. "Is that for official use, or are you just curious?"

I found myself grinning, and I told her that it was a bit of both.

"I'm Doctor Catherine Carr. What else do you need to know?"

I was tempted to ask for her phone number, but I thought that I'd better not push it.

"I was looking for information on Lee Scoular's fatal illness."

She looked puzzled. "I can't see how that could have any relevance to your investigation."

"To be honest, it hasn't really, but ..."

I sighed and held my hands up. "To be completely frank, I was involved in the investigation, which went horribly wrong, and a group of thugs literally got away with

164

murder. Perhaps I got too involved with the case and with the deceased's family – it was my first case after joining CID and I was probably a bit naive. Anyhow, when I heard that one of the suspects had died, I felt that I owed it to the family to find out the details, for a small bit of closure."

I looked at her, to see if I was getting anywhere. She had her head on one side, listening, as if to say, "go on".

"Look," I continued, "if it's against your medical ethics or something, it is really not that important. I was just hoping that you could give me the information off the record, as I'm here unofficially, so to speak."

"You are really a detective?" she asked, frowning.

"Of course I am. If you want to check, phone Springburn CID and ask for Detective Inspector Craig. He will vouch for my credentials."

She laughed. "No, I do believe you. I wouldn't want to get you into trouble."

"You wouldn't. You see, Andy Craig worked on the investigation, too, and I think he would probably like to know about this as well, but he doesn't yet know I'm here."

"OK," she said, "here's the deal. I'll give you some general answers to questions about the disease suffered by Mr. Scoular. You're the detective; you should be able to piece the rest together."

"Fair enough, I'll go along with that." I took out my notebook. "What was this disease that killed him?"

"Sorry, I can't answer that."

I must have looked annoyed, but she just looked at me and smiled. Suddenly, I caught on.

"What diseases are passed to humans from rats, and can be fatal?"

She gave me a look as if to say, "Well done, but it took a while."

"The most common disease passed to humans by rats is Weil's disease, which can sometimes be fatal, especially if untreated. It is caused by the anaerobic spirochete, Leptospira Interrogans, which can result in severe liver disease, leading to jaundice and possibly death."

"Whoa," I said, "go a bit slower with all those big medical words; I'm only a humble copper."

She repeated the names of the killer bug, which I wrote down to the best of my ability – I would look up the correct spellings later. I continued with the questions.

"And do cases occur regularly in the west of Scotland?"

"Cases occur regularly, but they can be mild. There has only been one fatal case recorded in this hospital in the last two years."

"Why would some cases be more severe than others?"

"That would depend on a number of factors, including the level of infection, the person's ability to fight infections, and whether prompt treatment was initiated, amongst other things."

"What are the symptoms?" I asked.

"Initially, flu like symptoms, with headaches, nausea, fever, and sometimes a rash. Often the patient improves after a few days, but they can then suddenly deteriorate, with haemorrhage, jaundice, and multiple organ failure. If left untreated, especially in the later stages, the patient may never recover."

I really wanted to ask if the bastard would have suffered, but I hadn't yet thought of a way to without looking bad.

"And how would this disease be picked up?"

"Mostly, it's through contact with rat's urine. Infection passes in by the mouth, the mucous membranes of the eyes or nose, or through cuts or grazes. Shallow freshwater lakes with low flows of water through them can be a problem, and in fact many of the cases we see are water sports enthusiasts. Heavily contaminated areas can also include crates of food or drink left in stores, or outside. The last outbreak we saw was caused by a convenience store that kept their crates of soft drink cans in an enclosed alleyway; people were purchasing the cans and drinking out of them without cleaning them first."

I made a mental note to always wipe the top of a can before drinking out of it in future.

"That outbreak was quite big – over twenty people were ill with it, but most of them weren't too serious and they all recovered with treatment."

I couldn't imagine Lee Scoular windsurfing or canoeing, so I would probably go for the knocked off cans of Irn-Bru that had been sitting in the back yard of some pub or mini-market as the cause of his infection.

"Well, thank you for that information, Doctor. It may seem sad to say it, but it may give a little bit of comfort for the deceased's family to know that one of the bastards isn't around any more."

She bridled a bit at that and I was sort of sorry I had said it, in a way.

"Look, I'm sorry. I shouldn't have said that, especially with you being a doc and all that, but there are still a lot of people hurting from this crime and sometimes that exposes some unpleasant traits in otherwise good people."

That seemed to mollify her a bit. "I suppose it must be difficult for them, but don't forget that Lee had a family who cared for him, too."

I thought of Lee's family and couldn't find much sympathy for them, but I kept that to myself.

The interview seemed to be at an end, but I chatted to her for a few more minutes, mostly about what she was doing in Glasgow, and wondered if I had the balls to ask her out for a drink. Although she wasn't spectacularly beautiful, she had the type of looks which, combined with her obvious intelligence and a good sense of humour, I found very attractive.

~~o~~

I didn't speak to Francis about Lee, but I did corner Andy the next day and explain what I'd found out.

"I can't say it is the brightest idea that you've ever had; it's the sort of thing that'll come back and bite you on the arse. Having said all that, it seems unlikely that you'll get into bother – the doctor seems to be discreet and it is nice to know some of the details of how the bastard copped it." He paused. "Have you spoken to Francis yet?"

I replied that I hadn't told him the details, and explained my reasons for not having done so. "He didn't seem as interested as I would have expected when I told him that Scoular had died. I wondered if he was beginning to move on and if further debate would just prolong the agony."

"I doubt it," he said. "Just wait for the right moment – or he'll get round to asking you, take my word for it."

"I'm not so sure. I think Deborah leaving him has given him a wake-up call."

"Yeh, that was a shock, wasn't it? I never saw that one coming. It just shows you. You think a couple are one hundred per cent solid, but you can't take anything for granted."

"What got me was that it was completely out the blue. I knew that she was away a lot of the time, but I never put two and two together." I told him about the friend that she had down south. "Francis and she just didn't act like a couple who were coming apart – when she was there, everything seemed as normal."

"John, we don't know what was going on behind closed doors. All we can do is be there if Francis needs someone to talk to."

"It's very difficult to get him to open up about anything, and when he does, it's on his terms only."

"That's the man he is," Andy replied. We agreed to try and meet up together with Francis in the not too distant future and left it at that. I was just about to go home for the night when one of the uniforms shouted that there was a phone call for me.

I found the nearest phone, picked it up, and told the girl to put me through to the caller.

"Hi there, it's Dr Carr here. I hope you don't mind me phoning?"

"No, not at all," I replied, "the pleasure's all mine. What can I do for you?"

"I enjoyed talking to you yesterday, but I did wonder why you didn't ask me out."

I burst out laughing. "Bloody hell!"

"What's up? You never been asked out before?"

"To be honest, no, not since I left school, anyway." I was still chuckling away to myself. "You're not shy, are you?"

She laughed now as well. "Normally I am, but I enjoyed chatting with you yesterday."

"I'm not perfect, but I'm not the worst either."

"Well ...?"

"OK, then, you've talked me into it. I'm off early tomorrow, if you fancy a bite to eat."

We agreed to meet for drinks first and we hung up. I did a little dance around the phone, but cut it short as two uniforms came round the corner.

169

My sister got married later that year and I took Catherine along which, of course, sent my Mum and all my aunties into a spin of engagement and wedding speculation. I didn't do anything to dispel the myth, but I knew that Cath, as I called her, wasn't intending to stay in Scotland for long. Once her internship was over she was first heading back home and then to Canada, where a friend of hers had emigrated. She and I both knew that I wouldn't be following her and that this was always going to be a fleeting relationship. It was fun, however, to wind up all the old fishwives in my family. I had been right about Catherine as well; intelligence and sexiness in the one package, with the addition of a good sense of humour to seal the deal.

In addition, she taught me a hell of a lot about the medical side of things. I would incessantly question her about pathologists' reports and other medical evidence that I came across at work and she would patiently explain the reasons for the long words and the complicated language that was invariably present, while I massaged her lovely neck or we snuggled up in bed in the dingy little flat she either used as a bolthole or to keep her independence. I didn't care because, other than the occasional busy on-call night, she had effectively moved in with me within a month of us meeting.

When her internship was up I saw her off on the Aer Lingus flight to Dublin, parting as good friends, neither of us even asking the other if we wished to go or stay. My mum and the whole female side of my family didn't speak to me for three months afterwards, because I'd let her go.

In fact, by the end of the eighties, it was my relationship with Francis that had developed into something like that of an old married couple, far more than any relationship I had with the opposite sex, and we were both very set in our ways. I was coming to the end of my playing days; I'd dropped back down to playing Sunday league football after struggling with injury the year before, but I wasn't enjoying it and I was gradually coming to the conclusion that Francis had made the right move when he'd retired before he started to go downhill. I intended to quit at the end of the year, but I felt duty bound to see the season out to avoid letting my new teammates down. We were actually doing all right, beating everyone else in the league apart from the top two teams, who were running away with it.

Francis had retired as coach from Glenhill the year I left, after a very successful stint – we won the league three years out of ten and never finished worse than fourth. We also did well in cup competitions and may well have reached a record-breaking second round of the Scottish Cup proper if we hadn't come up against a Cowdenbeath side who were striding up their own division in the Scottish League. Francis' retirement may have partly spurred me on to move down a league or two, although the attraction of one more year with some of my old mates who still tied a pair of boots on every weekend was also a factor. Francis would come and watch us most weeks and, to be fair on him, he managed to keep in check any impulse to criticise or give advice when we played poorly. I think he just enjoyed being able to watch a game of football without having to think about it. The guys, bless 'em, welcomed Francis into the fold and he often stayed for a few drinks afterwards, not saying much, but quite obviously soaking up the banter that was more widespread at this level than it ever was at Glenhill.

By now I really was his unofficial apprentice in all but name. I only occasionally received pay, but if we were away on a trip to an exhibition or a long distance delivery I never had to put my hand in my pocket and, at the workshop, I had the use of all the machines or workbenches and Francis supplied every bit of wood I required, along with ironware, glues and finishes, at no cost at all.

I never brought up the subject of Patrick's murder or trial, but occasionally Francis liked to talk about it, probably more to make sure that there were a few of us who hadn't forgotten than for any great need on his part to get it off his chest. Occasionally Andy would join us for a meal out with a few beers afterwards, all very comfortable in each other's company. When we occasionally discussed the

171

single lifestyles that Andy and I had chosen, all he would say was: "One day, boys, one day …"

We laughed away his predictions, citing our shallowness as protection against such a disaster, and the next few years seemed to bear out the confidence we had in our ability to avoid "the marriage trap".

CHAPTER 9   BARLINNIE

[Friday 16th February 1990]

Barlinnie prison is one of those places that should have the effect of discouraging criminals from their chosen profession – the grey imposing exterior is matched inside by a cold drabness that no amount of modernisation and bright paint can cover up. We had to visit it occasionally to interview a remand prisoner, or a convicted prisoner who was a witness or suspect in an investigation. Being inside the Bar-L, as it is known in these parts, was not a pleasant experience for me. I always felt a depressing chill, despite the fact the prison was physically warm enough.

On the particular day in question, a couple of us were there to interview a lifer who was a significant witness in an old case that we had re-opened after further evidence had come to light. Since I'd been promoted to Detective Sergeant, I'd been following up unsolved cases that, in the light of advances in forensic science, were being looked at again with a view to them being re-investigated. This case was slightly different, however.

We were trying to place our suspect near to the scene of the crime and his alibi, holding up under pressure, had him over in Northern Ireland at the time. We had been tipped off (which is why the case had been re-opened) that the suspect had been present in Springburn that day and, even more significantly, had been present in the flat next door to where the crime had taken place. The tenant of that flat at that time was none other than the current occupant of a Cell 2/22 of C Hall in the Bar-L, eight years into a life sentence for a Glasgow gangland killing which you may have read in the papers at the time: "The Kwik-Fit murder", so called because it had taken place in a tyre and exhaust fitting outlet and involved the bizarre use of a hydraulic vehicle ramp as the murder weapon.

Normally this wasn't the kind of guy who would provide evidence in another inquiry, but three things were working in our favour. Firstly, his business interests were currently being run by his wife and teenage son and, while they seemed to be managing adequately, he was anxious to make his stay in prison as short as possible and parole boards were very amenable to prisoners who were willing to provide help in clearing up unrelated crimes. Secondly, there was a strong sexual element to the crime we were examining and many of the Glasgow hard men hated rapists and other sex-offenders. Lastly, our suspect was at best a peripheral part of the Glasgow gang culture and could not rely on the normal level of protection that other lowlifes could often expect.

Anyway, we were waiting in the reception area for security clearance and had been told to take a seat for a while. Usually, a ten-minute wait was the longest we would have expected so, after half an hour, I approached the warder standing behind the counter and asked him what the problem was.

When he replied, I noticed that he had a strong Ayrshire accent.

"Sorry, we should hae kept you informed. There's been an incident in one of the wings and we've had tae shut down various areas to get things sorted oot. Some of your lot have been called in. It looks pretty serious."

"I didn't see anyone come through. Were they here before we arrived?"

"Just in front of you, but they didn't come through here – they went straight in. I think there were five or six of them."

"So what happened, or can't you say?"

"It's no secret, the whole place is talking aboot it anyway and by this time, half of Glasgow will ken as well. One of the prisoners got chibbed pretty badly. They took him to hospital, but I think it's touch and go. Funny thing is, this guy had asked to go into 'protection' last week. Normally only paedos and other sickos ask for that and they're usually up at Peterhead. He was doing three years for a serious assault; he must hae got on some cunt's tits in here."

I wondered if it was someone I knew of, so I asked the warden who had been assaulted.

"I think it's some guy, Sornie. Can't remember his first name, but as far as I ken, he was an evil wee bastard anyhow. Apart from the hassle we'll get for this happening in our jail, none of us will lose any sleep ower it."

He must have suddenly seen my face. "What?" he said.

"Was it James Sornie, by any chance?" I was suddenly sure it had to be him.

"D'you know, I think that wis his name. Is he one of yours?"

"No, no," I answered, "but I did come across him in another investigation where we didn't get a conviction. You'll probably remember it – the young student who was kicked to death and the gang got off after the trial collapsed. About ten years ago, it was."

He thought for a moment. "Aye, I think I remember – there was some kind of screw-up wi' the investigation, wasn't there?"

"Yeh, there was. The bastards got away with it. Well, James Sornie was one of them, so I'll not lose any sleep over him getting a doing."

Shortly after we were allowed in to interview our witness who, as I half suspected, gave us enough to completely destroy the suspect's alibi meaning we could put another case to bed. As I was leaving, the same warder called me over.

"That guy Sornie, DOA at the Royal Infirmary. We just got word back."

"The shit will hit the fan now for you lot. A murder inquiry will make life pretty difficult for you, won't it?"

"Ach, aye, but we get them every so often; with all the heid-bangers in here, it's always a risk. It will blow over after they get the offenders and some poor warden gets his knuckles rapped."

"Thanks for telling me. I know the murdered boy's family and I can tell them that the bastard is dead. Perhaps it will help a little."

I turned to go, but had a sudden thought. "If you hear anything further about this, can you do me a favour and give me a bell?" I handed him one of my cards. "Sorry, I didn't catch your name."

"Just ask for big Sanny Fairbairn. I'm well kent around this place." He looked at the card I'd handed him. "John," he said, "I'll gie you a phone if I hear anything interesting."

I phoned Andy, who by now was a DI at Baird Street and told him that another of the gang was dead.

"Christ, what happened this time – sleeping sickness?"

"No, he was in the Bar-L and was assaulted today, died in the ambulance on the way to hospital."

"Have they got anyone yet?"

"No details have come out so far, but seemingly he'd applied for protection a week ago, so he had obviously been threatened."

"If that's on record, someone will get a bollocking." He suddenly asked, "You told Francis yet?"

"No, I was going to phone him earlier, but part of me thinks we shouldn't say anything at all to him. It might just stir it all up again."

"He does seem to have got over it all now, if that's possible."

I shook my head. "He's just found ways to bury it as deep as possible, but you occasionally get a glimpse of what he's really feeling."

"You know him better than me, so I'll take your word for it. But I'd still tell him if I were you. You don't want him to hear it from someone else and wonder why you didn't tell him."

When I phoned Francis later that day and told him about James Sornie's death, I was glad I had. After initially being shocked, he seemed to be more relieved than anything else. It was as if he felt that, finally, a little bit of fairness had crept back into the world.

~~o~~

About two weeks later I got a call from the warden I'd spoken to the day James Sornie died. It took me a few seconds to work out who "Big Sanny" was, but once I'd got his broad Ayrshire accent clocked, I listened carefully as he told me that the results of the investigation into Sornie's murder inquiry were doing the rounds of the prison. They had charged three inmates with the murder and the word was that the police were pretty certain of convictions. It turned out that pictures of Sornie shagging an eight-year-old lassie had been circulating around the prison for a few weeks before he was killed, but the prison authorities hadn't known about it so when he asked for protection there were no valid reasons for them to allow the request. Obviously, in hindsight, Sornie had known he was a marked man, but there were to be no direct repercussions for the prison or its staff.

"But," Sanny added, "they did turn up one o' our boys who had previous, so he got a P45 in his hand for that. They seemingly got a tip-off about it."

"The guy would probably have got away with it if this murder hadn't happened, no?"

"Aye, but he's no loss. There's enough criminals in here, without having them on the staff. Anyhow, they've arrested the three inmates who assaulted Sornie, so the whole thing will blow ower."

"In a way, I'm slightly surprised Sornie turned out to be a paedo. His nickname was Pervo to the rest of the gang, but it was a kind of badge of honour with him – he had a taste for filthy sex with slutty women, and a liking for porn of the harder and kinkier kind, but there was never any question of him being interested in kids."

"You never know with that kind, it can be just under the surface. Mind you, he wasn't the usual type you associate with these dirty bastards; he seemed too much of the hard man for that."

I thanked him for phoning me and asked him to let me know if he heard anything more. I phoned Andy, and told him the details.

"No surprise, then, that he was murdered and that they got his killers; the only question is: did the wardens turn a blind eye and things went a bit far, or did they genuinely think that the guy was just bullshitting them when he asked for protection? If you really want to know, have a quiet word with Gordon Logan over at London Road. He was involved in the investigation, and he trained at Tulliallan with me. Just tell him I told you to call." He paused for a second. "Wait, I'll phone him myself. He might be more likely to give me the inside on the incident. I'll let you know."

Two days later, he phoned me back. "No joy, I'm afraid. They think it was a genuine case where the staff couldn't justify putting him into protection because there was no history of Sornie having committed any sex offences, and he couldn't be specific about any threats that were being made, if there were any. He said it was pretty straightforward, the three cons who assaulted him were lifers with a lot of time left, must have thought it was worth it."

"Thanks anyway, Andy. I owe you one."

I didn't hear about Gallagher's death until a few weeks after he died; I must have missed it in the Bulletin. I had known that he was ill and that he'd been a chronic alcoholic, so it didn't surprise me. Ironically, his last four months on earth were his only entirely sober ones as an adult, as he spent them in a terminal cancer facility with liver and pancreatic cancer eating him away from inside. I knew this because Francis told me – he had received a letter from Gallagher asking Francis to visit him in hospital. If Gallagher had wished to get something off his chest, Francis never gave him the chance. A polite letter of reply was all he ever received from him. Whether or not it contained any forgiving words, I can't tell you, but Gallagher died shortly afterwards and Francis said nothing to me about the whole episode until a few months later.

No one from the force attended his funeral, and I'd heard that the undertakers and gravediggers outnumbered the mourners two-to-one.

Of the three of them, Gallagher and the two fat sergeants, there were none left – Tommo had only lasted a year after his leg was amputated, and his body had lain for over a week in the house until someone complained about the smell and the police broke down the door.

CHAPTER 10   PINKY

[Thursday 19th November 1998]

When Pinky McNiven was killed by Malky McGovern part of me put it down to the violent and unpredictable world they lived in, but I was still shocked when I heard about it. I had worked with two of the investigating officers earlier in our careers so I managed to get pretty much the whole story as it developed.

They were quite close friends, those two, and did a lot of business together on the fringes of the criminal fraternity. Pinky had a stall that he transported around Central Scotland in an old Transit van. He made a living selling cheap tat, some of it knocked off items, rip-offs of more expensive designer type gear or illegal copies of CDs and films. He would venture as far as Ingleston Market in Edinburgh, but mostly you would find him in and around Glasgow or in central belt towns like Coatbridge, Airdrie and Motherwell.

Malky was slightly heavier duty, with connections that made him more of a middleman – or "wholesale", as he liked to call himself. He usually did his business from whatever version of BMW or Merc that he owned at that moment, not quite last year's model. Small stuff, like jewellery, he moved about in the back of the car; with bigger items he would pay somebody else to do the donkey work. Sometimes Pinky would cart things about for him, earning himself a few notes in the process, and in return Malky would supply Pinky with stock at more competitive prices than the cash and carry. Both would know that at least half the stuff was knocked off, or the proceeds of an insurance scam, but there would be enough bankruptcy stock or "seconds" to give both their operations an air of legitimacy. Fuck knows what the Inland Revenue or the VAT man thought of it all.

From what I was told, Pinky may well have stepped over the mark and sourced some stuff direct from one of Malky's usual "suppliers", probably having come in contact with him through fetching and carrying for Malky. As often with these things, where a sit down, a ticking off and an apology – with perhaps a few quid thrown in for good measure – would have probably sorted things out, instead it escalated, each accusing the other of being a cheating cunt, culminating in a stand up fight outside Pinky's flat. Neighbours subsequently said that it came close to serious assault that day, and each of the former friends was as bad as the other.

The upshot of it was for the six months leading up to early October there hadn't been any contact between them. On the day of Pinky's death he had picked up a half a dozen large boxes of watches from a warehouse on the south side and taken them in his van to his flat, where he stashed them in his spare bedroom with some of his other surplus stock. This was a much larger volume than he would have normally dealt with, but my impression was that Pinky was maybe trying to move upmarket, so to speak, cutting himself a bit of the wholesale trade by selling stock to fellow stallholders.

Whether the deal was done under Malky's nose or whether the resentment eating away inside Malky just boiled over into violence, nobody knows, but when police were called to an industrial estate just off Maryhill Road, they saw Malky legging it from the scene of a crime that involved the fatally broken body of Pinky McNiven beneath the wheels of Malky McGovern's latest BMW sports saloon, having been run over at least three times in both forward and reverse directions. The car was a bit newer than Malky's usual wheels, but it was definitely registered in his name. Malky was detained for questioning in connection with Pinky's death an hour later, someone having noticed blood on the corner of his coat when he had taken cover in the Crystal Tavern, a mere half mile from the murder. It smacked of the familiar arrogance that I remembered from his part in Patrick's murder inquiry, but this time we'd got lucky and the local CID had him banged up for it within a few hours of the crime.

Usually a ned in that situation will say nothing, demand a lawyer, and try and wait it out and see if they can get away with it. But I'm told that Malky had argued till he was blue in the face that he'd had nothing to do with it; that his car had disappeared earlier that day and that he'd received a phone call saying that someone had seen it behind the Post Office compound on the Strathkelvin Industrial Estate. When he'd got there (he'd hailed a taxi), he found the car door open and the interior light on, and it wasn't until it occurred to him to look round the car for damage that he'd found Pinky – he hadn't even known who it was at that point, not until he'd turned him over. Even then he'd barely recognised him as half his face was just mush. When asked if he'd driven the car that night, he'd said, "No, but I briefly sat in the driver's seat before getting out and discovering the body." And yes, he'd panicked and run when he heard the siren as he knew he would get fitted up for it anyway. Had he reported the car stolen? No. Why not? Citing the low success rate for solving vehicle theft didn't exactly endear him to the guys doing the interview, but they weren't caring. The whole of CID were delighted that he was talking, even if he wasn't saying the right things. Anything he said that could be easily refuted later on by forensics or witnesses would make it all the more difficult for him to spin any kind of plausible story. Most of them were very surprised that he talked at all, and indeed, when he did finally get to speak to his lawyer, he was told to shut up if he was to have any chance of staying out of prison.

By the next day Malky had been charged with the attempted murder of Stewart McNiven, pending the results of a post-mortem examination. Once this had been received, he was further charged with his murder and remanded in custody until his trial, three months later.

His lawyer claimed that he hadn't been cautioned, but that was a load of crap – half the pub had seen his arrest and the officers concerned knew that he had been read his rights. In the meantime, his lawyer was also desperately trying to find the taxi driver who had picked Malky up that night, and the prosecution team also made it a priority to find this crucial witness, to ensure that Malky wasn't telling the truth. Not surprisingly, no one had come forward to confirm this journey. In addition, there was no sign of Malky's car being broken into, the car's original set of keys were in the ignition, his were the only fingerprints anywhere on the car, and the DNA recovered from the car belonged to Malky and two of his former girlfriends, both of whom had sound alibis for that evening. There had been a phone call to his flat at around the time he claimed to have been tipped off, but it was from the phone box next to his local and could have been anyone. Unfortunately, the CCTV camera near the phone box had been recently vandalised and not yet repaired. No one had seen him leave the flat or get in the taxi, which in itself was not a surprise. It was a cold Thursday evening in November and the streets would probably have been deserted. Nope, everyone reckoned Malky was definitely going down for this one.

At the trial, the pathologist, giving his expert opinion of events, said that the murder was likely to have been premeditated, as it was difficult to imagine any other scenario where so much damage could be done on such a short stretch of road. The initial impact had been to the lower half of the body, which had been struck from behind by the bumper and the edge of the bonnet, breaking both legs and possibly causing some of the pelvic fractures that were also found to be present. From the blood and tissue marks on the road and on the car, he suggested that the car had then carried on over the body, causing multiple abrasions to the head and forearms, which would have been used to try and protect the face. It was likely that Mr McNiven would still have been conscious when the car then reversed over him, the rear wheels on the driver's side crushing his upper abdomen and lower ribs, causing a diaphragmatic tear and rupture of the left liver lobe. The front wheels must have been turned slightly at this point, because the front off-side wheel then drove over the neck and chin area, fracturing and dislocating the jaw, and crushing the hyoid bones of the larynx. After this Mr McNiven would have had severe breathing problems, a result of the combination of the crushed larynx and torn diaphragm, but may still have been alive for a further few minutes. He died at the scene shortly before the paramedics arrived.

Perhaps more brutally, one of the first officers on the scene later said of Pinky's body, "The cunt's legs looked like a swastika, an' his heid looked like a burst melon."

Further forensic evidence obtained from Malky McGovern at his arrest matched blood found on his clothes and hands to Pinky McNiven. The phone records from Pinky McNiven's flat showed an incoming call made from a phone box near to the industrial estate around about an hour before he was found, which the prosecution maintained had probably been made by Malky. Unfortunately, the phone box had been professionally cleaned by a company sub-contracted to BT for the upkeep of its public telephones before any fingerprint or DNA evidence could be obtained from it, and there were no CCTV cameras monitoring that area.

The defence had never managed to produce the taxi driver who had supposedly picked Malky up that night, and no other prints were found anywhere on the car.

In the end the jury retired for forty-three minutes and returned a guilty verdict. The judge, handing down the obligatory life sentence, made it clear that the murder had been a premeditated execution and recommended that the minimum time to be served before Malky McGovern should be considered eligible for parole would be nineteen years. At that point Malky had started shouting and swearing, repeating that he had been set up, and that, "The arse loving pigs, the bastard lawyers, the sad prick o' a judge and the stupid cunts that called themsel's a jury had fucked up and sent the wrong man tae prison." He was still shouting and struggling as they dragged him away to start his sentence.

I have heard, but have not had it confirmed, that Francis was in the public gallery when Malky was taken away, and that Malky had looked up, recognised Francis, and the pair of them had just stared at each other for a second or two until he was dragged away, kicking and screaming. If it was true, Francis certainly never told me.

~~o~~

In February 2002 Malky sparked off a small riot at Barlinnie. I first heard of it on the radio as I drove home with a couple of friends along the M8 between Edinburgh and Glasgow. We'd spent the previous night at a Radiohead concert at Meadowbank in Edinburgh. Andy came with us to the concert and then took us to a few of his haunts in and around the top end of Leith Walk and, after a few drinks, we had dossed down in his flat. It had been good to see Andy again and we had done a fair bit of catching up, something we hadn't done since he'd moved through to his new post as Chief Inspector of the Scottish Crimes Drug Enforcement Agency, based in Edinburgh, six months previously.

As it was a Saturday afternoon we had the radio turned on to listen to the football, but before it started the Scottish news team had broken the story of a serious disturbance at Barlinnie, involving the prisoners on one floor of D-Hall. Two prisoners had made it on to the roof and there was the usual standoff with the prison authorities. Let's face it, nearly everyone thinks that a couple of fire engines hosing cold water up there would soon bring them down one way or the other. I joked about the scene in *Porridge* where Fletcher talks McLaren down off the roof. You know the one; the coloured Scotsman with a chip on each shoulder.

I got in late that night after meeting my latest girlfriend, Caroline, one of the civvies from the station, for a meal and a few drinks, followed by a few hours at her place pleasantly naked, taking full advantage of her youthful enthusiasm and a figure that made me feel almost young again.

I left her flat about half past one; I wanted an early start in the morning as I was helping Francis with a big job over at the workshop and I knew that if I stayed I would be reluctant to get up early.

When I got back I automatically turned on the TV in my bedroom as I got ready for bed and I could hear the news in the background as I brushed my teeth and had a wash. As I came out of the bathroom and headed to pour myself a glass of water in the kitchen I heard the newsreader starting on about the Barlinnie riot, so I quickly poured my drink and hurried through. I sat on the bed watching the scene on the roof unfold. I had to look twice, because the first time I thought that one of the prisoners straddling the ridge of the prison roof was Malky McGovern. The second time I looked, he was turning away a wee bit and I was less sure. I watched until the end of the news and when nothing new came on about it I channel hopped, trying to see if any of the other news channels had different footage. It was mostly the same everywhere. Channel Four had a long-lens shot which showed the two men facing the camera, but it was so distant and pixellated that it could have been Terry Waite and Bishop Desmond Tutu for all I knew.

In the morning I quickly scanned the papers before leaving for Francis' place, but again the pictures were telephoto shots that really didn't help any further. I stopped at a phone box and phoned Sanny Fairbairn, who I knew was still working at the Bar-L, although he had only a year to go until he retired.

"John, nice to hear from you. What is it you want this time?"

I laughed. "Sanny, you know me, I'll buy you a pint any time, just name the place."

"I might take you up on that, but anyway, you definitely must be after something if you're offering booze."

"OK, fair's fair, I am after a little info. Were you working yesterday?"

"Aye, I was. Now let me guess. Riot, Malky McGovern?"

I spluttered. "How did you know?"

"Hey, you're not the only detective round about here. Firstly, what's by far the most interesting thing that's happened at the Bar-L for the last week? Second, I knew that Malky used to be a mate of that guy Sornie who you were interested in, they both lived in the same street."

"Right, how the fuck did you know that, then?"

"Well, I'd the job of going through Sornie's personal stuff before we disposed of it, 'cause nobody claimed it, and by sheer chance I was also covering for Davy Wilson on prisoner reception when he was off sick with the shingles on the day McGovern came in. I knew he'd be an awkward cunt; his attitude was shite from the moment he arrived. We practically had to pin him down to do a search on him. He was one angry little fucker."

"So it was Malky on the roof?" I asked.

"Aye, sure it was, him and some mate he palled around with. Both claim they've been stitched up, that they never did 'any fucking murder'. They persuaded some fellow inmates to get involved in their protest and before long the whole thing had blown up into a full-scale riot. We'd just got control back on the wing when I left work last night, but those two nutters were still on the roof. Far as I know, they spent the night up there. We even had to send up food, hot drinks and fucking space blankets to the bastards. Me, I'd have let the silly twats freeze tae death."

"Malky claimed at his trial that someone else had murdered Stewart McNiven, but the case was as tight as you could get it, there were no doubts on that score. The bastard just wants to cause trouble. As far as I'm concerned, the way he's behaving, if it'll keep him inside longer, it's no bad thing. If you hear more about it, let me know."

"Aye, nae bother."

I said I'd make a point of looking Sanny up after he retired and was just about to hang up when he said something else.

"Sorry, I didn't catch that."

"I meant tae phone ye a while back. I've got something for ye, connected tae yon Sornie fella."

"Right, I'd be interested in that. What've you got?"

"Another one of thae photos turned up afterwards. I asked the boss what needed done wi' it and he told us just tae put it in the bin. I kent that you'd be interested so I kept it for ye, but Ah kept forgettin aboot it."

He gave me his home address and about a fortnight later, when I was set to interview a witness out Riddrie way, I called in to see him. He happened to be on his days off so we took a wander down to his local, where I bought him a couple of pints. I just had the one then it was on to the orange juice for me, but Sanny was in good form, recalling a few stories from his days at Barlinnie. He also filled me in on the outcome of the rooftop protest. They had got them both down the next day and they had been put in separate wings, with a high security status on the pair of them. Sanny suspected that their performance would earn the pair of them at least an extra two years inside.

In a lull in conversation he reached into an inside pocket of his jacket and pulled out a small brown envelope, which he handed to me. "That's the photae I spoke to you aboot."

The pub was busy, so I slipped it discreetly into my back pocket and ordered another pint for Sanny. We spoke for about an hour all together; I left him sitting at the bar and continued on to meet up with one of my DCs to see the witness.

~~o~~

The day after the riot, I had asked Francis if he'd seen the whole thing on TV. He had seen it and was quite dismissive. "The bastard deserves all he gets. He may not have been there when Patrick was killed, but it was down to him that the rest of his mates got off."

"They aren't doing so well, are they?"

188

"Who?" asked Francis, sounding slightly puzzled.

"Oh, the gang members. Two are in prison, one of them for a very long time, one has been murdered by one of his mates, and two are dead. It's almost as if they have some sort of curse on them. I hear Billy Green isn't in the best of health, either."

"Are you keeping tabs on them?"

I shook my head. "No, not really, but I hear things at work; a lot of folk know I'm interested and they fill me in on any gossip that goes around about them. Andy hears a fair bit as well, although he is a bit out of the loop now, through in Edinburgh."

"Is he enjoying it through there? I haven't seen Andy in ages."

"I'd not seen much of him for ages until this week. It was a good chance to catch up on old times. He asked how you were getting on. I told him you were fine, by the way, and he said that he will call in and see you the next time he's through."

"It'd be nice to see Andy again; he was pretty decent to me, you and him both. It's nice to see that he's doing well. That's quite a promotion he got, wasn't it?"

"Oh, yes, he's on the up, is Andy – he's always been a bit of high flyer, in a nice sort of a way. Usually you have to brown-nose a bit to move up the ladder but, to be fair, Andy's done it on hard work and ability."

"You'll be next, wait and see. The pair of you will make chief constables yet." He laughed.

"Not me, I'm happy enough where I am. Too much politics to deal with up there. Anyway, I don't think I'll do much more than my thirty years, I'll have had enough by then."

"I thought you liked your job. You always seem to be happy enough."

"Don't get me wrong, I do enjoy what I do, but by the time I hit fifty, I think I'll be ready for something else."

"What will you do, if you retire?"

I grinned. "I'll come and work for you – do you fancy having an apprentice?"

Francis and I both laughed at the thought of me doing my City and Guilds, attending college with all the other young apprentices.

"No, I don't think you could be an apprentice. Anyway, you know as much as a fully time-served apprentice already. You just need to brush up a bit on some of the technical side of it and, of course nowadays, on the health and safety aspects."

"God, no. I think I'll just stay as a keen amateur, thanks."

"Well, I'll give you a job; just don't expect too much pay."

When I got home that night, just out of interest, I took a sheet of paper and made a list of all those involved in Patrick's death, and against each I made a note of what had happened to them.

NOLMAN

Prison. 3-5 yrs, serious assault

SCOULAR

Dead, Weil's disease

SORNIE

Dead, murdered

PINKY

Dead, murdered

MALKY

Prison, Life, > 19 yrs, 2 added for riot

BILLY GREEN

Ill, unknown cause

DAVID JOHNSTON

Whereabouts unknown

DEREK (SPAZ) DAVIDSON

Habitual prisoner, but released at moment

JOHN (WHITEY) WHITE

Whereabouts unknown

I thought for a minute, and added three further names

GALLAGHER

Dead, alcoholism, cancer

TOMMO

Dead, thrombosis?

PETE

Dead, heart attack

I had been right – many of the individuals connected with Patrick's murder weren't doing so well. I was a sceptic when it came to any religious or supernatural forces, but a little irrational part of my brain questioned whether there was some sort of malevolent cloud hanging over those involved in Patrick's murder, and those that had contributed to their getting away with it. I wondered if

Deborah had run away to a witches' coven; was she sticking pins in little ned dolls? Perhaps after all there was a god, and he was just setting the record straight. Suddenly, I had a burning curiosity to find out more about the gang members on the list, from Billy Green downwards.

I started with Billy. I talked to a few of his neighbours on the pretext of investigating the reopened case of a schoolgirl who'd gone missing twenty years ago. It had crossed my desk during the time I had spent on old cases, and been shelved almost immediately. As a result of my enquiries I learned that Billy had some sort of lung cancer. At his age this surprised me, although I knew that most of the gang smoked thirty or forty a day.

David Johnstone, the only one apart from Malky to be found not guilty at the trial, had a low paid but safe job at a packing plant, as a line supervisor. He was married with two small children and lived in a purchased council house on the edge of a former council estate which was undergoing a fair bit of development; cloned yuppie houses in close juxtaposition to blocks of concrete flats awaiting demolition. I thought to myself, at least one of them was doing OK, but it kind of blew my theory out the water.

Derek Davidson was working as a security guard for one of the many Glasgow security firms that provided "protection" and he was involved with some very dodgy characters. He'd moved around a bit and earned himself a reputation for being a reliable hard man. Ironically, he had worked briefly for the same team that Tommo had worked for, although the two of them hadn't been there at the same time. He had avoided prison, more by luck than judgement.

Finally, I had heard reports that John White was heavily into hard drugs, mainly smack, and was homeless. Living on the street, he had been in and out of prison frequently over the last few years, mostly for petty crime carried out to feed his drug habit.

[Friday 16th August 2002]

Single again, I phoned Andy and invited myself through to Edinburgh to see Noel Fielding at the Fringe. After the show we did a few of the pubs in the Grassmarket; it was absolutely heaving with folk, as Edinburgh always is around the time of the Festival. We had just left the Grassmarket Inn and were heading for The Last Drop when a group of women came round the corner and almost ran into us. They'd obviously had a few drinks and they were full of apologies, but laughing at the same time. It took me a few seconds, and it must have been the same for her, because we both recognised each other at the same time.

"Sarah," I said, "what are you doing here?"

"It's John, isn't it? I live in Edinburgh now. What are you doing through here?"

"I'm through visiting Andy. Do you remember Andy? You met him once at the flat, I think."

"I do, vaguely. I'm afraid I was a bit of a wreck at that point."

She looked absolutely amazing. Unbelievably, she was one of these women that seemed to get more attractive as they got older. I guessed she must have been in her forties, a good few years younger than me. Her friends had stopped politely a few yards further on as we spoke, but she waved them back and introduced them to us. To this day I can't remember all of their names; I think one was Carol, and there might have been a Claire, but I can't be sure. She explained who we were to them and there was a slightly awkward silence for a few seconds as they realised the circumstances in which we'd previously known each other, but it quickly passed. Andy started answering their questions about his job in Edinburgh and Sarah and I were left almost to ourselves.

"How are you getting on?" I asked her, a bit lamely.

"Oh, I'm doing well now. It did take me a long while to get my life back to anything near normal, but life goes on, as they say." She turned away as she said that, but I saw her face cloud over. "Sorry," she muttered.

"Hey, don't worry. It must be a shock, bumping in to me after all this time and bringing it all back."

"No, it's really nice to meet you again. I never got a chance to thank you for being so kind to me at the time."

I was surprised. "I was just doing my job, but I did really feel bad having to ask you all those questions when you were so obviously devastated."

"No, you were really sweet. I could see that you were trying not to upset me, and you found it difficult to ask me all those questions which, deep down, I knew were necessary. The other policeman that interviewed me before you was nowhere near as nice; he just seemed to want it over and done with. I felt he wasn't very sympathetic."

"I just try and put myself in the other person's shoes in that situation, if that's really possible."

"At least that means that you care. Some folk think of it as a weakness if you do that." She paused. "Francis said that you've been an absolute lifesaver to him; you, and Andy as well."

I could feel myself blushing. "Oh, we only tried to help. Besides, Francis is different. He's turned out to be a really good friend to me. We played football together for a while and I help out sometimes at the workshop."

"I know, Francis has told me. I still keep in touch with them both, you know."

All this time Andy was chatting away with her friends and they were all quite enjoying it, judging by the sounds of their laughter.

I turned back to Sarah. "We were just trying to find somewhere a little quieter to have a drink. Do you fancy joining us for one?"

"We were doing the same. There's no room to move in the pubs around here, and getting a seat is nearly impossible."

"I think Andy will know somewhere, I'll ask him."

I asked Andy and he thought for a moment. "Aye, there's a wee place not far from here. It's more of a restaurant than a pub, but you can go in and sit at the bar area even if you're not going in for something to eat."

Sarah had a quick word with her friends and we all made our way there together. It was probably no more than a five minute walk. Andy was as good as his word. It was quite a nice little place and although the dining room was full, the bar area was deserted and we could all sit in the soft seats that were clustered around a low table. The drinks were a bit pricier than in the pubs, but it was worth it just to get a seat.

The three other girls still hung on every word of Andy's, so I more or less had Sarah all to myself. We continued our conversation, mainly talking about Francis and Deborah's separation and how they were both coping. Sarah had visited Deborah on a number of occasions, but had never been back through to see Francis. They spoke occasionally on the phone, maybe once or twice a year, and if Francis did an exhibition in Edinburgh he would sometimes arrange to meet Sarah for a bite to eat and a chat.

I talked a little about work and she in turn explained that she travelled a lot with her job, that her office was based in Edinburgh and it was convenient for her to live in the capital. She worked with the Overseas Development Institute, liaising with other European government organisations in the supply of long-term assistance to third world countries.

Despite having previously met only briefly and in horrible circumstances all those years ago, we seemed to get on really well. I found her incredibly easy to talk to. The conversation quite often drifted back to Francis, and how I shared a passion for woodworking and fine furniture with him. For her part, she just knew him as someone who should have been her father-in-law, someone she could talk to at any time and who had felt the same way as she did about Patrick. In time, as the pain and loss faded, I think she had kept in contact with him because they found that they simply liked each other as people.

I think Andy and the others must have finally discussed how rude the two of us were being, because when I came back from one of my frequent visits to the gents Andy had taken my seat next to Sarah and the other girls had moved across. As a result of the new seating arrangement the conversation became more general and, although I can't remember too much of the detail or all of their names, it was nice just to be there. But I knew that before the end of the evening, I somehow had to find a way to see Sarah Anstruther again.

The bar filled up as the restaurant emptied and I got the impression that Andy had maybe made a move on one of Sarah's friends, but he was pretty subtle about it. When I suggested a nightclub, however, the two other girls declined the offer, citing husbands and kids as good reasons to avoid the sort of place we were thinking of. Hugs and kisses all round for the girls, polite pecks on the cheek for Andy and me, and the four of us were left on our own. I realised that it had been a polite withdrawal of two women who had satisfied themselves that their friends had not fallen into the clutches of two serial perverts.

I was prepared for a couple of hours dancing and drinking before perhaps a promise of meeting again, but we had only been in the club for half an hour when Sarah told me to get our coats, that we were going.

"Wait, I'll have to tell Andy. I was supposed to be kipping at his gaff tonight."

"It's OK, I already told him. He said that it's fine and to tell you that you've to call in and see him tomorrow before you go home." She laughed.

196

I put my hands up in mocking surrender. "OK, you're the boss, lead on."

We stopped twice on the way to her flat, for what we would have called an old fashioned snog when I was younger. The third time, if the surroundings had smelled slightly less damp and I hadn't suddenly thought of what the effect of being found in flagrante delicto in an ancient Edinburgh alleyway would have on my remaining career, we might well have done the deed before we even reached her flat. As it was, we were barely in the door when I had managed to get most of her clothes removed, and not quite so successfully removed my own, before finally reaching her bed and having what I can only describe as the best sex I have ever had. I would have bet on Sarah being a touchy-feely candles-and-romance type lover, and later on I would get to see that side of her, but that first time, to say she was a bit of a wildcat wouldn't have been an over-exaggeration.

I was pleased that I had had a fair skinful that night because otherwise I would have lasted maybe two minutes tops, but due to the significant amount of alcohol, I was able to stretch it to what felt like half an hour. Needless to say, despite the numbing effects of an evening's drinking, she didn't quite arrive at the same time as me, but I like to think it was bloody close.

Anyway, it gave me the excuse, shortly after I had started breathing normally again, to explore all the wondrous parts of her body with my hands and my tongue, this time giving her the satisfaction that I'd had already had. She was much softer and gentler this time, until near the end, when she did get more than a little animated again. Afterwards, she fell asleep first and, just before I covered us up with the duvet, I took a little while to admire her absolutely gorgeous naked, beautiful form. OK, there was a little tiny mound of a belly, if I was being ultra-critical, and at close range she had the start of little crow's feet at the corners of her eyes when she smiled, and I think that her hair colour might have been artificially enhanced to retain the same shade that I remembered from twenty years ago.

197

Looking back, she may well have taken me home the first night like that to try and remove any possibility of romance or real depth to our relationship, or it may have been simply that she hadn't had sex for a long time and I was a safe choice. Certainly, the violence of her initial lovemaking would bear out the latter, but it was also true that she never quite gave one hundred per cent of herself to me, not so much physically, but quite certainly emotionally.

When I woke up in the morning with a negligible hangover and a slightly embarrassing hard-on, and saw Sarah sauntering around her flat in a dressing gown and apparently little else, I thought that I had finally landed in heaven. I lay on my side for a while, supporting my head with my hand, elbow in the bed, watching her move from room to room through the open bedroom door, the dressing gown only partly hiding what I now knew was a body that I could truly worship, giving little tantalising glimpses from time to time of areas etched into my memory from the night before.

I heard the sound of the kettle, plates, knives and stirring spoons, could smell the toast and coffee, and prayed to the god of men-things that she was coming back to bed for breakfast. I quickly gathered a towel conveniently hanging on the back of the bedroom door, covered myself up, and scuttled to the bathroom. Surprised that my bladder had lasted that long, (perhaps the erection had persisted all night, and suppressed the tendency to pee every three hours), I managed to finally produce a urinary stream, after persuading my penis that a temporary deflation to allow this to happen would be a good idea. I then gave the whole area a quick but thorough wash and dry in case we repeated last night's pleasures. In the same vein, I quickly gave my teeth the old finger-brushing, checked my hair in the mirror for unattractive one-sided flatness, and applied some Dove antiperspirant, on the grounds that smelling slightly effeminate was better than having sweaty pits.

I made a lot of noise coming out of the bathroom to make sure that she knew I was awake. She shouted to me that I should go back to bed, that she'd be through in a minute, so I thanked whoever I had previously prayed to and made myself comfortable, just draping enough duvet to cover myself, but vainly hinting at a reasonably taut and manly body underneath for a man of my age.

I should have known better. She took one look at me as she came through the door and started laughing, so much so that she nearly dropped the tray. I must have looked a little bit hurt, because she tried to stifle her mirth, and came over with the tray to the bed. She smiled at me, and I lifted the covers to let her in beside me. She gave me a nice little kiss that tasted of coffee, and handed me a cup of the real thing.

"There's sugar there, help yourself, and stick into the toast, there's more if you want it."

I added the sugar and sipped the coffee with pleasure, sitting up in a strange bed with this beguiling woman leaning against me. We spoke a little as we ate, just silly stuff, skirting around anything hinting of last night or the future. After we had both finished, she reached over and placed the tray on the chair close to the bed, turned round to face me and asked if I'd had enough to eat. In her hands she held the open marmalade pot, the spoon still in it. To this day, I always get an erection when I even get the hint of the smell of marmalade, and even the tang of someone peeling an orange can have me adjusting the contents of my jockeys.

Being a thorough and thoughtful lover, with the additional attraction of being a clean and tidy individual, I endeavoured to ensure that no stickiness would remain to mark the sheets or the duvet; I think I must have licked marmalade from every possible surface, from every little nook and wonderful cranny of her. I don't recall exactly how much there was in the jar at the start, but it was certainly half full at least; by the end, the jar was almost empty. If you had asked me to eat a jar of marmalade for a bet I would probably have thrown up before I got to the bottom, but eating it this way, I could have managed three jars if that's what it took to give that much pleasure to one of the most exciting women I had ever met.

And it wasn't one-sided; she was no slouch when it came to handing out some joy of her own. I'll not say exactly what she did as I do respect that a girl needs a little bit of privacy, but I will say that she did things with her fingers and her lips that still send shivers down my spine at the thought of it.

Nor was our parting awkward in any way. We had slept again until lunchtime and I had returned the favour that was breakfast by throwing together a nice little prawn tagliatelle, one of my easy-but-tasty impress-the-ladies dishes which had evolved over the years, and readily cooked with the ingredients found in most kitchens. A few of those instant bake crusty rolls, a quickly tossed salad, and lunch was served.

Sarah fortunately brought up the subject that I was inwardly struggling to find a way to mention.

"John, last night and today has been wonderful. I really needed someone just to be with for a while, and you have been lovely …"

I sighed to myself. "But …?" I said.

"Yes, there's a 'but'." She smiled. "But it's not what you think."

I must have looked slightly less depressed at that, so she carried on.

"I'm trying to be completely honest with you here. I can't do a heavy relationship at this point, but I could do with this sort of thing from time to time. Can you handle that?"

I thought to myself that this was the type of relationship I would normally bite my hand off to have, but I already knew that I wanted more from this girl. However, the rational part of me screamed caution, to take what was offered and see what would come of it.

"I think I can do that, but how would it work?"

"Well, I'm away a lot and you live in Glasgow, so even if nothing else gets in the way, there aren't going to be many times we can get together, anyway. I'll call you if I need a bit of company, and you can do the same. If either of us isn't up for it, there could be lots of reasons why we couldn't get together, so no one gets hurt if the other begs off. Just don't put too much pressure on me; I need my own space at the moment." She rather sweetly held my hand at that last bit.

So that's the way it started and in many respects it was the most wonderful time of my life. In reality, we probably managed to meet up once a month, and that could be for a night or a weekend. Once that first year we went away for four days to a little hotel down in the borders, where normally I would be bored to tears, but having Sarah with me for four days made it magical.

Right from the start we had both made it clear that this was not an open relationship, that we should be monogamous, and I knew deep down that this wouldn't be a problem for me. Funnily enough, I completely trusted Sarah. I wasn't even sure that she'd had many sexual partners since Patrick, if any. It was never said, but I just got the feeling that she hadn't been with anyone else. Even the times when there were almost two months between us getting together, which happened on a few occasions, I still had no desire or need to go elsewhere.

Although we were only together on an irregular basis, she made up for the infrequency by being enthusiastic, skilful, teasing, lustful, funny, daring, attentive, considerate and occasionally just plain dirty, but she never really let me inside her shell; I supposed it was the one she'd put on when Patrick was killed. Sometimes, I would think I was getting somewhere and I would look at her expecting happiness and there would be a tear at the corner of her eye, or, if I was trying to be serious about our relationship, she would go into hysterical giggles, or change the subject when I started talking about us as a couple.

My problem was that I could normally, if I wanted, have shallow, medium-term relationships which revolved

201

basically around casual sex, good food, wine, humour and very little else.

Just not this time.

None of my previous relationships had prepared me for anything like this and even though I had been genuinely fond of most of the women I'd been with, until now I'd avoided the desperate neediness that goes with completely falling for somebody else, to the degree that you think of very little else.

After my first night with Sarah I turned up at Andy's flat at about three o'clock expecting a combination of questions and amusement, but Andy just asked very quietly if I'd had a good night. I didn't give him too many details, but old Andy; he knew that I'd been done for. He smiled and told me that I was a lucky bastard if it all worked out, and that I would still have been a lucky bastard if it didn't. I asked him if he had had any luck himself, and he just smiled and shrugged. "That's under development – we both went home on our own last night, but I'll phone her. She was very nice, and I'm just about settled into the job now, so I can afford a little distraction."

"Tough year, eh?"

"Yes, it was pretty high pressure at first; a big, big learning curve, so I just didn't have the time for anything outside work, sleeping and eating; my social life was watching a little TV, snack on lap, and falling asleep shortly afterwards. On days off, I would mostly just catch up on paperwork."

"You've just nailed it for me – I'll give it a miss."

"You could do DI no problem, I can't really see why you wouldn't give it a go. Give me one good reason why not."

I knew deep down that he was right, that I could do the job, that I'd done all the courses I needed and that there were jobs coming up where, if I indicated an interest in promotion, I could be seriously considered for the posts.

" I'd have to give up working with Francis and I've only got another three years to go before I finish anyway. Why make that time harder than it needs to be?"

~~o~~

I didn't see Francis the day I got back from Edinburgh; in fact, because I had to do twelve-hour shifts for eight days in a row, it was the middle of the following week before I caught up with him. I kind of dreaded telling him about Sarah with her having been Patrick's girlfriend, but I knew I didn't want him to hear about it from anyone else, so I made a point of going over and seeing him the following evening. It was nearly eight by the time I got there, but the workshop lights were still on. He must have heard me coming in because he was at the door of the workshop when I came into the yard. He closed the door over and motioned towards the house. We went in and he made us both a coffee.

"Something to tell me?" He grinned.

My face must have been a picture. "How did you know?"

He laughed. "I was on the phone to Sarah. She told me you two had got together. Hey, I'm pleased for you both."

I looked at him. "I thought you might feel a bit strange about it."

"Why? I would never have expected Sarah not to have relationships after Patrick was murdered; in fact, I've been telling her for years that a pretty girl like her should have more fun. Just don't do the dirty on her, or you'll have me to deal with. I'm quite fond of her."

I actually blushed. "Francis, I won't. In fact, being realistic, I think the boot is on the other foot."

He laughed again. "You can't blame me for saying that I told you that you would cop it one day. There would be a lot of women applauding Sarah if they could see you now."

"OK, OK. I can see I'm going to suffer. I just hope I can keep this to Andy and you, because if it ever gets out, my life is going to be a misery."

I must have looked thoroughly miserable because he came over and put his arm around my shoulder. "John, just take it as it comes, don't force it, and things will likely turn out all right."

He was taking such a perverse joy in this that I felt I needed to even it up a bit.

"Anyway, all these weekends and weeks you are away, can you honestly tell me there's not a woman involved?"

He smiled. "No, John, I can't deny it. Or confirm it, for that matter. But I will say one thing; everyone is entitled to a little bit of comfort."

I didn't know what to say. I just watched him and he had a little half smile at the corner of his mouth. I remember thinking it was one of the saddest things I'd heard him say.

I next saw Francis on my days off, when we had three carcases to assemble and glue. We clamped the first one up on the low central bench that we usually reserved for assembly, then put it on the floor and slid it along to the other end of the workroom. I couldn't have been paying attention, so when it suddenly jerked to one side, my hand was trapped between the upright and the edge of the bench, giving me a couple of painfully squashed fingers. Amid all the cursing, Francis just stood there, waiting. I eventually calmed down, as the pain in my fingers reduced from excruciating agony to a dull, painful throb.

"Well ...?"

"That bloody floor," I grumbled, "It's forever catching something. I'm going to take a plane to it one of these days."

"I wouldn't do that, it's been like that since I was a lad. I said the same thing about it as you did but my father told me to leave it be."

"Why the f…?" I retorted.

He showed me. He picked up a partly made frame that had been lying around and placed it on the floor, against the slightly raised board, and proceeded to plane the edge of the frame, without the frame sliding all over the place and without Francis having to grip it very tightly.

"I'll not say it was put there on purpose, but my father found a use for it so it stayed."

"OK, OK, but that doesn't help my fingers."

Francis reached into a small cupboard near the workshop doors and came out with a small packet. "Here's some aspirin. Take one before it swells up too much."

"I never realised there was a first aid cabinet, Francis."

"I showed it to you when we did the health and safety induction on your first day here."

After we had stopped laughing at that, we completed the assembly of the carcases and called it a day. I turned up the next day, fingers strapped together, but being honest, my pride was hurting as much as my swollen digits and it had taught me to concentrate more in the workshop, no matter what I was doing.

However, my hand was still throbbing a bit, so I helped myself to another aspirin from Francis' first aid cupboard. As I put the box back I had a quick look at the contents for future reference, although hoping I would never need to use them. In addition to the usual bandages, eyewashes, plasters and the like, there were three inhalers, one of which, on closer examination, seemed to be empty. I shouted over to Francis, "I didn't know you had asthma."

He came over. "I don't, but before we used dust masks, and when we used a lot of rosewood, I developed a very wheezy chest and, in addition to advising me to start wearing masks at all times, the doctor prescribed an inhaler for me until it resolved. I very rarely need it now, but I always keep one handy just in case."

I had noticed that the wearing of dust masks was one of the areas he seemed almost paranoid about; he insisted on us wearing them if any of the machinery was being used, if we were sanding anything (even by hand), or if we were cleaning the workshop. All the large machines had dust extractors fitted and there was a portable extractor that could be connected to any of the small power tools, so the place was kept as scrupulously free of dust as was possible.

[Monday 3rd February 2003]

I learned about Billy Green's death from the paper. I'd started to read the intimations page of the *Glasgow Herald* to my old man as his eyesight was getting poor and he couldn't look through the deaths section himself. All his friends and acquaintances were of the age when many of them were dropping off their perches, and he would get very annoyed if he didn't know about it.

I found the time and place of Billy's funeral in the small death notices, under his name and a line that stated that he'd died peacefully after a long illness. I went to the cemetery but stood well back near a large gravestone that I could lean on, getting a good view of the graveside ceremony without risking being seen by the family. I didn't see any of the other members of the gang, but I realised there were very few of them still alive. I half expected Kevin Nolan and Derek Davidson to make an appearance, but either or both of them could have been in prison, so perhaps it wasn't a surprise after all when they didn't show.

A little niggle at the back of my mind made me think that Francis might show up, but I didn't see any sign of him and, when I called in on him immediately afterwards at home, he was firmly ensconced in the workshop, looking like he'd been there for hours. I told him about Billy, but he already knew. I didn't say I'd been to the funeral, but we talked a bit about Billy's illness. Francis had heard a bit more than me – Billy had died of some asbestos related disease, probably caused by him hanging around the many derelict shipyards on the north side of the Clyde, within easy reach of where he was brought up.

[Monday 28th April 2003]

I'd promised Francis that I'd call over to check the kiln. I knew he had some wood drying out for an upcoming job, and that he was away for a week. It took me ages to get there; the traffic all over the West End was completely snarled up because of a gang related triple shooting in Maryhill, so I hung around for a while in the workshop, tinkering with a clock case I was making while I waited for the congestion to clear. It was at times like these, working alone among the benches and toolracks, that I almost felt as if I belonged there.

CHAPTER 11   DEATH

[Wednesday 30th April 2003, 3.40 a.m.]

I quite often get phone calls in the middle of the night, invariably from work, but it always gives me a horrible jolt when it happens. I usually wake up quickly, however, and I go from not quite knowing where I am for a second or two, to being lucid and in full grasp of my mental capabilities by the second or third ring.

Very rarely, however, do I get a knock on the door in the middle of the night.

Anyway, this night was in the middle of a week off. I'd been out for a few jars with a couple of mates and didn't get in until the back of two, so when doorbell rang I wasn't quite myself and fumbled for my bedside light twice before finally managing to switch it on. I rushed to the door, stubbing my toe on the corner of bed in the process, cursing under my breath. I unlocked the Yale and the deadlock, and opened the door. Under the yellow glow of the landing light, I was looking at a uniformed officer whom I was sure I'd never seen before.

"Hello, I'm Sergeant Bill Thompson, traffic division, Strathclyde Police. Are you DS John McDaid?"

I had fully woken up now. I replied that I was DS McDaid, and I told him that I was currently on leave.

"This isn't work-related. Your name and contact details have come up in relation to a road traffic accident we are dealing with."

"Who is involved?" I asked, outwardly calm, although I could feel my insides turning over. I quickly wondered about my sister and her family, but I hoped that none of them would have been driving at this time of night.

"Do you know a Mr Francis Hare, of Crow Road, Glasgow?"

"Yes; is he OK?" I knew that Francis had been away for a week. For the last few years Francis had been spending the odd weekend away travelling and occasionally, perhaps a couple of times a year, this extended to a week. He never discussed the details, but I suspected that there was a female companion somewhere.

The sergeant's next words knocked a hole in me. "I'm sorry, I'm afraid it's not good news. We believe that Mr Hare was the driver of the vehicle and that he and the other two passengers were all killed."

"Shit, I can't believe it. There must be a mistake."

I just couldn't take it in. Francis was always such a careful driver. For a moment, I thought I was going to be sick and I could feel myself shaking.

"I'm sorry; it's true, I'm afraid." He said nothing for a few moments. "Do you know of any relatives of Mr Hare that we could contact?"

"His wife is the only relative I know of, but they have been separated for quite a few years. She lives somewhere near London, but I couldn't be more specific than that."

"If we can't find a relative, would you be willing to identify the body at some point?"

I felt awful and I didn't want to say yes, but I knew I had to, for Francis' sake if nothing else. Then I had a sudden thought.

"Listen, I have a key for his house. He'll probably have his wife's address somewhere, on letters if nothing else."

"We could arrange to pick you up in the morning and go to the house with you, if you like."

"Yes, that would be all right, or I could meet you there."

"Right, shall we say ten o'clock then, at Mr Hare's residence?"

I confirmed that that would be OK, and I was just about to shut the door when a couple of questions suddenly came to mind.

"How did you know to contact me?" I asked.

"We found a notebook in the car and your name was in the inside cover, along with your rank, Detective Sergeant. We looked you up in the Force Directory, presuming that you were Glasgow based."

"Fair enough. Did you trace Francis through the car registration?"

"No, there were some business cards in one of his pockets with his name on. In addition, a bank card and credit card were also found with his name on it. The car was registered to a Miss Swann, from Henley in Oxfordshire. One of the passengers was a woman and we are working on the assumption that she may have been the car owner, but we have been unable to contact anyone at the address held by the DVLA." He said nothing for a second, and then asked me if I knew of this Miss Swann.

"I can't remember Francis mentioning anyone of that name, but I think he had a girlfriend that he kept fairly quiet about. What was this woman's first name?"

"Hold on, em, here it is, Deborah Swann, born 18th November 1940, that's the info from the DVLA."

I felt like I'd been kicked in the balls. I really couldn't understand what I was hearing. I struggled to breathe for a few seconds, until I heard the sergeant's voice saying something.

"Are you all right, DS McDaid?"

I struggled to speak, but eventually I managed to splutter. "I might be wrong, but I think that could be his estranged wife; I seem to remember her birthday was mid-November, she was about five years younger than Francis, and he would have been born in nineteen thirty-five or six. Her married name was Deborah Hare and she lived down south somewhere."

I knew that I was rattling on and I didn't sound very coherent, but I was sure that I was right. What I couldn't get to grips with was the fact that Francis and Deborah were in the same car, and that they had both been killed. Almost immediately, I remembered that there was another person in the car.

"Do you know who the other passenger was?" I don't know why, but I had a sudden dreadful fear that it might be Sarah.

He immediately dispelled that theory. "We have no identification on him yet, but he was between thirty-five and forty years old, dark hair, white, heavily tattooed, about five-eleven. Ring any bells? He was wearing sports trousers and a zipped hooded top, T-shirt and trainers. We thought it was a little strange with the other two being quite well dressed."

"I can't think of anyone like that who would have been travelling with Francis. How did the accident happen?" I still couldn't take it in. One half of my mind was asking and answering questions rationally, the other half was shell-shocked.

"The car hit a bridge parapet on the A74 motorway just North of Beattock, travelling north. The road was coned off at that point for repairs, so the section of crash barrier at the bridge was missing. Strange thing is, there were no skid marks on the road, although quite a few of the cones had been knocked away. We are currently working along the lines that Mr Hare fell asleep or became ill at the wheel, but a damaged mobile phone was found on the floor in the passenger footwell and we can't rule out him being on the phone at the time. We will be making appeals through the media for witnesses to come forward urgently. Obviously, we'll know a bit more when we get all the data from the crash investigators, and of course the post-mortems should help as well."

"I just can't take it all in," was all I could say.

"How well did you know Mr Hare?" he asked me. "I'm guessing fairly well by your reaction."

"Francis was a great friend of mine; in fact my closest friend, if I'm honest. We spent a lot of time in each other's company."

I explained the circumstances of our first meeting, how I'd got to know him during Patrick's murder investigation and how, through football and cabinetry, we'd come to be as close as we were.

He apologised for having to contact me and said that he had expected that I would have been a much more casual acquaintance. Because I was on the force he had hoped that I would be able to provide him with the next-of-kin information that he required, quickly.

"Listen, that's OK, thanks for letting me know."

He gave me his phone number and left, after agreeing that it would still be worthwhile paying a visit to Francis' house, if only to confirm that the woman in the car had been Deborah.

My first thought after closing the door was to contact Sarah, but I remembered that she was out of the country and, as was normal with the way we did things as a "couple", I didn't have a contact number for her when she was abroad. I left a quick message on the answering machine at her flat asking her to phone me as soon as she got back. I phoned Andy next and he, like me, had been asleep. Like me he woke up pretty quickly when I told him about Francis and Deborah.

"Fuck's sake, how in Christ's name did that happen?"

"There's a question that Francis might have been using a phone when it happened, crashed into a bridge parapet, they both died instantly, along with another passenger, they haven't identified him yet, he ..."

"What?" Andy, anxiously questioning why I'd suddenly stopped talking.

"Andy, what day is it?"

"Wednesday. Why?"

"No, the date, the fucking date." I could just imagine him looking at his watch.

"It's the thirtieth today. What about it?"

"Patrick died twenty-five years ago yesterday; they must have got together for that, maybe some private sort of memorial thing or something."

"Fuck, you're right. Did Francis not say anything to you?"

"No, and me being stupid I never even gave it a thought. I should have remembered. I wonder if the other passenger was a relative? Mind you, I've never heard Francis speak about anyone." I thought for a second. "Maybe Sarah would know, but I can't get hold of her at the moment. She's abroad. I've left a message on her answering machine."

"She'll be gutted as well; can't you get a message through to her via her work? Do you want me to pop into her office in the morning and ask them to arrange for her to contact one of us?"

"Aye, that would be great. I think that would work better than a phone call from me."

Andy had another thought. "Why were they only coming up the road last night, if the anniversary of Patrick's death was yesterday?"

"Maybe they did something for it down south and were heading back home?"

"That seems strange. He was buried in Glasgow. Maybe they just got delayed or something. They could have intended to be up the road earlier."

"That makes more sense."

We stayed on the phone for another twenty minutes, not saying much of anything but neither of us wanting to hang up and be on our own with our thoughts. I got dressed and moved restlessly around my flat for a few hours, until I decided that I might as well get out and get on with something useful. I jumped in the car without having had anything to eat or drink, feeling slightly nauseated, and drove over to Francis' house, letting myself into the workshop.

I'm not ashamed to admit that I could feel the tears welling up in my eyes as I sat on the stool by the workbench for a few minutes, suddenly realising that I would never spend time there with Francis again.

I knew that he kept a spare key for the house in one of the drawers on the bench, along with all the other keys that cabinetmakers tend to collect over the years, and it didn't take me long to find it.

I opened the front door feeling a little strange, as if I was breaking in. I wondered if I was technically correct to be in the house, or should I perhaps have waited for Bill Thomson in the morning. I'd taken a note of his number on the back of a betting slip, so I phoned him and told him that I couldn't sleep and had driven over to Francis' house to see if I could find Deborah's address. He told me that he didn't have a problem with that, but he would meet me there in fifteen minutes and that I shouldn't rummage about too much.

While I waited for him I walked round the house thinking of Francis, until I came to his study-cum-den. It contained a desk and chair, and a two-seater couch; an old wooden filing chest and a couple of bookcases took up almost an

214

entire wall. His computer, now a PC rather than a Mac, sat in one corner, and a drawing board on a stand stood by the window, with a high draughtsman's chair beside it. I noticed that the computer had been left on and made to shut it down. I waggled the mouse to get rid of the screensaver. Seeing only the log-on screen, I made a few attempts at guessing the password and was surprised that my third try, "Patrick", was successful. I didn't get much further as a cursory look at the hard disk turned up nothing of interest. I opened Notepad and pressed control-V to see if anything had been copied to the clipboard. "Glenhill" appeared at the cursor. I smiled. I pressed control-alt-delete to start the task manager and printed out all the programmes and processes that were running. I then shut the computer down, thinking that I would go back to it later.

I took a look in the top drawers of the desk and almost immediately found his address book, an old tatty notebook that had seen better days. Sure enough, Deborah's address was in it and it tied in with what Bill Thomson had been saying. When Bill himself arrived, he confirmed that the two addresses matched and that there was no doubt in his mind that the woman was Deborah Hare.

He had stopped to pick up two steaming Styrofoam cups of coffee and he gave me one. I took it gratefully, as I was beginning to feel a bit light-headed. He produced a couple of fresh scones for us from a paper bag and while we munched away, sitting at the kitchen table, I asked him if he thought that it would be OK if I still used the workshop occasionally. He replied that I had better talk to the lawyer handling Francis' estate and suggested that the best place to find out which firm of solicitors were involved was to look in the filing cabinet, where there might be a copy of the will, or at least some legal correspondence which would point me in the right direction.

However, my mind wasn't fully functioning and I forgot all about it. I went back to my flat and phoned into the station, explaining the situation, and took some extra annual leave, although the DI said that I should just take a couple of "sickies".

~~o~~

The worst part was identifying the bodies. I had observed this process from a police officer's perspective during many murder inquiries, but it only partly prepared me for the emotions that I would feel, and although I wasn't a relative of Francis we had been very close friends for a long time now. I had phoned Andy to see if he could come, but he was tied up with a high level conference somewhere in Perthshire, so in the end I went on my own.

Deborah looked older than I remembered, but otherwise you would not have known that she had been in a car accident at all. The car had seemingly hit the concrete pillar head on, but more to the driver's side. Apart from a couple of scratches on the face and a few more on her hands, presumably from flying glass, she looked as if she was just lying there sleeping. (She must have put her hands up to cover her face at the last moment.) The subsequent post-mortem showed that her only major injury was a fractured spine at the third cervical vertebrae level.

Francis, on the other hand, was pretty badly smashed up. I couldn't get to grips with the difference between the two of them, having both been in the same car. From one side his face was still recognisable, but the other side was all caved in and, although some cleaning up had been done, there was still a lot of blood staining the face and stuck to the hair. Crazily, what really freaked me out was that Francis had started to grow a beard and moustache. Initially, because of this, I had almost thought that it was someone else, but on looking closer I could tell that it was him. There were also massive chest and abdominal wounds as the car must have embedded itself in the pillar, but because his body was covered in a sheet I couldn't really see those. I was told afterwards that the estimated speed of the car when it hit the bridge was in excess of one hundred miles an hour.

I've seen many murder victims over the years. Stabbings weren't so bad, as their faces often looked quite serene. The worst were the victims who had died of head injuries after being repeatedly kicked or stamped on, or in a few cases beaten to a pulp with hammers, baseball bats, or

216

pickaxe handles. Francis fitted more into that last group, but I could see enough to be able to give Bill Thomson confirmation that that the two bodies were those of Francis and Deborah Hare.

Bill was very good. He trod a fine line between giving me a bit of support and not trying to be too "fussy", probably knowing that as a police officer I didn't want to be seen to react like an ordinary punter. Stupidly proud, I know, and fairly typical of the way most of the guys on the force would react, but I began to understand how people felt at times like this. I wasn't thinking clearly and was asking questions that I should have been able to answer myself; I was acting like Joe Public rather than an experienced DS. I resolved to show more empathy with victims' families in future, and be more patient about repeated requests for information.

After we had completed all the paperwork, he took me aside and asked if I wouldn't mind looking at the other passenger.

"I wouldn't normally ask, but with you being on the force, I know you'll understand my position."

"Of course," I said, "I'd do the same if it was the other way about." Not really feeling up to it, but curious to know who the passenger had been, I followed him through to the other room.

When they pulled back the sheet, I thought that there was no chance that I could help Bill as the head looked as if it had been through a mangle, but Bill pulled the sheet further back to reveal a badly damaged torso, still with the distinct markings of a tattoo, an elaborate dragon swirling round the body, the tail extending to the right arm, curling around the biceps, and ending near the wrist.

I stood still, not really taking in what I was looking at. I'd seen that tattoo before, when Gallagher and I had called to speak to Kevin Nolan. That was the only time I had ever seen him stripped to the waist, at the top of a dimly lit stairway in his mother's house, but the picture of the tattoo on his bare chest and his arm came flooding back to me.

Of course, I'd seen him at the station and during the trial, but always fully dressed. Incredibly, the body in front of me was his. I asked Bill if I could look at what was left of his mouth, and he got the mortuary assistant to show me. Sure enough, I could see the rotten teeth that I remembered from Nolman's smug grin.

Bill, seeing my reaction, looked at me expectantly.

"The guy's name is Kevin Nolan. Why in Christ's name was he in the car with Francis and Deborah?" I gave him the rest of Nolman's details. I told him that he was one of the thugs that had killed their son, and I could see that he was almost as shocked as I was.

He asked me if there was anyone else who could confirm my identification, and I gave him Andy's number. Bill said that he would also contact Kevin Nolan's relatives.

I think he thought that I'd seen enough for one day. He took me round the corner and bought me a stiff double in the Roxburgh Bar. After chatting about Francis for a while, we discussed the crash and its outcome. He explained that the passenger's body had to be literally shovelled into the body bag, having flown through the windscreen, hit the edge of the bridge pillar and been catapulted down the road for a further seventy-five yards, finally coming to rest wrapped around a piece of crash barrier still under repair. I asked Bill when the funerals were likely to be and he had told me that a firm of solicitors had come forward and indicated that they would be dealing with Francis' affairs. In the light of that, the bodies would be released by the Fiscal as soon as the paperwork had been completed to his satisfaction.

"John," he said, "we've been contacted by a witness saying that a car of the same description passed him on the motorway at high speed and we also have a couple of other witnesses saying that they had seen the driver using a mobile phone; one of the witnesses was a retired policeman travelling the same direction. I'm really sorry, but it does seem as if there is a possibility that Francis' use of the phone while driving may have caused this."

I really didn't want to hear that and while it wasn't Bill Thompson's fault I did get a little shirty with him, telling him that there would probably have been skid marks if Francis had veered due to being on the phone because after hitting the cones he would have taken some sort of evasive action.

"I still think it's much more likely that he fell asleep or he became ill or something," I finished, having said my piece.

"I don't blame you for being upset. I admire your loyalty to your friend. But the post-mortem showed no medical conditions that would have been likely to cause a blackout or similar and your argument about the noise of the car hitting the cones making Francis aware of the danger would equally apply if he had been sleeping. I'm just telling you all of this to warn you, because I can see the way this might go. There is a growing feeling that mobile phones are causing more and more accidents so the Procurator Fiscal, the courts and ourselves are under more pressure to look into the role of mobiles when accidents are investigated and, if there is any evidence at all, it is likely to be brought to the fore at the Fatal Accident Inquiry. We'll have a better idea anyway once we get hold of the records from the mobile phone company."

"Even then, that doesn't prove anything – Deborah could have been using it," I countered.

"Don't forget the witnesses. They all seem pretty reliable. Look, just be warned. I simply wanted to give you a heads-up on this, so it didn't come as a shock."

I slumped. "I'm sorry, I shouldn't take it out on you. I appreciate all you've done; I just don't want Francis to be remembered for killing himself and others through being reckless."

He put his hand on my shoulder. "Listen, from what you say he was one of the good guys. If he made a serious mistake, that doesn't change the rest of his life."

As soon as I'd left Bill, I phoned Andy to tell him to expect a phone call from Bill Thompson, and about Kevin

Nolan; he also found it hard to take in. We both struggled to think of a reason why he would have been in the car, but the only plausible one was that he'd approached the couple to show some kind of remorse, and that at some point something had been said that resulted in a struggle in the car which led to the accident.

That night, I got a phone call from Sarah. She was crying, but I got the gist of what she was trying to say. Despite my insisting that I would come and see her, she said that I was better staying in Glasgow and that she would come through to the flat. It was one of the few times she stayed with me in Glasgow. I phoned the DI and told him I'd be in later the next day. When she arrived, we spoke about our friendship with Francis, and Deborah to a lesser extent. Ours weren't really shared reminiscences because, apart from at Patrick's funeral, we had never been in Francis' company together, but Francis had sometimes talked to me about Sarah, and from what she told me, he often spoke to Sarah about me. Perhaps one of the reasons that we got together was that we knew more about each other than we both realised before our chance meeting in Edinburgh, and the fact that Francis always seemed generous in his praise of my friendship with him may have made her feel safer with me than anyone else.

Unlike me, Sarah had not been surprised that Francis and Deborah were in the car together. Being in touch with them both, she knew that there was at least limited contact between them. I had known that the separation was not acrimonious but had always felt it was a case of two people simply going in two completely different directions, when the one thing that could have held them together had been taken away from them.

I looked her straight in the eyes.

"The passenger in the car when they were killed was Kevin Nolan."

I let that sink in.

She seemed as shocked as I'd been. We sat for ages, trying to get our heads round what it meant.

It made everything much easier to cope with, having Sarah with me, so I was disappointed when she had to go home the next day but pleased when she said that she would catch up with me the following week.

I was surprised and relieved that the press did not go over the top with the story of Francis' and Deborah's deaths; it was reported as any road traffic accident of that severity would be. The third passenger was named as Kevin Nolan and it was said that the police were appealing for any further witnesses to come forward. The press made no connection with Patrick's murder until much later.

~~o~~

A few days afterwards I received a letter from Mitchell and Cameron, a Glasgow firm of solicitors, asking me to contact them to discuss my role as an executor of Francis' will. I'd forgotten that Francis had asked me some years previously if I wouldn't mind being an executor; not thinking it would involve me doing anything in the foreseeable future, I'd agreed. Now I was being asked to oversee the dissolution of everything that was Francis Hare.

I phoned the solicitor and his secretary pencilled me in to go for a chat after I had finished work the next day, but typically, three entirely unconnected serious assaults came in within an hour of each other, so I had to postpone. It ended up being almost a week before both the solicitor and I could schedule a meeting.

The following Thursday I finally presented myself at his offices in Park Gardens, a fine old Georgian townhouse with high ceilings and ornate cornicing which, like most of the terrace, had been converted to offices for solicitors, dentists and chartered accountants. The receptionist motioned me to sit in one of the plush chairs, but I had only just sat down when the intercom buzzed and she informed me that Mr Cameron was ready for me. I walked through the door that she held open for me and was met by a balding, elderly gentleman, rather sartorially dressed with a brown waistcoat and a spotted bow tie. He had a smile on his lips as he introduced himself, and he shook my hand firmly.

"Mr McDaid, nice to meet you, I'm Douglas Cameron. Please, have a seat. Hang your jacket up over there," he said, beckoning to an old-fashioned coat stand in the corner. I did as he suggested and sat down, waiting for him to speak as he quickly scanned through a document on his desk.

"Now, we have the sad task of disposing of Francis Hare's estate, and from what Francis told me, you were a very dear friend to him, so this must be a doubly onerous task for you. However, we are here to make it as easy as possible and, in reality, your position is in the main nominal. I need you to sign a few bank and insurance affidavits to release policies and access accounts; we will need to collect any outstanding income, settle all outgoings and complete an inventory. There isn't as much for you to do as it sounds; we do the bulk of it for you."

He explained that once the Procurator Fiscal had released the bodies of Francis and Deborah, the funeral arrangements would have to be made.

"Francis, in fact, left quite simple instructions for his funeral, and, indeed, his wife's, even down to the detail of which funeral directors he wished to use." He glanced at a sheet of paper in front of him. "Harold Grayson and Sons. Furthermore, from discussions I had with John Grayson yesterday, they had been instructed a number of years ago as to the arrangements that should be made in the event of either or both of their deaths, so there is very little needing done in that department, other than sorting out a time, and contacting anyone who would wish to be present."

I remembered that there was something I needed to ask him.

"Mr. Cameron, can I ask you a question about the workshop?"

"Sure, go ahead."

I pulled the keys out of my pocket. "These are the keys for the workshop and the house. Would it be possible for me to use the workshop until everything is disposed of? I'd like to try and finish a couple of things off and arrange to get my own stuff packed up ready to be moved." I explained that I had a collection of tools and a few pieces of unfinished furniture in the workshop.

"As an executor, you can have access to the house anyway, and the workshop, as long as you don't remove anything that isn't yours from either of them until we sort out the will. Feel free to use the workshop. Although technically you probably shouldn't, I somehow don't think Francis would have wished it otherwise."

~~o~~

I was in the extraordinary and completely unexpected position of being the "chief" mourner at the double funeral which took place the following Friday. No relative of either Francis or Deborah attended, and I didn't know if any existed.

There hadn't been too much of a delay because of the swift post-mortems, and as a result of the funeral being both simple and prearranged. A short mass in the local Catholic church and an interment in the cemetery in Duntocher was followed by a meal of soup and crusty bread at the Clan Head, where Francis and I had often sat and had a couple of pints. In addition to me, Andy, Sarah, and Douglas Cameron, there were about sixty other mourners, a mixture of Francis' customers and fellow craftsmen, churchgoers in Deborah's congregation, and Deborah's friend from Oxfordshire, who introduced herself as Margaret Baird. It fell to me to say a few words in the church and, although I was very choked up, I managed to convey my admiration and fondness for Francis and Deborah in a short and hesitant tribute to their lives. I mentioned Deborah's quiet courage and Francis' unflagging loyalty and supreme skill as a craftsman, but most of all, I tried to put over how much I was going to miss my good friend.

Margaret Baird then spoke about what a tower of strength Deborah had been during a serious illness that had nearly cost her own life, and that it had been a privilege to have known such a strong and supportive woman.

After the meal, during which there was a subdued murmur of conversation all around the room, there was a fairly swift exodus, as if the lack of family meant that there was no focus for the mourners. In the end, only Andy, Sarah, Douglas Cameron and I remained and, again, Sarah left shortly after, citing the need to get home and prepare for her trip to Sudan the following day. I had a brief word with the solicitor and he confirmed that a date had been set for the Fatal Accident Inquiry, one month exactly from the accident.

Bill Thomson had been right. At the inquiry, much was made of a twenty-one minute phone call from Francis' mobile that terminated at the approximate time of the crash. The number that had been dialled had been traced, but the phone was second-hand, having been sold by the original owner through a "Snips" small ad in the *Evening Times*, and was on a prepaid tariff, so we couldn't know who the call was made to. The phone company was able to give the locality of the mast used by the receiving phone, but that only narrowed it down to a large section of the West End of Glasgow. The witnesses who had reported seeing the driver using the mobile phone had also proved to be very reliable, although neither could positively identify the driver as Francis due to the night-time lighting conditions. The phone did have the fingerprints of both Francis and Deborah on it, but Francis' were the most prominent. The small splashes of blood on the phone belonged to Francis, but this was not thought to be significant because the phone was found in the passenger footwell, which contained a fair amount of his blood anyway. CCTV footage from the roadside cameras had not shed any further light on the journey, other than that the speed of the car had averaged around the seventy mark. The lighting had not made it possible to see much detail of the occupants of the car on the road, but a camera in the petrol station of Lancaster services on the M6 had captured Francis filling the Audi up two hours prior to the accident. His credit card had been used to pay for the fuel, three cups of coffee and a packet of biscuits. A bag containing the empty cups and biscuit wrappers was found in the car at the scene of the crash.

I attended much of the inquiry which, to be fair, was a balanced and well-conducted affair which returned a verdict on all three of the deceased as death by dangerous driving. I was gutted, but not surprised. It also turned out that neither Francis nor Deborah had any living relatives, which saddened me a little, as I realised how much they must have invested in Patrick.

Douglas Cameron was there on the last day of the Fatal Accident Inquiry, and I saw him chatting to the Sheriff, who had made a point of seeking the solicitor out after all the formalities were over. After they had finished talking, and had shaken hands, Cameron came across to me and shook my hand also.

"Very sad, but inevitable, I'm afraid."

"Yes. Bill Thomson, the officer in charge of the case, warned me right at the start that this would happen, so it's not a shock."

"It still doesn't make it any easier to accept, especially for his close friends."

I commented that it was unusual to have no surviving relatives and he told me that they had completed a search, independent of the Procurator Fiscal's investigation, and there were definitely no relatives alive that anyone had been able to trace, although they were still looking.

I made to go towards my car, intending to go out to the workshop and immerse myself in a bit of work to blot out my feelings of loss, but he called me back.

"Just before you go. I've provisionally scheduled for the will to be read on Thursday afternoon. Will that be convenient for you?"

"Yes," I replied, "I can take a day off. I'm due a few days before the end of the month or I'll lose them."

"We'll make it about three o'clock, then, if that's suitable."

"Yes, that'll be fine." I asked what to expect, curiosity having got the better of me.

"I can tell you that representatives from two charities will be present, and there are several small bequests for his friends, but I can't go into details."

"Right, I'll be there at three sharp. See you then."

As he walked off, I had a sudden thought and turned back into the court. I asked if I could speak with the Sheriff. I was told that he might already have left, but when the clerk knocked on the door of his office I heard a voice shout, "Come in!" The clerk stepped in and I could hear a murmur of conversation. The clerk came back out and told me just to go in.

I introduced myself as a good friend of the Hares and the executor of Francis' will, and asked if it would be possible to receive a copy of the Fatal Accident Inquiry documents. He said that all "interested parties" would receive a copy of the results of the inquiry anyway. I told him that I'd like a copy of the transcripts as well, if that was possible.

He looked at me, and said, "I know that you're in CID. If you really want a copy, you'd be better to find some way to request it through police channels."

I took the hint, thanked him, and left. I did receive the official Procurator Fiscal's report and threw it in the desk drawer in my flat. I asked one of the women in admin if they could get a copy of the Fatal Accident Inquiry transcript and she asked me if it was official or unofficial. I told her that I could make it official, I didn't think there would be too many objections, but I would prefer for it to be unofficial. She told me to leave it with her and she'd see what she could do.

[Thursday 5th June 2003]

I was running late on the Thursday as I'd had to go into work after all. Sod's law. I swear these silly bastards wait until I'm just about to go off duty before they decide to start knocking lumps out of each other. I dived up the steps at one minute to three, having parked two streets away in the only available parking space for two square miles. I felt sweaty after the dash from the car to the solicitor's office, so I was slightly uncomfortable when I was shown into the same room as before. It was hardly full: apart from Douglas Cameron, there were only two other people present. The first was introduced as John Ardglass, Scottish area executive for Fight for Forest – you'll have seen their adverts on TV; they're the ones who "buy" trees to stop them getting cut down, or something like that. Funnily enough, although I didn't see Francis as a rampant environmentalist, he had always tried to source his wood from renewable resources, often using reclaimed or second-hand wood where possible, so I wasn't surprised at his first choice of charity. The other one made even more sense. Chris Anderson worked for the NHS and was in charge of a teaching workshop in a local psychiatric hospital, where they used commercial contracts to allow patients being treated for drug or alcohol abuse and the like to learn various crafts and skills, from making household and garden furniture to picture framing and re-upholstery. They had had a number of notable successes with patients who had gone on to get qualifications in carpentry and associated trades. Even those who didn't gain a career out of it seemed to have a better recovery rate than average. The general public, who placed their orders because of the reasonable prices, did so on the understanding that the work was being done by trainees, closely supervised. Jobs could take a while as they didn't rush things, with no constraints from targets or the bottom line.

I had met Chris before when I visited the workshop with Francis, who had helped out occasionally on a voluntary basis, teaching the basic steps of finishing and polishing to the students, and I was pleased that they were going to benefit from Francis' estate. We all shook hands and chatted for a couple of minutes, each of us saddened by the reason we were all there.

227

"Gentlemen, can we get started?" Douglas Cameron called the meeting to order. We all sat down in comfortable armchairs placed in front of the large modern desk and he took his place behind it, opening a folder and looking rather dramatically over the top of his glasses. He began by stating that there had been no will left by Deborah Hare, or Deborah Swann as she was sometimes known, but that she was still legally married to Francis Hare and that her estate was considered to be a joint estate with his.

"Firstly, the dwelling house at 621 Crow Road, Jordanhill, Glasgow, will be placed on the property market by an appropriate estate agency at the direction of Mitchell and Cameron, solicitors and notaries, and will be sold by auction to the highest bidder. The proceeds of the sale, after deductions for all reasonable costs, will be divided equally between the registered charity, Fight For Forest (Reg No: S19873542) and a new charity, The Patrick Hare Foundation, to be set up by Mitchell and Cameron, solicitors, and run by a committee including Mr Douglas Cameron of that firm, and Mr John Reid McDaid, if he accepts the position. The funds will be used to support and develop in any way deemed suitable the furniture and craft training workshop that is part of the services currently run by Greater Glasgow Health Board at Kelvin Vale Psychiatric Hospital."

He again looked over his glasses at us, and smiled. I was quite pleased that Francis had thought to include me in his plans for the funds gifted to the workshop, and I hoped that I could do the job as well as he would have expected. I was kind of half-listening to the lawyer as he continued.

"The remaining part of the estate, including the shop, yard, workshop at 621 Crow Road, Jordanhill, Glasgow, all contents of these buildings, including the contents of the previously named house, and any other property or monies that were the property of Francis Hare, after the payment of any fees or taxes due at the time of the settlement of this will, I bequeath to John Reid McDaid, of Flat 1\2, 123 Appleby Street, Denistoun, Glasgow."

He looked at me across the desk. I sat stunned. I wouldn't have been surprised if Francis had left me some of his hand tools and maybe a small monetary legacy, but I just couldn't get my head round this. Later on, I realised that as Francis' closest friend, and with none of his relatives still alive, it shouldn't have been as much of a surprise as it was, but at that moment I was speechless.

"That concludes the reading of the last will and testament of Francis Hare." Cameron looked at us all, and spoke to each of us in turn. "We have currently valued the house at about two hundred and ten thousand pounds. If the costs of selling and other legal costs are allowed for, both your organisations should benefit to the tune of one hundred thousand pounds each. I trust that this is satisfactory to both of you?"

Both men thanked Douglas Cameron profusely, but he pointed out to them that he was simply the messenger, that Francis' generosity was what they should be really thankful for.

"As for you, young man," he said, smiling at me like a benign elderly uncle, "Francis talked very highly of you, and also very fondly, and I am sure that he felt that you would make the most of it. Of course, there is a quite significant inheritance tax liability, but there will still be a quite reasonable surplus at estimated market values," he added, more to give me some time to get my thoughts together than anything else.

Aside from the absurdity of being called young, I also felt strangely unequipped for this unexpected gift. I stammered some crap about being gobsmacked, and how out of the blue it was, and that I couldn't really take it all in. Cups of tea were brought in, although I somehow expected something stronger in the circumstances. The guy from Fight For Forest spoke briefly of how much good this bequest would do before making an exit, and the three of us remaining discussed how the fund was to be set up, what the administrative structure would be and what would be the most beneficial ways to spend the fund for the long-term good of the project. We set up a meeting for the three of us to sort out some of the people we wanted to bring in to help us run the thing, and Chris left to let the staff and trainees at the workshop know of the windfall.

When he had gone, Douglas Cameron turned to me, grinning.

"I could see that you never saw that one coming."

"No, I must say that it took me completely by surprise. I still can't believe it. Could you not have warned me?"

He chuckled. "Not allowed to, I'm afraid, and anyway, how could you spoil an old man's fun?"

I smiled at that. "Why didn't Francis just leave it all to the charities?"

He put his hand on my shoulder. "Listen, you may not realise this, but when Francis re-made his will about three years ago he told me he never got over Patrick's murder; however, with you around, he almost felt as if he'd had another son. While he mourned for Patrick, he took comfort from your friendship, especially as the two of you got on so well and shared a passion for furniture and football, his two loves outside of his family. He also said that you'd stuck your neck out for him on a couple of occasions – I'll not ask how – and that he felt that you had given him one hundred per cent loyalty. So don't feel guilty about this. It's a message from Francis that simply says, 'Thanks'."

I thought about that. "I can tell you that Francis was a big part of my life and was, in lots of ways, a massive influence on me. He got me serious about my football, he introduced me to working with wood, for which I am eternally grateful, but more than that, I just enjoyed being his friend."

"There, you see what I mean? Just enjoy the gift and don't waste it – pay off your mortgage, spend a little and invest a little, and don't forget him. Buy something significant that will last, a painting or something, and always have it to remember him by."

I don't know why, but I was suddenly sure of what I should do – I hadn't really had time to think about it, it was just a gut feeling, but it was one of these times when you know it is one hundred per cent the right thing to do.

"Mr Cameron, I'm going to keep hold of the workshop and the shop. I spend a lot of my time there anyway, and I don't want to lose that."

"Call me Douglas," he replied. I was quite warming to him by now. "There's no problem with that – there might have to be some negotiation about access for the house, but that's not insurmountable." He paused. "I'm sorry, but I assumed that you would want to sell up and use the money elsewhere. It never occurred to me that you would want to keep the workshop, never mind the shop."

I took a deep breath. "There's something else. I think I want to try and buy the house. Would that be possible?"

He seemed quite taken aback. "If you mean by that, is it possible to do a deal over the house with the two other beneficiaries, that would leave us open to all sorts of possible redress, but there's no reason that you can't bid for the house at auction."

"No, I didn't mean anything underhand. It was just me thinking aloud about how the best way to do it would be."

"The fact that you are an executor and will be a trustee for the beneficiary of the sale of the house may pose a few questions, but in principle, if you make the highest bid, then there should be no problem. What we must do is make sure that the process of bringing the house to auction is done totally transparently and correctly, so that at no point in the future can anyone make any criticism of the way the house was sold."

He looked very thoughtful. I was just about to ask him another question when he spoke first.

"Why do you want to keep the whole thing anyway?"

"It honestly just came into my head and it feels like absolutely the right thing to do. Even now, the more I think of it, the more it makes sense. I want to keep a workshop, and I will never get as good a workshop anywhere else for my purposes, and if I have the workshop, it might as well be right next to where I live. I have a flat to sell and a little bit of money to add to that, along with a mortgage, so from what you say, I should be able to afford it unless it goes for silly money."

"I suppose what you say makes sense. I was just hoping you weren't doing it for the wrong reasons, some morbid sense of duty to keep things as they were."

I felt slightly embarrassed. "OK, part of the reason is that I would like to keep the business going, at least until I've sold the remaining stock that Francis had, but part of me thinks I could continue even after that, part-time until I leave the force. It would keep the Hare and Son name going, at least for a while anyway, and I will be looking about for something to do with myself in a few years when I retire. As well as that, I've met quite a number of Francis' clients and they seem the sort of people who would like it to be kept going."

I think he was quietly pleased. "Do you know, I think Francis would have approved. Hell, he might even have known that you would think of doing that!"

"What sort of timescale would be involved?" I asked.

"There's no real reason for delaying anything, but it might be advisable to move a little carefully on it – it will let you think more clearly about it and give you time to change your mind if this sudden decision doesn't look as sensible in the cold light of day. It will also give you time to sell your current property if you decide to go ahead. You do realise it will be a bit of a gamble? You will need to have the finance in place by the auction, which means selling your flat first, and there are no guarantees that you will definitely get the house – you may be left homeless for a while."

"I could always sleep in the workshop, or even in the shop, if it came to that."

"The one good thing," he said, pointing to a property flier on his desk, "is that flats are selling very briskly at the moment and the prices for smaller properties have increased faster than those for larger properties. However, that can't last, so we don't want to wait too long. What if we say that the property will be ready for viewing in six weeks, with the auction three months from now?"

With that, it was all finished. I walked out of the lawyer's office a good deal better off than when I went in, but my overriding thought was that I would have much rather had Francis still alive so that I could nip round to his place and spend another few hours in his company, working away in the warm tool room, listening to him as he chatted about craftsmen he had known or footballers he had played with.

I phoned Sarah first, then Andy. They were both delighted for me and wished me all the best with the house, and the business. Andy jokingly predicted that I wouldn't last long in the force, with a more important career to think of. We arranged for me to go through and have a night out in celebration, and toast Francis' memory.

~~o~~

Douglas Cameron was as good as his word. The auction took place in early September, just two days over the three months that he had originally suggested. Those three months could have seen me anxious and worried, but they were so busy that I didn't really have time to think. Work was exceptionally hectic – if it had stayed that busy for longer, I might not have needed a mortgage with the amount of overtime I was pulling in. In addition, I had to sort my flat out, get it all ready for sale and put it on the market. If that wasn't enough, I had to decant the contents of Francis' house to the workshop, as it also had to be ready for viewing and we had to be seen to make every effort to make the house as attractive as possible to potential buyers.

Andy came through and gave me a hand. We emptied all the drawers, cupboards and shelves into boxes and bags, hundreds of them, and stored them in the loft area of the workshop. We put most of the furniture into the woodshed.

When we took all the drawers out of Francis' desk and emptied them, it took us ages to get them back in, as each drawer seemed to only fit one set of runners. I'd always thought that Francis' accuracy meant that everything that looked as if it should be the same had exactly the same measurements, so it was quite nice in a way that I'd found out that he wasn't always completely perfect. Perhaps that was why he kept this desk for himself – it was a "reject"! I had a laugh to myself at the thought of such a beautiful thing being a "second". I looked at the date on the back of the desk – 1957 – so maybe he had still been learning his trade.

A lot of what we did was very sad. Packing away all of Francis' clothes, shoes and personal gear, like shavers and toiletries, made it seem like we were trying to get rid of him quickly, even though we knew that the homeless shelter would be very grateful for all the stuff.

We found some slightly unusual objects – in the back of a cupboard were an old Epson photo dye printer – popular before the widespread availability of inkjets, but horribly expensive to buy and run – plus an early copy of Photoshop for the Mac, although we never found the Apple Mac itself. It made me realise that Francis was into computers and technology much earlier than most people, in contrast to his almost pathological avoidance of anything that took away the need for good old-fashioned hand tools when working with wood. Even up until his death, he would often choose a hand plane over a machine planer if time was not a major issue.

There were some funny moments as well. The strangest item we found was a priest's fancy dress outfit and we both gutted ourselves laughing at the thought of Francis and Deborah dressing up as a priest and a nun, until we realised that it had probably belonged to Patrick.

On Douglas's advice we hired a company that specialised in preparing houses for sale, to ensure that we had done everything possible to maximise the potential sale value. The house was listed with a well-known West End estate agent and the date was set for the auction. I had temporarily declined the post of trustee to the Patrick Hare

234

Foundation while the sale was going through and Chris understood and agreed completely when we told him the reasons. He had seemed pleased at the thought of Francis' business continuing, even if it was on a reduced scale, but he also warned me that he would do everything possible to maximise the sale price of the house, even if it meant walking round the streets with advertising boards and a loud hailer!

Deborah's small home sold very quickly and the price achieved was slightly better than predicted, but the sale of my flat came down to the wire – missives were concluded three days before the auction, although we achieved well above the asking price. Douglas Cameron had given me a conservative figure that I could expect from the savings and investments, with the tax and costs deducted, and I had had a meeting with my bank manager to arrange what turned out to be a workable mortgage to cover the expected shortfall. I had about another five thousand in various places if push came to shove and I was even willing to sell my car to one of the guys at work if it came down to the difference between getting the house or not.

In the end I managed to hold on to my car, but I did need a little of my five grand stash just to make sure I was the final bidder. It did cross my mind that Fight For Forest had planted a "buyer" in the auction to push the price up a bit, but I was assured that bidders had to register their details, thus ensuring that they were bona-fide buyers. I was happy to have got the house, but part of me wondered how weird it was going to be living in Francis' and Deborah's home. The presale team had painted everything a bland off-white and put new drapes and stuff up, so the house did seem a little different, which made it easier.

I then had to repopulate the house with furniture. I knew that it would be morbid to just return all Francis' and Deborah's furniture to its original locations in the house, but most of it was beautiful and well suited to the rooms, so I didn't want to discard it just for the sake of a fresh start. In the end I came to a compromise. I kept the stunning dining room furniture in its entirety, and I bought two new settees for the living room, but kept the large coffee table for the centre. I moved my own bed, which I'd made myself, into the main bedroom, and used Francis' bed in the spare room, along with the other bedroom furniture.

I returned Francis' office almost to its original state, adding a La-Z-Boy chair and a flat screen TV to make it into a real den, and it was where I ended up spending most of my time. The kitchen table and chairs were ideal, and the built-in shaker-style cabinets made by Francis at least thirty years earlier were far better than anything you could buy today. By the time new carpets had been fitted, a couple of the rooms papered, and new curtains, cushions, lamps and other miscellaneous furnishings added, the house retained most of the charm I'd always known it to have, but was different enough to avoid any feeling of living in the past.

Douglas Cameron called in on me a few days after the sale and told me that the insurance company were looking for confirmation that the offer made to settle the claim for the car was acceptable. He mentioned the amount and it seemed fair, so I agreed that he should contact them and confirm that the offer was satisfactory. I asked him what had happened to the car. He replied that he didn't know; the police had impounded it while the investigation was underway and usually, after that, it would be released to the insurance company, who would eventually arrange to have it sent to a wrecking yard.

"I hope you don't think it's weird, but I wouldn't mind having a look at the car. Can you find out where it is?"

He looked at me rather strangely but agreed to find out.

"I just find it hard to believe that Francis would have been so careless as to cause the deaths of himself and two other people. I keep thinking that I should at least do something to put the record straight and I've got a feeling that there may be an answer in the vehicle, so I want to see it before it gets destroyed."

"I can understand that. I must admit myself that I was very surprised at Francis doing something like that. He was always so careful about everything. I'll ask the insurance company where the car has been sent when I tell them the claim settlement is acceptable. But from what I read, I don't think there's any explanation other than that Francis screwed up."

I sighed. I knew that he was talking sense. "You're nearly certainly right, but there's just something doesn't quite sit properly in the whole thing. At least I'll feel that I've done all I can."

That was one thing about Douglas Cameron: when he said he was going to do something, you could consider it done. When I spoke to his secretary, she told me that the car was currently at a breaker's yard in Cambuslang and that while they were happy for me to have a look at it, it would have to be within the next couple of days. I wasn't looking forward to it. I had thought of asking Andy to come with me, but I felt strange enough about doing this without having someone else there to witness it, so I arrived at the yard on my own. I parked in the only clear area I could find. I was a bit nervous that they might lift my own car as scrap, being that it was past the first flush of its youth, so when I asked the guy in the old caravan that doubled as an office where I could find the boss, I also made a point of telling him that the car currently sitting in the yard was not due to be crushed. He said that the gaffer had nipped out to the bank, but if I was the guy here to see the wrecked Audi, I was just to go ahead and have a look. He pointed out to me where it was and I clambered over a pile of radiators to get to it.

Having seen Francis' body, I was not shocked at the state of the car. What surprised me more was that Deborah's body had looked relatively unscathed. The front end of the car had completely caved in, and the right hand side was almost unrecognisable. The front passenger door had been cut away, presumably to get Deborah's body out, and sure enough, there was a sizable pocket formed by the seat, the dashboard, the front footwell and what was left of the windscreen. I couldn't really get access to the rest of the car and I realised that I wasn't really going to be able to learn anything further without having time to take it apart piece by piece, and this was certainly not the place to do that.

I poked around anyway, more to kill time than anything else, and had just prised open the boot when I heard a shout and a heavyset man in very dirty blue overalls climbed over the pile of scrap towards me. I waved to him and he came over, walking around the car and shaking his head.

"Friends of yours?" he asked.

"Sorry to say, aye." I didn't really want to have to give long explanations and, to be fair, he just grunted.

"Did you see what you needed to?"

"Not really. I can't really get to anything. I'd need to use cutters on it."

"Haven't got the space or the time, I'm afraid, I only held it because I knew you were coming today – if you'd come tomorrow, it would've been gone."

"Listen, how much do you get for these?"

He looked at me, puzzled but interested. "About four hundred pounds. Big, heavy car, you see. Why, you want it?"

"Yes. I'll give you five hundred for it, that gives you a bit extra."

"I'll think about it. What about delivery?"

"Can you deliver it for me?"

"No, I've no time, but maybe young Davey would drop it off for you when he's finished. Bung him a ton, and he'll likely oblige."

"OK, so what about the cost of the car? Is five hundred OK?"

"Call it five fifty, for the use of the lorry and the diesel, and you can have it."

I wondered why I was doing it, but I agreed, and I gave him my address.

"Davey'll drop it off tonight, I'll see to that."

I shook his hand and left to get somewhere ready for the car to sit. I didn't want anyone to see it, so I decided to put it behind the workshop in the area that Francis usually reserved for large timbers awaiting splitting. There were only a few of those at present and I could use them to sit the car on, allowing access underneath.

I spent the afternoon clearing the area, and levering two large timbers cross-wise, ready for the car when it arrived. It was nearly seven o'clock before it finally reached the yard. Young Davey, who was about forty-ish, reversed in and lifted the car over the corner of the woodshed on to the waiting timbers. I covered it over with one of the thick tarpaulins that Francis used to protect any wood that he kept outside.

[Thursday 18th September 2003]

Because I had left work early the day before I had missed the note left on my desk, and due to circumstances beyond my control, I didn't get it until the day after that. I phoned the number on the note and found myself speaking to Joe Harrison, who I hadn't heard from since the days of the botched investigation into Patrick Hare's murder.

"Joe, long time no hear. How are you keeping?"

"I'm fine. How are you holding together? I heard about Mr and Mrs Hare."

"Oh, I'm getting by, getting by. It's been a sad time. What are you up to these days?"

Well, it turned out Joe had been busy. He was a DI, and he was married with three "bloody kids", one of whom had already left school and was at some college or another.

"I see the doc was right, then," I joked.

"Yeh, it all happened fairly quickly after that. We've been lucky."

I brought Joe up to speed with my life and told him about my new part-time career as a cabinetmaker, having taken over Francis' business.

"That's what I'm phoning you about," he said.

"What, you want some furniture made?" I interjected.

"No, no, I don't think from the sound of things that I could afford any of that stuff, having kids is too expensive. No, I didn't know if you'd heard about Derek Davidson."

For a second, I couldn't think who Derek Davidson was, then I remembered. "Spaz Davidson?"

"Yes, he got himself killed. Do you not read the paper?"

"No, I hadn't heard. How did that happen?"

"You know that big shoot out up at Maryhill Road? He was one of the fatals."

I was surprised I'd missed it, and I said that to Joe.

He explained. "It was just before the Hares died, and the names weren't given out for two or three days."

"I took a bit of annual leave round about that time and I didn't really look much at the papers for fear of what they would say about the crash."

"Anyhow, I thought you should know."

"Listen, thanks. If there's any consolation from all this, it's that very few of those bastards have outlasted Francis, and the ones that are left aren't doing so well."

I thought long and hard about Joe's call. It was ironic that Patrick's murderers had nearly all died young – the only ones left were John White and David Johnstone. Oh, and Malky, but he wasn't going anywhere for a long time.

~~o~~

My curiosity aroused, the following weekend I decided to track the pair of them down, as discreetly as I could.

Finding John White was simple. In and out of prison for years, he was a smackhead and had recently been admitted to a rehab unit as a psychiatric patient.

Finding David Johnstone wasn't so straightforward. He had no criminal record and he seemed to have accepted that he'd made a big mistake; he had turned his life round and got on with it. I didn't want to approach him at work or at home, so I followed him at a distance one day after he'd left the house. As luck would have it, I chose the one day of the week when he went to the pub, to play darts. I went in and made a point of standing at the bar where he would be sure to come over and buy drinks. When he did, I engaged him in conversation by asking him about the darts. He told me that it was his only vice, but it was great just to get out for the night, and that all the guys in the team were good mates.

"Not like your old mates, Nolman and Billy Green then, David," I said.

He turned pale instantly and looked quickly around, shocked and nervous.

"Listen," I added, "don't worry, I'm not going to cause a scene, and I only approached you in here to avoid contacting you at home or at work, OK?"

He stammered as he answered. "OK, but w-who are you? I've seen your face before, somewhere."

"I was one of the officers on the Patrick Hare murder enquiry, but you didn't see much of me."

"So wh-what do you want now? It was years ago, and I've had fuck all to do with that crowd since. I can't cope with this all getting out again."

"David, calm down, it's not going to get out; I just need a bit of information. When would it be suitable for us to have a chat?"

"Not at home. Can you meet me after work tomorrow? I can tell Mary that I'm working late, or going a message for the boss on my way home; yeh, that's it, a message."

"OK," I said, "but I'll meet you somewhere for a coffee, so none of your workmates see you with me."

He looked relieved, arranged to meet me at the Light Bite on the Main Street, and went back to his mates. I wouldn't like to have seen his scores that evening; I reckon he would have been lucky to hit the fucking board.

The next afternoon, at half past four prompt, he walked into the coffee place and sat down opposite me. I went over and got him a cup of coffee, and a fresh one for me.

I asked him about his job and his family to try and relax him a bit and he spoke of them as if they really mattered to him. He was a line supervisor at a local packing plant, but had recently applied for a management post and was waiting to hear about it. He had a nice house, the mortgage was getting lower every year, he and the wife got on well in the main, and both of them doted on their two girls. I can't remember what they were called, but it was something suitably flowery.

"How long have you worked in the plant?" I asked him.

"Oh, about, let me see, twelve or thirteen years, I think."

"And what did you do before that?"

All of a sudden, he seemed to stiffen up, and looked edgy.

"Look, if it was anything dodgy, I'm not interested," I told him.

"I was with the prison service," he mumbled.

I didn't know if I'd heard him right. The way he was acting, it was as if he'd been in prison.

"You were a prison warder?" I said, staggered that he should have chosen that as a job, with his history.

He laughed, harshly. "Yes, I knew you'd react like that. Mary's dad was in the service; he kind of got me the job. He's always been very good to me."

"How did you get in? You'd been tried for murder, for fuck's sake."

"I didn't tell them and somehow it wasn't picked up on, I don't know how." He was almost in tears now.

My heart went out to him. A girl who he'd married and her father had not only believed in him, but had stuck their necks out for him, and he must have always had in the back of his mind the nightmare that was me, or someone like me, turning up out of the blue and upsetting the whole apple cart.

"So why did you leave?"

He was very quiet now, embarrassed and afraid. "I was asked to leave."

I could see his bottom lip tremble. "Why?"

"They said I was p-passing stuff to prisoners, but I swear I wasn't. Why would I have spoiled everything? I'm not stupid."

"Whoa, calm down, you'll have a nervous breakdown here. Take a drink and a few big breaths."

I thought quietly as he took a few minutes composing himself. Something was buzzing around in the back of my mind, but I just couldn't put my finger on what was bothering me. "What prison did you work in?"

He looked up slowly, resignation in his eyes. "I worked at Barlinnie."

It all tumbled into place. "Sornie," I said.

Nothing was said for a few seconds.

"You were the prison officer sacked after he was murdered."

"Yes, that was me. I only spoke to the b-bastard once, you know, not long after he came in. He tried to get me to do stuff for him and I told him that I would resign if he asked me for anything, that I wasn't going to have anything to do with him. He left me alone after that. I suppose he thought that at some point in the future he could make me change my mind. Anyway, when he was killed I was relieved, to be honest. I thought I was OK, but the investigation into his death picked up on who I was. They told me that if I went with no f-fuss, there would be no criminal charges."

"So you didn't have anything to do with his death?" I had to ask, although I knew in my own mind he hadn't.

He looked at me scathingly. "What do you think? How could I have done it? I wasn't even working that day. Besides, they got his killers."

I must admit, I tended to agree with him.

"Listen," he said, "I will always regret, to my dying day, being there when that Patrick boy was killed. I tried to stop them at the end, but I was scared shitless. I know I can never get that scene out of my mind, but since then I've done everything I can to make a decent life for me and my family."

"I know, and you should probably give yourself a break now."

"I wrote to him once, you know, a few years ago."

"Who, Francis?"

244

"Yes, I couldn't go on without them knowing how sorry I was. He sent me a letter back, saying I'd been punished enough. Couldn't really understand. I suppose he meant the guilt thing."

"You do know he's dead, don't you?"

"Yes, I read it in the papers. I wondered if it was suicide."

That stopped me in my tracks. I felt quite annoyed. "Why would you say that?"

He looked at me, puzzled. "You mean, you haven't thought about that?"

I told him, "There's no way Francis and Deborah would have done that. I mean, Deborah especially was a devout Catholic, and that's a big no-no with our lot."

I must have been getting quite annoyed, because he apologised. "I didn't mean any harm, I had just thought with it being twenty-five years to the day, and all that …" He petered out.

"Look, let's just leave it at that. Go and get on with your life, you'll not hear from me again."

He fumbled in his pocket, and produced three pound coins. "You're a Catholic, aren't you? Will you do something for me?"

I told him I was, but that I rarely went to mass or anything.

"The next time you are there, can you light a candle for each of them for me?"

With that, he put the coins in my hand, stood up, and walked out.

I'd almost forgotten about my request for the Fatal Accident Inquiry details, but one morning a fairly thick buff envelope appeared on my desk, marked:

PRIVATE & PERSONAL, DS John McDaid.

I knew it wasn't my end of year appraisal, so I had a peek at the contents and quickly realised what it was. I took the Fatal Accident Inquiry Report home to have a good look at it when I had the time, but due to pressure of work and possibly a reluctance to drag myself through the whole thing again it was over a week before I started to look at it. Deep down, I knew I wasn't going to find anything that would change the outcome of the Fatal Accident Inquiry, but I just felt that it was so out of character for Francis to have been so careless that I forced myself to trawl through it all, just in case there was something. When I'd finished, I was no further forward

CHAPTER 12   DISCOVERY

[Monday 3rd November 2003]

Many of Francis' customers had contacted me in the weeks and months following his death, either by phone or, more frequently, notes they popped through the shop letterbox. Most of these were just passing on their regrets, but one or two were from people who had outstanding orders and, while they all made a point of stating their understanding of the situation and not wanting to appear insensitive, reading between the lines I could see that they really wanted to know if the furniture that they had ordered was in any way available. There were not many of them and I contacted everyone who had written. I gave those customers that I knew had partly finished orders the option of taking their unfinished furniture away to another cabinetmaker, who would then complete the work, and said I would charge accordingly. I felt it only right that I should offer a partial refund, although this would have been unlikely to cover the additional costs of completion.

As an alternative, I offered to finish the items myself. By then I had seen enough of Francis' techniques, and practised them under his guidance, to be confident of achieving a quality that would match most of the other craftsmen, if I was allowed time to do it at a pace suited to my experience.

To my surprise, every single one of them asked me to complete their orders. Most of them told me that Francis had often commented on his "apprentice", and had showed them pieces that I had made or was in the process of making. They had almost come to accept me as Francis' assistant, and my confidence in making the offer to complete their orders seemed to encourage them to believe that I could successfully keep the business going, at least in the short term. I warned everyone that I would not be considering any new orders until the outstanding ones had been completed. I also warned them that I was not yet capable of producing work as complex or intricate as Francis had been capable of, nor were my design skills anywhere near approaching those that Francis had. I explained that it meant I could make furniture based on the designs Francis had left, or simple modifications of them, as long as the designs involved were not too technically difficult for my capabilities.

Again, I was surprised how many of them asked to be contacted when I was ready to start taking new orders. In the event, I finished the outstanding orders quicker than I had expected. There was surprisingly little cutting, planing and jointing required as many of the parts had already been cut, ready for assembly, as if Francis had known that I would carry on. I found it a little tricky on my own so I enlisted Andy, who was visiting one weekend, as an extra pair of hands.

I then had four or five items ready to be polished and over the next two months I spent my spare time sanding, applying finishes, polishing and waxing until I had everything completed to my satisfaction.

I still had the rather frightening experience of presenting finished pieces to our customers.

In the event, they were all delighted and promised to place more orders when I was ready, even though I'd pointed out a few minor flaws in each piece that I knew would not have been present in a Francis Hare masterpiece. They appreciated my honesty and, to a man, said that I had exceeded their expectations, if not quite coming up to Francis' level of perfection.

Feeling quiet satisfaction, I then started to plan ahead. I knew my technique and my ability to produce a consistent quality would improve, so I started looking for new projects to start. I contacted a couple of Francis' favourite clients, hoping that would be a little more forgiving if I didn't come up to scratch.

A fairly simple bookcase and a television cabinet were the first two requests. I decided to use or modify a couple of Francis' designs as a starting point.

Francis kept his design books, large leather-bound albums containing drawings, notes, materials, and pictures of completed pieces, in the upstairs office in the workshop. They filled two shelves, all the way across one wall of the office. I removed five or six of these at a time, starting with the top shelf, and sat them on the desk, browsing through them to find designs that matched my requirements. I had no idea how Francis organised his collection, but I could tell that it wasn't alphabetical or chronological, so it meant hauling a section at a time off the shelves, going through them, and leaving out any volume containing anything that was promising. I had completed the upper shelf and was starting on the lower one, pulling out a manageable stack of the books at each go, when I noticed that the lower shelf went back further than the top one and, in fact, the books in some places were two deep. It was the slope of the roof that allowed the bottom shelf to be twice the depth of the top. I almost groaned as I realised that this meant there were probably an extra twenty or thirty books for me to go through.

However, only the first half of the shelf had books going all the way back and by the time I got to the middle I realised that there were boxes instead of books at the back of the second section. I presumed that they would be loose plans or perhaps archived accounts from previous years and decades, but on extracting one of the boxes and opening the lid, I recognised the contents after reading the first few pages of the bunched files.

This was Francis' safe hiding place for the comprehensive record of the murder investigation, the trial, and the subsequent internal inquiry that he'd shown me all those years ago. I smiled sadly at my memory of Francis collecting and collating everything connected with the case, including a pile of press clippings from the newspapers of the time. The next section of files contained the dossiers of the men accused of Patrick's murder. Puzzled, I thought to myself that some of them were thicker than I remembered and, when I counted them, there were only five in the box. I thumbed through them, starting with Kevin Nolan's. The missing dossiers were Derek Davidson's, John White's and David Johnston's.

In all the dossiers, sketchy but almost biographical details of their lives – and in some cases, their deaths – had been added. Francis had obviously kept tabs on them all, not always in great depth, but all the facts told of wasted, brutal and pointless lives, with an underpinning thread of cruelty and a casual disregard for other people. There were more recent photographs of some of the gang members, which Francis must have taken from a distance. He may well have had a long lens fitted to that fancy camera of his, which I hadn't yet come across.

I slipped the box back into place and took a few of the more promising books I had chosen downstairs and over to the house to examine at my leisure. Over the next few days I drew my own revised sketches and planned out my new pieces. The bookcase was straightforward and I intended to begin with it, but thinking that I might need to order special hinges for the TV cupboard, I thought I should look in the workshop to see if Francis had anything like that in stock.

I looked through all the drawers, not finding anything suitable, but discovered a myriad of useful bits of ironmongery and other hardware, along with all sorts of odds and ends that eventually could come in useful. Halfway through I realised that a thorough inventory would be useful to save me from repeated searches every time I need to find a handle or catch, so I restarted, listing each drawer's contents as I went. After the drawers were completed, with nothing suitable found, I started on the cupboards and shelves. Again I found nothing that I wanted, although there was a stack of stuff suitable for use in the future.

I found what I was looking for in the open space below a bench that ran along the wall and which was home to a variety of containers. In a plastic bucket, wrapped in pairs within waxed paper and placed in plastic bags, were hinges similar to the ones I required. They were too large and a slightly different shape, but being brass it wasn't going to be too difficult to modify them to suit.

Seeing as I had come so far in making a complete inventory, I thought that I might as well finish it. I realised that a similar list of all the stocks of wood that I had was something that would also be worth doing.

The next day I repeated the whole exercise for my stocks of wood. It was while shifting a stacked pile of various hardwood off-cuts to count and categorise them, and get rid of the ones that had no potential use, that I spotted a dusty canvas bag in the back corner. Thinking that it might contain more scrap wood, I pulled it out and emptied its contents on to the workbench. It contained a mixture of apparently random objects, including a face mask, a disc from an angle grinder, a plastic funnel, a jam jar and something that looked like a brake disc, only larger and thicker than any that I'd seen on a car. A large section was missing from one side of the disc, but it didn't look as if it had been shattered, more as if it had been worn away.

Puzzled, I examined it all more closely and thought *what a load of old rubbish*. I was trying to think of one good reason why Francis would have kept any of those things when, in a cascade of connecting synapses, a fact stored insignificantly in some recess of my brain for years suddenly slammed into my consciousness. I remembered that lorry brake discs contained large amounts of asbestos, to provide abrasive friction and be able to withstand the heat.

For about five seconds, I unsuccessfully grasped at an idea just beyond my reach, and just when I thought it was slipping away, it all meshed together.

Billy Green

Asbestos

Mesothelioma

Brake disc

Within seconds other connections were made, this time with devastating consequences for the way I viewed the world from that moment on.

Inhaler

Asthma

Billy Green

Asbestos

Mesothelioma

Brake disc

Francis

When the last one clicked into place, a few other things did, too. I ran upstairs to the office and pulled out the box containing the dossiers, grabbing for Billy Green's. Opening it, I skimmed through looking for something that I knew would be there. I found it fairly quickly, on the printed sheets that were part of my contribution to the dossier – a description of Billy Green's confession, extracted by Gallagher by withholding his asthma medication. The word asthma had been circled twice. In red.

I sat stunned for maybe five minutes. I tried to work out in my mind how Francis could steal Billy's inhaler and return it to him unnoticed. Three or four possible scenarios buzzed around in my head, but I couldn't see that any of them were feasible.

I went out, found a call box, and phoned Billy Green's mum. I told her that I was from the Transport and General Workers' Union, and that I was an investigator charged with the task of fighting for the rights of workers killed by asbestos-related disease to receive full damages for government and industry neglect.

"We know that Billy's case is slightly unusual because of his age, but we feel that including it will add fresh impetus to our campaign."

I could hear the pound signs whirring around in Billy Green's ma's brain, like a fruit machine paying out. Over the next ten minutes she gave me all the information I needed to know. She admitted that he'd never worked, that he was one of the victims of the lack of jobs on Clydeside, but that Billy used the old shipyards as playgrounds. "Always playing in the piles of rubbish," she said.

She asked me if the union could try and claim for Billy and I told her that he would have had to have been a member of the union, but as he had never worked or been a union member, the union could not help him specifically. I did point out to her that if the union were successful, Billy's case would be easier to claim for and that she could go down the route of suing the government herself.

She also indicated that she would like to sue the hospital as well, for letting a dying Protestant's last days be spoiled by allowing a Roman Catholic priest to see him. "The poor wee bastard lyin' there breathin' his last, an a cunt o' a Fenian priest comes in and gies him the last fucking rites, no wunner the puir wee soul wis writhin' and groanin', near killed him there an then."

She also gave me the name of Billy's doctor and said that she would phone ahead and tell him to expect a call from me.

When I phoned, Billy's doctor was just as helpful. He had seen a lot of cases, but usually in men of fifty to seventy years old. Around Clydebank, nearly all of the victims had been shipyard workers. Billy's case was unusual, and a puzzle to him. He had even thought of writing it up for *The Lancet*.

Returning home, I asked myself, @i Why Billy? He was no worse than the rest of them, was he? Had he maybe said something to Francis at some point, to push Francis in to striking back?"

253

Then it hit me: it wasn't just Billy. Was Francis and Deborah's car accident a botched attempt at Kevin Nolan's life that went horribly wrong, killing them all? Could any of the other deaths be connected with Francis?

I got the list from my wallet, where I'd kept it since making it a few years before. I looked at it, and scored out a few bits and added others.

NOLMAN

Prison, 3 – 5 yrs, serious assault Dead, RTA

SCOULAR

Dead, Weil's disease

SORNIE

Dead, murdered

PINKY

Dead, murdered

MALKY

Prison, life, > 19 yrs, 2 added for riot

BILLY GREEN

~~Ill, unknown cause~~ Dead, mesothelioma

DAVID JOHNSTON

~~Whereabouts unknown~~ Married, 2 kids, line supervisor

DEREK (SPAZ) DAVIDSON

Habitual prisoner, but released at moment Dead

JOHN (WHITEY) WHITE

Whereabouts unknown

GALLAGHER

Dead, alcoholism, cancer

TOMMO

Dead, thrombosis?

PETE

Dead, heart attack

I needed a look at the other three dossiers, but where the hell were they? I had already thoroughly searched the workshop, so I went to the house and walked through each room, looking in all the places that they could be concealed in.

I drew a blank downstairs and headed for the bedrooms. I hadn't noticed anything when we'd moved all the furniture about or when we'd thrown out all the stuff I didn't want to keep. My bedroom had been gutted and the spare bedroom had been, too, except that Francis and Deborah's bed, wardrobes, chest-of-drawers and dressing table were still in it. I closely examined all of these, but we'd emptied them previously and I would have noticed the dossiers then.

Just to check, I had a good rummage through the remaining bags and boxes of Francis' stuff, which I'd kept in Patrick's old room along with the decent furniture that had belonged to him. I found nothing useful in the bags, but decided to look in the cupboard in case we'd put any bags in there. The only things in the cupboard were Patrick's guitar and remaining records. I'd kept them, thinking that Sarah might want them.

Just then, I remembered the last time I'd searched that room and wondered if Patrick's stash was still where I'd planked it. I emptied the cupboard of the records and the guitar, and pulled back the carpet. On lifting the floorboard, I actually burst out laughing – sitting there was the Golden Virginia tin that I'd hidden twenty-five years ago. I picked it up, thinking that the contents must have disintegrated by now, and opened it very carefully, turning away from the expected cloud of dust that might escape when I prised off the lid. When I couldn't smell anything foosty, I looked at the contents. The inside of the tin was shiny clean, its former contents gone, replaced by two small keys and a laminated badge of the type worn in workplaces.

I pocketed the keys and looked at the badge.

DAVIDSON PHARMACY

Francis Hare

I couldn't grasp why I'd needed to see that badge to work out how Francis had killed Billy. I remembered Francis' stint at a chemist's shop to help out a friend when he was stuck, but had thought no more about it until now. Whatever way he had engineered it, he had access to Billy's prescriptions at source and it would have been simple for him to lift an inhaler from Billy's prescription bag and substitute it with one he'd prepared at the workshop. Even if Billy had only used it once, the concentrated fine asbestos dust that flew deep into his lungs would have been the equivalent of thirty years of casual exposure to the lethal powder that the ship workers had experienced.

I looked up Davidson Pharmacy's phone number in the Yellow Pages, but it wasn't listed. There were only two other chemists in Clydebank and both were part of large corporate groups. I tried them both and found a woman at the second shop who told me that Mr Davidson had retired shortly after selling the shop to a big chain pharmacy and that he still lived in Beechwood Drive in Bearsden. I thanked her and found the retired chemist's number easily. He confirmed that Francis had worked for him, after he had advertised the part-time job to try and ease the problems of using taxis to deliver prescriptions. He told me Francis had been very reliable, but had moved on to a job elsewhere with full-time hours.

This changed how I looked at everything. I knew now that if Billy's death was down to Francis, I would have to take a long look at all the others, although I couldn't see how he could have been involved in them all. Part of me was feeling very uneasy about what I had uncovered, but I had an overriding desperate need to discover the truth about what Francis had done to the gang members, which allowed me to ignore my inner misgivings.

I made an appointment to interview John White, ostensibly as part of a reopened investigation into Patrick's death. I hoped that he would never check this and although there wasn't much risk, I'd primed my DI some time ago by telling him that I kept tabs on the guys who'd murdered Patrick, as it was a case that had always annoyed me, and because of my friendship with Francis. Although he'd advised me to let it go, I suspect he had a grudging admiration that I was still annoyed that the guys had walked.

To get access to John, I first had to talk to his doctors. He was being kept in the semi-secure wing in Gartnavel Psychiatric Hospital and they weren't keen to let strangers near their patients, to avoid upsetting them. John White had been in and out of the place, sometimes as a result of being arrested for mindless assault or robbery, a couple of times because his family had had him sectioned and, according to the doctor who vetted me on the way in, once when he self-declared. That was his latest admission and the doc said that it was unusual in patients suffering from John's illness. He told me what it was, but I forgot to write it down and didn't want to go back and ask. All I know is that he was a mad, violent bastard.

When the doc was satisfied that I was who I said I was, and that I had a legitimate reason for wanting to interview John White, he gave me a few warnings about how he might react and what I should do if things started getting out of shape, but I felt quite safe as I was escorted to his room by the biggest brute of a female nurse I have ever seen. I was surprised when I was taken to a smallish single room with a bed and a built-in dressing table cum desk in one corner. It looked not unlike a cheap, no-frills hotel room. John White sat on the bed staring at the wall, so the nurse motioned for me to sit on the room's only chair.

"I've got to stay with you," she said. She turned to John. "John, there's a nice man here to see you."

He didn't respond. I'm not surprised; she was talking a load of bollocks. In no way would he regard me as a nice man, especially when I started asking questions.

"He can be a bit vague at times, with his medication." She spoke as if he wasn't in the room, but again, not a flicker.

"I'll manage," I said. "John," I said, turning to face him, "do you know who I am?"

No response. I tried again. "John, I've a few questions I'd like to ask you, if that's OK?"

I heard a grunt, which I took for a "Yes." I carried on anyway.

"You remember the guy you were accused of killing back in the late seventies?"

Again, a grunt. This was going to be a great interview.

"Has anyone, apart from me, been in contact with you about it recently?"

A different grunt this time. All of a sudden, he became very agitated, mumbling incoherently. I had to listen very carefully, but I could make out a word here and there. "letter", "brown letter", and "top" were really the only recognisable words.

At that point there was a knock on the door and the nurse answered it. She spoke briefly with someone, then came back in.

"I'll be five minutes, I've got a phone call I've got to take. Just watch yourself."

"I'll be OK, just carry on."

She slipped out and I tried again. "John, can you try and speak slowly and clearly, I'm having trouble understanding you."

As I was speaking I became aware of his body tensing up, but I wasn't ready when he suddenly lurched to his feet and rushed towards me. I didn't even make an attempt to defend myself, it was all so quick, but instead of attacking me, he passed by and pulled a drawer open on the desk. He pulled out a carrier bag and threw it over to me.

"Have I to look in this?" I asked, still shaken by his sudden lunge.

Another grunt. I emptied the contents of the carrier bag on to the bed. In among an assortment of loose papers, which seemed to consist mostly of DSS letters and the like, were five or six rather unusual looking envelopes, thick and heavy, gusseted, about nine inches by six. I looked at him, and he nodded towards the envelopes. I picked the first one up and looked at the outside of it. It was postmarked London and the address, presumably his home address, was on a typewritten label. It had been carelessly ripped open, so when I tried to empty it on to the bed, the contents caught on the torn edges and wouldn't come out; I put my hand in and fished them out.

There was one A4 sheet of paper. A series of different typefaces, text colour and backgrounds had been used to produce an effect similar to the archetypical ransom note typically seen in the movies. I read the note.

JohN,

HaVe ONE oN us You MuRDerInG BastArd

A GhosT

I looked at him, but he had sat down on the bed with his head between his legs.

I examined the other envelopes, which were all identical. They bore a variety of UK postmarks, and the dates made it look as if he was getting one of these letters two or three times a year. He looked up at me with hollow eyes, as if there was nobody home. He nodded towards the remaining envelopes. One of them, dated three months before, was unopened. I looked at him, and he nodded again.

I used my nail to peel open the envelope, and peered inside. Another of those notes, I could see that, but there was something small down at the bottom, so I turned the envelope upside down to retrieve it. As it fell on to my hand, I gasped and looked around.

I couldn't believe what I was seeing. I was standing in the middle of the secure wing of a psychiatric hospital with something that looked remarkably like a bag of smack in my palm.

"How the fuck did that get in here?"

It might as well have been a rhetorical question as there was no response from the recipient of the gift, who was now rocking back and forth on the seat, muttering again. I quickly gathered up all the envelopes, pocketed one, and put the rest back in the carrier bag. Stepping into the small cubicle that served as a toilet, I emptied the small bag of powder into the WC, putting the plastic bag in for good measure, wrapped in toilet paper so that it would sink, and pressed the lever to flush the toilet.

I stepped back into the room and looked at John White just as the nurse came back. The guy was a shell, and although I couldn't be sure how he'd accomplished it, I felt sure that Francis had somehow engineered his descent into madness.

~~o~~

Gallagher had been right about one thing. Big Mags White had always been a hard cunt of a woman, and even in her old age you could feel her malevolent influence on the surrounding neighbourhood. Her extended family, now including three great-grandchildren, was one of the main reasons why the millions of pounds of regeneration money that had poured into the social inclusion zone that the council estate had been designated were largely wasted; each of her offspring and their malicious progeny had their own specialised ways of terrorising the decent souls who had the misfortune to have been assigned a house in their patch.

Physically, she was a shadow of her former self, the trademark jugs that poured over her spare tyre to hang down almost to her waist were withered, the stomach itself shrunk to a hard lump, as if she was pregnant and about to deliver a bowling ball. I wondered if she had cancer or some other disease that was causing her to melt, and could imagine all the inhabitants of the estate who had hammered nails into fat Mags White dolls over the years were now quietly claiming success to themselves, and anyone else they could trust to keep their mouths shut.

Funnily enough, she was quite willing to talk to me. She had a strange relationship with the police: they generally gave her a wide berth and in return she kept her boys in check from the worst of the excesses that they could have undoubtedly unleashed on the town. She had no fear of us and could carry on a frighteningly normal conversation with our boys as if we were all business associates, but when she lost her temper, she could be the most foul-mouthed bitch you could ever meet. Unsubstantiated rumours of threats to local policemen's families and properties abounded and it may have been simply fear that kept anyone from blowing the whistle on her.

When I talked to her after my visit to her son, however, she was a pussy cat. More sad than mad, only a couple of times did anything like her famed temper erupt onto her face. Talking was obviously an effort for her, because she would make a small grunt after every sentence.

We spoke about nothing but John White. I knew that preamble and small talk was wasted on her. She told me, missing the irony, that John had been a good boy until

261

he'd got mixed up with the wrong crowd and some bastard had started him on hard drugs. I thought it was rich, coming from someone whose other sons supplied seventy-five per cent of the drugs used by the estate's junkies, that she should lay the blame for John's addiction on some mythical third party, but I didn't say any of that, of course.

He'd more or less changed overnight about twelve years before, and despite repeated attempts by her and his brothers to wean him off it, he always seemed to fall back into the slime of drug addiction. I wondered how she would have reacted if I had told her that Francis had probably been responsible, at least in part, for this state of affairs, but thought better of it, as I wanted to be able to live the rest of my life without fear of retribution through my association with Francis.

I left her, hoping, but not holding my breath, that she might have had just a glimpse of the pain and suffering her family had caused others over the years.

~~o~~

I got a phone call from Sarah roughly one weekend before I was expecting it. "You're coming through this weekend?" she asked. We very rarely spent time in Glasgow. Somehow our relationship suited Edinburgh more, perhaps because it was where it started, maybe because Sarah was more in control of it there or, more realistically, because Glasgow reminded her too much of the lowest point in her life.

My answer to her question, as usual, was, "Yes." I could rarely bring myself to refuse her invitations and when I did, it had to be for a very compelling reason. She seemed to have an instinctive knowledge of my duty rota, because I always seemed to have time off when she needed me.

As a result of our short conversation I travelled through to Edinburgh for the weekend. As we often did, we arranged to meet Andy for drinks and something to eat on the Friday night. Andy sometimes made it four with his latest girlfriend, but more often than not it was just the three of us, an arrangement that we all found remarkably acceptable. I'm sure there were some Edinburgh residents who concluded that we were a threesome!

Those weekends spent in Edinburgh with Sarah were the best times of my life. We would more often than not stay in the flat, eating food delivered from one of the many exotic restaurants in the area, watching rented films and making love to each other as little or as often as we desired. I was always amazed that her appetite, for food and for sex, often equalled or surpassed my own. On more than a few occasions, I have been met with the sight of Sarah in her most tantalising nightwear opening the door for me after my short trip over from Glasgow.

It was after a beautiful couple of hours we'd spent in bed on the Saturday afternoon that I told her we needed to talk. Instantly, I could see a shutter coming down and she looked at me with a combination of annoyance, worry and concern.

"John, I told you I can't do serious just yet. Don't go all slushy on me, please."

She had such a pleading tone in her voice at that last bit, I felt quite sorry for her, but I laughed.

"No, no, it's not about that, I promised to take it as it comes, and I am doing," I said quickly, adding "not that it's easy at times, right enough."

"Oh, that's all right. You had me worried for a moment." She paused. "What is it you want to talk about, then?"

"You're not going to like this, but hear me out, would you?"

"OK, but now you've really got me worried."

I was kneeling on the bed facing her, where she was lying, but she then got up and knelt opposite me, pulling the covers around her to keep warm.

I took a deep breath. "I have been clearing up around the place, in the house and in the workshop, and I've found a few things that are a little bit strange."

"What do you mean by strange?"

"Just shut up and listen," I said, although not unkindly.

She looked a little hurt, but she did stay quiet.

'Well," I said, launching myself at it, "I think that Francis might have had something to do with Billy Green's death, and that of some of the others."

She looked shocked but she didn't take it as badly as I'd feared. She said nothing, but put her hand over her mouth and looked a bit pale and unsteady for a few seconds. I asked her if she was OK.

"No, I don't believe it," she said, not even hearing my last question.

"Billy Green died of a type of lung cancer called mesothelioma. It normally happens in older guys who've worked all their years in shipyards, or with building contractors. It's caused by inhalation of asbestos."

I paused to see if she was taking it in.

"I found an empty inhaler in a cupboard in the workshop, and I know that Francis wasn't an asthma sufferer. I also found an angle grinder disc, an old lorry brake disc, partially ground away, and a plastic funnel, all in a sack under a pile of wood."

"So? That doesn't mean anything."

"No, but I found this." I showed her the badge. "Look at the name of the chemist on the badge, along with Francis' name. That chemist is in the middle of Clydebank, near Billy's home."

"Francis did help out a friend of his who was a pharmacist, way back, delivering prescriptions to pensioners. That's surely where the badge was from."

She hadn't stayed quiet for long, but I didn't mind. She hadn't stormed off as soon as I had started, as I was worried she might.

"I know that. I remember helping him out at the workshop when he was doing it."

"I still don't see ..."

"Francis knew that Billy was asthmatic." I told her about the case files that Francis had, and the dossiers for each of the gang.

She said nothing this time, so I continued.

"I think Francis put asbestos into Billy's inhaler."

She shook her head. "It's all too far-fetched, I think you're wrong about this."

She looked numb. I just wanted to put my arms round her and hold her, but I knew I had to finish.

"And someone's been sending John White letters with packets of heroin in them." I showed her one of the letters.

Now I could see a tear slip slowly down one cheek. I reached out and lifted up her hand. It felt cold and limp, so I reached out with both arms and pulled her towards me. She was sobbing quietly now, and I felt like an absolute shit, but I needed to tell someone and Sarah was the only person who knew Francis even half as well as I did.

I heard her mumble something, but I didn't catch what she'd said. I moved my head away, looking at her now red eyes and runny nose. I lifted a tissue from the box beside the bed and gave it to her.

"What did you say? I couldn't hear you."

"I said, it can't be right. Francis was a lovely man and even though I wouldn't care if they all died, Francis couldn't have done it. You must be wrong."

"OK, I can't prove anything, but who else would send John White letters like that? I saw the drugs with my own eyes. And why would Kevin Nolan be in the car with Francis and Deborah when they died? Have you ever really understood that?"

"I don't know why," she was almost shouting now, "but I won't believe Francis would kill someone, even monsters like them."

"I don't know why Kevin Nolan was in the car either. Perhaps he was trying to say sorry after all that time, perhaps Francis and Deborah were trying to confront him about the truth, but I presume at some point there was a scuffle, and either Kevin grabbed the wheel or Francis lost control and the car crashed. That fits in, because he didn't have his seatbelt on."

She looked at me, puzzled. "How do you know so much about this?" she asked.

"I've studied the Fatal Accident Inquiry documents, I've looked into every aspect of it, and I've just got too many unanswered questions that keep buzzing around in my head."

I didn't tell her that I had the car out the back of the workshop.

"Why didn't you tell me about all this, what you were doing?" She was close to tears again now. "I just don't understand."

"I didn't want to say anything until I was sure, that's why I didn't tell you, but I am sure now. I can't think of any other explanation."

"How can you be so sure?" she asked, obviously still doubtful.

266

"I interviewed John White; he showed me the letters and the drugs. How they got into a supposedly secure unit, I don't know. I spoke to his family. He was OK up until about ten years ago, when he started on smack. Now he's just a shell; he can hardly speak. The hospital says that every time he cleans up, he just goes back on the drugs right away. So would you if someone was sending you a quarter ounce every few months!"

I paused for a moment, then continued.

"I've asked around Billy's family. He never worked anywhere, far less with asbestos, although they did say that, as a young kid, he used to play around the shipyard rubbish piles."

I ploughed on. "I spoke to Billy's doctor. He's seen a lot of older men with asbestos related illnesses, because his practice is in the middle of what was once the biggest collection of shipyards in the world. He's never seen it in anybody of Billy's age, and he said that the men who got the disease had usually worked for years with the stuff."

"Who all knows about this?" she asked, catching me by surprise.

"Just me. And you now, of course. Why?"

"Are you going to say anything to anybody else? They'll think you're mad."

"I was going to say to Andy, but …" I trailed off.

"What?" she said

"Something stopped me, I don't know what. I think I want to find out more about it first."

"Oh."

"I don't want Francis' name pulled through the mud, either."

She still looked devastated, but less shaky than she'd been.

"Can I ask you a question?" I said

"Yes, what is it?"

"When you were with Patrick, did you ever go to fancy dress parties?"

She looked at me as if I was mad, but she answered my question with a half-smile.

"Yes, we went to one, it was about two months before he died. Why do you ask?"

"What did you both go as?"

"Not that it matters, but we went as Robin Hood and Maid Marion. I might add that he looked very good in my tights." She laughed, slightly embarrassed. I took a bet that Patrick probably had looked pretty good, but I could imagine that Sarah would have looked even better.

"Did Francis and Deborah ever get dressed up for anything, as far as you know?"

"No, I wouldn't have thought so; they didn't socialise much, and they definitely weren't party people. What has this got to do with anything?"

"When we were clearing out the house, there was a priest's outfit in a bag, from one of those better quality costume places; we thought it had maybe been Patrick's. It was an adult size, not a kid's costume."

"I still don't see where this is going."

"The hospital staff told me that two days before Billy died, he had a visit from a Roman Catholic priest. Although he was in and out of consciousness by that time and couldn't talk because his breathing was too bad, Billy was extremely agitated after he'd gone. In fact, he'd nearly died at that point after his breathing became really distressed. His family are kicking up a stink, especially with him being a Protestant, but the nurses say that they had never arranged a visit, and nobody had seen the priest until he was leaving the ward. It was quite late in the evening and none of the family were around at that point."

"You think that was Francis, don't you?"

"I can't be sure, but again, it all fits together. Don't get me wrong, none of this would stand up in any court in the land, but I know in here," I put my hand on my chest, "that it has got to be true."

Numbly, she said, "What will you do now?"

I told her that I was doing nothing until I could find a lot more about what had gone on. "But I've got to be fairly discreet about it. Even if I knew more, I don't think I'd say to Andy. I don't want to put him in a bad position. Also …" Again I hesitated. "If it ever comes out, folk will think that Andy and I might have helped Francis in some way. We could even be seen as accessories."

"What do you mean?"

"Francis and I were like, best mates. Where does that put us?"

"But you never did anything, did you?"

"No, of course not," I said, firmly, "but they might not see it that way." I looked at her, and decided that I loved her, and I needed to tell her everything. "Andy and I supplied Francis with some information before and after the trial. What you might today call a 'leak', but that was all. We just thought that Francis deserved to know what was going on. It has nothing to do with what has happened since, but if it all came out …"

She gave me a hug. "If I were you, I'd drop it and forget about it, before you get yourself in any sort of trouble." Defiantly, she added, "Anyway, even if he did it, I still think he was one of the best men I ever met and I don't feel sorry for any of the other three."

"That's part of the reason I've kept it to myself. I feel like that, too, but there's also the question of the others."

"What do you mean?"

I showed her the list I'd made eighteen months before, slightly amended.

NOLMAN

Prison, 3 – 5 yrs, serious assault Dead, RTA

SCOULAR

Dead, Weil's disease

SORNIE

Dead, murdered

PINKY

Dead, murdered

MALKY

Prison, life, > 19 yrs, 2 added for riot

BILLY GREEN

~~Ill, unknown cause~~ Dead, mesothelioma

DAVID JOHNSTON

~~Whereabouts unknown~~ Married, 2 kids, line supervisor

DEREK (SPAZ) DAVIDSON

Habitual prisoner, but released at moment Dead

JOHN (WHITEY) WHITE

~~Whereabouts unknown~~ Heroin addict, secure unit, Gartnavel psychiatric hospital

I'd folded the paper so that the three police officers didn't show; there was no point in muddying the waters.

"Do you think the other three were killed by Francis?" she said, incredulously.

"No. I know Malky killed Pinky, and Sornie was killed in prison by other inmates, so that seems unlikely. Derek Davidson was killed in a gangland shooting."

"And Scoular, what's that he died of?"

"Some liver disease he caught from rat pish."

"So what are you saying, when you talk about the others?"

"I don't know, but does it not strike you as strange that they have all died relatively young?"

"I suppose so, but how would Francis have done it? Voodoo?"

"Don't be silly, although it did cross my mind when I made that list." I smiled, weakly.

"You're just being paranoid now. I'm going to have a shower and make something to eat. Let's leave it for now."

"I suppose you're right," I said, realising how lame some of it sounded. I also liked the sound of Sarah in the shower, and Christ knows, we both needed cheering up.

From then until early Monday morning, when I drove across the M8 to work, was the best time we'd had together, and it wasn't all about sex, going out for drinks or meeting friends, although we did all three. It just seemed, for the first time, that my feelings for her were being returned in full. We weren't even particularly sickening about it – in the pub with friends of Sarah we didn't even sit next to each other, but there was just a current in the air between us. If anyone noticed, they certainly didn't comment and anyway, it was an uproarious evening, as if our feelings of well-being had spread to the whole group. We were pretty drunk when we

271

got home and when Sarah said to me quietly when we got in the front door that we could talk about Francis if I wanted, I just put my finger on her lips and said, "Ssssh," and took her up to bed. Even in bed, there was no urgency to have sex, we just held on to each other until we fell asleep.

Coming out of a deep sleep with a beautiful naked woman trying her best to get you going is the one time you don't mind being awakened in the middle of the night. I lay there for a while, pretending to be still sleepy just to enjoy her efforts to wake me up, but I could only restrain myself for so long. Afterwards she fell asleep quickly, but I lay awake and wondered exactly where I was going on this one. There was no doubt that I, commitment shy in the extreme, was now at the stage where all my senses told me to hang on to this woman at any cost. Trying to separate that from my other big problem was no easier. Obviously, pursuing any further investigation into Francis' actions would risk me losing Sarah, but deep down I thought that she would really want to know the truth, even if it was unpalatable at the time.

We spent the next day dotting about, doing very ordinary things together. I fixed a few things around her flat that had been annoying her, then we went for a walk up Arthur's Seat, which I'd never done before. It was a warm day but with a cool breeze when it blew, so we didn't stay at the top for long. We ate lunch at a little bistro place off Leith Walk and took in a film. Then, back to the flat, poached eggs on toast, and back to bed to cuddle up and watch garbage on TV.

When I left the next day she was as sad as I'd ever seen her and as I drove back to Glasgow I was savouring her long goodbye kiss and thinking that life was rosy again.

CHAPTER 13   RESEARCH

[Monday 15th December 2003]

Sometimes you can have too much time on your hands. One month later we had the quietest week there had been since I had started working in Springburn and even allowing for the amount of outstanding paperwork to be done, we were still left twiddling our thumbs. The DI gave us a bit of leeway, letting two or three of us away early each day as long as one DS and a few DCs were always to hand and the rest of us had our mobiles switched on. As a consequence of this unexpected free time, I took the opportunity to investigate the other gang members on the list.

Lee Scoular's illness, whilst having a perfectly plausible explanation, had always bothered me. I asked myself if there was any way Francis could have engineered Lee catching this Weil's disease, and I started looking at his old haunts.

I doubted whether Francis could have been personally responsible as he would have been too easily recognised by the gang or their friends and relatives, who had seen him every day of the court case. That left me with the sudden realisation that Deborah must have been involved. In the light of her and Francis being together when they were killed, and the fact that they were still legally married, I came to the conclusion that their relationship hadn't ended, that their separation was just a pretext to allow them more freedom and secrecy to prepare and implement their own form of rough justice. If Francis' involvement in Billy's death had come as a shock to me, this in its own way was worse, as it meant that Francis had effectively lived a double life for the last decade or more.

All the holidays away by himself, the hinted at girlfriend; the fact that I had been deceived, wasn't easy to take, but although it hurt, in some way I was glad I hadn't known anything. My pride had taken a dent, but I could live with that.

Unfortunately, I couldn't see how she could have infected Lee with rat's piss without risking other people's lives, and I didn't think she and Francis would have done that. How could I be so sure about that, in the light of all the other things I had got wrong about Francis? Deep down, I didn't think it was a line they would have crossed.

I ruled out Lee's home as somewhere they could have got to him. I wondered about eating places Lee might have frequented, but I thought that rat piss would have been fairly detectable and anyway, cooking food would have probably killed off the bugs. Shops were the same – there was too much risk of infecting other people for it to be practical. Pubs were the most promising places where Deborah could have doctored his food or drink, but from what I'd learned, the leptospirosis bacteria would have been highly sensitive to alcohol and the salt in crisps or peanuts would have probably killed it off. I felt that I needed to find out a bit more about the possible methods by which the bacteria could be dispensed without alerting suspicion.

~~o~~

The Mitchell Library, the largest reference library in Europe, is Glasgow's main library; a large, impressive Edwardian building, beautifully domed, with a columned frontage, and built in the days when Glasgow was the industrial city of the empire.

Inside, the main entrance opens into an enormous atrium. The balconies of upper levels give onto this open space, and the whole is spanned by an ornately decorated dome. Each of these balconied floors represents a reference section and, after referring to the building plan located on the ground floor, I made my way to the science and nature section on the fourth level. On showing my standard issue Glasgow City Council library card, I had access to over a million books, over two hundred years of newspapers, and a multitude of other documents and local publications from all areas of public life in and around Glasgow.

I found the medical section and after a bit of reading confirmed to myself that it would be difficult to infect somebody by using rat's urine in food or drink, even if you could find an infected rat. However, on further investigation using various microbiology reference books, I realised it would be feasible to culture the bacteria and use this concentrated form to infect someone, although even this was difficult, as it was still just as sensitive to being killed. I was becoming more sure that Lee Scoular had been killed by Francis and Deborah, but I needed to find how they had actually infected him and there was too much information available for me to sift through. Later that night in bed, I suddenly woke up with a jolt, as it suddenly came to me that there might be a way of pinpointing which books in the library had the information that I required.

I returned the next day, showed my warrant card to the middle-aged, rather frumpy librarian, and asked if it was possible to check if an individual had used the library, and whether there was a record of their borrowing history. She must have been bored and seen it as an exciting diversion from her humdrum routine, as she allowed me to access the computerised lending record that the library used. I was able to print off the whole of Francis' choice of reading material for the past twenty years. Some of it was scanned paper records, so it would take me some time to go through it all to find the relevant entries.

What surprised me was the amount of time that Francis had obviously spent in the library; the lending history stretched to eleven pages. There was also a record of any photocopies he had made, as there was a strict copyright policy in place. It was going to take quite a bit of time to sift through this new information.

In the meantime, I decided to approach it from another angle as well – I would assume that Francis had found a way to infect Lee Scoular, meaning I just had to find out where and when.

Over the next three days I felt like I'd visited every bar in and around Clydebank and those heading in towards the city, especially in the Dumbarton Road area, but although a lot of the bar staff remembered Lee Scoular, nobody recognised Francis or Deborah when I showed them their photographs. I went back to the box of files that I had in the filing cabinet. Billy's file wasn't the only one that had been added to – Lee's was more up to date than I remembered from the last time I had seen it and it was full of detail about his life and habits. I examined every reference to public houses contained in the notes and this gave me a list of half a dozen additional pubs, scattered around the city centre and just south of the river, which I tackled next. By the time I had repeated my questions in four of the bars, I was completely pissed off and seriously considering dropping the whole thing when, out of the blue, I had a bit of luck.

The pub's name was the District Bar and it was one of these pubs that caught a lot of the after-work trade, especially on a Friday night. Despite being on his own, and kept reasonably busy, the barman was helpful. Yes, he knew of Lee Scoular, who had been a regular a few years back, and who was OK if he was on his own but needed watching if he was with his mates. Liked to pick up shop girls, and did all right out of it. He had heard that Lee had died and was not surprised, as he thought that he'd looked really ill the last time he'd seen him.

"Real yellow, he was. At first I thought he'd had a bad fake tan, you know, like Tommy Sheridan, but he looked thin and drawn, and kind of hunched up as if he was in pain."

"Aye, he died of some liver disease caught from rats," I told him.

"Fuck's sake, how did he catch that?"

"I don't know, but that's what he died of."

"What's it to you, anyhow?" he asked, suddenly curious as to my interest.

I had a story ready if anyone asked, so I told him that I was following up an investigation into a crime in which Lee may have been involved. "A fraud case, he may have been working with this couple." I showed him pictures of Francis and Deborah. "Francis Hare, Deborah Hare, though they may have used different names, Deborah Swann, perhaps."

He laughed, and I must have looked puzzled, because he immediately explained. "It was just when you said the name there; we had a nice young Irish lassie worked here for a few months, Debbie O'Hare." He emphasised the "O" in the middle, as if to highlight the difference.

I thought quickly. "This woman has a daughter, but we haven't had any reports of her working with them. What age was she?"

He gave me a description of a decent looking Irish girl, short blonde hair, possibly dyed, glasses, medium height, late twenties, green eyes, popular with the male customers. He made a motion with his hands that indicated she had not been averse to showing off her cleavage. I tried to look disinterested, and I half-promised to let him see a picture of the daughter if I was passing by again.

"Did you ever have any money go missing or stock lifted, anything like that?" I asked him. I needed to steer him away from "Debbie" as I was beginning to realise who she might be. I could feel that horrible lead weight in my stomach again – I knew Sarah had kept in contact with Francis and Deborah, but now I had to ask myself if she was part of all this.

As soon as I could get out of the bar I phoned her and told her that I was coming through to see her the next day, as I was off over the weekend. She said that was fine, that if she wasn't there just to let myself in, the spare key would be in its usual place. I told her that there was something I wanted to ask her about, but when she pressed me to tell her what it was, I chickened out and told her that she'd have to wait till I got through. I wanted to be face-to-face with her when I spoke about all of this.

277

For the last month I had been trying to pluck up the courage to ask her if she would move in with me, but I was afraid of what her response might be. During the last month, despite our argument over Francis being involved in the deaths of Billy and the others, I felt that we had definitely become much closer. In bed, after lovemaking, she would cling on tightly to me for a while, and in and around the flat we would touch more often, and I would catch her looking at me when she thought I couldn't see her. We were now seeing each other on a weekly basis, mostly at Sarah's request. The sex was still as wild sometimes, but it was becoming more about being close than being purely physical, and I was just happy that she seemed to be beginning to feel for me in the same way that I'd felt for her from day one.

I knew I had to confront her with what I suspected; I wrestled in my own mind with the choice I had to make, but deep down I knew that even if she did admit being part of Francis and Deborah's rough justice plan, I couldn't let her go.

Back at the house that night I made serious plans to find all the clues Francis had planted, for by now I was sure that he had deliberately left me enough information to piece the whole thing together, but only if I really wanted to. He had given me an opt-out clause: I could easily have ignored the small clues which had initially made me suspicious, but for two things. Firstly, it was my job to be nosey, it's what I did for a living and pride wouldn't allow me to let it go. Secondly, I thought I had known Francis, but it seemed not as well as I thought I had.

I repeated my search of the house in light of the new information that I'd managed to unearth, but could find nothing of interest. I had been hoping to locate some of the distinctive envelopes used to send the letters and drugs to John White, or the small plastic bags that contained the drugs. Other than borrowing one of the drugs squad's sniffer dogs, I could never be one hundred per cent sure that the house that I, DS John McDaid, lived in did not have a stash of class A drugs hidden somewhere within it.

I had a quick glance at Francis' library records and I noticed that among the many and varied subjects he'd studied, microbiology and pathology titles had figured prominently. I resolved to go back to the library when I had time, and to examine the books he'd looked at to see if I could narrow down the details of his research.

I wasn't looking forward to my get-together with Sarah the next day. I was rehearsing my conversation with her over and over, getting more and more depressed. As a distraction, I made myself go over to the workshop and do something useful rather than just sit in the house, moping. I began preparing some drawer fronts for a small chest that I needed to get on with, when I hit on a good idea. I had never made anything for Sarah, so, because I knew she had a couple of pieces that Francis had given her, I spent a pleasant half hour sketching out a few ideas in one of the hardback notebooks that Francis kept in one of the bench drawers for that purpose.

It was while I was doing this that I noticed the incubator we used as a glue heater was still switched on, its little red power light glinting in a gloomy corner of the workshop. I got up to switch it off, as I wouldn't need warm glue until I was just about to assemble my next furniture project. As I absentmindedly switched it off, I suddenly realised what I was looking at. While this incubator was covered in splashes of glue and varnish and the seal on the lid did not quite fit properly, I remembered that Francis had also purchased one as a spare, in case this one had ever broken down. I couldn't remember where I'd seen it, but a quick search of the small lean-to annex at the top end of the workshop, a place we used as a clean room to varnish and polish the furniture in, turned it up in one of the cupboards below the wide central bench. It was absolutely pristine on the outside and through the glass lid I could see some clear plastic packages. I undid the incubator lid clips and realised that I had been right. The packages contained a selection of plastic and glass dishes, burettes, tubes, pipettes and other unnamed items; enough, I reckoned, to run a small but perfectly adequate laboratory. Francis had been brazen enough to store his ancient microscope next to it. I wouldn't have thought that an old thing like that would have been up to the job, but I suppose Francis' relic would have been more advanced than anything someone like Louis Pasteur had access to. I popped a sample of the various pipettes and containers in my pocket as ammunition for the next day with Sarah, returned the incubator to its cupboard, switched out the lights and headed back over to the house to try and get a good night's kip.

I woke up several times that night with random thoughts buzzing round my head, such as how Francis would have passed off the labware if anyone had asked. "Mixing varnishes, stains and wood treatment solutions accurately," I could just hear him say.

[Friday 19th December 2003]

Eventually I woke up once too often and, seeing a faint glimmer of daylight through the curtains, gave up on sleep and headed downstairs for a cup of coffee. It was no later than six thirty when I left the yard in Francis' old but immaculate Jaguar XJ6 Mark II, which I'd kept purely because I liked the luxurious purr it made when you drove it. I'd also kept his van for business reasons, but had parted with the Morris Traveller. It was an indulgence I had no time to enjoy.

Despite a slow build-up of traffic as I reached Edinburgh, and the Jaguar's sedate but stately progress, I reached Sarah's flat by a quarter to eight. I didn't want to wake her up too early, so I dozed on and off in the car, parked in the street outside, until half past eight.

There was no sign of her moving about in the flat by then and the curtains were still closed, so I found the spare key that she hid in the flowerpot at the side of the house. I was tired of telling her that she was just inviting a burglar into her house; she never paid any attention, citing twenty years of freedom from theft as a good enough reason to carry on the way she had always done. I opened the door and shouted her name, not wanting her to come to the conclusion that this was her first ever burglary and clobber me with a pan or something. There was no answer, but she could be a deep sleeper sometimes and I'd seen that her bedroom curtains were closed. She normally opened them on waking, as she loved lying in bed with the light streaming in through the stained glass leaded lights of the large Georgian sash windows. I shouted again, wondering if I dared get into bed beside her and wake her up in a less orthodox manner. Mulling over the plusses (probable sexual relations) and the negatives (causing her to have coronary heart failure) I'd more or less decided that it was worth the risk, so I crept over to her bedroom door and peeked in. My heart missed a beat, as I could see that her bed was made up. I ran through the possibilities in my mind. She could have been called into work – it occasionally happened that she'd have to get a rush flight somewhere in the world to help out in some diplomatic wrangle over the delivery of aid. She could have spent the night at a friend's house after a few drinks: unlikely, as she knew that I was coming through, although she probably expected me much later in the day. The other possibilities, while gnawing away steadily in the back of my mind, I didn't want to think about.

I knew that if she'd known she wouldn't be here, she'd have left a note. Sure enough, when I went into the kitchen there was a small white envelope on the table, addressed to me in her distinctive handwriting.

I opened it and my heart lurched. I could actually feel the blood draining out of my face.

On a small white card was one word:

"Sorry."

The prickling feeling at the back of my head now became a painful throbbing. I looked around the kitchen – nothing looked out of place and as I walked quickly through the living room, it looked the same as it had done for the past year or more, as did her bedroom. With trepidation, I opened her wardrobe doors and knew then that I might never see her again. A few items remained, obviously stuff that she hadn't liked or needed, and as I looked in the drawers of her dressing table and the bedside cabinet, finding them also empty, I crumpled, and sat on the edge of the bed, just managing to hold myself together.

My mind must have been still active because part of me was thinking about ways to find her – she still owned the flat and presumably she still had her job. I looked around, shattered, as I realised that this flat, that had seen the happiest times of my life, was now the scene of my worst ever day, as I realised that my phone call to Sarah the previous night had precipitated her sudden departure. I forlornly opened all the drawers in the kitchen one by one, hoping optimistically that she'd left some other form of communication or a clue to her direction of flight. I moved on to the living room and looked quickly around, progressing eventually to the desk that Francis had given her at some point in the past. She'd emptied all the personal stuff out of it, but had left some of the normal desk debris and some unused stationery in one of the drawers. In the bottom left hand drawer, beneath a large A3 drawing pad that would have concealed them from any casual search, I found a half-full shrink-wrapped pack of gusseted buff envelopes, identical to the ones that contained John White's supplies of heroin.

Moving on to the other side of the desk, the drawers were empty apart from a small photograph album, pocket size, and a few paper clips. I lifted out the album, and when I looked through it, I could feel my eyes pricking with tears. Most of the photographs were of her on her own, but five or six at the start of the album were of Patrick and her, and two at the back were of Sarah and me. I could only remember one of them being taken, in The Starling, a pub we used to go to in the Canongate, and I could see part of Andy's arm at the edge of the picture, holding up a pint. Sarah and I were also holding up our drinks; it was the night I had celebrated the purchase of Francis' house with Sarah and Andy.

The other picture of us together was taken in the back of someone's car. We were both laughing and she had her arms round my neck, her hair blown by the draught from an open window.

I pocketed the album, as it was the only solid evidence I had that our relationship existed. I didn't even mind the pictures of Sarah and Patrick. After all, although I'd never met him, Patrick had been as large a part of my life as anyone. I continued searching morosely around the flat, just in case any other keepsake of our time together might surface. I thought of phoning Andy and as I lifted the phone to dial, a card fell to the floor. I picked it up – it was an estate agent's business card, the address not more than half a mile from Sarah's flat.

I closed the door of the flat for the last time, pocketed the key, and drove the short distance to the address on the card. The brightly lit shop front displaying the properties for sale and to let was no guarantee that the office would be open, but as I approached the door I could see that their Saturday opening hours were 9.30 a.m. – 12.30 p.m. I entered, the bell above the door jingling as I did.

A smartly dressed bright young thing asked me if she could be of any assistance. You could tell we were in one of the better areas of Edinburgh. Recklessly, I produced my ID and told her that I was concerned for the well-being of one of her customers. I gave Sarah's name and handed her the key for the flat, telling her that I had been there and, despite assurances from Miss Anstruther that she would be at home, her bed had not been slept in and she'd left no messages with family or friends. Most of this was technically true, but I may have led her to believe that I was there in an official capacity and not on a personal mission.

The outcome of this was that she retrieved the appropriate file from the bank of cabinets behind her and showed me the contents. I made notes as I examined each page, more for effect than for any other reason because I could see almost right away that I was not going to get any help from these files – Sarah had placed the flat on the market on the Monday after I had first mentioned my suspicions about Francis, with instructions that the house should be sold quickly, with no "for sale" signs displayed, and with an early entry date. Utilities would be cancelled by the seller on her departure and would be settled by her directly.

She also told me that a sale of the contents had been arranged, and she gave me the date and the name of the saleroom. "The proceeds are to go to charity," she told me, but seemed a bit miffed that the charity chosen was based in Glasgow.

"The Patrick Hare Foundation?" I asked.

Surprised, she told me that it was.

I asked her how the sale had been settled.

"That was the unusual bit. The money from our client account was paid to her as a banker's draft," she told me.

I thanked the girl and left, telling her that we would let her know if we needed any further information and that she shouldn't worry too much about it. I then found a phone box, as I didn't want my mobile number traced, and phoned Sarah's work, which I knew had a skeleton staff on a Saturday morning. I used a technique that I'd found successful with government employees before. I asked the girl at the desk for the accounts department and was told that it was closed. I made some noises as if exasperated, and asked if she had any access to personnel lists, as I was finalising the severance package for a departing employee, Sarah Anstruther, National Insurance number KJ277497C, having made up the number, but using the correct format.

I was relying on three things. Firstly, Sarah would have been noticeable, and known and well-liked by most of her co-workers. Secondly, only the payroll department would have access to Sarah's National Insurance number. Thirdly, I sounded official, and had produced all the information that I would have been expected to know about Sarah.

She asked me to wait, then informed me that Sarah's official leaving day was the following Friday but, in an aside, she added that Sarah had two weeks holiday lying and that her leaving do had been on Friday past. I thanked her and told her that she'd been very helpful.

I nearly tore myself apart wondering. Would Sarah still have been with me if I had just let my obsession with finding the truth go? Had my insatiable desire to know cost me the best thing that had ever happened to me? Looking back, I realised that during our last month together Sarah had been saying goodbye. I knew deep within myself that by that time she had become almost as fond of me as I was of her, but whether that was enough to compete with the love she'd had for Patrick, I don't know. Perhaps she thought that I would have come to hate her for what she had done if she'd stayed with me.

I knew a few things were certain. If I traced the account that the banker's draft had been paid in to, I would find that the money had been withdrawn as cash, along with any other personal money she had, and the account closed. If I checked, Sarah's credit cards would not have been used and would probably have been returned to their issuing bank. With her worldwide contacts, her fluency in many languages, and her abilities, she could settle anywhere with complete confidence. In all probability if she didn't want to be found then it was going to be difficult for me to find her, but it wouldn't stop me trying.

I only went back through to Edinburgh once more, to the sale of the contents of her flat. I bought a couple of small items, along with the desk Francis had made for her and, rather sadly, her bed. I took it all back to the house and put it up in the loft, just in case she came back. As weird as it might sound, I couldn't stand the thought of anyone else using it.

~~o~~

I was back in Glasgow the day after Sarah had gone, thoroughly depressed, and I moped about all weekend, unable to settle at anything. For a long while afterwards every time the phone rang, I was aching for it to be Sarah on the other end of the line, but it never was. I would desperately scan the post for any sort of letter or card from her, but there was never anything other than junk mail or bills.

I had been glad to go back to work the Monday following her disappearance, hoping it would take my mind off the shambles that was my personal life. I tried not to be irritable with people, but I could see my colleagues giving me sidelong glances when I was snappy. Sure that something was up, but not wanting to ask, they started avoiding me. Word must have filtered up because the DI called me in and asked if there was anything I wanted to talk about. I told him that there wasn't and he asked me why I was like a bear with two sore heads.

I didn't want to discuss it with anyone, so I mumbled that it was just a glitch, that I would be fine, hoping it would keep him off my case, but he persisted, asking me if I was still bothered about Francis' death.

"You've never been like this. Everybody's just worried about you."

"It's not about Francis," I told him, and asked him to give me a little bit of time to sort it out.

"What about taking a few days leave, buckshee?" he asked.

Knowing that I would not get peace otherwise, I agreed to take a few days off to sort myself out. His face softened as he spoke again. "Listen, John. We go back a wee bit, so if there's anything I can do, you know where I am."

I felt sorry for fucking him about because he was one of the best DIs I'd ever worked with and I knew he was genuinely concerned about me. However, I'd sort that out later. For the moment I just needed to be on my own, to try and work out where I was going from here.

On the way back home I took my copy of Francis' library records down to The Mitchell Library and had a good look at some of the volumes that he'd signed for. Incredibly, in some of the books the pages were still folded over where he'd been reading. As a result, I could see that among the many subjects he'd covered, asbestos, mesothelioma, leptospirosis, mucoid protective layers and bacteriological culture all figured extensively. Other subjects were more obscure, and too many to mention, but strangely, home cooking, photography and information technology were amongst them.

When I got back to the house I sat myself down at my desk and made a list of the jobs that I needed to do to give myself a chance of seeing this thing through and of letting me get my life back to some sort of normality. These included looking through the Hare and Son accounts, which I knew were in a cupboard in the workshop office, and investigating Francis' computer, which I'd never got round to doing. On a more domestic note, I had to sort out the boxes and bags upstairs in the house, throw out what was not needed, and retain only the essential bits and pieces.

I started with the accounts. They were kept in old-fashioned black and red ledger books, and signed off each year by Francis' accountant, whom I'd retained for the sake of continuity. Invoices and other papers connected with the accounts were kept in box files on the shelf above the account books, one for each year.

I went back five years at first, then ten, and finally twenty-five. I found it interesting to examine the financial side of Hare and Son. Turnover had tripled in that time and although costs of supplies had gone up as well, the profit Francis made on an annual basis had steadily climbed over the years. I was also intrigued to see just how many cash transactions had been made. Most of these, as I've said before, were itemised as legitimate purchases, but not all of them could be truly verified. Cash required to finance their campaign could have been easily hidden by the hazy nature of those transactions, but it would still have taken courage and nerve to buy items like the heroin used to ensure that John White never had a chance of rehabilitation.

I was searching through the second last year, having decided that anything over twenty-five years old would be irrelevant, when I noticed a transaction from property assets to personal drawings of fifty-five thousand and five hundred pounds. I wondered if the house had been part of the business originally and that for some reason Francis

287

had decided to transfer the house to his personal ownership.

There was no detail on the accounts themselves, but in the invoice folder I was very surprised to find a transfer of deed to Sarah Anstruther of the Edinburgh flat.

I wondered if the flat had been originally destined for Patrick and Sarah and given to her after Patrick's death, or if the flat had been bought specifically for Sarah. I could have delved further back to find out which, but it was of no real interest to me. The fact alone that Francis and Deborah had given Sarah the flat showed the strength of their feelings towards her.

I then forced myself to go through the boxes and bags in Patrick's old room one last time and set most of it aside to take to the dump later. The few things I retained, I put in the filing cabinet along with my own personal stuff. As I neared the end, I noticed two boxes I was sure I hadn't seen before. The first one was sealed with tape and had a piece of folded Mitchell and Cameron letterhead marked "Deborah Hare" stuck to it; scrawled on the side was, "for hand delivery to John McDaid".

I then remembered Douglas Cameron had phoned me to say that he was dropping off what remained of the paperwork connected with the estate for me to dispose of it as I wished. He must have still had a key to the house that had allowed him to put the boxes with the rest of the stuff, and sure enough, when I looked behind the front door, a key labelled "Hare" lay on the carpet.

I used a kitchen knife to slice the tape and folded back the lid to reveal a pile of old wage slips, bank statements, household invoices and various other odd items.

The bank statements confirmed that Deborah had always worked since she "left" Francis, and that her employer had changed at least twice over the last ten years. Like Francis, she had made sizeable cash withdrawals from time to time. The household expenses were unremarkable, borne out by the quick glance through the sheaf of invoices for the last couple of years. There were one or two photographs, which I kept, and a substantial pile of letters addressed to Deborah, obviously from Francis, dated at regular intervals during the years when they'd been supposedly separated. I placed them all in a large brown envelope, sealed it, and put it at the very back of the bottom drawer of the filing cabinet.

Her pile of wage slips made interesting reading. She had worked in various places since moving down south, but her job in a microbiology laboratory for a year really stuck out. Intriguingly, she had also worked as a coordinator in the Prison Reform Group. I thought that she would have been the last person to want leniency for criminals.

When I came across Deborah's student matriculation card, I cursed my stupidity at missing the fact that, as an Open University student, she would have had the use of most university libraries and online resources, but it would have been impossible for me to find out her reading history without going through official channels and drawing attention to the fact that I was conducting my own personal investigation.

But I knew enough to be able to say, with some certainty, that Deborah would have had access to a vast additional amount of medical and scientific literature, and with her experience in the laboratory and their joint research of the whole process, Francis and she could have succeeded in extracting the leptospirosis bacteria from rat's urine, cultured it to produce significant quantities, and mixed it with some kind of mucoid gel as a delivery system, to enable them to infect Lee Scoular in one of the sandwiches I presumed he'd consumed in the pub.

I thought of going back to work the next day, but I knew that the DI would have chased me. Whenever I needed a bit of time to think clearly or, perversely, needed to be distracted from something that was bothering me, I would escape to the workroom, where I would find a task that suited my mood. It might be sharpening tools or merely tidying the place up or, if I was capable of concentrating, continuing with the next stage of whatever commission was on the go at that time.

I started by vacuuming all the benches and machines, tidying away any loose tools and pieces of wood as I did so. To access the back of the bandsaw, I moved its dust extraction unit into the passageway between the machine and the long bench. I cleaned up all around, and as I slid the dust extractor back into place it caught on the floor and tipped over, landing with a clatter, scattering shavings everywhere. I cursed loudly and continued grumbling to myself while I cleaned it all up, and eventually got the place shipshape again.

I prodded the raised board with my foot, and said to myself, "Bugger Francis, I'm going to fix this bloody board."

On closer examination I could see that the problem was not actually caused by a raised board but by the short piece of abutting floorboard being slightly depressed, leaving the edges of the surrounding planks sitting proud. I got a couple of old chisels and was considering trying to lever the plank up, but I knew I would be lucky not to damage the surrounding floor if I did that.

I was just about to give up when I noticed a thin piece of metal glinting at one end of the board, as if a nail or a staple had fallen into the joint. I tried to fish it out with a small screwdriver, but as I pressed one end of it the piece of metal disappeared with a sharp click, and to my astonishment one end of the board sprang up towards me, causing me to hit my head on an overhanging part of the bench.

After a further bout of swearing and rubbing of the painful area, I examined the lifted board. It had a small finger-sized hollow in the exposed end, allowing me to lift it up further. It was hinged in some way at the other end and it swung up to reveal a fairly large recess below. I pushed it just beyond the vertical, where it stayed of its own accord. The little spring mechanism that had held the board in place was very ingenious, especially as it was obviously handmade. It was typical of the sort of thing that Francis sometimes incorporated into his furniture.

Grabbing a torch, I peered in and could see some sort of plastic box or folder. I reached in awkwardly and grasped it and, in keeping with how the day had gone so far, scraped my knuckles pulling the thing out.

It was a blue plastic ziplock folder and through the hazy plastic I could see a set of car keys and some paper. I stood up, opened the folder and emptied the contents on to the workbench. The car keys belonged to a BMW and were on a cheap novelty key ring.

There were two other items: one was the part of the DVLC car logbook document that is retained when a car is sold. I looked at it in disbelief, not understanding how Francis had got hold of this particular piece of paper. The buyer of the car had been Malky McGovern and the seller a Mrs Sylvia Fowler of Giffnock, Glasgow; the date of transfer was the 14th of February 1998.

I went over to the house, looked up the phone book and dialled Mrs Fowler's number, figuring that she would be in, Giffnock being the part of Glasgow with the highest percentage of wives who don't have to go out to work.

She answered after about six rings. I asked her if she was Mrs Sylvia Fowler and she distrustfully confirmed that she was, probably thinking I was somebody trying to sell her a new kitchen or double-glazing.

"Don't be alarmed in any way," I warned her, "but my name is Detective Sergeant John McDaid, and I am following up on an inquiry from a few years ago that involved a car that you once owned. Can I ask you a few questions?"

"Oh," she said, "that's a bit unusual. What's the investigation?"

I told her it was a murder, that someone had been imprisoned for it, and that I was investigating a related crime.

"Well," she said, obviously excited that she would have something to tell her friends about when they next met for coffee, "I'll try and help as much as I can."

I asked her if she remembered the car, and gave her all the details, including the registration number.

"Oh, yes, I remember that car. Ronnie bought it for me for my thirtieth birthday, it was lovely. Ronnie's my husband, by the way."

"Right, that's good, but you sold it in 1998 to a Malcolm McGovern, is that right?"

"I can't remember his name. Nice chap; Ronnie took care of everything to do with it."

"Would Ronnie remember his name? Can I speak to him?"

"Not at the moment, he's out of the country on business, but he'll be back in a week."

I told her that I would probably phone him when he came back.

On a sudden impulse, I asked, "This guy, what did he look like?"

"I would say quite tall. Slim-ish, in his late forties, quite distinguished looking."

"Are you sure about that?" I asked.

"Yes, he came in for a cup of tea, he was very polite."

"Did he pay by cheque or by cash?" I asked, but I already knew the answer.

"He gave us cash, I do remember that. Ronnie wouldn't hear of anything else, and the man had brought enough with him. Ronnie was going to do the paperwork for him, but the man said that he would do it himself as he wanted to get away."

I thanked her for her time and repeated that I would phone her husband if we needed any further information.

But I knew that I didn't need to.

I put all the stuff back in the folder and replaced it in its hiding place, closing the board over with a soft click. Once I had brushed a little dust over the edges, you would never have known that there was anything there.

I was having quite a productive day and, on a roll, I decided to look again at Francis' computer. I had paid very little attention to it, but after having found so much stuff elsewhere I cursed myself for not looking at it in a bit more detail before now. On closer inspection of the rear panel, I saw that Francis had fitted a card slot reader into one of the expansion bays. These are normally found on notebooks to take PCMIA cards. The card in one of the slots was a Vodafone mobile card and I removed it, excited now at the possibility that the phone call that had been made on Francis' mobile from the car had perhaps been made to this card. I removed the SIM card from it and placed it in my own phone. It was a pay as you go SIM, and a quick check of the Fatal Accident Inquiry transcript showed that it was indeed the same number that had been phoned the night of the crash. Obviously, Francis had bought a phone second-hand for cash and discarded it after removing the SIM. As long as he hadn't topped it up, the SIM, and its associated mobile number, would have been virtually untraceable.

I switched the computer on and waited for it to start up. I'd briefly looked at the PC before, but only in passing, and had almost thrown it out as it seemed to contain only personal stuff belonging to Francis, and a bit of business material.

However, this time I was more thorough. I discovered that the hard disk had been split into two partitions and there was a separate drive assigned to each partition. The E: drive had been renamed and its icon changed, so it wasn't immediately obvious that it was another drive. When I tried to access it, a message saying that the drive was encrypted flashed up on the screen, and asked for a sixteen digit encryption key to unlock it. I had no idea what the code would be, so I contacted Bruce Davidson from our Computer Crime Investigation Unit. He was a specialist in retrieving data from computers, if it was encrypted, corrupted or even in some cases, deleted, and was especially revered by the Serious Fraud Department and the Child Sex Crime Unit for his ability to get evidence from virtually any computer disk that was presented to him. I had used his department on quite a few occasions over the years and I'd also played football with him briefly for the Strathclyde regional team, although he was much younger than me.

I knew him well enough to ask if he could do a "homer", which was handy, because I could pass it off to him as my own computer's hard disk that had inadvertently been encrypted and say that I had no idea of the password. Because he was based at Pitt Street there wasn't much danger of me being spotted and word getting back to the DI that I was not at home recharging my batteries.

It took Bruce no more than ten minutes to unlock the hard disk's hidden partition, so I thanked him, chatted for a while about football and told him that I owed him a pint. He transferred the contents of the drive to a CD-R for me to make things easier. When I got back to the house I put the hard disk back in the computer out of the way, slipped the CD-R disc containing the decrypted files into my laptop, and opened it up in File Manager. I quickly searched around, copying interesting looking files to an empty directory on my C: drive as I went. The files ranged from business documents, mostly Word files or spreadsheets, to media files and photographs, mainly of furniture. There were a few downloaded videos, but most of the media files were music – there were hundreds of MP3s. I clicked on a few at random, and the files opened up in Windows Media Player, filling the room with instant music. It took me back to some of the journeys that Francis and I had taken around the country, listening to his music on the tape player in his van.

Getting back to work I noticed a larger than usual MP3 file, about twenty megabytes instead of the more normal three you would expect for a typical song. I clicked on it to open it up, and a new window opened on my desktop informing me that, "This file requires a password for viewing". I tried "Glenhill", remembering it from my first foray on Francis' computer, but that didn't work. I ran through all the passwords I could think of, even the obvious ones that Francis would have been unlikely to choose, "Hare", "Francis", "Deborah", "Patrick", I tried their middle names, "Peter", "Anne", and Deborah's maiden name, "Swann". Every time I tried a password the screen blinked and the message "Password Invalid – Please try again" flashed above the small white box where I entered each unsuccessful attempt.

I tried multiple variants of each password, upper case, lower case, lower case with first capital, but still got that infuriating message. I knew that I should be able to guess it – I was convinced that Francis had left everything so that if I really wanted to, it would be possible to access it. I tried all of Sarah's names, Francis' phone number. Hell, I even tried all of my own names.

I went through Francis' favourite books, films that we'd talked about and records that we'd listened to. I tried tools, wood types, names of joints and names of the workshop machines, like "DeWalt" and "Sedgwick". I started going through significant street names, birthdays, I even tried the name of the trial judge and all the names of the police officers involved. I went back to Patrick, this time giving "Pat" and "Paddy" a go.

Once or twice I lost my temper and entered some random abuse as the password, just to make me feel better when it was rejected, but mostly I kept at it, taking a break now and then. In the end I had to give up, if only for my sanity. I considered going back with the file to Bruce Davidson to see if he could unlock it for me, but I knew that I'd be pushing my luck, so I left it, meaning to go back to it in a couple of days with a fresh mind.

Looking elsewhere on the DVD, I opened a folder labelled "Mac" and examined its contents. I'm reasonably useful with computers as long as it doesn't involve anything too technical, so I was usually able to tell what type of file I was dealing with from its three-letter extension; I knew

"Cabinet.jpg" was a picture and "Letter.doc" was a Word file, for example. All the files in this particular directory had the same extension, ".MCF", which I didn't recognise. I quickly googled "MCF file extension" and discovered that it was an old type of file format used by early versions of Photoshop on the Apple Mac, and it wasn't compatible with current Photoshop versions for the Mac or Windows. I tried searching for filters and file converters on the Internet, but came up with nothing, becoming even more frustrated.

I went to the desk and in the pile of papers that had gradually built up since I had moved in, I found the printout I had made of programs that had been running on the computer at the time of the crash. I went back to the computer and went through the list, trying to identify each program or process. Most of them were programs that you'd expect to be running, but I found one called RECDMBL.EXE that showed up on none of the file identification sites. I tried the name in Google and was directed towards a file-sharing site. The program was described as a small freeware background utility for recording telephone conversations on a notebook connected to a mobile phone network, and although I couldn't get into it, I knew for sure that the large MP3 file was a recording of the phone call Francis had made from the car.

Still discouraged, I left that for a while and browsed through the rest of the files. In among them were the letters that had been sent to John White, and the address labels for the envelopes.

Not getting any further with the computer I took a break and, thinking about the hiding place under the floorboards, I started wondering if Francis had a multitude of hiding places, and groaned inwardly, wondering what the chances of finding them would be.

I started in the workshop, first checking the floor, but all the other floorboards looked normal and I assumed that any hiding place would be "identifiable" in some way. I started looking elsewhere. I tapped benches, looking for hollow places, the backs of cupboards, the bottoms of toolboxes. I measured and compared internal and external measurements, hoping to find a discrepancy. After I'd thoroughly searched the workroom, including the office, I moved over to the shop. Rather sparser, it was easier to check and it didn't take me long to draw a blank.

Moving on to the house, I concentrated initially on furniture that I knew had been made by Francis or his father, because I'd heard him say that he often would put little hidden compartments in his furniture at clients' requests. I think the customers may have used them as a secret store for cash or valuables, which was not very effective if a thief made off with the whole thing. If drug dealers could have afforded it, Francis' furniture would have been an ideal place to hold their stash!

I continued, checking the bed for hollow posts and the wardrobes for sliding panels, but I found nothing.

When I went into the den I looked at the desk and suddenly realised I should have looked at it first. *The drawers. Different sizes. Remember?* I thought to myself. I was getting too old for this; my brain just wasn't as quick as it used to be.

I pulled out the drawers again, this time labelling them to make putting them back a simple process.

The left hand drawers were about three inches deeper than the right hand ones. I measured the internal measurement of the right pedestal, and measured the outside. There was a four inch difference. Shining my torch through the space where the top drawer had been, I could only see the two drawer runners, the wood that divided the cavity off from the next drawer down, and the back of the cavity. There were no catches or movable panels or anything, so I tried the other drawer spaces, but they were the same.

I pulled the desk out from the wall and looked at the back. Definitely made by Francis, I could see the plate with his name on it, and the date: 1957, nearly as old as me.

Unusually for the back of a piece of furniture, he had dovetailed the frame holding the back panels in place.

Most would have considered it a waste, but I wouldn't have put it past Francis and his quest for perfection. However, I began to think that perhaps the dovetails were there for a reason. I got a magnifying glass and started by comparing the dovetails on the left side of the desk with the dovetails on the right. There was a difference, when you looked really closely: not all of the right hand ones were glued. I counted ten that weren't. I pressed a few of them but, although there was a tiny bit of give, nothing much happened. A single dovetail is made up of a pin which fits into a socket. These were quite big, as dovetails go. Despite not being glued, the craftsmanship was so good that you could not have got a single sheet of paper in the gap between the tails and the sockets. I knew that I could get in behind the panel by attacking it with a saw, but I couldn't bring myself to destroy Francis' work; I could almost feel him behind me looking over my shoulder.

One by one, I went down each dovetail, pressing each corner, pressing the middle, until I got to the last one, at the very bottom. Again, I should have realised. It was the one that would be least likely to be pressed by accident.

It only moved in about one millimetre, but it moved. I then tried the next one and now it did the same, and so on, all the way up to the top, apart from the last one. When I pressed it, the others popped back out. I repeated the process. The others only seemed to work if I pressed the bottom one first. That left nine, excluding the top one. I pressed them all again and tried to slide the panel, but it wouldn't budge. I pressed the top one again and tried different combinations, but had no success. I realised that I wasn't going to get it by luck. I figured that it was likely that each dovetail represented the digits one to nine, with no zero.

The most obvious series of digits to press was the date on the nameplate, 1957, so I tried it. I took one to be the bottom and nine the top, and pressed the dovetails in order.

Nothing.

I tried it the opposite way round, taking nine as the bottom number.

Nil.

I tried the date reversed, top to bottom and bottom to top.

Niente.

Bugger this, I thought, *there's more to it than that*. I thought of other significant numbers, but none of them worked. Then I remembered that Patrick was born in 1957, it surely had to be his birthday. I had to look it up, but quickly found that it was the thirteenth of May.

I wrote down 13/05/1957.

Zeros weren't an option, so I wrote it out again, without the zero or the backslashes.

1351957

Still it didn't work. I was convinced that it had to be Patrick's birthday, but as each attempt failed I began to see the saw as a more attractive option, when I suddenly thought that there was no point in repeating any numbers. I scored out the second one and the second five.

1351957

I pressed the top pin to reset the mechanism and tried the five numbers in order, and as I pressed the seven there was a loud click and all the dovetails slid in about an inch. I pushed gently on the back panel, sliding it down about two or three inches, revealing a dark, slim recess behind it. I thought that it was empty, seeing nothing in it at first. Disappointed, I slid my hand in as far as it would go, just able to touch the bottom, but even if I moved my hand along the length of the compartment from one end to the other, I couldn't feel anything there. I thought it strange, but I could feel that he'd lined the back of this compartment with some sort of card or paper. I got a torch from the kitchen drawer and shone it in. What I had assumed was a lining paper was in fact the back of a manila envelope almost identical in size to the size of the recess. Because it was such a snug fit, I couldn't get a grip of it to extricate it. I tried various tools to try and catch the edge of the envelope, to no avail, but eventually hit on the idea of some very strong duct tape, which I stuck on to the envelope with an opened paper clip underneath for me to grip it with. As I pulled, the tape started to pull off in the middle, but the envelope had moved enough for me to get my finger behind it and slide it out into the light.

I would have loved to have seen how the mechanism worked, but I knew that to find out I would have to take it apart and I didn't think I could do that without damaging it.

There was no writing on the outside of the envelope, but it was sealed. I used a paper knife to carefully open one end and tipped the contents out on to the top of the desk. There was a slim sheaf of papers and a plastic clip badge with Deborah's name and photograph on it. It was an access badge for Barlinnie prison, describing her as an Official Prison Visitor connected to the Prison Reform Group.

I looked through the papers excitedly hoping to find something significant, but at first glance there was just a newspaper clipping, invoices, and delivery notes.

There were quite a few of those; most were almost identical receipts from a wholesale wine and beer merchant, each for a crate of twelve bottles of The Gordon Highlanders Scotch Whisky or William Grant's Blended Whisky. There was also part of a carbonised copy of a receipt for a delivery company I'd never heard of, Speedy Parcel Delivery, whose marketing slogan was the catchy "Local Delivery – Local Price". I judged from this that it was probably two guys with a Transit van who sought to undercut DHL and UPS, but only if you wanted your parcel delivered within the Glasgow area.

The delivery address was missing, but it was dated 12/4/82. The office phone number was on the sheet, but when I phoned from my mobile the person who answered said that they had never heard of the company and that I'd phoned a private number. I apologised and hung up, not surprised at the demise of the Speedy Parcel Delivery company.

I took my list from my wallet. It was still folded over, showing only the gang's names. I slowly unfolded it and looked at the names of the three detectives, and wondered.

There was an invoice for the laboratory supplies I'd found in the incubator, which also showed quantities of various growth media that I knew from my library research were needed for bacterial culture.

The newspaper clipping described the outbreak of Weil's disease that Catherine Carr had spoken about. Francis had underlined some of the key areas. This must have been his inspiration for their method of dealing with Lee Scoular.

I turned the last sheet of paper over and found a photograph stuck face-down to the back. I carefully peeled it off, trying to avoid damaging it, and I almost succeeded, apart from a little piece in the centre, which was now an irregular white patch where the film had lifted away from the backing paper. It was a photograph that I recognised. Francis had used it for the front of one of the brochures that he had printed every two or three years to display in the shop, hand out at exhibitions, or to send after receiving postal or phone enquiries. It was a picture of the whole frontage of Hare and Son and he had taken it on a sunny day, when the old stonework contrasted with the glossed green wood of the gates, the shop door and the window surrounds. The windows themselves had reflections only in the corners, and the furniture displayed inside clearly stood out from the cloth backdrop. It looked very classy and had been ideal for the cover, summing up the timeless qualities of "Hare & Son, Cabinetmakers". I thought how it was strange that I noticed more looking at the photograph than I could remember from seeing the outside of the building a thousand times.

I looked more closely at the stonework. The craftsmen who built it had obviously taken a great pride in their work; there were some unusual details that elevated it from the humdrum, but it was so subtle that you only noticed when you looked closely.

I could see nothing helpful on the picture and I was just about to put it to one side, when I thought that just to make sure I ought to check the photo against the building. I quickly went out into the yard, stepped through the green yard gate and crossed to the other side of the road.

I was now looking at the building from where the photograph had been taken. I looked at it for a few seconds and I suddenly spotted what was missing from the photograph; something that I had so often seen before, but until now had never taken much notice of. Above the double gates, set into the large sandstone block at the top of the stone arch, was the year that the building had been constructed – 1872

Exasperated that Francis had made it so complex for me to get to this stage, I practically ran to my laptop in the den and impatiently waited for it to start up. As usual, it took forever, and even after the Windows logo had disappeared and the desktop was displayed, the little hourglass cursor seemed to persist for another five minutes. When I was finally able to open up File Manager, I went straight to the large MP3 file that had so intrigued me and tried to open it up. When asked for the password, I entered "1872" and banged the desk in triumph when Windows Media Player opened up and started loading the file.

I sat down and waited until it had finished loading. Just then, the phone rang. It was Andy, wanting a chat. I found it difficult to concentrate on our conversation and I'm sure Andy must have picked up on it, because he asked me three times during the call if I was OK. I'd already clicked the pause button to stop the clip from being played, so I wasn't worried about him hearing it, but I was desperate to find out its contents. Eventually, I managed to get him off the phone without appearing rude or arousing any suspicion that I was going off the rails. I took the phone off the hook and turned to the computer again.

CHAPTER 14   RESOLUTION

I played the clip. Then I played it again. I still couldn't believe what I was hearing. I got up and checked every room just to make sure that nobody else was in the house. Irrational, I know, but I just had that feeling that nobody else should ever hear it apart from me. I sat down again and played it once more. I made a transcript as I went along, as if it wasn't already etched into my mind anyway. For years afterwards I could, at any point, hear the full thing just by closing my eyes. I couldn't quite write fast enough, so I had to keep pausing the clip to catch up. I'll let you read it in its entirety, as that's the way I heard it first. I've also included some descriptive notes: noises inside the car, other vehicles passing, etcetera, etcetera. It sort of fills in the gaps.

DEBORAH

Do you think he realises who we are yet?

FRANCIS

I don't know; why don't you ask him?

NOLMAN

What ye sayin'?

DEBORAH

Michael; that's your real name, isn't it?

NOLMAN

Aye, Michael McBride. Why? Whit's it tae you?

DEBORAH

You know how you got this lift? Your friend Stevie knew someone who was coming up to Glasgow, could give you a lift?

NOLMAN

That's right, Stevie Sweeney, whit about him?

FRANCIS

Well, we gave him a couple of grand so he would organise that you would be getting a lift with us back to Glasgow, Kevin.

[Conversation paused, sound of car indicator, sounds of another engine, as a van or small lorry is passed, indicator sound repeated]

FRANCIS

Well?

NOLMAN

You're talkin' shite, man. Ah needed a lift up frae Birmingham and he said he knew someone that wis goin' up. And I don't know where you're gettin' aw that crap about me bein' called Kevin, ma name's Michael.

DEBORAH

Ah, that's where you're wrong, Kevin. We know exactly who you are. You're Kevin Nolan, aren't you?

FRANCIS

Know who we are, Kevin?

NOLMAN

Naw, I've never seen you before, an' I'll tell ye sumfin', I'm gettin really hacked off wi aw this, ya pair of cunts. Ye can let me aff at the next service station an' Ah'll get a lift wi' some other cunt, right.

FRANCIS

Kevin. [Short pause] That's not going to happen, you're staying right here with us.

[Sounds of something rattling, a few grunts]

NOLMAN

Listen, I don't think ye knaw who ye're dealin' wi' here, ye're fuckin' wi' the wrong guy, man. I'll fuckin have ye when Ah get out ay this seat belt.

[More noises of struggling, muttering, odd swear word]

NOLMAN [Shouting]

WHAT THE FUCK, WHAT'S THE MATTER WI' THIS FUCKIN' BELT; IF AH CANNAE GET THE CUNT OOT, AH'LL CUT THE FUCKER AFF.

[Extended sounds of struggling, swearing, then clattering sound, small squeal from Deborah]

FRANCIS

No point in losing the plot, Kevin, it'll do you no good at all. I mean, that knife could've hit one of us. By the way, the seatbelt looks normal enough, but it's locked tight and is made of a tough nylon webbing reinforced with fine steel wires, so it would be impossible for you to cut or break it in any way. It would take an angle grinder to get through it.

DEBORAH

Kevin, do you still not know who we are?

NOLMAN

305

NAW, AH FUCKIN WELL DON'T, AN' AH DON'T GIVE A FUCK, EITHER. FOR THE LAST FUCKIN' TIME, LET ME OUT, YA BASTARDS, YE.

[There was a pause, and I presume that Francis turned round at this point]

NOLMAN

Aw for fuck's sake, it's you. Jesus, what the fuck are you doin'?

FRANCIS

Well, Kevin, we've been meaning to have a little talk for some time now, but we've had a few things to deal with first.

NOLMAN

What ye talkin' about, ya mad cunt? I nearly didnae recognise ye wi' that beard ye've got. Ah widnae hae got intae the car wi' ye if Ah'd kent. Listen, if this is about yer son, we wernae the ones whit done it; the courts cleared us. You were there, ya daft bampot.

DEBORAH

No, Kevin, the verdicts weren't "not guilty", they were "not proven"; and you, us and everyone else in the world knows that you were all as guilty as hell, so don't even start.

FRANCIS

Kevin, before you get out of this car you are going to tell us exactly what happened that night. If you don't, this car is going to hit a concrete wall at over one hundred miles an hour. You will die, as will we, but that won't matter because you really killed us twenty-five years ago when you murdered our son.

NOLMAN

Listen, ya pair o' cunts, I'm tellin' ye that A didnae kill onyone's son, right. Wance and fur all, wid ye stop the fuckin' car and let me out.

[Car engine sound gets louder with higher pitch, sudden rapid thumping of catseyes, squeal of tyres]

NOLMAN [Shouting]

FUR FUCK'S SAKE, NO, NO [SCREAMS] YE'LL KILL US AW. Just slow doon an' Ah'll tell ye whit ye want.

FRANCIS

That's better, you'll be OK as long as you give us the honest truth.

NOLMAN

Are you cunts tapin' this? Cos if ye are, I'm no sayin nu'hin'.

[Sound of engine tone increasing again]

NOLMAN

OK, OK, YA BASTARDS, GIE'S A MINUTE, WID YE.

[Sound only of steady engine noise, heavy breathing for a couple of minutes, gradually subsides]

FRANCIS

Right, you've had enough time. We're not taping it, by the way. Start with this – had you met Patrick before the night you killed him?

NOLMAN

Fuck aye, man, he'd been round some o' the pubs we went tae, sometimes wi' his tart or his pals in tow, but sometimes on his own. Came once wi' his ain tart an' another wee skinny tart, right funny lookin' thing, ye widnae ride her fur money. [PAUSE] Listen, Ah need a fag, Ah've dropped ma packet, can yehs let me get them?

307

DEBORAH

No, I'll get them for you. [Pause, sounds of movement] There. Do you have a light?

NOLMAN

Yes, Ah've got one here. [Pause, sound of lighter, fizzle of cigarette being lit, long exhalation] Can Ah open a windae?

DEBORAH

No, we'll open one at the front. [Sound of window being wound down, rush of air – next part of conversation more difficult to hear]

FRANCIS

Carry on, Kevin, please

NOLMAN

Well, he was a bit smart assed, like, thought he wis wan o' the boys, swannin' down tae our haunts and thinkin' he could make himsel' at hame. Thing was, a lot of thae older bastards, pals o' ma faither an' that, they thought he was aw right, but hawf o' them widnae even say a word tae us, thought we were scum. Anyway, we'd gi'en him a warnin' about two weeks before, then Sornie tells me he saw him and his tart in the Bracken, pallin' it up wi' some cunts fae wan o' the works, just laughed when Sornie went up tae him and told him tae beat it. They others told Sornie tae fuck off an' all.

FRANCIS

So did you go looking for Patrick, then?

NOLMAN

No, fuck man, we wis just goin' alang Dumbarton Road intae town, huvvin' a few bevvies alang the way, when up pops yer boy and his tart. Now, that wan Ah would've gie'n a length tae, sorry tae offend ye like, but ye did ask fur the truth, Ah'm just bein honest, man.

FRANCIS

Just keep to the story. So you thought you'd follow him home, put the frighteners on him?

NOLMAN

Naw, it wisnae really like that, we wis just noisin' him up a bit, giein' him a bit of the verbals, an' he wisnae so clevir this time, wi' the girl there an' that, so we wis just tryin tae get him tae shite himsel', gie us a bit of respect, man.

DEBORAH

So what happened? Did Patrick say something back to you? Why did you attack him?

NOLMAN

Naw, he said nu'hin' at first, but then Sornie came out wi' a line about yer man taken his doll up the arse, and the boys were pishin' themsel's laughin'. So we stood around for a few minutes, letting them slink away hame. He wisnae such a smart cunt then. We went across the road an' got a couple mair pints ae swallow, an' when we came back out, who did we see but yer boy again. He took wan look at us and started runnin' back the way he'd came frae. Well, Sornie was still annoyed wi' the cunt, an' he was fairly jaked wi' the drink an' that, so he chases him; he's a wee fast cunt, Sornie, when he gets intae gear. Well, he must have been nearly home when Sornie caught him, an' he tried to shove his way past an' up the close, but Sornie just blocked him aff. We all caught up with him and kinda surrounded him. He was giving us a load of shite about how it had gone tae far, and he had some money we could have, an' that. Ah said tae him that it wisnae aboot the money, it was aboot him tryin' tae be a smart cunt an' aw that. Ah wis fuckin angry by that point, and the rest of them were an' aw, so I just pushed him a bit, but the cunt sorta pushed me back, so I nutted him. After that, Sornie and the rest joined in. To be honest, Ah can't remember a whole lot after that, we'd aw buzzed some glue earlier, an' wi' the booze an' that, we wis a bit wrecked. Next thing I know was, Ah was jumpin' on his heid, an' Davo was trying to pull us aff the cunt. Ah could see a pool of blood at his heid, an' Ah knew masel' that we'd hurt the cunt.

Each time I'd got to this point, I'd had to pause the clip. I couldn't imagine what Deborah and Francis would have been feeling at this stage, but in my mind I could see Deborah sitting up straight, tears falling quietly down her cheeks, Francis stony-faced and grim, knuckles white as he gripped the steering wheel. Once Kevin Nolan's confession had started, he seemed to almost be enjoying it. The way he was talking about Patrick, it was as if he was talking to a couple of strangers, not to his victim's parents. There was no remorse shown, or any attempt to spare them the brutal details. While it wasn't actually boasting, it was almost as if he had no understanding of how his actions might affect other human beings.

I poured myself a glass of whisky, and took a deep swallow. I clicked on the play button to restart the clip.

FRANCIS

What happened then?

NOLMAN

Next thing Ah knew, Ah was runnin' alang Dumbarton Road wi' Whitey and Scoular. Sornie, Billy, Davo, Pinky and Spaz had headed the other way, up towards Maryhill and out that way. Nae buses at thon time, but it didnae bother us, a bit o' a walk, we'd sometimes walk fuckin' miles tae get hame after a night oot. By the time Ah got hame, Ah was nearly fuckin' sober. Ah realised we'd done sumhin' a bit heavy, but Ah was fucked from baggin', along wi' the drink. Well, Ah got up the next mornin', man, there was blood on ma shoes an' on ma bed an' everythin'. Ma old dear came in an' she said Ah was a silly cunt, and got aw ma gear aff me and told me tae get in the bastard shower.

FRANCIS

Did your mother get rid of the clothes and stuff for you?

NOLMAN

Naw, she just put it in the machine an' washed it aw. She said that the cunts wouldnae find it if it wisnae bright red and hit them in the napper. Ah cannae remember whit day the fuzz came tae the hoose, thon big cunt Gallagher tried it on wi' ma old dear, but she told him where tae get aff. Ah spoke tae a few o' the boys, and we worked oot a story which would hae been fine, but Ah knew aw they cunts widnae stick tae it. Then when Malky came roon tae ma bit, he had heard whit went doon and was real pissed at missin' the fuckin' thing. But that was tae work oot aw right for us, man, 'cos he came up with this idea of confessin', an' if anyone else squealed, it wid fuck the polis up rid rotten.

FRANCIS

So you knew before the trial that Malky was going to set the prosecution up for a fuck up?

NOLMAN

Aye, we thought Pinky or Davo would be the wans, but we hadnae thought the pigs wid be clever enough tae keep Billy's inhaler aff him until he ratted on us an' aw. We didnae really blame the wee cunt onyhow, it wis right nasty whit they cunts did tae him.

FRANCIS

So it was definitely Malky's idea for him to give a false confession?

311

NOLMAN

It wis really Malky's, but Ah caught on as soon as Ah heard. Thae polis was fuckin stupid, man, thought they were too guid fir us.

FRANCIS

And when did the lawyers know about Malky?

NOLMAN

Malky told one of his lawyers early on, no' the big heid yin, but he told him that he should shut up, no' tae tell anyone until he gie'd the go-ahead. So that was whit happened, and we got away wi' a few months on remand, then oot. That was some night that night, when we got released at the end of the trial. Funny thing was, Ah wore ma underwear frae the night we done him fir the whole trial, fir luck, like. Put them bastardin' pigs in their place, if they kent.

FRANCIS

Kevin, is that everything, then? Was anyone else involved?

NOLMAN

Naw, the wans Ah've spoke aboot, that's aw.

FRANCIS

Your mates haven't done very well, have they?

NOLMAN

Whit? They've just been unlucky, man. Poor bastards.

FRANCIS

You're the only one left, no?

NOLMAN

Naw, Ah still see Whitey noo an' again, although his brains is fucked, if ye ask me.

FRANCIS

And all the rest are dead?

NOLMAN

Naw, ya cunt, they're no'. Big Malky's in the jail.

FRANCIS

And the rest?

NOLMAN

Aye. Don't know aboot wee Davo Johnstone, we never seen him efter the trial, he fucked off an' widnae hae nu'hin' tae dae wi' none o' us

FRANCIS

Do you want to know why most of them are dead?

NOLMAN

You sayin' you had somethin' to do with it? Yer a mad cunt, so ye are.

FRANCIS

Let's say we helped them along. Billy, Lee, Derek, Stewart, James, all of them. John, he's not doing so good these days; Malcolm, well, look where he is.

NOLMAN

No way, you are full of shite, the pair of ye.

FRANCIS

Oh, I think you know that what I'm telling you is the truth.

[Sounds of slight movement, then no sound except for the low drone of the car]

FRANCIS

Billy Green, remember what he died of?

NOLMAN

Aye, fuckin' asbestos, wasn't it? So what?

FRANCIS

Billy never worked a day in his life, far less with asbestos; work that one out.

NOLMAN

He was always around the docks, an' stuff, he could hae got it there.

FRANCIS

Recognise this?

NOLMAN

That's an inhaler, like the wan Billy used tae huv.

FRANCIS

No, it is the one Billy used to have.

NOLMAN

So, the pigs took one away tae try and get him tae spill. Did you take Billy's away when the poor cunt wis dyin'?

FRANCIS

You're a bit slow, Kevin. Have a think about it. How did Billy get the asbestos into his lungs?

NOLMAN

What the fuck are you going on ab...? Oh, you cunt, ye didnae, did ye?

FRANCIS

Well done, Kevin, we got there in the end.

NOLMAN

That disnae mean that ye did the rest o' them.

FRANCIS

OK. Scoular. What did he die of?

NOLMAN [Huffily]

Ah don't ken, some kind of disease frae rats.

FRANCIS

Yes, that's right, normally caused by drinking water contaminated with rat's urine. How did Scoular get it? Not water skiing, for sure.

NOLMAN

How can you gie someone rat's pish? Don't tell me yer tryin' tae say ye did.

FRANCIS

No, I didn't, but someone else did. You know that nice looking girlfriend of Patrick's? Well, she took a job in a pub. The District Bar. You know it?

NOLMAN

Aye, used to go tae it sometimes wi' nice totty, bit poncy, though.

FRANCIS

I'll make it easy for you. Sarah put contaminated rat piss in a cheese and onion sandwich, which she gave him as a freebie for a "favourite" regular. I think he took a bit of a shine to her.

NOLMAN

Naw, ye are talking shite now, I don't want to listen to any more of this crap. He would have recognised her, onyhow.

FRANCIS

See the woman that got out of the car when we picked you up?

NOLMAN

Aye, so whit?

FRANCIS

She looks a bit different, all done up; short hair, glasses, coloured contacts, bit of make-up, tarty clothes. Lee didn't recognise her either.

NOLMAN

That wisnae her, wis it?

FRANCIS

You'll just have to take my word on that, Kevin.

[A few minutes pause, sounds again of struggling and muttering]

FRANCIS

Here, Kevin, have a look at these.

[Sounds of movement]

FRANCIS

Recognise these pictures, Kevin?

NOLMAN

That yin's Sornie, [Pause] Fuck, what's that, it's some kid getting shagged, that's fucking rank, man, are you some kind of perv?

FRANCIS

Here.

NOLMAN

How the fuck! No way would Sornie be intae that shite. He liked a bit of right dirty sex, but only wi' birds over the age, like. Did you get that picture done by someone?

FRANCIS

No, Kevin, it's easy to do yourself, with a little effort – a few clicks on a computer, printed on photo paper. Even back then, the technology was available, although it was a bit pricey.

NOLMAN [Laughs]

So you killed Sornie. What, paid some prisoners to do it, or something?

FRANCIS [Laughs]

Didn't have to. Deborah, show Kevin that payslip.

[Pause, rustle of paper]

NOLMAN

So what, it's a fucking payslip; no' something they've given me a load o' over the years.

DEBORAH

Look closely. It says PRG, doesn't it? Prison Reform Group. I was employed as a coordinator for three years with them, but before that, for eight years, I was a prison visitor; you know, visiting long-term prisoners without families, or whose relatives refused to visit.

317

FRANCIS

And you did your visiting where?

DEBORAH

Oh, mostly down in England, but for a few months, in Glasgow. Barlinnie.

NOLMAN

YOU PLANTED THE FUCKING PHOTAES, IS THAT WHAT GOT HIM KILLED, YA CUNTS?

FRANCIS

David Johnstone? We gave him a bit of a rap on the knuckles, but left him alone otherwise. Do you know, he's the only one that showed any remorse and he was the only one found not guilty at the trial; for good reason, eh, Kevin?

NOLMAN

I don't think the wee cunt deserved any better 'n us; he wis there, wisn't he?

FRANCIS

Aye, he was there, but from what we know, he didn't actually take part in the violence that night, and as you said, he tried to pull you off, so he's been punished enough. The best thing he ever did was to get away from you lot.

NOLMAN

Fuck youse, ye didnae have anything to dae wi' Pinky – Malky killed him, silly cunts the perr o' them.

FRANCIS

Deborah, show him

[PAUSE]

318

NOLMAN

I don't unnerstan', how did you get in that picture? Did you get there before the polis came?

FRANCIS

Kevin, we were there before Malky came. Deborah, give him the other photos.

DEBORAH

Here.

FRANCIS

That's Malky arriving, after Pinky's dead.

NOLMAN

I don't believe it – Malky didnae kill Pinky, then?

FRANCIS

That's right, but he is doing a life stretch for it. Ironic, isn't it, how he got all of you off life terms for something you were guilty of, and he is doing life for something he didn't do. I hear he started a riot a while back, so he won't be out any time soon. Funny, he did that just after we sent him a wee souvenir of the murder. Nothing that would give him anything to appeal on, just enough so he'd know why he was in there. It's a wonder he never told you about it.

NOLMAN [Dully]

I huvnae spoke wi' him since he killed Pinky, so he couldnae hae told me. He did phone wance fir me, but Ah widnae speak tae him.

FRANCIS

I'm glad of that. It might have given you warning about our little trip.

NOLMAN

319

[In low voice] Fuck, you did kill Pinky, and you set Malky up fir a lifer fir it. You bastard.

DEBORAH

They both deserved what they got, Kevin.

NOLMAN

Cunts, the pair of ye. Whit aboot the others?

FRANCIS

Well, Spaz was easy; a few words in the right ears, spread a little doubt in the minds of men of violence, provide a bit of evidence that he's moonlighting for another firm. BANG. Done.

NOLMAN

See wance Ah'm oot ae this, youse is fuckin deid.

FRANCIS

John White, got a wee thing with heroin going. First time he tried it, he shot up with a pretty young thing. Well, he shot up, she just injected some saline. You see, she loved Patrick just as much as we did, and the lengths she went to .

NOLMAN

Did she shag him as well, the cunt?

DEBORAH

[Indignant] No, don't be stupid, she wouldn't have done that.

FRANCIS

But she WAS with him the first time he was shooting up.

NOLMAN

Ah don't think youse know who you're fuckin' wi' here, Ah know some heavy teams, anythin' happens to me, yer deid.

FRANCIS

Kevin, Kevin, you don't get the point; no one knows you're here.

NOLMAN [Laughs]

There's nae fuckin way ye can get away wi' killin' me, an' when ye dae get caught, a dozen o' ma friends wid do ye, wherever ye were.

FRANCIS

You still aren't getting it, Nolman, are you? Deborah, Tell him.

DEBORAH

Our life finished on this day twenty-five years ago at eleven forty-five p.m., so don't worry about us.

FRANCIS

What time do you make it, Nolman?

[Slight pause]

NOLMAN

It's just efter half eleven, an' whit's this ye've suddenly started callin' me Nolman? Only ma team calls me that.

FRANCIS

Nolman, it's exactly eleven thirty-six, which means that you've got nine minutes to live. And don't worry about the "Nolman" bit – we're the last people you'll ever know, so we should at least be on first name terms.

NOLMAN [Laughs, nervously]

How ye gonna kill me? Ye willnae get near me. Ah've another fuckin' knife here ... aw fuck, ye huvnae got a gun, huv ye?

FRANCIS

No gun, Nolman.

[Engine sound has been gradually getting louder and more high-pitched]

DEBORAH

You still haven't got it yet, have you?

NOLMAN [Shouting]

WHIT YE ON ABOUT, YA AULD MINGIN' CUNT?

DEBORAH

You won't be dying on your own.

NOLMAN [Shouting]

NO, MAN, YE CANNAE DAE THIS, YE'RE JUST TRYING TAE FRIGHTEN ME. YE WANT ME TAE SAY AH'M SORRY? AH'M SORRY, RIGHT? WELL, AH'VE SAID IT, NOW SLOW THE FUCK DOWN.

[Pause]

NOLMAN

Ma family will report me missin'. The polis will know it's me in the car, they'll know ye did it; it'll be all over the papers an' the TV an' that.

FRANCIS

Nolman, a delivery was made today to your mother's house. Nothing but a couple of hundred in small notes in it, but a rumour is circulating that you pulled off the big one before you were killed, and a big part of the stash is being kept at your mother's house. They'll be too busy fending off all the lowlifes in Glasgow to worry about kicking up a fuss about you.

NOLMAN [Shouting]

THEY'LL GET NO PEACE, IF EVERY CUNT THINKS AH'VE KEPT A LOAD O' DOSH THERE. YOU REALLY ARE EVIL CUNTS, SO YES ARE.

[Dies to mumbled cursing, occasional sobbing, and sound of engine. After a minute, the click of a lighter and sound of burning. Then rush of air as window open and closed]

I imagined at this moment that Deborah was burning the photos in the ashtray, and perhaps disposing of the inhaler out of the window.

[Long pause, sound of engine racing, sobs of Nolman continue]

FRANCIS

Deborah, I love you, and I loved our boy. You both were my life.

DEBORAH [Distinct shakiness in voice]

Francis, I love you and I loved our boy, too.

NOLMAN [Mumbling]

No, no, no, no, no, no, no, no, Jesus, no.

[Engine now racing loudly, sounds of Nolman whimpering, cursing, struggling constantly.

Soft click, loud scream for 4-5 seconds, then loud bang, then stillness. After 30 seconds, long bleep, then woman's voice, "Caller disconnected, please hang up", repeated for 2 minutes, then long continuous bleep]

I poured another whisky, three fingers this time, and gulped about half of it. I had known much of it before hearing the recording, but having it all confirmed and a few of the gaps filled in made it more final. I knew that some of the remaining questions I had would never be fully explained. Had Francis planned it down to the very minute to hit the only bridge that had the crash barriers removed for repair? How had Francis found out the information on Spaz Davidson that allowed him set up his shooting? How had he lured Pinky McNiven to the industrial estate to have him killed? And how had he tipped off Malky that his beloved BMW was at the industrial estate to entice him there, to be set up as the killer? How much had Sarah changed her appearance so that Lee Scoular or John White wouldn't recognise her? When did the three of them plan all this; were Sarah and Deborah involved from the start?

I now knew what the contents of the Mac directory on Francis' PC had contained. I could have probably asked Bruce Davidson for a File Conversion Utility to view the Photoshop files, but I'd already seen the results of Francis' efforts at manufacturing paedophilic photographs of James Sornie, and those had been convincing enough to get him killed. Deborah's access to the prison allowed the "evidence" of Sornie's paedophilia to be planted inside Barlinnie.

They'd taken a lot of risks, not least getting hold of a quantity of smack and keeping it hidden, Francis' "priestly" visit to Billy Green's bedside, just to let him know why he was about to die, "stealing" Malky's car from him with the spare set of keys, and switching Billy's inhalers in the chemist.

Of all of them, Pinky McNiven's death bothered me the most because he was the one Francis had killed in person, even if it was from behind the wheel of a car. I imagined a delighted Malky buying the BMW from Deborah, thinking he had got the bargain of a lifetime, not knowing that Francis had a key for it and could drive it away at any time. A thought suddenly struck me – it must have been Deborah, or even Sarah, I suppose, who was driving when the car ran over Pinky. It had bothered me how Francis could have been sure of hitting Pinky with the car, but I had just realised how it had probably been done:

Francis met Pinky, on whatever pretext, and talked to him while Deborah or Sarah drove the car along the road. Francis then gave Pinky a hard push off the pavement just as the car passed. As he lay in the road, they drove over him a couple of times just to make sure. That made more sense, and I felt another little piece of the puzzle fall into place.

They hadn't really made any mistakes – no unidentified fingerprints or DNA had shown up on Malky's car, the pictures of Sornie got into circulation in Barlinnie without Deborah's position being compromised, nobody other than Lee Scoular was infected with Weil's disease, Sarah wasn't recognised by John White or Lee Scoular, Kevin Nolan was successfully "snatched" and held in the car without him suspecting anything, and the police never found out the true nature of that journey.

Although the press eventually caught on to Nolman's presence in the car, their speculation followed a similar line to my own when I had first discovered that it was him who had died in the car with Francis and Deborah; namely that he had tried to make his peace, or had been confronted by the couple and a struggle between him and Francis had caused the crash. Ironically, because of the speculation, the explanation that the crash was caused by Francis' use of the phone had lost a bit of its credence. Nolman's family didn't kick up a fuss about his death. I heard that they'd had three break-ins within the first year, but that they wouldn't get the police involved.

I eventually got rid of the Audi. Before I did, I had a quick look inside in light of what I had heard on the recording made during its last journey. I found a length of wire cable under the passenger seat with a small metal "shoe" at one end, and a loop on the other. From what I could see, the seat belt fastener had been modified by the addition of a small spring welded inside the lock. I presume that when the seatbelt was clicked into place, it was permanently locked until Deborah pulled the wire with a sharp tug to release the belt just before the car hit the bridge. If you listen carefully to the recording, you can almost imagine a soft click just before Nolman starts screaming. When the traffic boys had examined the seatbelts it would have just looked as if the rear passenger had not been wearing his belt and the modification deep inside the seat belt mechanism would never have been examined, especially as, without the shoe in place, the seat belt worked normally.

I took the money I received from scrapping the car and gave it to the furniture project.

I continued to live in Francis' house and fitted a large and expensive wood burning furnace at the back of the workshop, which used scrap wood and fallen trees to provide a cheap source of heat and hot water for the house and the workshop. On the 25th April 2005, I got the news that John White had taken an overdose of heroin and died before they could get him to hospital.

EPILOGUE

[Sunday 27th April 2008]

Five years to the day after Francis and Deborah died, and thirty years after Patrick's death, I watched the furnace burn in the warm April sunshine.

When I'd discovered that they'd committed suicide I'd been annoyed that Francis didn't leave a note for me, but I came to realise that he *had* left me a message, it had just taken me a while to decipher it. I knew that all the clues I'd come across were for me alone to find and make sense of. If it all came out, Francis, Deborah, and Sarah would forever be remembered as killers. I also knew that if it became public knowledge, Malky McGovern would walk out of prison and, although it crossed my mind that technically he shouldn't be in there, I just couldn't do it.

I did struggle with the knowledge that Francis, Deborah and Sarah had lied to me from the day I had met them, and used me on some occasions as a source of information. I should have felt betrayed because of it, but I didn't. In reality I had provided very little help, apart from the copies of the investigation paperwork, and most of the stuff was public knowledge anyway. With Francis, I genuinely knew that my unconditional friendship was of much greater importance to him and that our closeness was not in any way calculated or false. With Sarah, I rationalised to myself that I'd got involved with her much later on in the day, that our getting together had been of no help to any of them, and that she had just needed somebody to fill a gap in her life at that time. I did feel a little stupid for having been so easily duped, but I knew that there hadn't been too many obvious signs that I'd missed, and that they'd been very discreet in everything that they did. More than anything, I just missed them.

And if I'd known earlier, what would I have done? I've asked myself that question a thousand times, and I always come up with the same answer:

Nothing.

I did my thirty years on the force, never getting any higher than a DS. I had thought of trying to pack the job in early, but two things stopped me. Initially, the financial stability the job gave me took some of the pressure off having to earn a crust making furniture and, by staying on, I was increasing the amount my police pension would eventually give me. But I also had access to a lot of information sources while I was working that I would lose when I retired, and I had needed those resources to disentangle the story that had so dominated my life.

Even before I'd retired, when I only just kept Hare and Son ticking over by spending a great deal of my spare time in the workshop, I had decided that once I'd left the force I would become a full-time cabinetmaker. So in late 2005, when I finally called it a day, having done my thirty years, that is exactly what I did. I stuck to the principle of producing top quality furniture as close to Francis' level of perfection as I could manage, although without matching the complexity and exquisite design of Francis' commissions. I retained many of his core customers and, although they always seemed pleased with the furniture I made, they would concede that I would never be in Francis' league.

I will always remember the quiet satisfaction when, before my first commission went out the door, I screwed the small gunmetal plaque on to the back:

P. Hare & Son, Glasgow.

J. McD. 2004

328

The business has come to be a reasonable little earner, which in conjunction with my pension, leaves me fairly comfortably off and all things considered, I am glad that I kept it going.

Why? Three reasons, really. The selfish one is that I love working with wood, the smell of the workshop, the solitude of the workbench. I love making beautiful furniture, seeing customer's faces when the furniture is collected or delivered, and I enjoy "talking shop" with other tradesmen, knowing that I am one of the dwindling tradition of professional craftsmen that dates back to the Bronze Age.

The second reason is that Francis was my greatest friend. I don't believe in an afterlife but I like to think that if Francis was still around somewhere, he would appreciate the fact that I'd kept Hare and Son going and that I hadn't judged him, but had accepted him for what he had been, and for the actions that he had taken.

For many years, since the last time I was with Sarah, in fact, I had a series of women in my life, mostly for a few months, occasionally for a bit longer. They were all lovely in their own way, one of them even moved in with me for a while. A few were beautiful, most were pretty. With some, it was a hoot, with others the sex was great, one of them was a fantastic cook and I put on a stone in six months. Another was an avid reader and introduced me to books and authors that I would never have read otherwise. They nearly all enriched my life in some way, and I still feel guilty that I could not commit to any of them, because just about all of them deserved better than that.

That brings me to the third reason: I knew that if Sarah Anstruther ever walked back into my life I would be unable to stop myself grabbing hold of whatever she was offering, and I knew that while I had the shop and the workshop it would always be easy for her to find me, if she wanted to.

I've no reason to believe she's still alive, or dead for that matter, and wherever she is, I don't know if I figure in her thoughts very much, or if she ever has any intention of looking me up sometime. I did make discreet enquiries about her while I was still working, but nothing ever showed up in the UK, Ireland or indeed Europe. I may well be a stupid soft bastard for even thinking about her after all this time.

But sometimes, not always, when the bell above the shop door rings, I look up, expecting to see her standing in the doorway.

THE END

ACKNOWLEDGEMENTS

I would like to thank Big Greig for being the first person to read the book, for reading it so quickly, for being so enthusiastic about it, and for checking that all the CID stuff held together. Many thanks also to Tel (The White Rhino) for checking it out from the legal angle and to Jim C. for correcting my grammar and punctuation, and for helping me tidy up the book's final structure.

The comments and support that I got from my other proof readers was very much appreciated. They were Cat, Michael, Karen, Gordon and Franko (by proxy).

I wouldn't have persevered without the positive feedback that I got from Zander, Claire, and Jon, professionals in the publishing trade. While they didn't take the book on, their comments and suggestions gave me the confidence that I had a book worth publishing.

Thanks to Cat for the cover; all that education finally paid off! Also thanks to Harvey for the tools we used on the cover.

In February 2015, when the book had finally earned enough to cover the costs, I retained Julie Lewthwaite to edit The Cabinetmaker professionally, and I appreciate the speed and the thoroughness of her work, and for her kind comments about the story.

Last of all, thanks to my wife, children and all my extended family and friends for putting up with me for all those years.

If you enjoyed this book, and wish to recommend it to a friend, they can obtain the opening chapters free of charge at: http:/www.thecabinetmaker.info. The website also contains additional material connected with the book, including a map and a glossary.

GLOSSARY

CABINETRY

[auger bit] fits into a brace, for drilling larger holes

[bandsaw] Thin-blade machine saw for curved cuts

[bed] thick cast iron surface on woodworking machines

[biscuit joints] simple wood jointing system

[block plane] small plane for shaping across wood grain

[block] holder for cutters on spindle moulder

[carcase] furniture without drawers & doors, etc fitted

[chamfer] a planed edge at 45 degrees for decoration

[chisels] used to hollow out square recesses in wood

[clamp] for gripping: G-clamps, edge clamps, etc.

[cramp] another name for clamps, eg sash cramps

[dovetail] complex wedged joint for two pieces of wood

[dry assemble] building furniture temporarily without glue

[fence] cast metal guide for woodworking machines

[frame] skeleton' of a piece of furniture

[gouge] like chisels, but curved

[inlay] material fitted into a groove for decoration

[jackplane] long plane for shaping wood along its length

[jig] a way of making repeated cuts identical

[jointing] any method used to cut out joints

[lathe] turning machine for cutting round profiles

[mitre] joint made at 45 degrees

[mortice] socket in a mortice & tenon joint

[moulding] a profile cut made along the edge of wood

[pin] The male part of a dovetail joint

[plane] a tool to remove shavings to make wood smooth

[rebate] a channel or shoulder cut into wood

[rip saw] a saw for cutting wood along the grain

[spindle-moulder] a machine for producing mouldings

[tail] the sockets in a dovetail joint

[tenon] pin in a mortice & tenon joint

[turn] using the lathe to make a pole or spindle

[turning] the results produced by the lathe

POLICE TERMINOLOGY

[CID] Criminal Investigation Department

[WPC] Woman Police Constable

[PF] Prosecutor Fiscal

[DC] Detective constable

[DS] Detective sergeant

[DI] Detective inspector

[QC] Queen's Council

[AD] Advocate Depute

GLASGOW SLANG

['tention] attention

[aboot] about

[ae] of

[aff] off

[ah'd] I would

[ah'll] I will

[ah'm] I am

[ah've] I have

[alang along

[an] and

[arenae] aren't

[baggin] sniffing glue

[Bairn'd] made pregnant

[Bampots] nutcases

[baw] ball, or testicle

[buckshee] free of charge

[cannae] cannot

[chappin] knocking

[chibbed] beaten up

[clevir] clever

[cos] because

[couldnae] couldn't

[cunted] exhausted

[dae] do

[deid] dead

[didnae] didn't

[doon] down

[d'ye] do you

[efter] after

[fae, frae] from

[faither] father

[fenian, pape] catholic (derogative)

[fir] for

[foosty] mildewed, damp

[footered] dithering

[fur] for

[gid] good

[gie] give

[gi'en] given

[gie's] give us or give me

[gonna, gonnae] going to

[gottae] got to

[granweans] grandchildren

[hae] have

[hame] home

[hasnae] hasn't

[hawf] half

[heid] head

[himsel'] himself

[hooring] prostitution

[hoose] house

[Houf] rough bar

[hun] protestant (derogatory)

[huv] have

[huvnae] haven't

[huvvin] having

[intae] into

[isnae] isn't

[jaked] drunk

[jakey] waster

[kent] knew

[kinda] kind of

[knaw] know

[mair] more

[masel'] myself

[mo'] moment

[moggered] drunk

['nads] testicles (gonads)

[nae] no

[napper] head

[naw] no

[ned] thug, waster

[noisin'] annoying verbally

[noo] now

[nu'hin] nothing

[nutted] head butted

[onyhow] anyhow

[onyone] anyone

[oot] out

[ower] over

[paedos] paedophiles

[pallin] being matey with

[perr] pair

[photae] photo

[pish] urine; rubbish

[pished] drunk

[pishin'] urinating; raining

[probs] problems

[puggys] fruit machine arcade

[puir] poor

[roon] round

[rozzer] policeman

[schemie] disadvantaged resident of a social housing development

[scripto] furious, mad, daft

[scuse] excuse

[shiting mysel'] afraid

[Shtum] quiet

[skinful] a lot to drink

[slagged] ridiculed

[sorta] sort of

[sumfin, sumhin] something.

[swallow] drink.

[swanning] sloping.

[tae] to

[thae] those

[themsel's] themselves

[verbals] chat (malicious)

[wance] once

[wasnae] wasn't

[wee] small

[wernae] weren't

[whit] what

[wi] with

[wid] would

[willnae] will not

[windae] window

[wis] was.

[wisnae, wisn't] wasn't

[wouldnae, widnae] wouldn't

[wunner] wonder

[wunner (in a)] in one go

[ya, ye] you

[yehs] you (plural)

[yer, ye're] your

[Yersel \ yerself] yourself

[ye've] you have

[you'se] you (plural)

26226814R00197

Printed in Great Britain
by Amazon